By JAKE C. WALLACE

Soul Seekers

Published by DREAMSPINNER PRESS
www.dreamspinnerpress.com

Soul
Seekers

JAKE C. WALLACE

Published by
DREAMSPINNER PRESS

5032 Capital Circle SW, Suite 2, PMB# 279, Tallahassee, FL 32305-7886 USA
www.dreamspinnerpress.com

This is a work of fiction. Names, characters, places, and incidents either are the product of Jake C. Wallace imagination or are used fictitiously, and any resemblance to actual persons, living or dead, business establishments, events, or locales is entirely coincidental.

Soul Seekers
© 2016 Jake C. Wallace.

Cover Art
© 2016 Brooke Albrecht.
http://brookealbrechtstudio.com
Cover content is for illustrative purposes only and any person depicted on the cover is a model.

ISBN: 978-1-63477-260-0
Digital ISBN: 978-1-63477-261-7
Library of Congress Control Number: 2016900166
Published June 2016
v. 1.0

Printed in the United States of America
∞
This paper meets the requirements of
ANSI/NISO Z39.48-1992 (Permanence of Paper).

Speed Demon, you make my stories possible and my life amazing. Thanks for seeing those special things in me that I can't. Love you.

CHAPTER 1

LEVI REED paced his bedroom, frantically shaking his hands. Like a caged animal yearning for escape, he wore the same tread repeatedly across the blue shag rug. Waves of fear lashed out, tearing into his fragile mind. He paused his pacing, then jumped up and down, as if the action were enough to shake off the icy grip of panic. No such luck. His life had always been about the fear, and after nineteen years that hadn't changed.

He resumed pacing. Terror threatened to drown him beneath relentless, suffocating waves. Since morning, the menace had been growing from a deep crevice within his mind. At first, there had only been a small grain, barely detectable. By midday, that small grain had coalesced into the burgeoning, familiar companion that had accompanied him for his entire life, always there, rarely resting.

"Think." The sound of his own voice did little to settle his nerves. The time for tricks of distraction and deception had passed. He was well into the throes of the nightmare. Fear, greater than any human should ever know, threatened his sanity. He cursed his ingrained weakness, which only proved the names, "sissy" or "queer"—less than a man—that had been used to describe him over the years. But he dared any man to deal with the ruthless panic, fear, and dread he had managed to survive without crumbling.

"You're safe." He repeated the mantra several times, but the words were a hollow attempt at self-reassurance. "Come on, Levi. Cut this shit out."

Rubbing his icy hands together, he fought to bring his focus back so he could formulate a plan. *Yes, a plan,* he thought, but the adrenaline pumping through his veins forced his thoughts to whirl about too quickly. Closing his eyes, he bent at the waist until his ears were level with his knees. The action accentuated the racing beats of his heart clamped beneath the ever-tightening muscles of his chest. The tighter they squeezed, the faster and harder his heart pumped. Any minute, he imagined his heart would shatter his ribs into a million sharp, bony pieces.

Willpower was the only weapon he had against the enemy—sheer determination to keep up his defenses. Achingly, his mind continued to battle the ever-surging breakwaters threatening to overcome their dam, the psychological wall he'd learned to construct years ago. The fear, if allowed to overpower him, would shred his sanity into tiny reflective bits that would only echo who he once was. His psyche had yet to smash but bore jagged cracks that had weakened its structure. Just a matter of time.

Not now. Not this time! His mind screamed at the unseen adversary.

"Focus. Breathe."

Steadying himself, Levi gripped his thighs, digging his nails into his skin through his gray sweatpants, the pain a faint and distant echo. He forced a deep breath into his lungs. "One… two…" He struggled to keep the air from escaping prematurely. "Three." With strained control, he steadily allowed the air to escape. Quickly, he drew in another breath and repeated the pattern several times. His attention focused solely on that one last life-saving act, but a noise interrupted his plan.

A closing door. Footsteps in the hallway. His thin, hollow core door was the only barrier. Levi bolted upright. A surge of dizziness threatened to topple him as the walls of the room slanted and tipped. Footsteps stopping at his door brought reality crashing down. Everyone should have been asleep. The distraction was the pause his internal enemy needed.

With unnerving ferocity, the fear breached the dam, forcing through fractures within the blockade constructed to restrain his foe. Panic pushed the release of adrenaline. His heart seemed to freeze momentarily as the hormone invaded. Levi gasped and slapped his palm against his sternum.

"No!"

The absence of the familiar thudding pushed his panic past the edge of reason. Just when he was sure his heart wouldn't start again, the muscle exploded into beats faster than he could count. Numbness crept into his right arm and leg. Blood roared in his ears.

Levi spun around as the door to his room opened slowly.

"Please, no."

The man entered casually, kicking at something on the floor that blocked the door. A blue NY Giants ball cap shielded his eyes from the overhead light.

"Saw you were still up. Knocked but you didn't—" The last word caught in the man's throat as he raised his head. "Levi?" Alarm replaced the relaxed smile on his face. Quickly, quietly, he closed the door behind him, his eyes never wavering from Levi. "It's bad this time?" Part question but mostly a statement.

The twist of fear and panic on Levi's face must have been a dead giveaway. The sight of his older brother rushing around the bed toward him, the determination of his stride, the familiar mask of worry on his face took any fight left within Levi. Surrender was his only option now. Clawing at his throat, Levi managed to whisper, "I... can't... breathe!"

The tightening in his chest rose to envelop his windpipe. Air everywhere but none of the oxygen reached his screaming lungs. *I'm dying*, he rationalized, *or worse.*

Logan gripped him firmly by his shoulders. Levi could barely feel the pressure.

Floating... I feel like I'm floating.

Blackness pushed into the edges of his vision. Beneath him, his legs threatened to buckle and send him crashing to the floor.

"Levi?" The voice wafted away on an undetectable breeze. When he didn't answer, Logan gently shook his shoulders and put more authority behind his name. "Levi. Look at me."

Levi's chin rested on his chest, and he stared off into nothingness. His head was so heavy. Fingers touched his chin. Levi looked up and forced his eyes to work together. He focused on his brother's face. Rigid, hard lines and narrowed eyes, masked slightly by the shadow of his ball cap, spoke to the seriousness of his demand.

"I... I... c-can't. The dam broke." Levi's voice was barely audible as torrents beat ceaselessly against him. He was losing the fight, the will to continue.

Logan nodded. "Listen. You're breathing as if you just ran five miles. Slow it down. It's just a panic attack." Logan pulled Levi's hands away from his throat where he'd been digging into his skin. Logan then placed Levi's palm against the center of his own chest. "Focus on my breathing." Logan exaggerated the movement of his chest. "In... out... slow it down... in... and... out. There's nothing to be afraid of, right? Nothing's going to hurt you."

Despite Logan's coaching, Levi had lost control of his body, which was now the domain of his primordial fear. Shortly, his mind would evict him, throwing him into the ether.

"Levi, you need to help me here." Logan's tone held an edge of annoyance. Logan raised his hand and lightly slapped Levi's left cheek. The contact echoed into Levi's skull and cleared enough of the fog smothering his brain to direct his attention. Levi's gaze lifted to Logan's face with confusion. "This isn't working. I think I'd better wake up Dad."

"No!" That thought brought a new wave of fear, one from an actual source. "Don't... tell... Dad."

"Okay, okay. Sit." Logan guided Levi back and had him sit on the bed. Logan placed his palm on the back of Levi's neck. "Put your head between your knees."

The action took some of the rush from Levi's head, and the roar in his ears faded slightly.

"You're okay," Logan crooned slowly and softly as if Levi were a child. "Nothing can hurt you while I'm here. Just listen to the sound of my voice." Logan's soothing tones entered his mind, searching for the panic as if it were an antidote. "You're strong. You can fight this. Focus on my voice." Logan rubbed Levi's upper back. "Focus on my touch. We've done this before. You're the one in control. You're the one who built the dam. You're the one who can put the fear back where it belongs."

Levi's shallow, rapid breaths slowed. Logan's voice filled his head, but Levi doubted his strength to corral the wild beast that still threatened him. Levi couldn't remember the last time the fear had fully escaped its enclosure. How had he put the menace back behind the dam last time? He shook his head to tell his brother he couldn't do what he asked.

"Yes, you can, Levi. Fight it, now!"

Obeying, Levi took in several deep breaths, held them in, and then blew them out. The muscles in his chest started to relax. The feeling of suffocation receded slightly. A surge of hope came with that small victory—a rise of strength.

Logan placed his hand on Levi's knee. Levi rested his cheek against the warm skin, soaking in Logan's reality.

Sure as the panic had come, it began to wane, its retreat like dark smoke being sucked slowly from a room. The withdrawal was not without effort on Levi's part, using a reserve of energy from deep within, with just enough coercion to hasten the momentary defeat of the enemy.

"That's it. You're winning." Logan had whispered, then sighed loudly, continuing to rub Levi's back.

Breathing came easier for Levi. Senses previously muted by the onslaught heightened. Replacing the terror was an overwhelming fatigue that rushed through every muscle of his body. Nerve endings in his arms, hands, legs, and feet screamed their discomfort, assaulted with tiny electric shocks from the influx of oxygen. No matter how hard Levi struggled, the muscles of his hands were too weak to form a fist, lacking vigor and strength.

Waiting patiently, Logan was silent. Replacing Levi's dread from the unknown fear was the discomfort of now having to face Logan—not that his brother hadn't helped him with his panic attacks in the past. Logan had never questioned Levi's irrational fears or their origin, had never made Levi think he was as crazy as he believed himself to be, had never let him down. But a nineteen-year-old man shouldn't be scared to death of nothing. A nineteen-year-old *gay* man should be more afraid of stepping out of the closet. Unfortunately, Levi's panic had kept him in a very different closet altogether, one where he often hid from his irrational, pointless fears. If he ever broke free of that small dark room, he'd be stepping into an entirely new version of that closet where he'd finally have to deal with being gay.

No one but his best friend Gia knew about his preference for men. Although, throughout high school, there had been those taunts of "queer" and one guy who actually had called him "fag" a few times. Levi wondered if they'd known he preferred men, like some crappy bully gaydar-type nonsense. Gia always said it was because Levi was too pretty to be a guy. Gotta love being male and being called "pretty."

"Hey," Logan said, finally breaking the silence. "Over?"

Unable to stall any longer, Levi nodded. Wisps of dizziness still spun in his brain. The heaviness of the upper half of his body almost knocked him over. He rested his elbows on his knees and nestled his head in his hands. His legs shook under the weight.

When Logan gently touched Levi's shoulder, shock waves reverberated into the core of his chest. *Damned overdeveloped startle response.*

"Levi." A noiseless pause. "Say something."

A simple request, but Levi's mouth felt as though it had been welded shut. Prying his tongue from the roof of his mouth, Levi managed a dry, hoarse, "'M okay," and then unenthusiastically turned up the corners of his mouth.

A relieved smile replaced the harsh lines that had bracketed Logan's mouth minutes earlier. A spark lightened his blue eyes beneath the shadow of the lid of his favorite ball cap. Curls of dark blond hair—a bit darker than Levi's—peaked from under the back of the cap. A scar, from an accident a few years ago, ran from the crown of his brother's head and ended just beneath his left eye. Still pronounced, the scar always made Levi shudder whenever he focused on the deep, red, jagged line, and he'd have to steady himself.

Fatigue quickly turned into exhaustion, overtaking Levi's mind with a ferocity that equaled the fear. Sleep would be his refuge but not yet.

"I'm sorry, Logan."

"For what?" There was a hint of surprise in Logan's question.

For being scared of nothing and needing you to rescue me, again.

"I'm not the one who just battled the demon." Logan punctuated this sentence with a light punch on Levi's arm but failed to lighten the mood.

Logan had helped Levi confront the monster more than once in his life, sitting with him and talking through the panic and mind-altering fear. Logan had always been Levi's safety net and connection to the real world, where Levi had felt he'd never belonged. It was as if an invisible barrier prevented him from truly living life as others knew it, always an arm's length away. He dwelled in that realm, which had been built on anxiety, dread, feelings of unreality, and invisible threats from a faceless enemy. Dulled emotions, the need to feel something—anything—had dominated most of his life. He was different from his family and friends and had always known that fact to be true.

Levi nodded, ignoring the imminent shutdown of his weary brain. "Yeah. It was bad this time."

"Why didn't you come and get me earlier? And why was this one so bad? The last time you had a full-blown panic attack was last November, right?" Logan's questions rolled out one after another until he uttered the one question Levi had been dreading. "Did you forget to take your meds or something?"

Out of the corner of his eye, Levi glanced at the small black zippered bag on his nightstand. Even when he'd been at school earlier, the contents of that bag had reached out, calling to Levi with promises of relief.

Logan's eyes searched Levi's face for an answer that he didn't want to give. Levi had quit taking his anxiety and depression meds over a week ago.

CHAPTER 2

LOGAN STOOD and turned away from Levi. Beneath his thin white T-shirt, the muscles in his back rippled and tensed, a sign that Logan was trying to control his anger. *Anger at me.* A painful stab penetrated Levi's heart.

Logan spun to face him. "You stopped taking your meds? All of them? The ones for anxiety and depression?" His brother's confusion quickly morphed into irritation and then into anger. "Do you know how awful it was watching you like that? You should've seen the look on your face. It was as if you were about to be murdered by some monster that doesn't even exist. I feel so damned helpless when this happens. If fear could truly kill a person, you'd be dead right now. That's how scared you looked." Logan shook his head violently, as if trying to rid his mind of a horrible image.

Levi drew back. This was the first time Logan had shown any anger or impatience for his mental illness. Levi had irrational fears, strange rituals to avoid the panic, late nights filled with dread. All of that had to be a major drain on his brother's life. Logan was always there helping Levi to live with his depression and anxiety as well as sticking up for him at school. High school hadn't been all bad. Mostly there had been a few jocks who'd picked on Levi because he didn't fit their idea of masculine. Logan had always stuck up for him, gave without getting in return. Now, the look of disappointment on Logan's face clawed at Levi's insides.

"Don't be mad. I can explain." Levi's eyes were gritty. Rubbing them didn't help. He squinted. *Is it getting brighter in here?*

Logan folded his arms over his chest. His posture warned Levi that his explanation had better be a good one. He couldn't handle the way Logan glowered down on him. Levi tried to halt his impending tears, but they were inevitable and burned his eyes.

You never, ever cry. Stop it.

Actually, it had been so long since Levi had even come close to crying that he assumed he'd either lost the ability or had just forgotten how.

Lowering his head, Levi hoped to stall long enough for his eyes to dry. He needed to be strong. He didn't need his deep-seated, innate weaknesses pulled further into the light.

A blink and a single tear left a moist trail, rolling down the side of his nose. Before he could capture the wayward drop, it rolled over the top of his lip and fell, splattering on his hand.

Damn. Betrayed by a tear.

"Are you crying?" Levi heard the innuendo in his brother's voice.

Poor, pitiful Levi. So fragile. Don't get him upset. He's so scared all of the time, unable to keep it together long enough to even go away to school or keep a job. Whatever will we do with him?

God, he *was* pathetic and weak. *Sissy boy.* That thought was enough to stop his tears and replace them with disgust. Who in the world lived as he did? Who lived in an empty shell where they rarely experienced emotions except for fear?

Levi definitely had the fear down pat, from low-level anxiety to full-blown, debilitating, scared-to-death terror. He was an expert. But all of those emotions that actually made a person human—like happiness, sadness, lust, love, anger—well, those emotions and sensations merely echoed inside of the hollow of Levi, never taking root, never growing in intensity. He was never totally pissed off or ecstatic or lust-driven or deliriously happy or any other extreme. He was generally flat—except for rare life-changing events with hit-you-head-on emotions. Like when his Nana had died suddenly (punch-to-the-stomach grief), or when he'd accidentally stabbed Stevie Haskins in the foot when trying to juggle knives (big-time remorse), or when Logan had crashed his snowmobile, flying helmetless into a tree and nearly dying (big-time-scary panic and fear).

Generalized Anxiety Disorder with Depressive Features. To Levi all that diagnosis meant was big stinking fear and being emotionally dead.

The pity he saw in Logan's eyes threatened Levi's long-standing resolve that he could never—not in a million years—do anything to hurt his older brother. But fuck if that anger wasn't stretching out and filling him up. Being an unfeeling shell, Levi had earned an F minus in dealing with emotions, and on those rare occasions when intense emotions entered his world, they seized control and called all of the shots.

Like now.

He was pissed.

Levi pointed his finger at Logan's chest. "Don't look at me like that. I'm so sick and tired of people looking at me like they feel sorry for me. You want to know why I didn't come to you? That look right there." Levi jabbed his finger into Logan's face.

Logan looked down his nose at the finger and then back at Levi, his surprised expression melting away. Logan's eyebrows furrowed and his jaw clenched, but he remained silent.

The heat of his anger flushed Levi's cheeks. "Dad's always giving me that look like I've failed him as a son and haven't lived up to his golden boy, Logan. He avoids me most of the time. And Mom whispering on the phone to her friends about how I'm just not right and praying to the great Lord that any girl I find will understand my 'condition,'" he said, adding the air quotes, "lest I will live life alone."

And he would live alone if girls were his only choice.

"No one seems to understand why I miss classes, or rarely leave the house to go for coffee or to the movies, or go on Spring Break or whatever else normal people do." He took in a deep breath, unable to cease his rambling. He was a prisoner in his head with unattainable freedom dangled in front of his face daily, and he was sick of it.

Logan shifted his weight, then returned to his inanimate posture.

"Excuses." Levi raised his arms, then dropped them to his sides. "That's the sum of my entire life. Excuses for my weaknesses and my inability to understand there really is nothing to be afraid of. Excuses to spare myself long explanations about what exactly is wrong with me *and then* evading those incredulous looks when people realize there really is *nothing* wrong with me. It's not like I have cancer or some other devastating physical illness."

"So, I decided if there isn't anything wrong with me, then I shouldn't have to take meds that make me numb, spacey, and unable to concentrate, make me feel like I live in an alternate universe parallel to this one. I want to feel something, anything real. I can't live like this anymore. I'm… I'm… emotionally retarded."

Levi desperately wanted to avoid Logan's stare, but he stiffened his spine and met Logan's eyes with an icy glare.

The momentary pardon from his previous exhaustion ended. He swayed a bit, desiring nothing more than to collapse onto his bed, crawl under the covers, and shut out the world. The intense emotions evaporated faster than snow on black pavement under the spring sun. Logan took a long moment and studied Levi's face, then cocked an eyebrow. What conclusion would he reach about Levi's ranting? He hadn't been privy to many of Levi's emotional overdoses, first because they were rare, and second because the last one had occurred when Logan had been in a coma for two weeks.

Lucky him.

Levi was about to break the awful silence when Logan's face relaxed and the corner of his lips curled. "Are you done?" He rocked back and forth on his heels, his smile stretching wider. "I mean, far be it from me to impinge on your pity party since, apparently, I'm the one who invited it with my piteous leering."

Levi frowned. "Piteous? Really, Logan?"

Logan returned the frown. "Golden boy? Really, Levi?"

The door to Levi's room flew open. He spun around. His hand went to his chest. Again, his heart shifted into overdrive.

His father stood in the doorway.

"What the hell is going on in here?" Their father blinked as his eyes adjusted to the brightness of the room. His salt-and-pepper hair was disheveled. Apparently, he'd come straight to Levi's room the minute his feet had hit the floor. "I can hear you two numbskulls all the way down in my room."

"Sorry, Dad. We were just talking and got a little loud. We'll be quieter." The sincerity in Logan's tone had an immediate calming effect on their father.

"You'd better." He pointed his warning finger. "Some of us have to get up early tomorrow." The door to the room closed as abruptly as it had opened. Footsteps faded down the hall, and a door slammed shut.

Levi turned back to Logan, still trying to recover from his father's surprise entrance. Logan's smile faded, and his expression returned to that of a worried older brother. He wasn't going anywhere. After twenty-five minutes of persuasion, Levi finally convinced Logan he'd be okay and his brother left. Levi flopped into bed at 1 a.m., more than exhausted. Morning would come quickly, and his statistics class started at 9 a.m. He so sucked at statistics.

LEVI HIT the snooze button three times before he rolled out of bed after 7 a.m. The previous day was a blur of memories, but the panic and fear were fresh in his mind. Jumping into the shower, he hoped the water would wake his groggy mind. Despite his lack of sleep, Levi moved quicker than usual, remembering he'd agreed to meet Gia in the coffee shop at school to review notes before class.

Out in the driveway, he found his father's truck gone as usual. Logan's black Ford F150 was still parked on the lawn by the garage. At least he was able to sleep in after Levi's nonsense the previous night. Even though Logan would never admit it, Levi's constant anxiety had to be draining, even if his panic attacks had become sporadic over the few years before he'd gone away to college last fall.

Yesterday's attack had been a result of stopping his medication. During his teens, the panic had been under control through medication and counseling. However, every day of his life contained some level of anxiety—a nagging uneasiness, apprehension, disquiet. Irrational fears thrived beneath the surface of his skin, a menacing presence in an unrelenting state of readiness. His tolerance for anxiety was probably higher than what most people could endure over the long term. Levi's problems arose when the menace found cracks in his barrier and the fears were let loose.

When he was younger, Levi's therapist, Dr. Ross, had helped him to visualize a mental "dam" to contain his panic and fears. Given the enormity of his anxiety, a dam seemed like the intelligent choice. Wasn't a dam designed to hold back massive lakes of water, thousands of cubic feet of pressure with steel-reinforced concrete? Lately, however, the pressure against Levi's barrier had been growing and fissures had formed, weakening the structure. Patching the holes created an enormous amount of mental strain and took precious energy. Stopping his meds had added to that strain, but tiny cracks had been forming in the dam over the years, branching out without being fixed. His experiment of stopping his medication had produced the major panic attack, but the long-term outcome of a daily life without those meds remained to be seen. Levi shook off the memory of Logan's disappointment. This was Levi's life, not his brother's.

Levi pulled into the closest parking spot he could find behind North Country Community College. He was in the liberal arts program since he had no clue what he wanted to do with his life. This small school in his hometown was Levi's consolation prize after having to leave Plattsburgh State in northern NY before the end of his first semester, his fear and panic worsening. Another dream stolen by the monster.

As he exited the car, his cell phone rang. Struggling to free it from the front pocket of his jeans, he sprinted across the parking lot to the annex.

"I'm here!" He skirted around students exiting through the front door. To the left was the Cyber Café, where Gia waved frantically from a table in the rear. Levi pushed through the bodies and slid into a chair at the small round table already covered with books, a laptop, and two large caramel macchiato espressos.

"About time. I'd just about given you up for dead in some horrific accident. Was already planning my vengeance." Her bright red lips were a stark contrast to her alabaster skin and darker-than-black hair. *Italian from head to toe, hairy and raised on revenge*, as she'd informed Levi when they'd first met in sixth grade. Levi had been unsure if he should have laughed or been mortified. *Italians are very hairy people. I've been getting electrolysis since the age of ten*, Gia had explained. *And yes, cross me or someone I care about, and they'll never find the body.* Four feet, eleven inches of pure, uncensored Italian. Levi had grown accustomed to what Gia labeled her "dark side." Though she'd always been sarcastic and a bit removed, that had increased since the death of her mother from cancer when they were in the eighth grade. Sometimes Levi felt it had become a defense mechanism.

"Rough night. Running on about five hours of sleep." He left it there.

Gia had some knowledge of Levi's anxiety issues, but not the magnitude of the iceberg beneath the surface. Not even Logan knew how truly behemoth that was.

"That's what happens when you're up all night having sex with random guys," Gia deadpanned. "Especially ones that scratch."

Levi's hand automatically went to the scratches he'd created during the panic attack. The touch of his fingertips stung the raw spots. He looked around, but no one seemed to have heard her comment. "Ha! Sex. What's that?" A quiver in his voice threatened to betray him.

"It's this nifty little thing that your virgin ass needs to get."

"Says you." Levi regretted bringing up the subject at all.

Gia's perpetual purpose on the planet was to "get" Levi some. He had bigger demons to fight than relationships and thoughts of groping a hot man and blowjobs and anal sex. When you're a hollow husk of nothing, sex tended to take a back seat. Gay sex especially, because that shit came with a whole other set of issues. Despite the lack of feelings, he had brought himself to orgasm through masturbation, but the act was purely physical, emotionless, and generally left him empty and unsatisfied.

Thankfully, Gia dropped Levi's taboo subject and moved on to statistics. Within an hour, they were seated in Mr. Cobbert's class as he droned on endlessly at the board. Levi fought the profound weight of his eyelids.

He craned his neck to whisper to Gia. "Keep me awake."

Gia snorted as if the likelihood of that was slim. Levi leaned his elbow against the desk and supported his chin with his palm, closing his eyes for a moment.

Just a moment.

As sleep overtook him, Levi startled, caught his head from rolling off his palm, and then righted himself. Eyes still closed, Levi mused at past memories of watching fellow classmates fight to doze with their heads upright. How many were currently entertained with his struggle? *Let them watch,* he thought, descending further away from Mr. Cobbert's monotone murmuring until the words were no longer discernible. A low octave hum followed him into unconsciousness.

Just as he entered sleep, Levi's psyche smashed into a barrier with the equivalence of a car slamming into a wall at eighty miles per hour. The crash rattled every fiber of his being. With the magnitude of a vocal cry, a guttural scream penetrated his subconscious, ripping Levi out of sleep. He started, disoriented as to his location. He gripped at the sides of his desk, the force dumping his books on the floor. The resounding boom echoed around the room. Heads turned, and dozens of pairs of eyes stared at him relentlessly. Levi could only grit his teeth as a roar filled his ears. Not the familiar roar of rushing blood, but of something coming. Something huge.

CHAPTER 3

LEVI COULD scarcely appreciate the magnitude of the force growing from some primitive pit deep within his mind. *It*—whatever *it* was—was surfacing, ready or not.

He had to get out. Running was his only solution, the only thing that made sense. A break with one's psyche had to be messy and definitely nothing a room full of his fellow students deserved to witness. It sounded like nasty business.

"Hey," Gia whispered, setting her hand on Levi's shoulder. "You okay?"

Gia's touch shot pain into his bones and was more than he could stand. He jerked away.

"Levi?" Concern colored Gia's voice.

Unprecedented pressure crowded Levi's mind, and, like a balloon filled past capacity, something eventually had to give. Terrifying visions of his gray and white brain matter splattering across student's faces, on pages of open textbooks, on Mr. Cobbert and that hideous tie covered with statistical equations, invaded his mind. Levi wondered how long he had before his head exploded.

Fumbling to gather what remained on his desk, he picked up his messenger bag and bolted for the door. What was happening to him? *God, anywhere but here.* The heat rushing through him spiked. A large black blur startled him as it passed by the window of the door. Taken back, Levi hesitated and then grabbed for the metal door handle. When he tried to pull the door open, a painful spark of static electricity crackled at his fingertips. Instinctively, Levi pulled his hand back as the shock snapped against his skin.

Don't let the door close!

Levi caught the metal monstrosity with his knee and squeezed through, allowing it to slam behind him.

Which way?

His car. In the back parking lot. To the right. The hallway was empty. As he ran, the unrelenting cranial pressure doubled him over in agony and pain exploded in his chest. Stumbling to remain upright, Levi steadied himself with his hand on the wall and then pushed off, propelling himself forward. His thoughts were vacant. He was in pure survival mode, true fight-or-flight, however something was wrong. No. Something was missing.

The fear.

Out the front doors. Blinding sunlight. Colored figures rushed past him, pushing and knocking into him.

So much pressure!

"Hey, watch it!" a male voice yelled as Levi bounced off a body.

When his vision came into focus, Levi was well into the parking lot, dodging moving and parked cars. Another blur of black passed nearby, but he ignored it, not giving a shit. His only objective: find his car and fast.

Again, he doubled over as the pain escalated, this time accompanied by roiling nausea. Where was his damned car?

Digging deep into his front pocket, Levi fought to free his keys. Just as he reasoned the piece of shit must have been stolen, there it was. He'd never been so relieved to find the old, rusting heap of steel. Juggling the keys, Levi managed to hit the button on the key fob, grateful for access to the locked car.

As he dropped into the driver seat, another wave of mind-numbing pain knocked into him, immense in his head and blossoming in his chest as well. *Not again.* His hands pressed against the sides of his skull. Maybe if he squeezed hard enough the counter-pressure would relieve the pain, or maybe it would simply crush his skull. When there was a reprieve from the pain, Levi revved the four-cylinder to life. Without hesitation, he backed out of the space, then slammed the gearshift to D, fleeing, as if he were being chased by every scary monster in the history of scary monsters.

On Main Street, he took a left, even though the route home was to the right. Barreling through the middle of town on autopilot, he took a left onto Howson and another left onto Lakeview, which ran along the east side of Lake George. The pressure that had threatened to explode his skull began to back off. The farther he traveled on the paved road, which eventually turned to hardpan, the further the force shrank. Dazzling pops of electric shocks still invaded his hands all the way up to his elbows. Not numb but alive and dancing. He watched as his hands twitched and jumped on the steering wheel, making it hard to hold on.

What the hell had happened to him? Should he go to the hospital? He couldn't imagine a mental breakdown would have been that painful, but more like a quiet, numbing slip into insanity. The intense pain had lessened into a low thudding ache. Maybe he'd had a stroke. Or maybe a brain tumor. Maybe he had one of those rare brain amoeba things multiplying in his head, feasting on his brain. Mad Cow Disease?

The pain had been so extreme he'd wanted to crawl into a dark quiet hole. Much like his mother did when she had one of her rare migraines. Hers tended to last for hours, mess with her vision and balance, and make her nauseated. This one had been quick. Maybe they were short migraines?

Whatever had occurred, Levi no longer felt as if he were going to die. He turned his attention back to the road, trying to distract himself. Large lakefront homes with well-manicured lawns that lined the left side of the road became fewer and farther between. Smaller camps peeked from behind overgrown brush and evergreen trees on the sides of the road, which narrowed even further into one lane. His rusted Ford creaked and moaned as it bounced over large holes and ruts. Levi's escape hadn't been as aimless as it first appeared, but why the hell he'd chosen to go there, he couldn't fathom.

Levi was no stranger to Lakeview Road or this southern corner of Lake George. His childhood summers had been spent at a small camp, which had belonged to his paternal uncle, Ray, and his wife, Helen. Hot and hazy summer days had been filled with hiking, swimming, fishing, and boating. Uncle Ray had died suddenly when Levi was around eight. After that, Aunt Helen had disowned their entire family. Why, Levi wasn't sure. And where Aunt Helen had gone or who now owned the cabin was a mystery. It had actually been so long since he'd been to the cabin that exactly where it was located eluded his memory. His anxiety tended to turn his memories into swiss cheese.

Reaching the end of the road, Levi pulled into the large dirt area cleared for the sole purpose of parking. SUVs and trucks had been parked at various angles, without care, their occupants either hiking the extensive trails or at the state campsite. The only access to the campsite was by boat or the well-marked trails.

Parking at the farthest end of the lot, Levi hoped no one would notice his car, but then, who would know to look for him there? Levi had an urgent desire to breathe fresh air and exited the car. The quiet of the woods rushed him. A beautiful requiem.

Something tried to tell him that he should pause to allow reason to creep back in—a moment to ponder his flight to this location. But no. Levi locked his car and jogged to a nearby path, failing to consider where he was going.

Years had passed since he'd been on the paths by the lake, and he proceeded in a slow jog. He couldn't remember if he'd been on this specific path as a child. Day after summer day he'd spent with Logan exploring practically every square foot of the towering forest surrounding the cabin—wherever that was.

Now, jogging on the wooded path, a powerful, overwhelming need pushed him farther, faster. Levi hurdled small puddles and protruding rocks and ducked through showers of low-hanging deciduous and evergreen branches. Leaning forward, he pushed his legs harder, digging his sneakers into the packed dirt. Fast wasn't enough.

Faster.... Faster.... Faster.

Beads of sweat trickled from his forehead, tickling his face. Heat rose from his chest and flushed across his cheeks. Picking up more speed, he pushed off with his right leg and flew over a large decaying tree to the right of the path. A cushion of littered leaves deadened his landing. Off-trail he ducked, weaved, and jumped, expertly creating his own trail through thick underbrush and around mature oaks, firs, and maples. The same predestined force that had driven him from the college seemed to drive him forward.

Only one thought pushed him. *Faster.*

Speed increased, foliage blurred, occasionally a stick whipped at the skin of his arms and face, but the momentary stings couldn't compete. Movement became a necessity for continued existence. A faint sensation ascended through mucky blackness of his mind.

A feeling? An emotion. Pure, uncontaminated....

Euphoria.

From the crest of a small hill, Levi could see Lake George peeking between the bare budding trees. Levi's blood surged, afire within his arteries, and his heart pumped harder and faster to fuel his muscles. He wondered at the rapturous feeling that expanded and magnified. Heat flowed through his pores, filling the air around him, easily negating any cool breeze he created as he cut swiftly through the sheltered forest. His body's internal temperature rose rapidly with only one thought—*more feeling.*

A burning current shot up both of his arms, energy similar to what he'd experienced earlier yet magnified hundreds of times. Ecstasy and elation faded into a fiery and all-consuming inferno that invaded his torso, his legs, his arms, his very molecules. Any minute, any second, he would spontaneously combust outward in a blinding light and reduce his surroundings to ash. There was no doubt in his mind.

He knew what he had to do. There was only one remedy for the searing heat rising relentlessly from deep within. Levi bolted to the left and went down the hill with a speed that threatened to throw him down the rocky and tree-laden hillside. Leaning back, he fought the forward momentum of gravity, the lake well within sight. Dead leaves and pine needles were kicked into the air as his feet slid toward the bottom. Tripping over a tree root and stumbling out onto a rock shelf jutting over Lake George, Levi pushed off with his left leg. That final effort sent him soaring into the air.

"Oh hell!" He flailed seeing the water was over twenty feet below him.

For a split second, he wondered what the heck had convinced him that throwing himself into the freezing lake was a good idea. Struggling to enter the water feet first failed, and he landed partially prone on his right side. Pain exploded into his ribcage as the numbing water enveloped him, icy claws digging into his skin.

An arctic blast extinguished every last bit of his heat and numbed his mind to rational thought. Darkness surrounded him. The cold cramped muscles and froze joints. In a matter of minutes, his body would be completely immobilized. Panic. *Can't breathe.* Fraught with determination, he pulled at the water above, fighting to inch closer to the daylight. Kicking his legs helped propel him, and just as his mouth opened for air, he broke the surface.

"Fuck me, that's cold."

As he dog paddled toward shore, his feet finally scraped against the stony bottom of the shallows. A problem loomed large above him in the form of the massive ledge of rock he'd just attempted to swan dive from. He could have sworn the smooth, unclimbable gray face of that rock silently mocked him.

Standing in about two feet of water, Levi wrapped his arms around his torso, numb to the core, and stumbled to a break in the shore. Just an hour ago, he'd been resting comfortably in statistics class, and now he had nearly become a drowned rat—a *cold* drowned rat. Was it the world that had tilted off its axis or him?

Wobbling on frozen feet, he climbed through the brush and collapsed onto the soft brown carpet shed by a grove of cedar trees. Staying on the ground would mean death from hypothermia. Not that moving was necessarily going to guarantee survival either, but the odds were better.

Levi sat, doubting cell service reached this far down the lake. Rolling his eyes, he muttered a string of obscenities as he pulled his phone from his pocket. Water leaked from every orifice of the electronic device. Levi chucked the worthless phone into a watery grave. Could the day possibly get any worse?

Rapidly the numbness fled, giving way to full-on cold. Wearily, Levi stood, his feet aching from the pressure exerted on them. Tentatively, he walked, as if barefoot on hot sand. Each painful movement definitely ruled out trekking back to his car, whatever direction that was from his current location. What new form of stupidity had surfaced the second he'd started jogging on the trail? Cardinal rules of the wilderness. You never go into the woods without telling someone. You never leave a marked path. And you definitely never, *ever* jump into an Adirondack lake in the middle of fucking March—no matter how hot you are—and with your cell phone in your pocket!

He let out a nervous laugh. "I'm not lost. Just temporarily misplaced." His levity did little to improve the situation.

Maybe at the top of the hill he could see something, anything—a path, a camp, a quick way to get help. Whatever energy had propelled him to sprint through the dense woods now evaded him. And what was with the nagging need to go off-road in the woods, much less run doing it? Better yet, what was with the need to be in the woods at all? It wasn't so great now that he was there.

With great effort, he reached the apex of the hill and practically threw himself the last few feet. Pain screamed in his fingers and toes, even the tips of his ears burned. Real fear surfaced that frostbite would warrant amputating parts of his body. Important parts. In this cold climate, it was more common than he cared to think about. Fiercely, Levi rubbed his hands to create friction, then studied his fingers. Red, numb, and cold. Not good.

It was imperative he move. His body shuddered in an attempt to warm itself, and his jaw had unclenched and his teeth chattered. Looking around, Levi realized moving south would eventually bring him toward the camps along the lake.

Eventually.

Ignoring the pain in his feet, he pushed through the undergrowth near the shore. Each step forward caused searing agony, especially if he stepped onto a rock or accidentally bumped his toes. Although the air was probably a good thirty degrees warmer than the water, the wet clinging clothes fueled the cold in his body.

"Survive a life of a fear-laden hell, thinking I would die from some phantom illness or disease only to die from hypothermia in the middle of the woods. Classic."

A loud screeching noise suddenly echoed through the trees. Squawking birds flew wildly from their hidden roosts. A momentary fear gripped him icier than the coldness. Wait. That was a chainsaw.

A chainsaw!

The possibility of rescue quickened his movement. The whining of the two-stroke engine grew louder, and Levi prayed it continued until he located its operator. Another moment in time, running across a chainsaw-wielding stranger in the thick of the woods would have brought Levi an uneasy feeling. At this point, he would have sold his soul—maybe more—for any bit of warmth.

The brown wood siding of a cabin appeared through a clearing ahead of him. The screaming chainsaw wound down and stopped. Staring ahead with the goal line in sight, Levi plowed through brush and thicket that threatened to stop him. To be this close and fail was not an option. As he rounded the front of the cabin, the sight of a figure halted him in his tracks. From the darkened edge of the woods about fifteen yards away, a set of eyes assessed Levi. A man in a bright red parka leaned forward, his bent leg propped up on a log. The chainsaw still in his hand, a set of safety goggles were resting on the brim of the ball cap that sat low over the stranger's eyes. The sight of Levi moved the man from his relaxed state. As he stood upright, Levi could see just how long his legs

were. The speed at which he covered the distance between them made
Levi cringe. Way too determined. Way too fast. And still, the chainsaw
was in his hand.

Oh hell. Two minutes ago Levi hadn't cared if Jack the Ripper had
saved him. Now he really fucking cared.

CHAPTER 4

LEVI TOOK three steps back as the large man quickly covered the space between them. Looking down, he searched for something to defend himself—a large limb, a rock—anything. His only thought: no one would hear him scream.

Continuing forward, the intimidating man emerged into the daylight from beneath the shadows of the thick pine canopy. He was close enough for Levi to see his face was twisted with confusion. The growing panic retreated as Levi recognized the ball-capped man.

"N-Noah?" Yes, it was. Noah Macy from college, and high school. Whoever would have guessed he'd be so thankful to see him, especially when Noah had been one of the jocks who'd picked on Levi in high school. *Pretty Boy* had been the nickname Noah had branded him with; however, it had never been said with disdain or intended as bullying—at least that was what Levi had believed. And as far as Levi knew, he wasn't a psychopathic killer. Well, Noah didn't look like one at least but, then again, killers rarely looked like murderous monsters, so strike that.

Noah's recognition of Levi kicked in, and an incredulous look crossed his face as he surveyed Levi from head to toe. For a moment, Levi's heart stopped. What if Noah took advantage of their secluded location to beat down Levi?

"Pretty B—I mean, Levi? What the hell? You're soaking wet." The last question stuck in his throat. Noah's eyebrows rose in a quizzical manner, his green eyes overflowing with—concern? Noah stripped out of his parka and wrapped the jacket around Levi's shoulders. His black T-shirt flowed around his lean frame. The residual warmth of his body made a small dent in the aching cold inside of Levi. "What happened?"

Biting down on his lower lip, Levi pondered his reply. *Well, I was falling asleep in stats, and I thought my head was going to literally explode, so I fled to the woods, running like a possessed maniac, and left the trail—which I know you should never do—but then I felt something— shit, yes—I actually felt something real, an emotion, then I was hot, so fucking hot, that I jumped into the lake in the middle of March. So what's up with you?* Yeah, that's exactly what Levi should have said.

"I f-f-fell into the l-l-lake." Close enough to the truth.

Noah frowned, giving him the standard that-was-dumb-look. Levi shrugged, way past the point of caring about anyone's opinion. He was just friggin' cold. Briskly, he rubbed his hands together.

Noah grabbed Levi's hands between his, and they all but disappeared inside of Noah's. "Don't rub. I doubt you've got frostbite, but if you do, you could damage the skin, tear it." Noah was oddly gentle.

The comment might have actually halted Levi's nagging amputation fears if he could have felt Noah's hands touching his. Nope. Nothing but numbness.

"We have to get you inside and warm you up, get you out of those wet clothes." Noah surveyed Levi. His clothes clung so tight to his body Levi was sure they had melded to his skin. "You shouldn't walk just in case your toes are frostbitten." He paused, assessing the situation. "I'll carry you."

Huh?

Levi's exaggerated frown brought a curl to the side of Noah's mouth. Before any form of protest could fall from Levi's lips, Noah effortlessly scooped Levi into his arms, climbing the stairs and pushing through the green door of the small cabin. Levi may have been small, but damn, he wasn't some kind of damsel in distress.

"Fuck, Noah, put me down." Levi struggled to free himself from the tight grip.

Noah chuckled, then deposited Levi onto the sofa that sat across from an impressive river-rock fireplace. A hand-hewn mantle, about a foot thick, was covered with more Adirondack-style knickknacks and memorabilia. The inside of the cabin was typical Adirondack style—high beam-exposed ceilings, knotty pine walls, wide plank flooring, the requisite Adirondack chairs, wood floors, walls decorated with antique fishing rods, creels, deer heads and antlers—fishing and hunting stuff were a must; however, this was a higher-end Adirondack style with several expensive pieces of furniture crafted out of limbs and logs from the area. It called to mind memories of his uncle's cabin.

Levi pulled his knees to his chest and sunk inside the down parka. Searing pain spread through his toes and fingers as if flames licked at them. A nagging ache crept up his right side and under his arm. He swore he would never be warm again. At least his teeth had stopped chattering.

"Not sure what I can find here for clothes." Noah's voice startled Levi. He'd been waiting for some form of taunting from Noah or to be called Pretty Boy, but Noah was being nothing but hospitable. His voice faded as if he had moved out of the room. "I'm sure I can find something, though," he called out.

Footsteps signaled Noah's return, but Levi kept his head buried, focusing to block out the screaming pain. The couch cushion shifted as Noah sat next to him. He touched Levi's hair, and Levi flinched.

"Levi?" Noah's deep voice was soft with an undercurrent of worry.

Without raising his head, Levi spoke. "My toes and fingers feel like they're on fire."

When Noah had failed to reply, Levi raised his head.

Noah nodded with understanding. "As they warm up they'll burn, maybe itch, but don't itch." He pointed a finger at him. "I'm more worried about your core temp right now. Need to bring it up before you go into shock." He rubbed the nape of his neck. "Truthfully, I have no clue how you even made it here in such great shape."

The thought had crossed Levi's mind as well. "You're full of knowledge. You a Boy Scout or something?"

Noah cocked an eyebrow, then chuckled. "Yeah. Something like that. I found these." He motioned to the clothes in his lap. "They'll definitely be too big. Belong to the guy who owns this cabin, but they're warm and dry. You'll need to take off everything that's wet." Noah flashed a nervous smile.

Everything?

Yeah, that shouldn't be an issue because they were guys, and guys saw each other naked in the locker room. Not that he ogled the other guys, but Levi imagined it was a lot like a straight guy in a girl's locker room. You were going to look and you might get hard, right? Although he was pretty sure his dick was a frozen Popsicle at that point, Levi wasn't taking any chances getting naked in front of a guy, a straight guy. Levi reached a tentative hand out from under the coat for the items of clothing. "Is there somewhere I can change?"

Noah glanced at the room where he'd found the clothes but appeared unsure. Levi cradled the needed clothes to his chest, wondering why the hesitation.

"Ummm… why don't you change here?"

Here! In front of you?

"I-I mean…." The words stumbled out of Noah's mouth, and he drew in a deep breath. "What I *meant* to say is that I'll go into the other room while you change so you don't have to walk all the way over there." Again, the nervous smile. What the hell was that? Noah was one of those confident guys Levi had always envied. A guy who wasn't bothered by anything.

Levi's stomach did a flip. Warily, he regarded Noah's words and body language since he'd arrived at the cabin. Noah had been sending up signals that most gay guys would call gaydar. Levi didn't believe in that crap. He considered it a dangerous mistake to assume someone was gay. What Levi did know was when macho jock types were sending signals. It wasn't as if Noah was a stranger. Being gay in a small town wasn't exactly news, but being openly gay in public was. Noah was an acquaintance of Gia's from high school, but she'd never once let Levi know he swung toward boys—well, now men. If Noah was Gia's friend, Levi would trust him since Gia didn't tolerate losers. And Noah was trying to help him in what was one of the stupidest situations he'd ever allowed himself to be in.

When Levi didn't agree immediately, Noah spoke. "I'll go into the other room and promise not to look," Noah said, then held up two fingers and smiled. "Scout's honor."

"Okay." Levi twisted his upper body to lay the clothes on the coffee table. A stabbing pain ripped up his right side. He cried out. Instinctively, his left hand went up to protect the area as he fell toward the table. His right palm slammed into the floor before his head could strike the table's jagged corner.

"Shit, Levi."

Pain throbbed in his side. Muscles in his chest and stomach clenched tight, restricting his lungs. He gasped for air as if the wind had been knocked out of him. Frozen in pain, he struggled to remain upright as darkness clouded his vision.

A fuzzy Noah knelt before him.

"What's wrong?"

Levi could only manage to shake his head. With great effort and agony, he drew in enough air to grunt out two words. "Fuck…. Pain."

Noah immediately began inspecting Levi's body. "Where?" He pushed the coffee table away and moved to the side Levi protected with his left hand.

Levi signaled to his side. Closing his eyes helped him to direct his attention toward relaxing his muscles and away from his physical torment.

"Your side hurts?"

Levi nodded. Where the hell was the pain coming from? He still couldn't take a deep breath.

"Move your hand so I can take a look."

Levi shook his head, continuing to guard the vulnerable area with his hand. The intense pain slowly faded into a hot throb. No more pain was his current motto.

"Please, just let me look." Noah's voice was calm and oddly soothing. "I'm sure it's nothing. I promise not to hurt you."

Again, Levi refused. That shit hurt way too much. Call him a pussy and see if he cared.

"Just let me look, please."

"I'm okay." Levi had forced the words out. Now if someone would stop trying to rip his side apart, he wouldn't be called a liar.

An exasperated sigh escaped Noah. "You've always been so stubborn. Just trust me."

Was that a hint of aggravation in Noah's voice? And what did he know about Levi's stubbornness?

Glancing over his shoulder, Levi caught a glimpse of Noah where he knelt. His hands were planted firmly at his hips, his green eyes had darkened, and his face hardened. Just the sides of his shoulder-length auburn hair had been pulled back into a ponytail. Shorter, wavy locks hung at the sides of his face. When had he taken off his hat? His hard stare told Levi he was serious about checking his injury.

"Okay." Levi relented and removed his hand. He clamped his eyes shut, prepping for the pain.

"I'm going to lift up your sweater so I can take a look." Noah slipped his finger under the hem of Levi's sweater next to his hip. The tip of Noah's finger gently swiped Levi's skin, causing him to flinch.

"Did I hurt you?"

"No."

Why had he jumped?

Carefully, Noah peeled the damp fabric toward Levi's armpit. Reflexively, Levi wrapped his arm around his chest to prevent too much skin exposure. Noah didn't seem to notice his act of modesty. Yeah, that wasn't embarrassing or anything.

"Hell, Levi!" Noah startled him—again.

"What?" Levi craned his neck to catch a glimpse of the area, but the pain limited his ability to twist.

Noah squinted as if trying to get a better look. "What did you say happened? You *fell* into the lake?"

That's exactly what he'd said. "Yup."

"Did you hit your side against something?"

It had all happened so fast, he wasn't sure. He'd tripped coming onto the rock, but he hadn't fallen. Actually, he *had* fallen into the water—twenty feet into the water onto his side—the side currently holding Noah's attention.

Without getting too specific, he said, "I didn't hit anything, but I fell pretty far and landed on that side in the water."

"And *where* exactly were you that you fell far enough to crack a rib?"

Levi's head snapped around, igniting the pain. "I broke a rib?"

"Oh, yeah. At least one." Noah reexamined the area. "Maybe two."

No way. He had to be wrong. "How do you know they're—"

"Broken? The side of your chest is turning a reddish purple color from right here under your armpit to about here." He twirled his finger over a spot Levi couldn't see. "It's worse right in the middle. A deeper purple. Bruising like that generally means broken bones."

"But it didn't really hurt until now," Levi felt as if his entire body was on display for Noah's perusal. He grabbed his sweater and pulled it down.

Noah blinked. "Cold tends to numb injuries, and you fell into a huge pool of ice water." He stood and returned the ball cap to his head. "We need to get you to the hospital."

Oh, no way. "Are you kidding me? I can't go to the hospital. What am I supposed to tell my parents?" His father was going to go ballistic— Levi had screwed up again!

Levi managed to sit on the floor and tried to catch what little breath his ribs allowed. Definitely fucked something up.

"We aren't going to mess around with this." Again with the directness. "You need X-rays. You could have punctured a lung, or liver, or be bleeding internally. No messing around with this, Pretty Boy."

Levi frowned at the name, and didn't those injuries sound a little over the top? Levi decided he liked the reassuring, smiling Noah better than the direct, take-charge Noah, but thought better of arguing. Even if it seemed farfetched, the idea of slowly bleeding to death increased Levi's cooperativeness. He even changed into the oversized clothes while tears threatened to spill from his eyes.

"I can't really walk right now. Guess we'll just have to stay here, or you'll have to carry me to your car." The thought of walking across the room, much less a mile back to his car, sent phantom spikes of pain into his feet. The thought of Noah carrying him thrilled Levi even less.

Noah turned from the cabinet he'd just opened with a pile of fleece blankets in his arms. "You won't have to walk."

"So, how do we get out of here?"

"By boat."

Right. Why hadn't Levi known that?

CHAPTER 5

THE ENTIRE agony of the trip to the hospital—walking to the shore, the boat ride, lying in the back seat of Noah's SUV, bumps and turns—blurred in Levi's mind as he lay on the gurney in the ER. The flimsy pale blue curtain around his bed did little to drown out the noises of the hospital. X-rays had been taken, blood drawn, parents called, and pain medication administered. The pills took the edge off the pain and clouded his mind. If only he could sleep before his parents arrived. *If only I could crawl into a hole…*.

"Hey, Pretty Boy."

"Hmmm?" Levi didn't open his eyes. The floating sensation was kind of nice.

"How's it going?" Noah whispered as if it were a requirement.

"Oh, just peachy. Your original diagnosis was correct, Dr. Macy." Levi couldn't help the giggle that escaped as he looked up at Noah. "Minor frostbite and one broken rib." He waved a finger in the air.

Oh, how he hoped they'd send him home with more of that pain stuff. What had he felt earlier in the woods? Euphoria? Yeah, this was a lot like that.

Noah circled around the gurney. His hat was off again. More locks of hair had escaped their tie and floated wildly around his face. The pools of his emerald irises were deep and inviting. Such long eyelashes. Soft, rounded lips. When Noah gently rested his hand on Levi's forearm, goose bumps sprung to life, and an unfamiliar warmth spread from beneath Levi's navel, twisted and turned, and traveled south. Levi gazed up at Noah with a wide smile. He had a desire to reach up and pull Noah to him for a kiss. That thought didn't even register as odd.

Noah cocked his head to one side, raised an eyebrow, and a lopsided smile curled his lips.

Had he always been so good-looking? Levi's need for Noah increased, filling him as he lost himself in those green eyes. He'd never lusted for someone before. "Feeling pretty good right now?" Noah asked.

Levi nodded. He couldn't lie. He felt awesome. "They should put this stuff in the water."

A loud burst of laughter filled the room, and Levi lost himself in the laughing man before him.

UNFORTUNATELY, ALL good things must end, and within two hours, Levi was in his own bed. A nagging ache in his side and the same old anxiety replaced the medication-induced euphoria. No such luck being sent home with those little magic pills, no chance of extending the artificial high. He'd been given something less impressive. And halted just as swiftly as it had surfaced, the lust he'd felt for Noah.

Only the skeletons of that former glorious rapture remained. A growing black hollow expanded through Levi's chest, adding to the enormous sense of loss weighing heavily on him. Fear of never feeling another emotion so vividly again fueled his anxiety. It felt a lot like mourning.

Closing his eyes, Levi tried to take slow, deep breaths, but the bandage wrapped around his ribcage restricted the expansion. Scratch deep breathing from his list of anxiety-fighting tools. Muscle relaxation, number two on the list. Yet the thoughts whirling about his head kept focusing on those moments on the gurney, the warm feelings, and Noah. No matter how far from this day he traveled in time, Levi doubted he could forget his emotions as he'd gazed up at Noah. The next time Levi saw Noah, he wouldn't feel anything.

A wave of panic spilled over the top of the dam.

Levi's attention shifted to the black zippered pouch still on his nightstand. One pill could strengthen the dam, make it taller and stronger. Why suffer with another panic attack when it was preventable? Except for the brief time he'd spent at college in Plattsburgh, his meds had faithfully squashed the panic for years. A low level of perpetual anxiety had remained, but it hadn't crippled his life as the panic had. So why continue to abandon the proven method of his medication?

Because he'd *felt* something earlier.

Not the fake euphoria from the pills at the hospital. That had been a lie. What he'd felt in those brief moments when he'd run through the woods had been genuine emotion. Was his mind finally waking up from its long antidepressant-induced slumber? God, how long had he been on meds? Ten years? A short week of abstinence apparently wasn't long enough to make a significant difference. Hoping the feeling part of his brain would flip on like a switch when he'd quit the meds had been wishful thinking, but something was happening. It was as if that part of his brain was trying to restart, but in fits and starts, sometimes allowing small amounts of emotion through, like when he'd cried with Logan. Other times, his emotions were revving into overdrive like the euphoria in the woods. Despite the malfunction, something was changing, and that brought him a single ray of hope.

Maybe I can finally be a real boy, he mused to himself.

That would have to be enough to sustain him as he waited for his emotions to emerge from their slumber. He needed to stay positive.

God, I need to take a piss!

Levi's bathroom was only ten feet from his bed, but relief might as well have been a million miles away. The relentless searing-hot poker thrusting into his right side made movement not only scary but near impossible.

Voices in the hallway caught his attention. His mother spoke right outside of Levi's door. During the car ride home from the hospital, Levi had endured his mother's lamenting of his accident. Why hadn't he been in class? Whatever had possessed him to go to the lake alone? What had gotten into him since he'd left Plattsburgh State? All questions a frightened, caring mother had the right to ask. Questions Levi had failed miserably to answer because he didn't know.

Levi willed his mother to go away, too tired to face another interrogation. The door opened slowly, and Levi clamped his eyes shut. Fake sleeping always worked. His mother had no problem waking her children but get the sniffles, skin your knee, or anything worse, and she'd let you sleep for a week if that's what it took to heal.

"Levi?"

Soft footsteps on the rug, rustling of fabric, a gentle hand on Levi's forehead, and then her retreat.

Out in the hall, his mother spoke again. "He's sleeping."

"What did he say happened?" The booming voice rattled across Levi's nerves. *Ugh*, his father.

Luckily, he'd been out on a job with Logan when the hospital had called. Levi held his breath as they spoke.

"He said he slipped off a large rock and fell into the water." His mother's attempt at whispering had failed miserably.

"And what the hell was he doing at the lake in the first place?" Levi was convinced his father's voice could crack concrete if he became loud enough.

"He said he needed a break."

"A break?" His father snorted. "That boy just needs to buckle down and focus on school."

The words sank Levi's heart. His father always went there whenever Levi struggled with his anxiety. Buckle down, work harder, stop the nonsense, do what he needed to do, and Levi would be fine.

"Art, you know he has issues, and they aren't going to go away just by trying harder." At least his mother defended him.

"I think he needs to see Dr. Ross again," his father said.

His therapist?

His mother chuckled dryly. "He saw that woman for over eight years, and a lot of good that has done. I think he needs a new therapist. I'm worried, especially after today." There was a short pause. "Art, what if this wasn't an accident?"

Huh?

"What do you mean?"

Levi lifted his head to hear better. God, his bladder was about to explode. Wouldn't wetting the bed just add to his freakiness?

"When I called Logan earlier to tell him about Levi, he said not to give him a hard time about this. When I asked him why, he told me that Levi's been struggling with his anxiety. He said that Levi stopped taking his meds over a week ago."

Levi gasped. Logan had told their mother! How could he have betrayed him, and to their mother of all people?

"Is he taking them now? He needs those meds." His father's volume rose and was tinged with urgency. Levi had no clue his father gave a crap if he took his pills, much less went to his therapist or not.

"Listen, Art." Her voice shook. "You don't think Levi tried to intentionally hurt himself, do you?"

Holy shit! Did she really believe that Levi had tried to… commit suicide? Oh, Logan was so dead.

"That's nonsense." Apparently, his father was having none of that. "Levi may have some issues, but the boy's not suicidal, so get that out of your head."

Levi was surprised by his father's words. He closed his eyes, trying to block out their voices. Surely this would blow over after Levi assured his mother it had been an accident, even if his spring swim had been intentional. However, before any of that happened he was going to murder Logan.

"Mom, don't say stuff like that," Logan said, his annoyance apparent. *Speak of the devil.*

"I'm going to eat dinner." Levi heard his father descend the stairs.

"Logan, you said it yourself he stopped his—"

"Mom, Levi didn't do this to himself. I know he didn't, so cut him some slack. You and Dad are always giving him such a hard time."

Any anger Levi harbored for Logan faded fast.

"We're no harder on him than we are on you. In fact, we've cut Levi more slack than we ever did for you. It's just... I'm...." Her voice wavered slightly.

Oh great. Was she crying?

"Levi's going to be fine. Don't worry." The softness in Logan's tone confirmed that his mother was indeed crying. Well, didn't that just make him feel like a selfish asshole?

When his mother finally spoke, her words drove the asshole point home even further.

"I'm just so tired. Ever since he was little.... He's draining me. It's always something with him. When will it end?" Her confession struck Levi hard.

"Let me talk to him," Logan said, and then there was silence. Levi wondered if Logan was hugging their mother, trying to comfort her.

Levi laid his head on the pillow. When Logan entered the room, Levi closed his eyes.

I need to take a piss so badly!

When he didn't sense Logan near, Levi peeked out of one eye. Logan grabbed the chair at Levi's desk and swung it around to the side of the bed. When Logan glanced in his direction, Levi shut his eye, let out a little snore, and waited.

"I know you're awake. You may fool Mom, but I ain't buying it."

Levi pursed his lips and opened his eyes. Logan straddled the chair he'd set down backward. He rested his forearms over the back, his ball cap swinging casually in his hands. His mouth curved into a mischievous smile. He still wore his work clothes—plaid flannel shirt, blue down vest. His faded jeans and work boots were caked with dried mud. Every inch the Adirondack man. His attire spoke to just how upset their mother had truly been. Any other time, Logan wouldn't have made it past the back porch with those dirty clothes much less the boots.

"Hey, Crash."

"Ugh." Levi moaned and wrinkled his nose at the long-forgotten nickname. Logan had bestowed that name on Levi after he'd run his bike into a tree and broken his leg. "Crash" had stuck to him like superglue for over a year. The wry smile on Logan's face told Levi it might stick again after an eight-year hiatus.

"So a broken rib, huh?"

"Yup."

Pulling at a stray thread on his comforter, Levi intentionally avoided looking at his brother. The world's most uncomfortable silence filled the space between them. Biting hard on the inside of his cheek distracted him further as he waited for Logan to just say it.

"You know Mom and Dad are really worried about you."

There it was.

Levi snorted. "Dad worried about me? Yeah, I don't see it."

Logan sighed and looked down as if studying his hat. "I see it in his face. He may not say it, but he looks… worried… maybe even sad."

The words Dad and sad in the same sentence were an oxymoron.

"And Mom—"

Levi cut Logan off. "I heard Mom. She's tired of me." He folded his arms over his chest.

"That's not true. All she said is that she's tired." Logan had always played the peacemaker between Levi and their parents.

"Same difference." Levi stared straight ahead stubbornly.

"She was crying. Don't you even care?" Logan asked in what sounded like sheer exasperation.

Like most people would, Levi really did want to care. What kind of a person wouldn't be distressed knowing they'd made their mother cry? Only someone who was dead inside, someone who lacked the ability to feel on a deeper level, someone like Levi. Yes, his mother crying had bothered him, but it bordered more on annoyance than anything else.

"She always treats me like a baby."

Logan had stopped twirling his hat in his fingers. The hard lines of his mouth and jaw, the furrow in his brow, his cold hard stare, told Levi that Logan was either too enraged to speak or debating if he should say anything more.

"You know, Levi, sometimes you can be such a brat." He'd muttered the last word, but Levi had heard it all the same.

"Well, we all can't be as perfect as you, Logan." He'd tried to volley the hurt delivered with Logan's statement, but truthfully, hurting his brother was the last thing he wanted to do.

Damn, they were acting as if they were kids again.

"Yeah, I never get tired of hearing that."

The crestfallen look on Logan's face and defeated tone told Levi he'd hit his mark, and he hated that he'd gone there. Fatigue dulled Logan's eyes to a grayish-blue color. His weariness wasn't due to a lack of sleep, but most likely from the realization that the long, hard battle he'd been fiercely fighting was an act of futility.

Levi cringed. What was he doing pushing Logan away? Guilt stabbed into his chest. And then the pressure, that sudden sharp pain, was back, rapidly filling his skull.

Logan closed his eyes and pinched the bridge of his nose. Levi either had to get Logan out of his room or get away from him. *Bathroom!* Flinging the covers off, Levi bolted to a sitting position, fighting to suppress his cry of pain.

His movement brought Logan to his feet ready to assist. "Where're you going?"

"Bathroom. I can do it myself." Levi twisted away despite the pain when Logan reached to touch him.

Just as in class earlier, the force rose in his head, squeezing nerves to the point of screaming. He willed himself to rise. After successfully pushing off the bed, Levi stumbled as the agonizing pain in his side matched that in his head. He slammed into his desk, gripping the edge to remain upright. A painful pressure expanded in his chest.

"Are you okay?" Logan went to Levi and put his hand on Levi's shoulder.

Levi clenched his teeth. Air hissed through his lips as he tried to breathe through the never-ending pain. Lowering his head, he tightened every muscle, searching for the power to overcome the force working to destroy his mind.

"Is it another panic attack?"

Levi shook his head. That's when he saw something out of his window—a large man standing beneath the streetlight across the road. Dressed in a black sweatshirt with the hood pulled low over his face, the man looked right at Levi.

"Is it your ribs?" Logan squatted, looking up at Levi.

Another wave of agony shuddered through Levi as he clamped his eyes shut and dug his fingernails into his scalp. Tendrils of pain whipped around his brain. His rib cage seemed ready to bust open. A warm, wet rush washed down his legs.

"What do you need? Do you want me to get Mom?"

Levi grabbed Logan's wrist, unable to reply, muted from his battle to save his sanity. What kind of demon had his mind created to assault him so ruthlessly? And how long before it took over completely?

Weakness invaded Levi's legs. He wavered. Maybe this was a stroke? Or a second stroke? No. He didn't know how, but for some reason he knew this wasn't caused by something physical. Somehow his mind was creating this hell.

"I got ya." Logan wrapped an arm around Levi's waist. The pressure in his head lessened to a dull throbbing ache, the pain in his chest gone, returning his attention to his screaming ribs. Looking out of the window, Levi saw that the man had vanished, if he'd even truly been there.

"Let's get you back to bed," Logan whispered, guiding Levi away from the desk.

That's when Levi felt the wetness of his sweatpants and the awful realization that he'd pissed himself. A dark stain covered the front of his sweats. Even his socks were wet.

"Fuck!" He could only stare in disbelief.

"What?" Logan looked at the front of Levi's pants and for a minute appeared to be flustered.

"I don't know what happened. I didn't mean...." Tears flooded his eyes.

Logan shook off his bewilderment. "Hey, it's no big deal. I'll get some dry clothes. Sit in the chair."

Suddenly, as if a bucket of icy water had been dumped over him, Levi was submerged within a cesspool of overwhelming sorrow, immersed in a swelling sea of grief—heartache… sadness… loss… misery. The swirling anguish overtook his senses. No longer was he an empty shell, but one overflowing with the sadness and agony of a million tormented souls. A never-ending despair reached deep within him, twisting and turning his heart, scratching at his insides with razor-sharp claws. Hopelessness ripped through his mind filling every dark corner.

"Oh God, Logan." Levi cried as Logan guided him to the chair. "I… I c-can't do this anymore." Large sobs wracked Levi's body. Tears streamed from his cheeks onto his already wet sweatpants. He grabbed Logan by his forearms, frantically searching his brother's face for any comfort or reassurance.

Logan crouched in front of Levi, who threw his arms around him in one desperate motion. The desolation and misery were mind-numbing and crushed Levi's will to exist.

Logan pulled him close. "It's okay. Whatever it is, it's going to be okay." His reassurance was immediately crushed by Levi's despair.

"I'm an awful person. I don't deserve you or Mom or Dad. You're right. I'm a selfish brat." He sobbed and couldn't stop. "I only care about myself. Please don't hate me for ruining your life."

Levi squeezed his eyes shut, witnessing the gray barren plane of his existence—*Oh God*—the sadness, the utter hopelessness. Millennia of desperation rotting inside of him while hundreds of ghostly claws descended on his body, ripping huge gashes into his skin, digging into muscles and ligaments, gouging at his eyes, ripping out the protective bones of his chest, devouring his heart.

Only one way to stop the pain. End it now.

CHAPTER 6

SELF-INFLICTED METHODS of death flashed before Levi's eyes—a gunshot, slitting his wrists, electrocution, jumping from a great height, overdose.

Pills.

"What would ever make you think I hate you?" Logan's voice shook. "Just take some deep breaths and calm down. It's not that bad."

It was *that* bad, worse than an atomic bomb, a tsunami, a hurricane. Any moment he would be swept away into oblivion or disintegrate into a pile of dust.

Levi released Logan. He jumped up from the chair, the black bag on his nightstand his sole focus. Within it, salvation from a world of suffering. A sweet release.

After pulling out a bottle of meds, Levi worked at the child-safety cap. He had to open it. Swallowing all of them was the only thing that would save him.

Logan plucked the bottle from his hand. "I'll open it."

Levi reached for the bottle of pills prescribed to halt his panic attacks, intent on swallowing every last one. "Just give it to me." He tried to snatch the bottle again, then crumpled onto the bed from the pain.

I can't take this anymore!

Logan held out his hand, palm up, where two tiny pills rested.

He needed so many more.

"Levi, take these now."

Levi grabbed the pills and swallowed them dry. "I need more. Give me the rest of them, please."

Logan frowned, looking at the dosage again. "It says to take two."

"I need more."

Logan paled then steeled his expression. "No." He pushed the bottle into his front pocket and stared at Levi who wiped the wetness from his face. "I'm going to get you some clean clothes."

Levi wrapped his arms around his head. The intense anguish, distress, sorrow, were slowly fading and morphing into grief.

Logan returned to the bed with fresh clothes. Levi's eyes burned, ribs ached, the bone-crushing pressure now a small headache. Most importantly the imprudent plot to end his life was gone, the hollow in his chest once again empty.

Logan knelt on one knee before Levi. "Feeling better?" His tone was tenuous.

No, I was going to hurt myself, and I don't even know why. But he couldn't tell his brother that. "I'm okay."

Logan's expression was neutral, but the fear was evident in his eyes, as if he was unsure of what Levi would do next. Levi felt the same way. His life had gone from merely out of control to fucking crazy.

"Levi, what just happened?" Logan had never been afraid to ask the hard questions.

Too bad Levi didn't have any answers. First, there was the crushing pain at school followed by the euphoria that had burned so hot he'd propelled himself into a cold lake, his lustful desire for Noah, and again that terrible pressure in his head, and then a gut-wrenching despair worthy of ending his own life. What if Logan hadn't been there?

What if Levi had…?

"I can't remember ever seeing you cry… well, except when you hurt yourself or when Nana died, but other than that…. Now you've cried twice in the past two days." He shrugged, seemingly at a loss.

What could he tell Logan? The entire day had been crazy. Logan deserved the truth, honorable, reliable Logan, who'd never let Levi down. How could he tell Logan that his mind was crashing and would soon take him with it? Would he become a drooling shell, slumped over in a chair, unable to move or communicate, trapped in a hell designed just for him, or would he explode like a dying star and fill the air with his displaced molecules? Doubts began to surface that stopping his medications had been the cause. Actually, there had been periods of time when he'd gone without certain medications. Dr. Ross had called them "medication holidays." That had been only a few times in the last ten years, and he couldn't remember why they were stopped. Even during those times, which had been as long as two weeks, nothing like this had happened.

Levi licked at his dry lips and told a bold-faced lie. "A headache. They said something about a possible concussion at the hospital. I think it got worse when I stood." Yeah, that sounded good. "I thought my head was going to explode." Right, because he only cried from pain. So easy to lie when you were in the middle of a break with reality. "And yesterday I think it was because I hadn't been taking my meds."

Logan tilted his head, his face blank and expressionless. Levi couldn't tell if Logan had bought his lie or not. Logan's eyes softened, but not before he flashed an incredulous look at Levi. "You should talk to Mom. Maybe see your therapist again. I know going away to school and then having to come home was hard on you. And you know you can talk to me too." The earnest look on Logan's face was mixed with an underlying sadness. Levi couldn't blame him for worrying. Levi was worried himself.

"I know. Maybe, if things don't get better soon...." He didn't want to promise Logan anything he wouldn't do.

Logan spared him from having to go on. "Do you want me to help you get changed?"

Levi wrinkled his nose. "Fuck no. My own brother? Get out!" He forced a smile, hoping to bring levity to the anything-but-funny situation.

"I thought the same thing after I said it." His brother chuckled slightly, exaggerating a shudder.

Logan's smile quickly faded. Levi could tell he wanted to say something more. Questions were forming, doubts layering.

"I really meant it when I said I was sorry for, you know, everything," Levi said.

"That's what big brothers are for."

Levi highly doubted they were made to put up with all of his nonsense.

"Get some sleep, Crash. I'm right in the next room if you need anything."

Logan really meant that, but Levi also knew he wouldn't be bothering Logan, no matter what.

On his way to the door, Logan stopped and turned around. "Oh, I forgot. Gia called for you. She was freaked out by your exit from class. She said that she called your cell about a hundred times, and it went straight to voice mail. You should call her back or at least text her."

Levi sighed heavily. "Unfortunately, my phone sleeps with the fishes."

Logan laughed out loud. "You dropped your phone into the lake too?"

More like chucked it. "Unfortunately, yeah."

"That really sucks." Logan covered his mouth to hide his amusement.

"Yup, and since that was my second phone since November, Dad is going to kill me, especially after what happened to the last one. I will be phoneless for the foreseeable future."

Logan rubbed the stubble on his chin. "So, what's worse? Dropping your phone in the lake or dropping it in the driveway where Dad runs it over with his truck?"

Levi already knew the answer to that one.

"The Dad one most definitely," Logan said, answering for Levi, his blue eyes reflecting the light from the ceiling.

"Good night, Crash." Logan waved as he shut the door.

Levi smiled, but it was short-lived. He was going to miss Logan the most when he lost his sanity. Luckily, he'd avoided questions about what had happened at the lake. Unfortunately, the avoidance had come in the form of his head nearly exploding and pissing his pants like a toddler. Don't forget his near suicide attempt.

LEVI MANAGED to avoid further interactions with his mother and father for the night. Sleeping with a broken rib was even harder than it sounded. The ringing of the house phone startled him from a dead sleep. Levi was surprised by the sunlight filling his room. He snatched up the cordless phone from the nightstand and pulled the covers over his head. Gia screamed at him through the other end. Even with the phone six inches from his ear, Levi heard her loud and clear.

"Levi! What the hell happened? You're in class one minute and gone the next. Then I find out you fell into the goddamned lake and broke your rib? And I have to find out from Noah Macy that he brought you to the hospital."

"I'm fine." Noah was quite the blabbermouth, wasn't he? Levi rubbed his head. It was way too early for this.

Gia huffed. "Now spill all of the details and leave nothing out."

Levi knew if he didn't give her something juicy Gia would be at his bedside within twenty minutes. He gave her a story about a panic attack, the unplanned trip to the lake, tripping over his own feet, falling into the lake, cell phone and all, ending with the heroic rescue by Noah.

Hopefully that would satisfy her, but apparently she was hoping for a more exciting explanation.

"Are you sure you weren't at the lake for a rendezvous with Noah, but your hot and steamy lovemaking burned with such intensity that your only saving grace was to jump into the freezing lake?"

Close with the reason for jumping into the lake, but not the cause. "Wait. What?" Levi crawled out of his blanket cocoon. "You think I was having sex with Noah Macy?" Maybe she was as crazy as Levi was.

"No, I meant punching him in the friggin' face. Duh." She did sarcasm so well.

Levi rubbed his eyes. Was he still asleep? "Noah's not even gay."

"Do you even live on the same planet as the rest of us? Jesus Christ, Levi, last week at lunch Noah stopped and talked to us. When he left, I told you that he had his foot out of the closet."

Levi remembered something about Noah and a closet, but he hadn't thought Gia had been talking about that kind of closet. "Gia, when you tell me a hot sports jock like Noah Macy has stepped up to bat for my team, and my jaw doesn't scrape the floor and my eyes bug out of my head, then you can be fucking sure I'm not listening no matter what planet I'm currently visiting!"

So, Levi hadn't been wrong about the signals. Could be interesting if he was still hopped up on endorphins, but thinking of Noah Macy right then did nothing for him at all.

"You're the worst gay person I know."

Subpar at everything else, so why not the gay part as well?

"When you just shrugged I thought you weren't interested because, well, you're never interested."

But fucking lonely.

Shit, where had that come from?

Levi pondered what she'd said. "So just a foot out of the closet? How does that work?" You're either in or out, right? Who knew there were shades of being in the closet?

"Again. Worst. Gay. Person. Ever," Gia said emphatically, but Levi heard that underlying warmth few people got from her. "It means he's told a few people he trusts, but he isn't advertising. I think he told me because *you* and I are friends."

"But why would he... ohhhh." Levi realized his stupidity. Shit, had "pretty boy" been a compliment? That so wasn't important right then.

"Wait, how does he even know I'm gay?" Definitely wasn't anything Levi had ever advertised.

"I don't know. Maybe it's because you've never been out with a girl."

"I've never been out with a guy either."

"Sweetie, what that screams to most people is a guy in the closet."

Technically, Levi was in the closet since he knew he was gay, hadn't told anyone, and didn't hook up or date. There hadn't been any reason to tell anyone. He couldn't get into the dating/relationship part since emotions were required for that.

"Only you, Gia."

"A girl can have hope for her best friend, right? So speaking of hope, Noah asked me for your cell phone number, but—"

"Don't you dare give him my home phone number! I don't need a stalker."

"Hell, Levi, when a sweet piece of meat like Noah Macy asks for your number you rent a billboard to make sure he knows it. My God, he saved your life and all."

"Whatever. And now I'm going to do something I promised myself I'd never do in a million years because your Italian ego is big enough for ten people. I agree with you. I'm not interested in Noah Macy."

"While I revel in your coming to your senses and agreeing that I'm always right, I don't want to be right about this." A long silence followed, and Levi wondered if she'd hung up. Wouldn't be the first time she'd been pissed off enough to hit the End button. When she spoke again, her tone was uncharacteristically soft. "Sometimes I really worry about you Levi." And he knew she did.

Get in line. "Really, I'm fine. And I never said you were *always* right. Just this time."

"Your delusions are your own. And whatever about Noah."

Levi knew it was far from over with her where Noah was concerned.

Levi ended their call assuring Gia it was pointless to visit him, giving the excuse that the pain meds made him tired. That day, Levi was hiding from the world.

CHAPTER 7

A SHORT while later, there was a soft knock at his door.

He sighed heavily. If only the world would leave him alone. "Yeah?"

He heard his door open. "Levi, I... Levi? Where are you?"

"Right here, Mom," he said, really wishing he were anywhere else.

"What're you doing under the covers?"

"Nothing much." *Just hiding.*

"I'm not talking to a blanket, so get out here."

Levi threw the covers off.

"How're you feeling? Is the pain bad?" His mother bent over and picked up some of his dirty clothes.

"Just when I breathe," Levi muttered, picking some stray hairs from his black shirt.

"I'm sure you'll be good as new in no time."

If there was one thing Maggie Reed was good at, it was painting the ugliness of the world with sunshine.

She turned abruptly to face Levi. "But you are to stay in that bed until then."

Levi snorted but wouldn't argue with her when she used that "motherly tone." Would a month in bed be pushing it?

His mother disappeared into the bathroom still muttering something about having to go somewhere with someone today. Emerging from the bathroom, cradling a pile of dirty towels, she continued as if Levi had been listening all along. "You know Logan is very worried about you." His mother's statement was so matter-of-fact Levi had almost missed it.

"Logan? Really?" Levi tittered to himself. "Logan's worried" was Mom's code word for "I'm worried."

Averting her gaze, she continued. "Of course he is. Especially about this whole business of you stopping your medication."

The air hung thick and heavy. Levi knew he should end this quickly. "Well, I'm sure Logan is no longer worried since he watched me take my meds last night. He actually handed them to me."

His mother's mouth dropped open slightly, then closed. "Really. He didn't tell me that," she said, shaking off her surprise. "Well, I'm sure he's relieved that you took them."

Levi nodded. "Yup, *he's* relieved."

His mother surveyed the room, appearing to search for anything more to tidy. "Your father's at work. Logan had to run an errand and said he would check in on you later. Need anything before I leave?"

Where should I start?

"I'm good." Especially since the house would be empty soon.

"Okay, sweetie, I'll see you later."

Levi pulled the covers back over his head as his mother vacated the room. Sleep would have been a sweet escape, but the throbbing in his side and another knock on his door wouldn't allow it.

"Mom, I *still* don't need anything."

The door opened anyway. "Hiding under the blankets won't block Supermom's powers."

Peeking from under the covers, Levi found Logan leaning against the doorjamb, smirking. He was dressed in his usual work uniform—flannel shirt, white T-shirt, jeans minus the hiking boots (because their mother wasn't that upset anymore), and his Giants cap.

"Not even if it's made of kryptonite?" Levi winced as he struggled to sit up.

"Not even kryptonite can stop Supermom."

Logan stayed in the doorway. Levi surmised his distance was due to the events of the previous night—not to mention the night before that as well.

"Mom said you had to run an errand? What about work?"

Logan rarely took a day off, but occasionally it happened.

His brother raised his eyebrows. "Took a day off, so I thought I'd run out and pick up a little something for my little bro, Crash." Logan was enjoying the resurrection of Levi's nickname way too much.

"And what exactly dragged you out of the warmth of your bed on one of your rare days off?" Levi's interest had definitely been piqued.

Logan pulled a white plastic bag from behind his back and then, with a grin, tossed it onto the bed beside Levi.

Levi opened the small bag, pulling out a box. He glanced at Logan still looming in the doorway, the same satisfied grin on his face.

"An iPhone? Are you serious?"

"Just try not to get this one wet... *or* drop it in the driveway."

"But how did you get Mom and Dad to...." Levi bit the inside of his cheek. "They don't know, do they?"

Logan pursed his lips and shifted his shoulders, folding his arms across his chest. "No, and they don't need to know another 'Levi phone' bit the dust. Just consider it an early birthday present—and Christmas, Easter, Hanukah. You know, all of the major ones."

Knowing how expensive the phone was killed Levi's elation. Yes, he'd wanted an iPhone for over a year, and no, he hadn't been able to save the money, and yes, here was one in his hands, and, no, he couldn't keep it. Still living at home, Logan's sanity held on by tiny frayed threads. He'd been saving to move out. The phone must have taken a chunk of his savings.

Logan shook his head. "Jeez, I'd imagined a tad more excitement. I mean, every other word out of your mouth for the past year has been iPhone."

Excitement couldn't begin to cover how he felt with the phone in his hands, and he didn't want to appear ungrateful. "It's just... I mean, I love it, really I do, but... it's too expensive. You need the money to move."

Logan lifted an eyebrow, and a quizzical expression crossed his face as if he hadn't expected that reaction.

"Anxious to get rid of me?"

"You know I didn't mean that." Levi never wanted him to leave.

"Enough arguing." Logan raised his hands and shook his head. "It's all set up with your number. Of course, yours truly is already in the contacts because, hey, I'm awesome." He beamed a cocky smirk. "Just turn it on, and it's all set. I've only got about twenty minutes before I have to meet Melissa so we can spend some 'quality time' together." He had added the air quotes and then rolled his eyes deeply. "I'll check in later. May even send you a text."

Before he could beat a hasty retreat, Levi said, "Thanks."

Logan bowed slightly and was gone. The house was oddly silent.

LEVI SPENT the remainder of the day playing with his new phone. He received dozens of texts from Gia expressing unabashed jealousy over Levi's new toy, and making sure he kept up on the gossip, which Levi couldn't have cared less about. When Gia's last text mentioned Noah, Levi ignored her.

True to his word, Logan sent a text complete with a picture of him with Melissa. Levi couldn't glean where the photo had been taken, but he was certain it wasn't anywhere Logan truly wanted to be. Melissa tended to lead while Logan followed. True love.

Levi dragged his laptop across the bed and logged into his Facebook account, which he rarely checked. The last time had been over a week ago. Besides Gia, there weren't many people Levi considered true friends. Compared to others on the social network, his friends list bordered on the pathetic side, filled mostly with relatives. Some friends on his list were people from his current college classes. A few were from Plattsburgh State, including Professor Winston who'd taught Levi's philosophy class. For some reason, they'd clicked and kept in touch on Facebook since Levi had abandoned college for the safety of home. She'd been trying to get Levi to visit, but he'd declined each time. For the most part, Levi had accepted many of the friend requests, being nice. Now, the small red box with the white number one at the top of the screen made him wonder who he'd be friending out of nicety this time.

When he clicked on the red box, Noah Macy's small face beamed back at him from the request. *Fuck.* He let out a moan and threw his head back onto the pillow. Why was this guy constantly invading his life? Gia must have put him up to it. Levi bit down on his lip and tapped his finger against the keyboard. What harm could come from friending the man who'd saved him from freezing to death? Gia had been prepared to offer up his phone number. This act might serve to silence the subject, giving time for all of the hoopla to die down.

Two choices: Accept or Not Now. Tentatively, he pointed the white arrow to Accept. *Just do it.* With a press of his thumb, the request was accepted. He was now "friends" with Noah Macy. No big deal, right? But if it wasn't, then what was with the nagging intuition that Noah was about to complicate his life?

Probably a premonition because Noah showed up at Levi's house that night.

CHAPTER 8

NOTHING. NOT a twinge, or a skipped beat of the heart, or an inkling of the warm lust Levi had experienced yesterday as he'd gazed up at Noah from that gurney. He assessed Noah sitting on the couch across from him, studying the contours of his cheeks, the shape of his lips and tried to recreate that perfect moment in the hospital. Nothing. Both relief and remorse struggled to be recognized.

Earlier, Levi had been relatively pain free and comfortable in his bed. Reluctantly, he'd moved to the couch in the living room after his father's announcement that Noah would arrive at 6:00 p.m. No amount of arguing or excuses got Levi off that hook. The question of the day? How did Noah get an invitation to his house and from his own father no less? Impossible, Levi had thought, yet there Noah sat across from Levi. Noah's wavy auburn hair had been pulled neatly into a ponytail. None of those pesky, errant waves from yesterday were visible. In his button-up blue shirt, khakis, and leather loafers, he'd come dressed to impress.

Levi's father had monopolized most of the conversation so far, which took the pressure off Levi. Yet Noah kept insisting on dragging Levi in. After a play-by-play of the events after he'd stumbled to the cabin, Noah went on to explain why he'd been there in the first place. To Levi's surprise, Noah was an Adirondack guide as well as a college student with plans to study law. He'd done a summer internship with a lawyer downstate and was now the caretaker of the cabin the lawyer owned. Most weekends, Noah guided fishermen, hunters, hikers—anyone who wanted the mountain experience—through the Adirondacks. During the week, he attended classes and kept up the cabin. A bonus, he added, was his unlimited use of the cabin since the owner only visited the area a few times a year. Noah flashed Levi a wide grin with that last bit of info as if it would impress him.

Levi's mother stepped into the living room, asking Noah, for like the tenth time, if he wanted anything. Again, his answer was no. Apparently, he wasn't getting that saying yes would have saved him from her incessant hospitality. Unfortunately, his mother's mission that time wasn't to serve as much as to drag his father from the living room.

Great, he was alone with Noah.

Unease filled Levi's gut. Noah may have saved him, but Levi felt as if he owed Noah something. He didn't like the feeling. Small talk wasn't Levi's forte. Any kind of social interaction involving him holding up one end of the conversation was something he tended to avoid. What would a normal person say in that situation?

Noah stretched his arm and rested it across the back of the couch. Levi could swear there was nervousness underlying his cool façade.

Silence rarely bothered Levi—in fact, most of the time, it was his saving grace—but he chose to break it first.

"I'm not sure if I said it at the hospital"—Levi could have said anything given the drugged state he'd been in—"and... well, I just want to thank you for helping me out yesterday." He breathed a sigh of relief. He'd spoken and lived to tell about it.

Noah sat forward and propped his elbows on his knees. His face brightened, and a gleam flashed in his eye. His smile was a bit too wide. "No problem. Kind of a freaky day, huh?"

The understatement of the century. "Yeah, I guess." So, he'd said thanks and now wanted to know when to expect Noah's departure.

When Noah sat back, getting comfortable again, Levi feared it was going to be a long haul.

"So, exactly how did you end up here, at my house, tonight?" The question sounded ruder out loud than it had in Levi's head.

Before Levi could retract the question, Noah answered. "Your father called me. He actually knows my mom. He surveyed some land for her a couple of years ago. Your dad said he appreciated what I'd done for you and then asked me to visit." He shrugged.

Probably more like getting the story straight from the horse's mouth. The fact that his father trusted a stranger more than he trusted Levi was a sickening kick in the stomach.

"So how're the ribs doing? That was a nasty bruise. I can only imagine what it looks like today."

Levi's cheeks heated at the memory of Noah lifting his sweater yesterday. It increased his unease tenfold. "I haven't taken off the wrap that the doctor put on. He said not to remove it for a couple of days. Something about keeping the swelling down. Really, I have no desire to see it."

Time to leave, right?

"You're lucky you only broke a rib. At that distance, you could have been knocked out."

The enormity of the distance he'd fallen hadn't hit Levi until they'd taken the motorboat from the camp. When Levi pointed out the massive stone ledge, Noah had shaken his head in disbelief and questioned how Levi had walked away with only a broken rib.

"Yup. I'm the lucky one all right." Levi groaned silently. A dental visit would have been less painful than their conversation, but how did he end it without being totally impolite? Then, as if on cue, Logan walked into the room, Melissa following close behind.

My hero!

Levi introduced them to Noah. Logan vigorously shook Noah's hand, showing his appreciation.

"Hey, thanks for taking care of *Crash* here for us. We just never know what he'll do next." Logan winked at Levi.

Levi glared at his brother and crossed his arms.

"Logan, don't pick on Levi. How're you feeling?" Melissa asked, flopping into a chair with a magazine she'd been carrying.

Levi knew he liked her for a reason. "Good."

Noah chuckled with an impish smirk. "*Crash?*"

"Logan, you're gonna get it," Levi murmured, but first he had to remove himself as the focus of the conversation. "Hey, did you know that Noah's an Adirondack guide?"

That statement not only removed the focus from Levi but also saved him from further conversation with Noah. By eight o'clock, Levi's ribs pulsed as the worthless pain meds wore off. Levi excused himself for the comfort of his bed despite the forlorn expression on Noah's face.

Logan assisted Levi off the couch. Climbing the stairs was a slow process, his ribs pained with each lift of his right leg. Some relief came in the form of crappy pain meds and escape into sleep.

TWO DAYS in bed, and Levi truly believed he'd lose his mind faster than he'd expected. When Gia called Sunday morning, Levi begged her for a speedy rescue. Another day at home with his mother, and Levi wouldn't be responsible for his actions.

After a brief argument where his mother had insisted he remain in bed or suffer the consequences, Levi was in Gia's Honda and free from the warden and her prison.

"You're a life saver!"

"If it wasn't for my cousin Alice's wedding, I would have rescued you yesterday. Hey, do you know what you get when you put an ugly woman in a three-thousand-dollar wedding dress?" Without waiting for a reply, she said, "Yup, an ugly woman in a three-thousand-dollar wedding dress. No amount of money was going to save that wreck of a woman. He's definitely marrying her for the money."

Levi held his side as he laughed through the stabbing pain, but it was so worth it. When he could finally breathe, he asked, "Isn't she your mother's cousin? The one who…." Shit, he hadn't thought that through. "Sorry, I didn't mean…."

Gia was quiet for a moment. "No, it's okay, Levi. Alice was the one who helped take care of my mother when she was sick."

Gia's mother had died from cervical cancer, already stage four when it was discovered. Her death two years ago had been a blow to the Alberici family especially Dario, Gia's father. He called Cara Alberici his soul mate, and Levi had been in awe over how he'd worshipped his wife. While he'd mourned her passing, Levi had been sure he'd be lost without her. Instead, he was the man Levi had always known—strong, commanding, confident, loving. Levi had asked him one day how he was coping so well. Dario had told Levi his wife would always be in his heart and that someday they would be reunited. He'd told this over and over to his daughters and Levi, as if knowing that would ease their pain. If anything happened to him, he would be with his Cara. Until then he had daughters and an adopted son to raise. Levi had always viewed Dario as a father figure, and Gia was like a sister.

"Did your father go?"

"Yeah, and he did okay. I figured after all of this time seeing my mom's twin sister would be really hard for him…." She visibly swallowed. Her mother's death hadn't been too easy for her. "But he smiled and laughed and was really okay."

Levi nodded. "I'm glad it went well."

Their first stop was Gia's house. She lived outside of Ticonderoga, on Lake Champlain, which bordered the east side of town. Levi had spent so much time there over the years that he'd taken over one of the many guest rooms as his own. Gia's father often traveled for his business, which had something to do with extraction and storage. Whatever that meant. Gia's older sister, Rachele, was in college in Burlington, Vermont, about an hour and a half away.

Gia's house was an amazing modern log cabin with all of the amenities. Huge cook's kitchen, large family room with massive floor-to-ceiling windows, a deck overlooking the lake, walk-in showers, and to top it off, a heated pool if the lake was too cold for a swim. It was definitely posh and paled Levi's house immensely. Mostly Levi came to Gia's for the quiet and solitude.

She dragged Levi into the kitchen, which wasn't necessary since his nose would have done the job for her. Homemade Italian spaghetti sauce simmered in a pot on the stove. The sauce took Gia's dad three days to create and was enough to make Levi's stomach sit up and beg.

"Tell me it's done." Levi's mouth watered as he drifted closer to the large metal pot on the six-burner stove.

Gia gave Levi an evil smirk as she held up a large spoon but remained silent.

"So help me God, Gia, if you brought me here to torture me, then I will never speak to you about—"

"Gia, don't tease Levi," a deep voice said.

Dario walked into the kitchen, his dark brown-and-gray hair slicked back. He had the classic Italian look—long, thin nose with the bump in the bridge, olive skin, bushy eyebrows, almond-shaped brown eyes, thin, well-defined lips. Levi had to admit to having a boyhood crush on Dario when he'd hit puberty. Nothing sexual, just a young gay boy noticing a handsome man.

"Hey, *la mia amica del cuore.*" Dario squeezed Gia, kissing her on the head.

"Hi, *Papà.*"

Dario smiled wide.

Their family was highly affectionate and touchy-feely. At first, it had freaked Levi out given they weren't family and were constantly touching and hugging him. Gia explained it was an Italian thing, well, at least in her large extended family. When her relatives came to visit, they were always hugging and kissing cheeks and sitting close. They had no clue what a personal boundary was. Once Levi had gotten used to the handsy lot, he'd become more comfortable and even a little jealous of their openness.

Dario gently wrapped an arm around Levi's shoulder in greeting. He then took the spoon from Gia. "Levi, how're you doing? Gia tells me you that you fell into the lake and broke some ribs? You do realize it's March, *si*?" He gave Levi the cursory what-the-hell-were-you-thinking look. Yeah, that was the look he'd gotten from everyone.

"Just one. It was a stupid accident. I'm doing much better." He ducked his head to hide his embarrassment.

"Well, if you're injured, you must eat." Dario pulled out a plate for Levi, who snorted. Every occasion in the Alberici household was a reason to feed people. You pass a test, you eat. You stub your toe, you eat. If it's a day ending in "y," you eat.

Dario piled the plate high with pasta and smothered it with the thick sauce laden with sausage, pork, and chicken. Levi closed his mouth to stop any drool from escaping. He was damned sure that the sauce could cure any human ailment.

"*Tieni, manga*," Dario said in his boisterous yet deep voice. He set the plate before Levi and then affectionately ruffled Levi's hair.

Levi immediately stuffed the tomato-y goodness into his mouth. He grinned around a mouthful of pasta and sauce and gave a muffled, "Thank you."

Dario poured himself a glass of red wine. "How are your parents, Levi?"

Levi swallowed his mouthful of spaghetti. "Good. Dad's busy with surveys. Logan's still working with him. Mom's busy, too, but everyone's good."

"*Molto bene*. That makes me happy to hear. And school? You studying hard?" Dario raised his eyebrows in that expectant look parents give their kids that said, "The answer had better be yes."

"School's good." If you didn't count fleeing from the building like the hounds of hell were on your heels, it was good.

"Keep it that way. My beautiful Cara, God rest her soul, always made sure our girls took their school work seriously, and I'm sure you do as well, *figlio mio*."

Levi nodded.

"*Bene. Bene*."

Then Dario stepped right next to Levi. Sitting on the stool, Levi was at eye level with Dario. His stare was intense. "You're a smart boy." Levi was stuck in that intensity, unable to look away. His heart rate sped up.

"Life is full of tests. There are great obstacles that you must overcome to get what you want and to keep what you have. This will take great inner strength. And you are strong, *figlio mio*. Don't ever forget that. Trust yourself." Dario held his stare, and Levi squirmed under the scrutiny. Realizing Dario was waiting for a reply, Levi nodded.

"I have work to do in my office. Gia, get Levi some bread," Dario said as he left the room.

Levi looked after Dario, wondering what the heck that had been all about. When he looked to Gia, she raised a brow. "The vague prophetic wisdom of my father." She shook her head. "Half the stuff he says to me I have no clue what it means. Stopped asking years ago. Don't take him so seriously. You know he likes to keep us all on our toes."

Levi couldn't help the shudder that ran through him as he recalled the words. *There are great obstacles to get what… keep what you have.* Probably had something to do with his mental health issues, which he was sure had tested him plenty already.

"So, what about my bread?" Levi asked, knowing exactly the response he'd get.

"Get your own fucking bread. I swear whenever you're here you're like the prince of the house."

Levi shoveled more of the yummy goodness into his mouth and grinned around the pasta and sauce, some dripping off the corner of his mouth.

"Oh, a real prince." She threw a towel at him.

Levi snatched the towel and wiped his chin. "Are you sure you have to go to this thing at the college? Couldn't you just skip it and we could hang out here or something?"

"Nope, you have to suffer the Annual Spring Icebreaker with me." Gia had that stubborn set to her expression that told Levi no argument was going to change her mind.

Levi moaned. The annual Spring Icebreaker was a sort of thank-god-spring-is-here-themed fair. Different groups at the college were doing their own tributes to spring. Levi had repeatedly refused to attend, adamant about continuing his avoidance of all things school until Monday.

"It's going to be a blast. We can make fun of the theater geeks in their togas. They're doing some crap from ancient Rome or something." She scrunched up her round face in disgust. "Like I don't get enough of that Italian crap at home. If my dad talks about the 'old country' one more time, I may scream."

"I don't think ancient Rome really has anything to do with the 'old country.'"

Gia wrinkled her nose. "It's all the same. And you, *fratello mio*, are going."

"Ugh," Levi groaned, then shoveled more pasta into his mouth.

"Don't whine. I'm going to get ready. Oh, and when you're done, would you go and see if my father has the envelope he wants me to drop off at the bank?"

"You mean go into *his* office?" Levi had never been inside. It was off-limits to everyone, kind of like the Batcave.

"Yes, Levi, the *scary* office. Just knock on the door, chicken." She shook her head and left the kitchen. She would have made an excellent older sister with that wit and sarcasm. After finishing the pasta, Levi rinsed his plate and placed it in the dishwasher. He wandered down the hallway and stopped at the thick carved door to Dario's office. Although he always had a smile for Levi, there was something formidable beneath the surface of Dario Alberici. He was a successful businessman from what Levi understood from Gia. The way he held himself with confidence, controlled his environment, commanded others, Levi could see him crushing business opponents easily. That part of Dario unnerved Levi.

Levi knocked, the sound absorbed by the hard wood. After a minute, he knocked again louder, his knuckles stinging. Shit, he couldn't hear anything through the door. He should wait for Dario to answer, but what if he was telling Levi to come in and he couldn't hear him? Shit. One more knock and no answer. Levi sucked in a breath reached for the handle. Slowly, he turned the knob and pushed open the door. "Dario?"

No answer, so Levi peeked in. The office was large, decorated in the same light modern style as the rest of the house. A massive mahogany desk sat in the middle of the room facing the windows overlooking the lake. Best view in the house.

The room was empty. Levi was about to leave and find Gia when a noise to the right startled him. Along one wall was a set of bookcases. Levi's mouth dropped open when one section swung open like a door and Dario stepped out.

When he saw Levi, his brow furrowed. "Levi?" The tone of his voice said he wanted an explanation for Levi's uninvited intrusion.

"S-sorry, Dario. Gia sent me here to get something…. You wanted her to drop off something at the bank. I knocked a few times, but you didn't… I didn't think…. I mean, I thought you didn't hear me." Damn, he sounded guilty of something.

Dario shut the bookcase and smiled slowly. "All right."

He walked to the desk with a sideways glance at Levi. He picked up an envelope and slowly extended it across the desk. His expression almost dared Levi to come and get it. Levi stepped forward and reached for the envelope. When he gripped the smooth paper and pulled, Dario didn't release it. Levi swallowed hard.

"Now, Levi. What you've seen here today is our little secret, *si*? Can I count on you to keep this to yourself?"

The set of Dario's jaw and the hardness in his dark eyes was enough to make Levi agree to anything, even liking girls.

"You mean the office?" Was it really that big of a secret?

Dario cracked a smile. "The bookcase, Levi. Behind there I have a room where I store some very valuable assets for clients. Assets that my competitors would like to get their hands on and wouldn't think twice about hurting someone I love to get to it. Which is why it's a secret from *everyone*." He raised his brows again in that Dario way. Levi knew who he meant by "everyone"—Gia.

That wasn't too dark and menacing. And why did he feel like he was getting some kind of warning? *Paranoid much, Levi?*

"Sure, no problem." Levi nodded vigorously. He just wanted out of the office.

Dario released the envelope. Levi smiled tenuously.

"Tonight, I am heading out on a business trip. Keep an eye on my Gia."

"I will."

Levi quickly slipped from the office feeling as if he'd been caught doing something wrong. Envelope in hand, he went to find Gia and head to the Spring Icebreaker. He couldn't get away from the house soon enough.

At the college, Levi followed Gia into the lounge where their usual group of friends had gathered. Actually, they were Gia's friends and Levi merely a tagalong. From an outsider's perspective, Levi appeared a legitimate member. In reality, he stayed on the fringe and rarely hung out with the others unless he was with Gia. The phrase "alone in a crowded room" was his motto.

Levi sank tentatively into a chair next to Gia. He closed his eyes briefly, trying to calm his shakiness. His ribs and head ached. He was still on edge about being caught in Dario's office, which was stupid. Dario was a nice guy. Maybe Levi should have just stayed home, but then, he'd have to admit his mother had been right. That would mean hell had finally frozen over.

Gia turned to Sarah Morgan and her boyfriend, Josh Finn, who sat on a sofa, and then she frowned. "You know, Sarah, you'll never meet anyone nice if you keep taking him out with you."

Josh gave Gia the finger and then cracked a smile. Gia had a way with people, even if it was an evil way. Yeah, Levi was jealous of her ease with others.

As they talked, the crowd streaming through the lounge toward the classrooms swelled. Levi's claustrophobia and restlessness increased. The air was heavy and hot, and Levi found it hard to breathe. He rubbed his hands together in his lap. In his chest was a faint yet familiar tightening. *Just breathe.* Since the night he'd taken two of his pills, the anxiety had been on the lowdown. Now, he feared losing control in the crowd with no way to escape.

Closing his eyes, he took several centering breaths, but the bandage around his torso constricted his lungs. When he opened his eyes, Levi spotted Noah making his way through the crowd, coming toward him. Shit, Levi couldn't handle the overly friendly man right then.

Levi told Gia he'd be right back and squeezed through the crowd toward the men's room. The closest bathroom had a long line, so Levi headed toward the one located downstairs, which meant he had to get through the crowded hallway. Not even a quarter of the way down the hall, Levi regretted the decision. The hallway was filled to capacity with crushing bodies. Elbows poked at Levi from all angles. A surge from the crowd trapped him. He couldn't move, couldn't breathe.

He had to get out.

Someone knocked into Levi's side, and the sharp pain contracted his rib cage. Levi worked his way to the side of the hall and hugged the wall. Sweat broke out on his forehead, and blood rushed in his ears. The exit was back near the lounge. He had to escape, or he was sure he'd die.

Pressure ripped through his skull, killing off every bit of the fear. Grabbing his head, Levi fought to keep from crumpling to the ground.

Instead of slowly growing in intensity as in the past, his mind was slammed with a full-on assault. Sharp stabs of pain filled his chest as bodies continued to push past him. Fighting the crowd and the debilitating crush in his brain, he managed to turn and fight his way back in the opposite direction.

Have to get out of here!

Levi focused on moving his feet and pushed to move through the masses of bodies on his left and tried to avoid being pounded into the wall to his right.

Bam!

Levi ran into a hard wall of chest. The collision pushed him back a step. Protecting his side, Levi was about to go around the large person until he saw it—a large red dragon in a sea of black—the black of a hooded sweatshirt.

Was this the man who'd been outside of his house? Was he some kind of a modern-day Grim Reaper, exchanging the hooded cape for a hooded sweatshirt, a hipper, up-to-date version of Death? When Levi looked up, a pair of dark eyes glared down on him. The man's stern mouth was clamped shut. His jaw clenched so tight the muscles bulged at the sides. Then a ripping pain traveled straight to the center of Levi's brain and doubled him over.

Levi cried out, his shout absorbed by the noise of the crowd.

When he managed to stand, the man towering over him laid his large hand on Levi's shoulder. The contact brought on a swell of horrific pain, ringing in Levi's ears and stinging tears to his eyes. Levi tried to muffle the deafening rumble by covering his ears, but the sound increased. Within the pain, a distinct sensation emerged, a pulsing energy licking at his brain and filling his chest with the heat of a thousand suns—and it was coming from the large man. Memories coalesced and sharpened. That man in the black hoodie had been that black blur outside of Levi's classroom and in the school parking lot. He'd been outside of his house. And there he was right in front of Levi—an assailant with an invisible weapon.

Was the stranger trying to kill him?

Whatever his motive, Levi had to get away from this harbinger of… whatever he was a harbinger of. Yanking his shoulder away, Levi turned and struggled to pass through the dense crowd. Terrified, he refused to look back to see if the man followed.

Levi heard his name called from within the crowd. Melissa waved frantically from across the hall, but Levi continued weaving through bodies to escape. Finally reaching the end of the hall, Levi burst through the exit, into the stairwell, and leaned against the railing. The pressure in his head had subsided slightly, the burning in his chest tolerable. Just when he thought it was over, another attack surged with great intensity.

The door opened behind him. Whirling around, he faced the dark-eyed man again. The door slammed with a thunderous echo behind the man, his stare fixed on Levi.

"Stop it!" Levi screamed through clenched teeth.

As hard as he tried, Levi couldn't keep his gaze on the man. The nauseating pain forced his hands to his head. Boots scraped against the floor, echoing through the stairwell. As the man came closer, Levi scrambled back and hit the wall.

"Leave me alone!" Levi swung his fist toward the dragon-covered chest, but he missed.

Another sickening wave struck, and a warm trickle seeped from Levi's left nostril. Swiping his nose with the back of his hand, there was a bright red streak across his skin.

Blood.

"Y-You're *killing* me!" The words came out as a guttural cry. "Go away!"

The footsteps stopped. Levi peered up expecting the menacing face to morph into a hideous monster. Instead, there was only a bewildered man, seemingly stunned as blood ran down Levi's face and soaked into Levi's gray sweater. The stranger's mouth opened, as if to say something, but there was only silence. He stepped back, his eyes unwavering.

Levi grabbed his head again and closed his eyes for a few seconds. He heard the heavy boots of the guy pounding down the stairs. He peered up and was alone.

The door flew open, and Noah barreled through, almost missing Levi, then his face was horror-stricken when he saw the blood. He glimpsed down the stairwell and then back at Levi.

"You okay?" His wide eyes darted from Levi to where the man had disappeared and back.

Levi nodded, and Noah descended the stairs.

Levi slid down the wall and sat on the floor. The bleeding from his nose had slowed. His stomach churned, threatening to empty. He swallowed hard. The sickening force in his head subsided as rapidly as it had emerged, a ghost of its former self. A warm tickle in his chest was all that remained.

Rapid footsteps echoed on the stairs, and Noah reappeared, hastening to Levi. On Noah's face was enough anger to break someone in half.

"He's gone. What did he do to you?" Noah knelt beside Levi.

What did he do? To Levi, it felt as if he'd tried to rip his brain out through his nose, but the man had only touched his shoulder. What could he say that wouldn't sound totally insane?

"Did he hit you?"

Levi shook his head and lied. "No. He didn't touch me."

Noah frowned, appearing puzzled. "But you're bleeding?"

How did Levi answer that?

CHAPTER 9

LEVI GLANCED down at the obnoxious deep red stain on his gray sweater.

"It's just a bloody nose."

Levi brushed at his nostrils with his fingertips to make sure the bleeding had stopped. "I was in the hallway when my head really started to hurt. I literally ran into that guy. When I came out here, he followed me. I guess I got a little freaked."

That was putting it mildly.

"So he didn't touch you?"

"No, really. He didn't." The lies were piling up. He had touched Levi, and then, if Levi's warped sense of reality was correct, the man had tried to kill him with some kind of freaky mind meld or something equally weird. "How did you know where to find me?" Levi surveyed the blood staining his hands.

"Your brother's girlfriend. She mentioned you ran out here acting all strange. That was quite the bloody nose. How about we get you cleaned up?"

Noah reached for Levi's hand to help him to his feet. Levi accepted his help. Goose bumps covered his skin again, and a foreign warmth stirred in his chest. Noah's green eyes had softened. Concern for Levi reflected in their deep richness. A slight smile, and Levi felt a flutter in his chest. Of course, Levi thought he probably looked like a walking corpse, but Noah didn't seem to mind.

Noah led him down the stairs to the lower level, avoiding the crowded hall. Levi was on edge, waiting for the man in black to jump out at him. What did he want? Was Levi just being paranoid thinking this man was following him? Maybe he really hadn't been present each time Levi had felt that skull-crushing pain, the breath-stealing agony in his chest. Maybe he was hallucinating.

Downstairs, the bathroom was vacant. Noah waited outside. Levi gaped at his reflection in the mirror. Damn, he looked like the walking dead. The blood wasn't the only horror. His skin had taken on a gray, waxy pallor, highlighting deep black circles beneath his eyes. The color had drained from his lips. Turning on the water, Levi wet a paper towel and scrubbed at the dried blood on his face and hands. For having just survived a near miss with a trendier version of Death, Levi felt surprisingly good.

Stripping off his gray sweater, Levi found the blood hadn't soaked through to the white T-shirt he wore beneath. The sweater went into the garbage can. No way would he chuck that into the laundry for his mother to uncover. Her gloating about being right would never end. Kind of like Gia's.

Again, Noah had come to his rescue. A surge of heat flushed Levi's cheeks, bringing him back to life. A knot twisted in his stomach as he thought of Noah's green eyes, his seductive smile, and long, dark lashes. And that hair, all wild and unruly. Levi imagined the strands would feel soft as he ran his fingers through the auburn curls. He shuddered thinking of Noah's arms wrapped tight around his waist, Noah's hot breath on his neck, Noah's lips touching him. Fuck, that image was hot.

Pushing open the bathroom door, Levi found Noah leaning his shoulder against the wall, arms folded across his chest. Like the day Noah had rescued him, just the sides of Noah's hair were pulled back. When he smiled, the smallest amount of breath escaped Levi's lips. He wiped his sweaty palms against his pants. Pangs of desire rose quickly, and right then he knew he had to feel Noah.

"Wow, you clean up nice." Noah gave him a coy smile.

Levi stood toe to toe with Noah, lightly skimming his palm over the fair skin of Noah's cheek. For a moment, Noah appeared confused, then playfully curled up one side of his lips. An unknown force fueled Levi's desire. Each movement, each breath from Noah was driving him crazy. Unable to control the voracious need, Levi hooked his finger in the waistband of Noah's jeans and drew the man against his body. He laced his fingers at the nape of Noah's neck. He guided Noah until their lips touched. Noah wrapped his arms around Levi's waist and returned the kiss in earnest.

Tongues dueled and teeth gnashed as their kiss deepened. He pushed his growing erection against Noah's groin, and a groan escaped between their lips. Shit. Noah returned the pressure, and Levi thought he'd cream his pants right there. Noah's hard bulge pressed against Levi's hip. He needed more even if somewhere deep down it all seemed wrong.

Noah worked his hands under Levi's shirt, running his nails across his back. Levi shuddered. A fever rose within him that prickled across his skin. Sensations he'd never experienced before battled to be at the forefront—lust, want, need, desire. He *had* to have Noah, possess him totally. The man was *his* and could only be *his*.

Levi pushed his hips harder against Noah, crushing him against the wall, the pressure undeniably exquisite. Frantically, Levi kissed Noah, harder, faster, holding the back of Noah's head with balled-up fists entangled in his hair. When Noah tried to pull away, Levi pressed against him harder. He raked up Noah's shirt and scratched the warm skin of his lower back. Every muscle in Levi's body tightened, straining to get more contact. Rutting against Noah, the pressure in Levi's balls escalated. A frenzy of heat burst forth in his gut and with it a crazed need to hurt Noah, to cause him pain. The desire clenched the muscles in Levi's jaw and curled his fingers, digging his nails hard into Noah's skin. Levi's teeth caught hold of Noah's lip, and it took all of his might to keep from biting clean through.

Noah yanked his head back, his brows furrowing. "Did you just bite me?"

Levi ignored his question and went for Noah's mouth, his nails digging harder into flesh.

Noah avoided his lips. "Levi… slow down." He blocked Levi's advances.

But Levi kept going at Noah with a ferocity he couldn't control. He was chasing his orgasm while a screaming need to do harm, inflict pain, rode next to the pleasure. The rage overtook any of the wrongness he should have felt for trying to hurt Noah.

"Levi, what in the hell are you doing?"

Levi gritted his teeth and pummeled his fists against Noah's chest, who caught his wrists and held him back. The shock from Levi's actions covered Noah's face. Levi struggled against his grip, the need to destroy him seizing his free will.

"What…. Are you okay?" Noah's tone was filled with doubt. Shadowing his eyes was what Levi believed was disbelief.

No, he wasn't okay. He wanted to *kill* Noah.

He ripped his wrists from Noah's grip and took several steps back. The urge to hurt him raged like a thunderstorm in Levi's chest. If the man didn't want Levi, then no one would have him. Levi's heart raced, breaths rapid, fists clenched at his sides, the muscles in his legs ready to pounce on Noah as if he were prey. The all-consuming rage ate up Levi's humanity like an underfed lion.

Noah stepped forward, his hand held out to Levi. He knew that touch, the feeling of Noah's skin against his, would propel him across a line from which he feared he might never return. Levi drew back again, stopping Noah in his tracks. Noah straightened, pulling his shoulders back, his eyes narrowing. The action renewed Levi's ire. A war of wills raged in his mind, a single voice winning out.

Run.

Levi bolted past Noah and took the stairs by twos. Nothing stopped his escape. Not Noah yelling his name, not the crowd of bodies he pushed through with a vengeance, not the burning in his ribs. He flung the front door open and then ran into the cold afternoon without a destination. Fleeing the college was becoming an unsettling habit. At least last time, he'd had his car for the getaway.

The fury within him was dying away, the wrath of the monstrous entity releasing its fiery grip on him. He sprinted until he reached the Quick Stop two blocks from the college. The heat that had brought the flush of fever to his skin diminished. The chill of the unseasonably cold spring air raised the hair on his arms. His sweater gone, his jacket back at the college, Levi was freezing. Reaching into his pocket, he pulled out his new phone and chose Logan's name from the contacts list.

"Logan, please answer."

Levi wrapped his arms tight around himself, trying to shield against the coldness. After the fourth ring, he almost gave up hope, and then....

"Hey, Levi. What's up?"

Thank God! "Logan, can you come get me? I need a ride."

"I thought you were with Gia? Where are you?"

"I'm at the Quick Stop on Main Street. Gia's at the college. It's a long story. Can you pick me up? Please?" His teeth chattered.

"Are you okay? You sound funny."

"Yeah, I'm good." Huge lie.

"I'll be there in about twenty."

"Logan, wait. Please don't say anything to Mom and Dad." If he did, Levi would certainly face an interrogation when he arrived at home.

There was a short pause. "Okay."

"Thanks." Levi ended the call, already trying to piece together a convincing explanation for when Logan showed up.

Levi entered the semiwarm store. He texted Gia to let her know he'd left the college and Logan had picked him up. Of course, she wanted to know "what the hell happened," but Levi said he'd explain later. God forbid if Noah told Gia about how unhinged he'd become. Probably would blab it to everyone. As if Levi wasn't enough of an outsider already.

A cup of hot chocolate sounded good right about then. The machine spit the piping-hot chocolate drink into his cup. Dousing the volcanic liquid with milk, he wrapped his hands around the cup and took a huge gulp. "So good."

He paid for his drink, then wandered through the aisles pretending to look for something to stay out of the cold until Logan arrived. Turning the corner at the end of an aisle, Levi almost plowed over an older woman. She dropped a box and a can she'd been carrying.

"Shoot! I'm so sorry. My fault. I wasn't looking where I was going." Levi bent down to get the box.

The tall, thin gray-haired woman leaned down to retrieve the can as it rolled across the floor. "That's quite all right, dear."

As the woman stood, Levi watched as shock crossed her face, filling her grayish eyes. She grasped the cross on her chest. She shuffled back a few steps.

"Are you okay? Do you need help?" Levi asked.

Please don't die right here in front of me!

Leering back, the woman muttered over and over, "*Dio mio.*" Her face hardened, and she leveled an icy glare on Levi.

"I'm sorry. I don't understand. Is something wrong?" Her actions freaked Levi out.

The woman pointed a finger at Levi. "*Senz'anima.*"

"Excuse me?" Levi was annoyed with the woman's odd behavior. "I don't understand."

The next words uttered from the woman sent an arctic blast through Levi and froze him where he stood. "I see you. You are hollow, empty, unfeeling. Not even human." She'd spat the words out as if they tasted bad.

The cup of hot chocolate slid from Levi's hand and hit the floor, the light chocolate-colored liquid creating a puddle between them.

"What did you say?" The whispered words had barely escaped Levi's throat.

"*Senz'anima*," the woman hissed again. "Your kind will be cleansed from the earth." She narrowed her cold eyes, her gaze steady, sending an icy current through him. "*Il Giudice*."

"What? Do you think that's my name?" Something stirred in Levi's thoughts. That word sounded familiar... *almost* right. A creeping chill covered his skin as he stared at the elderly woman. Damn, she looked as if she'd seen a ghost and wanted to slay him at the same time. "I... I'm s-sorry...." Levi backed away as the woman glowered at him.

"You can't hide."

Levi ignored her rants. Damn, she was crazy.

Keeping his head down, he quickly exited the store. Outside the air had grown colder, but Levi was already numb from the woman's prognostic ranting. Levi rushed forward when he saw Logan standing near his truck.

When Logan spotted Levi, he smiled but that dropped off quickly. "Where's your jacket?"

Levi looked over his shoulder to the store and then to the truck. "Can we just get out of here?" Levi pulled open the door and jumped into the warm cab. He slammed the door, locking it behind him. Logan climbed in, shut his door, and reached behind the seat, pulling out a flannel shirt and handing it to Levi.

"Thanks." Levi slipped into the shirt that smelled like Logan and helped him to calm down.

Logan started the truck, which rumbled after coming to life and shook the cab. He then turned to Levi. "Are you gonna tell me what happened? Like why you're here"—Logan gestured toward the store—"without your coat?" His voice had taken on that big brother tone.

"I'd rather not." Levi heaved a sigh.

Logan stared out over the front of the truck. Levi rubbed at his temples with his fingertips. There was too much to tell, so much that didn't make any sense. Attempts to put the recent events into words would sound like the ramblings of a soon-to-be madman.

Logan put the truck into drive and pulled out of the parking lot. Within the cab, the silence crept into every crack and crevice. Levi tried to focus on the sound of his breaths, the hum of the oversized truck tires, anything to avoid the cascade of confusion and mystery of the past four days.

Logan's voice startled him. "You know you can tell me anything, don't you? I mean, haven't I always let you know that?" Logan's gaze didn't waver from the road. His tension showed in lines around his eyes, his mouth, and in his jaw. "But you keep me at arm's length just like you do everyone else."

Hearing the strain of anguish in his brother's voice, Levi winced. He wanted nothing more than to let Logan and the rest of the world in, but he had no idea how. Nothing connected within his hollow body. The elderly woman's words haunted Levi, wrapping invisible fingers around him and holding tight.

"I don't mean to do it. Really. It's just the way I am… all that I seem able to be." He was like the color white, absorbing all of the colors of the rainbow and reflecting nothing back.

"Yeah, I know," Logan said in exasperation. "But lately you're acting…."

"Stranger than usual?"

Logan let an ironic laugh escape. "That too, but I was going to say more distant. You used to tell me everything you did, everything you wanted. You were always dragging me into the middle of your life. I mean, it was nothing deep or anything, but you always included me. At times, I had to take 'Levi breaks' to recharge. And please, don't take this the wrong way, but I used to wish for you to tone down the drama a notch." He shook his head slowly. "Now I wish you'd say anything at all to me."

Levi could use a "Levi break" too. "I'm sorry" was all that he could think to say.

"I think it's gotten worse since you came back from college. It wasn't a huge difference, but I noticed." He glanced at Levi as if he needed to know Levi understood, if he agreed.

And yes, he did.

Going away to college had appeared to be such a simple step in the progression from teenager to adult. Applications were completed, the SAT taken, letters of recommendation acquired, and then acceptance letters, scholarships awarded, the dorm room paid for. It had all become a large boulder rolling down a hill, unstoppable, sweeping Levi along. His parents' expectations, in fact, the expectations of teachers, relatives, friends—even societal value on higher education—had all pushed Levi to attend college. So he went, and within three short months—months that had seemed to stretch into years—it had all crumbled.

Debilitating panic attacks had kept him from many of his classes, had interfered with homework assignments, and had even kept him from driving home on weekends. Fear and anxiety filled most of his hours, spiraling out of control until he'd crashed headfirst into the ground. It had changed him. The entirety of the trauma, the failure, had drawn him further into himself than he'd ever been before.

"What do you want from me? I can't just change who I am… what I've become."

Or what I'm in the middle of becoming.

Logan was silent, almost statue-like, and then spoke. "Can't you?"

The question had been like a slap with words.

CHAPTER 10

LEVI FORCED himself to ignore the pain Logan's comment caused. That was the same attitude most people had. They couldn't understand the relentless, raw fear, the perpetual anxiety, the ache to bond with another human on any level, the longing to escape the loneliness of his existence, none of which he'd been able to change. Dr. Ross had mentioned something about an attachment disorder, stemming from a failure to form a significant bond with his primary caregivers as a baby. Levi couldn't fathom how experiences from infancy could reach out and affect his life years later. Now anything seemed possible.

Despite the warmth of the truck, a chill crept into Levi. When he failed to answer, Logan became quiet again, his eyes unwavering from the road. The silence stuck the entire way home, and Levi could feel a wall building between them.

In their driveway, Levi jumped from the truck as it rolled to a stop. He entered through the mudroom to avoid questions about his lack of a jacket. Levi's mother looked up from her food prep as he tried to pass undetected through the kitchen.

"Did you have a good time? How do you feel?"

"Had a great time. Feel good. Have homework to do," he said, as he breezed past her to exit the kitchen.

"Levi."

The deep voice stopped him. When he turned, Logan's body filled the doorway to the mudroom. His keys dangled from his fingers at his side. His stern look of indignation hit Levi hard.

"Logan? I thought you were in your room?" A puzzled look crossed their mother's face.

Logan's gaze burned into Levi, who fidgeted, then crossed his arms. Was Logan going to turn him in, rat him out? Their mother looked between the two of them, as they regarded each other in silence.

A moment longer, and his mother started to speak, but Logan cut her off. "I was in my room, but I had to run out for a minute. Got some paperwork to do, so I'm heading up there now." He stuffed his keys into his pocket.

"Well, dinner is at six." Her tentative tone matched her baffled expression.

"Okay." Logan passed by Levi as he left the kitchen.

"He's acting strange." His mother narrowed her eyes with the implication that Levi was the culprit.

"He's just strange anyway," Levi said, deflecting his mother's suspicions and backing out of the room.

Levi raced up the stairs in time to catch Logan opening the door to his room.

"Logan, wait."

Logan's hand was on the knob of his partially opened door. When he looked at Levi, he still wore the same expression of indignation.

"Thanks for not saying anything to Mom." Levi smiled, but Logan didn't reciprocate.

"Yeah, whatever." He turned from Levi, entered his room, and closed the door.

That single act of turning away held great significance for Levi. Logan was telling Levi without words that he'd had enough. He was leaving the game, no longer interested in playing. Levi had never imagined a greater feeling of loneliness was possible, but there it was. A closed door, and the only person he'd ever felt the slightest connection to was hiding behind it.

Hiding from me.

Levi rested his palm against the cool wood. An aching sadness along with a faint need to cry resonated in his chest, but he couldn't grasp it. He willed it forward, a deep need to react as most humans would in that situation. Squeezing his eyes tight, he was determined to shed at least one tear. Logan deserved at least one tear. But nothing came, and it was as if he'd failed Logan all over again.

LEVI TOSSED and turned most of the night. The dark-eyed man, his touch, the crushing pressure in his presence was unfathomable. Was it even in the realm of possibility that another person could create such a mind-crushing physical reaction in Levi's body, because to say it aloud was just... crazy. No. His mind had to be playing tricks on him in his descent into madness. He grasped at explanations based in reality and to explain away the crazy.

So why had the man touched Levi? Strangers rarely went around touching each other. Well, Levi had been crying out in pain. Maybe he'd been trying to help. But he couldn't forget the surge of energy—bone-splitting electricity—that had rushed through his being when that dark-haired harbinger of death had laid a hand on him. Coincidence? If so, it was a scary, unbelievable coincidence.

And what about the woman's reaction in the store? Now that was beyond scary. It was as if her aged eyes had looked straight through to Levi's soul.

"Hollow. Empty. Unfeeling."

And what had she meant by *"you can't hide"*? He shuddered. "Not even human," Levi said to the darkness. *"Senz'anima."*

Those words rang with familiarity in his ears. Italian. How did he know that? And where had he heard it before? School? Yes. But where? In class. Dr. Winston's Philosophy 101. An article they'd discussed in class. What had it been about? He threw off the covers and then switched on the light. In his closet, he pulled out boxes that Logan had packed from his dorm at Plattsburgh State. Levi hadn't even been able to return to get his belongings, so Logan and Melissa had made the trek to retrieve his stuff.

Removing books, notebooks, and papers from the boxes, Levi knew what he was looking for, if only he could lay his hands on it. His philosophy folder or book didn't hold the answer. His notebook. He sifted through the pages of handwritten notes. At first, the pages were filled with extensive writing for each class he'd attended, each entry dated. As he flipped further, the dates became further between, showing the classes he'd missed. The sections of notes got shorter and spoke of the anxiety and panic that had followed him into the classroom, becoming his sole focus.

Scanning his notes, he turned page after page. That word had to be there, he knew it, but when had it been discussed in class? Then it caught his eye, on top of the page dated October 25, in between doodles of some strange symbols he had no recollection of drawing.

Senz'anima—soulless.

Nothing else was on the page. He continued to flip through the pages, but nothing else was written about the word. Closing his eyes, he tried to remember the contents of the article, but the word was all he could see.

He frowned. Why would that old woman call him that?

Levi rose with the notebook and grabbed his laptop, taking them both to his bed. Sitting against his pillow, he typed the word into the search engine, adding the quotes. The search results were in Italian. Opening another window, Levi pulled up Google Translate, and with the translated page, he searched the short synopsis under each result. One was a chapter of a fiction book, another about vampires, a question pertaining to the soul-stealing Dementors in the Harry Potter novels, a Facebook page mentioning the word, another page proclaiming the Euro as soulless money. Levi had to chuckle at how the word soul was attributed to so many different subjects, but nothing referenced the article his teacher had passed out and discussed.

He typed *soulless* into the search engine. First was a definition of soulless from a dictionary… a Victorian romance with the same name… a band in Cleveland, Ohio… a computer game… more books. He went back to the definition and clicked on a link. *1. A person lacking sensitivity or humanizing qualities. 2. Lacking facility for deep feeling. 3. Heartless; mechanical.*

Damn, if that didn't speak directly to the very essence of who Levi was, except maybe the part about lacking humanizing qualities. Maybe the old woman was empathic or something and had sensed his emptiness, his lack of emotion. That didn't make him soulless and did little to reassure him of the woman's intent.

Levi typed *soulless person* into the search engine. A word in the title of the first website smacked him hard.

Psychopath.

He let out a nervous laugh to ease the tension inside, but what if…? No way. Yet after what he'd felt toward Noah, a savage, raging, primal anger laced with the covetous desire to own and destroy him all at the same time. He definitely sounded like a psychopath.

A notification box popped up on his computer screen. A Facebook message from Dr. Winston? They'd chatted online often since his departure from school. Also, when he'd first been accepted to the SUNY school, she'd contacted him since he'd indicated his interest in philosophy on his application. Their discussion had ended with him enrolling in two of her classes that first semester. So it wasn't odd she'd message him. What *was* odd was the timing.

Levi clicked on the box, and the message opened. Levi gasped, covering his mouth with a shaky hand.

I know about the man who is following you. Come to my office at noon tomorrow. It's urgent.

SLEEP EVADED Levi most of the night. The man in black *was* following Levi. How could his professor possibly know about him? Levi hadn't told her, or anyone else for that matter. The thought made his skin crawl.

Around 7:00 a.m., Levi called Gia. Again, Gia questioned Levi's abrupt departure from the college. Levi lied and said that his mother had sent Logan to pick him up, still upset about him going out. Levi held his breath waiting for Gia to mention anything about Noah, but he stayed out of the conversation to Levi's relief. The real reason Levi had called Gia was to tell her he was skipping classes, feigning pain in his ribs. The amount of lies coming from Levi's mouth grew each day. Maybe he *was* a psychopath.

At ten fifteen, Levi sat in his car, which was still parked in his driveway. His heart raced, his palms were sweaty, and at any second he might throw up. Plattsburgh was an hour and a half away, and Levi hadn't been there since November, four months earlier. His last trip home, he'd had to pull to the side of the road, unable to breathe, too light-headed and dizzy to see straight, convinced he was going to die on the side of I-87. Again, Logan had come to his rescue, bringing along his friend, Dave, who drove Levi's car home. At the time, Logan had been the buffer between Levi and their parents when he'd refused to return to school and they'd freaked. Logan had never let him down. So why was Levi constantly letting his brother down?

Levi summoned up the nerve to start the car and move forward. Driving solo that distance with his fear and panic was iffy, but even more so because of this mystery man who may or may not want to harm him. Closing his eyes, Levi started the car as he had hundreds of times, but this drive was different than all the others. He had excited expectation and dread to deal with on top of his anxiety.

"Just go." He wasn't sure if that had been a demand or a plea.

Driving north finally, Levi fought to relax as he reached the dreaded highway, blasting his music with the windows wide open. Anything to distract him from worrying when the panic would surface, praying he wouldn't lose it in the middle of nowhere between exits. Cell service was spotty in the dips and valleys of the mountains. Walking or flagging down a stranger wasn't at the top of his list of things he wanted to do.

Around eleven forty-five, Levi pulled into the parking lot a short distance from Champlain Hall where Dr. Winston's office was located. He was a little sweatier and a little shakier, but he'd made it there. Being back on the campus stirred feelings he hadn't expected, least of them longing—longing to return to a seminormal life, one without fear, to be a student who only cared about getting classes out of the way so he could move on to the fun.

Levi gripped the door handle firmly and entered Champlain Hall as if he belonged there, like any student, not a dropout. Taking the stairs to the third floor, he passed the occasional student and wondered if he would run into anyone he'd known. No one stood out to him until he rounded the corner and practically ran into Milo Covington, Dr. Winston's teaching assistant.

Milo's eyes widened. His expression was one of surprised apprehension. Levi had to be imagining the reaction. "L-Levi. My God, what're you doing here?"

"Hey, Milo. I'm going to see Dr. Winston."

Milo bit on his lower lip. "She's not here, I don't think." His eyes darted about, then settled on Levi. His body relaxed, and then he smiled. "I mean I think she's out but.... How have you been?"

"I'm good. You?"

"Good, man. Hey, how about a cup of coffee? Catch up?"

Catch up on what? They'd never been close and had only seen one another in classes. Levi fidgeted, very uncomfortable with their interaction.

"Wish I could, but I told Dr. Winston I'd meet her." He looked at his watch. "Now actually. I'll see you some other time."

Milo only nodded as Levi stepped past him. When Levi looked over his shoulder, the man was gone. Levi remembered him as being jumpy and skittish, but he was even more so now. It only reminded him of his nervousness as he stepped up to the professor's door. Again, he questioned why he'd come. What was waiting for him behind that office door? Steeling his spine and locking his knees, he knocked gently, almost hoping the professor didn't answer. Unfortunately, she did.

The door opened to her smiling face. "Levi, so good to see you." Dr. Winston wrapped Levi in a sustained hug that took him aback.

"Uh, hey, Dr. Winston." Levi had to extricate himself from the hug.

"It's so good to see you. Come in."

Moving aside, she motioned him inside.

Dr. Winston was an older woman, possibly in her early fifties. Shoulder-length, ash-brown hair with a limp curl, amber eyes, a little hippy on the bottom but quite slim on the top. As usual, she wore a flowing multicolored skirt. A heavy-beaded necklace made with glass beads in teals and a gold flaming sun crystal bounced about her bosom. Never one for discreet jewelry, her matching earrings were long and heavy. All matched her personality: large, gregarious, expressive.

"I saw Milo in the hallway. He thought you'd gone somewhere."

She cocked her head, her lips thinned for a moment, and then she raised her brow. "Nope, I'm here. Sit, please." She motioned to a chair near her desk.

Nothing had changed in the office since Levi's last visit a few weeks before leaving Plattsburgh State for good. Tall bookcases lined three of the walls and were filled to capacity with books—new and old—idols of deities from dozens of religions, totems, ancient representations of myths, mystical creatures, and dozens of jars and ornate containers. On the walls were paintings, many mythological figures, along with some woven tapestries with strange sigils. Dr. Winston wasn't just a professor of philosophy and ethics, but also presented classes on Greek and Roman mythology, folktales, ancient cultures, and even the occult, among a few others. Her office was the least boring place on campus.

Dr. Winston sat in her plush desk chair and swiveled to face Levi. Her usual wide smile was painted on her face, her hands relaxed in her lap. Levi played with the zipper on his fleece jacket, begging off the intense need to flee.

"It's so nice to see you in person again, Levi. Chatting on Facebook just isn't the same as good ole face-to-face contact. Don't you agree?" The words seemed to bounce as they fell from her mouth.

Levi nodded. The knot in his stomach tightened.

"You left school so abruptly, and I know you said it was for health issues. You look well. How're you feeling?"

Like at any minute I'll be jumping off the edge of insanity.

"Good. I'm doing good. Taking classes at North Country this semester, so that's good. Everything is good." The word *good* took on an air of falseness with its repetition.

"I'm so glad to hear that. I was so upset when you left school. You're a smart guy. And you did so well before you got sick."

Levi nodded and pursed his lips, feeling the familiar sense of unreality that came with his panic. He imagined bolting from the room at any moment.

"So, did you come here alone today?"

Levi tried not to frown. "Yes." His response sounded more like a question than an affirmation.

He pulled at the bottom of his jacket, adjusting the hem, wishing Dr. Winston would get around to talking about the man in black so he could leave.

"You live with your parents, don't you?" Her smile faded, and her countenance took on an edge of seriousness.

"Yeah, my mom and dad, my older brother, Logan." *And a tank full of tropical fish, but what does that have to do with the man in black?*

Dr. Winston nodded, regarding Levi intently. "What about a guardian?"

Levi didn't suppress his frown this time. Hadn't Dr. Winston asked him this question last fall? He answered as if she hadn't. "A guardian? Isn't that someone who legally acts like a parent?"

"Sometimes, in general terms, yes," Dr. Winston said, tilting her head to one side. Her earring swung about her neck, mesmerizing Levi. "Do you have any relatives you're really close to like an aunt or an uncle or family friend?"

Levi raised his eyebrows, not even remotely understanding the gist of this conversation. "Logan and I are pretty close." *Or were.* "Other than that, no."

"But he's not too much older than you, so too young."

"Too young for what?"

Dr. Winston sat back in her chair and tapped her fingertips against her peachy lips, rocking in short side-to-side bursts. Silently, she looked off somewhere beyond the walls of her office deep in thought.

Levi shifted in the chair, his annoyance and impatience growing. "Listen, your message said something about a man following me. What was that all about?" Levi wasn't going to acknowledge anything about the man until he heard what Dr. Winston knew of him. "I also wanted to get a copy of an article. You know the one about *senz'anima*. Do you remember that from class?"

Dr. Winston halted her chair, and her face took on a sharp expression of surprise. What had he said wrong?

CHAPTER 11

"WHY WOULD you need that?"

Levi shrugged, trying to seem unaffected by his intense need. "I liked it and wanted to read it again."

After a pause, Dr. Winston sat forward again with renewed vigor. "Levi, I need to tell you some things that may sound, well a little crazy, but keep an open mind. Do you think you can do that?"

Levi shifted uncomfortably in his seat. "I don't understand what you're getting at."

"You will. I just need you to listen carefully and with an open mind. Misunderstandings and lack of perspective come when people close themselves off to something new. Can you open yourself up to what I'm going to tell you?"

The intensity of her words, her poignant stare, cut right through Levi. His chest tightened slightly. *Breathe.* Levi would agree to anything if it brought Dr. Winston closer to the point of their bizarre reunion.

"Sure."

"Good." Dr. Winston clapped her hands together, clanging the metal bangles around her wrists. "The most logical place to start is that article, which actually is a chapter from a larger book, which I currently have at home. Anyway, *senz'anima* means soulless. Do you remember what it said about the soulless?"

Levi shook his head. *Ugh!* Not a lecture, just a copy of the article would be enough.

A slight grimace crossed the professor's face but quickly faded. "In this case the soulless aren't actually without a soul as much as their soul and body have been separated."

"By death?"

Dr. Winston pursed her lips and shook her head, her large earrings slapping against her neck again. "No, because the person is still alive, and not all of the soul is removed."

"Removed by someone, a Seer or something, right?" Facts from the article were coming back to him.

"Partially. A Soul Seer can see other people's souls. A Keeper is the one who removes and 'keeps' the soul. There are many reasons for removing a soul—greed, power, salvation. The latter is the only reason that is allowed under council rules."

"Salvation?"

"Yes, salvation. This is the part I really need you to understand. Seers are born with innate power to peer into a person's soul. The soul is a misunderstood entity. Christians believe, for the most part, that since man was created by God, then all souls were as well. Actually, the idea of a soul or some essence of a human that continues after death has been written about extensively for thousands of years. Plato and Socrates even delved into the subject. Life after death is a concern for all sentient beings. The idea of becoming nothing is unfathomable to most."

The thought brought a wave of stomach-churning panic to Levi. Fear of death was very real to him.

"Anyway, Traducianism is the belief that the soul is actually a creation of the parents and not of God. If God had truly created the universe and rested on the seventh day, then he's not responsible for creating new souls. The idea is that the only soul created by God was that of Adam. Since Adam is believed to be the father of all of mankind, it is through generation that new souls are formed, as is true with the body. What this means is that the souls and the bodies of the parents create the soul and body of their offspring." Dr. Winston paused as she did in her lectures, as if waiting for questions from the class.

The only question Levi had—*What does this have to do with the man in black?*

Dr. Winston continued. "Seers see the energy a soul creates and feel its power. Everything in the universe has its origin in energy. Vibration of that energy takes on different forms, creating everything."

"How exactly do you remove a soul? It's not like a heart or kidney? Cut the skull open and pop out the toy surprise?" *Kinda gross.*

Dr. Winston ignored his attempt at humor. "No. It's not something most people can see. But it can be done. Seers view the soul as a ball of energy, colorful, something like an aura. And the soul is located within the heart, not the head. Its energy powers the essence of life. True feeling comes from the soul, which is why emotions seem to emanate from the chest."

Levi placed his hand over the hollow beneath his sternum. Was his soul malfunctioning?

Dr. Winston continued in focused lecture mode. "Seers aren't rare but aren't numerous either. A Seer can see disparities in a soul, impurities as you might put it, which place that person at risk. Innately, these disparities come from the joining of the parents' souls."

"So it's the parents that mess up the kid's soul?" *That explains so much*, Levi mused to himself. "Okay, so what would warrant something as serious as removing a soul?" *Holy hell*. How much longer did he have to endure this? Probably would end much quicker if he stopped asking questions.

"It's nothing small, I can tell you that. There has to be such total disharmony within the soul that allowing it to continue in the body would place the individual in jeopardy and continually spill out discordant energy. This affects those around that person most, causing dissonance, tension, conflict."

"Is the person evil or something?" *A psychopath?*

"Innate evil is very rare, but it does happen. No, mainly what humans consider evil is created through experience and wrapped up a bit in genetics, as well."

"Okay. So that's how people become soulless. Well, thanks for the rundown of the article. I have to be home soon." Just a small lie. "Is there anything else you want to tell me, like about that man?"

Dr. Winston narrowed her eyes. "Why do you think I went into such detail explaining this concept to you?"

Easy A. "Because I asked about it."

"And why did you ask about it?"

Levi nervously swiped a shock of curls from his face. "I was looking through my notes from class and wrote those words on a page but didn't take any notes." Damn, he'd just admitted to not paying attention in class.

"Levi, I'm trying to tell you something about yourself. Something that from the first day you came into my class I thought you knew, had to have known because not to, well, it's just impossible… the safeguards in place, the planning. But I can tell you have no knowledge of this."

Levi grasped the sides of his seat. It had been a bad idea to come there. "Of what?"

"Levi, you don't have a soul."

Crazy covered Levi like a second skin, but he hadn't known Dr. Winston was part of the club. Levi actually cracked a bit of a smile, but it faded. "Okay... umm... yeah, I'm going to get going now."

Levi rose and headed for the door.

"Fear."

Levi halted and turned slowly, trying to keep his expression blank.

"Fear, anxiety, nervousness, maybe even panic? Do these sound familiar?"

"Yeah. I have an anxiety disorder. That's why I left school."

It's why every day of my life is hell on earth.

Dr. Winston shook her head slowly. "No, you don't."

"I think I would know."

"It's not the source."

"I suppose lacking a soul is the real reason." Levi was unable to control the sarcasm that coated his words. He wished he'd asked Milo for the article when he'd seen him in the hallway. Too late for that.

"Please, sit and I'll explain."

When Levi failed to move, she went on. "Our bodies need energy to exist. Yes, energy from food but most importantly the energy of a soul. Without it, the body tries to compensate by continuously drawing in whatever energy is available. Everyone's soul gives off a hint of energy. The more energy around, the more that will be drawn inward, filling the body, overdosing it in a way. How do you feel in a room full of people?"

It made his skin crawl and most of the time drove his panic to astronomical levels, but he wasn't going to confirm anything.

"You feel safer with as few people as possible around, probably even more so alone. Less energy to deal with." She studied him as if to see how much he'd bought of what she'd said.

Levi averted his gaze. "That doesn't prove anything."

"It *proves* everything."

"You think because I have issues with anxiety that I don't have a soul?" Levi wasn't the only one with issues.

"No, I think you don't have a soul because I can't see it."

Levi frowned. "You're a—"

"Seer. Yes. And the moment you walked into my class I knew yours wasn't there. That's why I handed out the article on *senz'anima*. I was trying to tell you I knew and figured you would come to me. Tell me, why did you ask for the article?"

Should he mention the old woman? Wouldn't sound any crazier than what he'd heard from his professor.

"A woman yesterday she... well... she said I was *senz'anima*, hollow, unfeeling... empty."

Dr. Winston's lips thinned. "Where was this?"

"In a store. She just pointed at me and said it." Even now the memory sent chills through him. "Then I remembered the word from class."

"She would have to be a Seer to have known that." Dr. Winston chewed on her fingernail.

Levi didn't like the look on Dr. Winston's face. "That woman was disgusted, even afraid." He so wasn't a scary person.

"Not all Seers feel that souls should be removed. There are *people* who believe removing a soul creates evil that will affect those around that person. They are quite... vocal about it."

Vocal?

"So this woman saw I didn't have a soul and decided to tell me I'm evil. Nice." Levi wanted to close his eyes and wake up in bed. "How do you know she was one of these Seer people?"

"Because she knew that you didn't have a soul. But Seers aren't supposed to approach the soulless for many reasons. Souls aren't just taken at infancy. At the age of consent, anyone can choose to part with theirs."

Who in the world would choose to part with their soul and feel the gut-wrenching agony of anxiety every day of their lives?

"So I have no soul?" Levi could play along. "Why am I still walking around? Within a soul there is the energy to power many worlds. Very little is needed for one life."

"You still have a small part, just enough to keep your life force going."

"Can you see it, I mean, *if* I had only part of a soul left?"

"No. It doesn't give off enough energy. I don't see anything, which tells me you've had yours removed."

Levi huffed. "If it's so horrible to go without a soul, why in the hell would anyone remove it in the first place, because, I have to tell you, my life hasn't been a picnic."

Biggest. Fucking. Understatement. Ever.

"It's not supposed to be like that."

Levi smirked. "And what's it supposed to be like?"

"What's left of the soul allows the person to feel and function and avoid the influx of energy from the environment. You, however, seem to be more affected by its absence than most. Guardians are people who volunteer to council and assist their charges through this process from extraction to reentry. If you'd had a guardian, then that person would have kept in contact with the Seer and Keeper involved and advised them of any issues that arose."

There was that *guardian* word again. "So this missing person would have intervened and not allowed me to suffer for all of these years, that is, *if* my problems were because my soul is missing. Figures." He grunted, then cleared his throat. "Listen, I really appreciate your concern for me, however misguided it is, but I have an anxiety disorder diagnosed by a real doctor, treated with real medication and counseling. Actually, until I came to college, it was pretty much under control." He just didn't feel much on the side of emotions.

"What about now? Is anything different?"

Except for panic attacks and his psyche preparing to crack into irretrievable pieces, and the crushing pain in his head, and the intense emotions driving his insanity, oh, and the whole psychopath thing, not much, except....

"I stopped taking my meds. I couldn't stand not feeling anything anymore. I was so closed off, so dull. I read that it can be a side effect of antidepressants." It really had been an epiphany at the time.

"When was that? Did your doctor take you off of them?"

Levi regretted saying anything. He knew full well that you never stopped meds without your doctor's okay, but... "Almost two weeks ago. I just decided to stop taking them."

"And what happened?"

"More anxiety, a huge panic attack."

"What else?"

What else did she want? She appeared to be digging for something.

A knock at the door startled Levi. He hadn't realized how tense he'd become. Even Dr. Winston looked a bit unnerved but regained her composure.

"Excuse me." She passed by Levi on her way to the door.

Levi stood and moved to the other side of the office to get some distance from whoever had knocked. Probably a student needing to meet with Dr. Winston, which would give him the opportunity to get out and fast. He'd indulged the fantasy world of his former teacher long enough. But he still needed to know about the man.

Dr. Winston opened the door and spoke to someone on the other side out of Levi's view. A few nervous glances at Levi, and then Dr. Winston drew back and opened the door wide.

Fuck me sideways.

It was the man in black.

CHAPTER 12

LEVI SCRAMBLED back into a pile of books, and they tumbled to the floor. His gaze froze on the dark-eyed man, sans the black hoodie, looming in the doorway. He'd never forget those dark eyes and their harsh, deadly glare. Adrenaline surged, readying Levi for flight; however, he was trapped in the far corner of the room like a rat by a big fucking cat, the only exit blocked. Levi raised his hands to his head ready for the mind-exploding pain and pressure… but nothing happened.

Dr. Winston and the tall man—not as tall as he'd previously appeared—watched Levi. He wore a black T-shirt that stated "I'm the evil twin" in white letters.

Even without the bone-crushing force he'd experienced last in the man's presence, Levi was terrified. Sweat formed on his brow, pushed out by his rapid heart rate. That man was there, seventy miles from Levi's home, in his professor's office, stalking Levi.

Dr. Winston looked to the man who raised his eyebrows with a slight nod. Her expression told Levi they were acquainted.

The man returned the look and shrugged. "Looks like it worked." His voice was rough and low, almost like a growl.

Their gazes returned to Levi. If he ran fast enough, he might be able to knock the man back and get into the hallway. But then what?

Dr. Winston walked tentatively toward Levi, raising her hands as if she knew he was ready to bolt. That was so Levi at that minute. "Levi, it's okay. I know Jeb."

Jeb.

His stalker had a name. Levi gripped the windowsill behind him. They were on the third floor. He looked down at the ground. Jumping for a quick getaway was out of the question.

Jeb, the stalker, leaned his shoulder casually against the doorjamb, settling in. His large hand went to his chest, and he fingered a long object hanging from a silver chain around his neck. Maybe a crystal?

A rush of calm came over Levi. His hands relaxed, his shoulders dropped. What was he afraid of? Dr. Winston knew this man. She'd never allow Jeb to hurt him, right? If so, then why did part of his brain scream "lies" at that logic?

Levi looked into the eyes of the stranger, which weren't black, but a deep, dark chocolate. Now that he wasn't trying to kill him, Levi noticed the sharp line of his jaw and his high cheekbones. His black hair was wavy, swept across his thick dark eyebrows, and curled toward his ears. Jeb reminded him of Logan with his air of confidence, but this guy bordered on cockiness.

"Levi, we have a lot to discuss, so why don't you sit?" Again, Dr. Winston motioned to the chair where Levi had been previously seated.

The idea of talking seemed okay. Thoughts of fleeing left Levi's mind. He returned to his seat.

Jeb passed before Levi, sauntering toward the windows. As he passed, the calm within Levi faded, replaced with trepidation and apprehension. What was he thinking staying there a moment longer? Grasping at the arms of the chair, he decided to wait until Dr. Winston sat, and then he would bolt. However, Dr. Winston didn't sit but leaned against her desk. Would she try to grab Levi if he ran?

I have to get out of here!

Jeb leaned against the wall between the windows, regarding Levi with unnerving silence. What was he looking at? Levi had almost said it aloud but bit down on his lip. Levi's eyes darted between them. A puzzled looked on Jeb's face gave him pause.

"Relax. You look terrified. Jeb's a nice guy," Dr. Winston said.

A nice guy who was stalking Levi and had practically caused his head to implode. At least he hadn't been deliberately trying to hurt him, as Levi had thought. But he still wasn't convinced Jeb wouldn't release his mind meld on him again.

Jeb continued playing with the crystal, eyes intent on Levi. Levi took a deep breath, relaxing his muscles and rolling his shoulders to release the tension. He leaned back against the chair and released his grip on the arms. Out of the corner of his eye, he glanced at Jeb and thought he saw a ghost of a smirk.

"That's better," Dr. Winston said. The smile returned to her face.

"Who is he?" Levi kept an eye on Jeb from the corner of his eye.

"He's a friend, and part of the Seer community."

"*You're* a Seer?"

Jeb snorted, still playing with that necklace. He had quite a fetish for it. "No."

"I sent Jeb to check on you." Dr. Winston said without a hint of remorse.

Levi straightened in the chair. "You what? *You* sent *him* after me?"

Dr. Winston's lips thinned. "Not *after* you. Do you remember the last conversation we had in this office before you left school?"

He did. Dr. Winston's concern for Levi missing so many classes, his attention wandering in class, his reluctance to participate had been apparent. At the time, Levi had failed to mention he'd already decided to leave college. "Yes."

"I sent Jeb to try and find out who your guardian was. I'd feared that person hadn't taken their role seriously and neglected the oath they'd taken to be there for you once your soul was removed."

Back to the soulless thing.

"Mine's right where it's supposed to be." Levi pointed to his chest, not wanting to say "soul" aloud in front of Jeb.

Dr. Winston sighed heavily and turned to Jeb.

"Having some difficulty accepting the truth?" Jeb had muttered as if Levi wouldn't hear.

Dr. Winston only nodded with a faint glimmer of pity in her eyes. God, he knew that look well.

Levi glared at Jeb. "So you believe this? You think my soul is gone too."

Jeb didn't answer, just continued to stare expressionlessly at him.

Levi dropped his hands into his lap. Despite the enormity of the situation, he'd remained quite calm. From under the fringe of his bangs, he gave Jeb a sideways glance. Jeb continued to silently play with that damned crystal, his steely control apparent in every movement, every breath. "Evidently, he didn't find a guardian, because I don't have one."

But I do have a soul. I have to.

"You're right. He didn't find anyone. In fact, you're quite a solitary person."

Rubbing the tension at the base of his skull, Levi knew he was going to have one whopper of a headache. "Tell me something I don't know."

As if the words had been a dare, Dr. Winston said, "Jeb has been watching you since the day you left school."

A sickening chill ran down his spine. Levi glared hard at Jeb, who truly had been stalking him. "W-why would you…? I would've known."

A smug smile crossed his stalker's lips. "No one sees me until I want them to."

Levi begged to differ. "I saw you at the college, outside of my classroom, in the parking lot—*outside of my house*. I ran into you in the hallway."

Jeb shifted his stance. Apparently, Levi had hit a nerve. "Those were times I *wanted* you to see me."

"Riiiight."

"I did ask Jeb to talk to you, to convince you to come and see me. I sent you several messages, but you kept putting me off. Can you tell me what happened whenever Jeb approached you?" Dr. Winston had moved to her chair, and she leaned forward. Her closeness made him want to push his chair back.

"What do you mean?" Levi was so ready to hit End and cease that conversation.

Jeb was about to speak, but Dr. Winston put up her hand and silenced him.

Good boy, Levi snickered to himself when Jeb obeyed.

"Jeb said he ran into some trouble whenever he got near you. What did you feel?"

"Nothing." He wasn't letting them into his personal shit. "That wasn't about him."

It couldn't be. None of it made any sense. Maybe Levi wasn't in that office. Maybe his body was somewhere, drooling in a heap in a padded room, his mind cracked. This had to be an illusion. A *very* real illusion.

"It had everything to do with him."

Jeb at least had the decency to look apologetic for what he probably assumed was his doing.

"If it did, then I wouldn't be sitting here right now. I'd be writhing on the floor in agony, blood pouring from my nose, and my head about to explode brain matter everywhere."

Dr. Winston raised an eyebrow and glanced to Jeb, who gave her what appeared to be an I-told-you-so look.

Levi startled when Dr. Winston reached above his head and retrieved something from the bookcase behind him. When she stepped back, a small, silver box was nestled in her palm. Crossing to Jeb, she opened the lid. Without being asked, Jeb removed the chain with the crystal from around his neck, placed it into the box with a jut of his chin, and snapped the lid shut.

Pressure as terrifyingly real as ever slammed into Levi. Leaning over in the chair, he grabbed his head, nearly falling over, a fiery heat consuming his chest. A hand grabbed his. The pressure quickly subsided, but it was too late. Blood dripped from his nose, splattering onto the Oriental rug below. A tissue was stuffed into his hand. Levi quickly pressed it against his nose to staunch the blood.

Slowly sitting upright, Levi was faced with Jeb, who knelt beside him. The warmth from his touch sent a shiver straight through Levi. He held the crystal loosely in his other hand. His expression was one of... concern? Probably afraid he'd be convicted of murder if Levi dropped dead. He yanked his arm away. The man was too close. Jeb stumbled back, surprised by the sudden movement.

"What did you do to me?" Levi stood on wobbly legs. Fuck, there was that headache.

Jeb pulled to his full height. He clasped the crystal around his neck but didn't answer.

Dr. Winston spoke instead. "I'm sorry, but it was the only way to show you that Jeb is causing your reaction. I haven't figured out why this is happening, but it's definitely Jeb's proximity to you. When Jeb told me about your recent reactions to him, I had my doubts. I mean, he's been close to you for months and suddenly this starts occurring."

Levi shuddered at the word "close."

"It didn't make sense. Now I feel it might possibly have something to do with stopping your medication. Past that I'm baffled."

Why did she have to mention that?

"The crystal blocks energy. For some reason, Jeb's energy is having an adverse effect on you. I've never seen anything like it."

"Nothing like it? Of course not, because it's all freaking crazy. So it was you every time I felt like my head was going to explode and my heart was being ripped out of my chest?" He pointed to Jeb accusingly. Jeb's arms were at his side, and he was very still. "Do you know what kind of hell you put me through? I thought I was going crazy, like losing my friggin' mind crazy. I thought my skull was going to disintegrate. I almost died at least three times."

Dr. Winston's head jerked in Jeb's direction, but Jeb didn't move.

"Yeah, that's right. After that first time at the college, I ended up in the lake, because I felt like my body was on fire."

A raised eyebrow, an evil smile, then a low chuckle came from Jeb. "On purpose?"

Levi sneered. "Yeah, only I don't see how dropping twenty feet into an icy Adirondack lake, breaking a rib, and then almost freezing to death is funny."

Jeb's smile faded.

Levi balled his fists at his sides. "The second time, when you were outside my house, I almost swallowed an entire bottle of pills, because I couldn't take the crushing sadness that filled my head. And then yesterday, when you touched me, my God, the pain… and then my nose started bleeding and, then… well… forget it." Levi plunked down into the chair, fingers digging hard into his throbbing temples.

"I'm sorry, Levi. We didn't have a clue it was that bad." At least she looked remorseful.

"Well, maybe if you'd asked before sending your goon after me, all of this could have been avoided." Levi wondered how hard he'd have to rub to crush his skull and end it all.

Jeb resumed his relaxed position against the wall, playing with that damned crystal, the only barrier between Levi's sanity and utter hell whenever he was near. The corner of Jeb's mouth curled, a mischievous glint colored his eyes. Was the cocky jerk enjoying his pain? Jeb tilted his head to the side and wrapped his fist around the crystal. His lips parted.

A startling warmth flooded Levi's core, expanding outward. He rubbed his palms slowly over the tops of his thighs. Jeb held Levi's gaze, then gave his bottom lip a slow, languorous lick. Levi's eyes followed the pink appendage. God, what would it be like to suck on that lip?

What the hell was that? Levi practically jackknifed at the thought, the action tipping the chair.

"You okay?" Dr. Winston reached out to steady the chair.

"Not really," Levi said blatantly.

Jeb unwrapped his fingers from the crystal but continued to hold it between two fingers.

Dr. Winston carried on. "I'm confused about some things you said."

Welcome to my world.

"What exactly happened that drove you to jump into the lake and contemplate swallowing pills? Once Jeb wasn't near you, the effect would have ended."

Levi explained the euphoria and the searing heat that followed. He described the sadness and overwhelming despair but stopped before mentioning the wanton need for Noah and his murderous desires.

"What about yesterday?" Levi glared at him, but Jeb continued. "After I left you, what happened?"

Levi looked down at his hands unsure how to answer that. "Let's just say there's this person"—no way was he outing himself there—"and, well…." He swallowed hard, trying to suppress his blush. "It was all nice and cozy, and then it wasn't."

"So what wasn't 'nice'?" Jeb leaned forward, scowling.

That expression pissed Levi off. "I wanted to kill this person, okay? If I hadn't gotten away from them, I might have done it with my bare hands."

Jeb cocked an eyebrow as if impressed with Levi's statement. "You just wanted to kill this person? Nothing else."

Levi narrowed his eyes, wondering what Jeb thought he knew. "Um, first I might have wanted to… you know…." Levi could feel his face turning ten shades of red.

"What?" Jeb wasn't going to let it go.

Levi gritted his teeth and flashed Jeb a murderous glare. "We were kissing, and you know, it got a little out of control, and then something happened… I felt… I mean it was like I wanted to murder hi—this person." Levi was unsettled sharing the information.

Dr. Winston leaned forward. She looked excited. "So after you left Jeb each time you experienced an intense emotion running the spectrum. On one end mild euphoria, which, when untethered, can turn to a raging, burning high. Sadness to utter despair and then lust to a murderous rage."

Sounded about right. Levi nodded.

"Absolutely fascinating."

Not quite. "Can you tell me why I had those emotions?

"Not really. I mean they're normal emotions. Something definitely triggered their intensity."

Levi shook his head. "You don't understand what I mean. I don't really feel intense emotions, *ever*. Except for a few times when something really bad happened, they just aren't there, more like echoes of feelings." Probably just enough to keep him from being a psychopath. Levi continued without trepidation. Might as well throw all of his most embarrassing details out there. "I'm as dead inside as they come. I don't even cry unless I break a bone or something more serious. I totally pissed my brother off yesterday, really hurt him, the only person in my life who's always been there for me, and I just did it. I felt a little guilty and tried really hard to cry when I saw how upset he was, but nothing." Levi was disgusted by his hideous behavior toward Logan. "My emotions are dull echoes except for the times I was near him." Levi jabbed a finger at Jeb.

Dr. Winston's jaw dropped. Jeb didn't move except to narrow his eyes. Levi really did want to punch him.

When no one spoke, Levi continued. "That's why I stopped the meds. I thought they were causing me to feel nothing, but…." The empty lonely echoing within had continued.

"But it didn't help," Dr. Winston said. "Oh, Levi. This just keeps getting stranger. I know this is a lot to take in at once, but we will find your soul and make this right."

Levi looked at the bloody tissue in his hand. Blood covered his palm as well. "Can I use the bathroom?" He could only imagine what his face looked like.

Dr. Winston nodded. "The door behind Jeb."

Of course it was. Levi stood and tentatively walked toward Jeb, wondering if he would move at all. Just as Levi paused Jeb stepped aside and motioned for Levi to pass.

Levi shut the heavy wood door behind him and turned the lock. He exhaled at his image in the mirror. Not much blood was left on his face. Quickly, he washed up. Frowning, he leaned into the mirror, focusing on his eyes, searching for any hint that his soul was missing. He didn't look soulless. He envisioned a gaunt, lifeless image, gray skin, white hair, black, dead eyes. No, he didn't look soulless, but fuck all if he didn't feel it in every cell. *"Hollow, unfeeling"* as that woman had said. Had she seen the gaping black hole where his soul should have been?

Loss overflowed within him. Overcome with misery, Levi squeezed his eyes shut against the burn as his eyes filled with tears. Warm droplets rolled down his face. He couldn't have been more surprised if blood had leaked from his eyes. With his fingertip, he trapped a tear as it rolled past his mouth. Closing his eyes, he pictured the incredulous look on

Logan's face, the defeat Levi had served him, and Logan turning his back on him. Gone.

Shudders wracked Levi's body as he was overtaken by sobs. *Logan, I'm sorry.* He grabbed his cell phone and called Logan, willing him to answer, but got his voice mail. The sound of Logan's voice pushed him further into remorse. Through blurry eyes, he struggled to text his brother.

I am so sorry. Please forgive me, please!

Levi hit Send. He needed to see Logan. He wiped all traces of his tears from his face and tried to fan his eyes with his hands. His eyes were red and puffy. There was no mistaking he'd been crying. Jeb would have a field day with that one. Realizing it was a lost cause, he exited the bathroom, nearly smacking Jeb with the door. So close.

"Feel better?" Jeb seemed overly optimistic.

Levi passed by him, refusing to answer.

"Well, it's been a lot of fun, but I have to get home. My parents think I'm at class, and my last one is over in forty-five minutes. If I'm late, they'll freak."

Levi walked purposefully toward the door determined to escape.

Dr. Winston raced past Levi, plastering herself to the door to block his exit. "Wait. Levi, there's more."

Levi had had enough, way more than enough. "I'm full," he assured his former teacher. What more could there be? "I get it. I'm soulless, and if you just keep Mr. Bad-Ass-Energy over there away from me, then all will be good."

Jeb grunted but said nothing.

"But you can get your soul back."

The possibility hadn't even occurred to Levi. "Got any lying around? I'll take what you've got."

"The only person who can remove a soul is a Seer, and the only person who can hold that soul is a Keeper. The entire point of removing a soul is to allow the person to gain a mature conscience. Then the soul is almost always returned. With an infant that is generally anywhere between seventeen and twenty-five. It all depends on the person's personal growth."

"So someone has my soul in a jar on their shelf, and they're supposed to give it back?" If the day took many more twist and turns, Levi was going to puke.

"In a manner of speaking. It's the guardian who decides the right time to return the soul, and only the Keeper can return it. There are strict rules that govern Seers and Keepers. And souls are not kept in jars. Breakable and all." Dr. Winston smirked.

Levi imagined the "oops" moment when a jar full of soul hit the floor. "But we don't know who my guardian is."

"No, we don't, but we can go to the next best person to tell us the Keeper's name. Only one person can give permission for an infant's soul to be removed."

"I really hope you don't mean God." Levi sighed with exasperation.

She shook her head. "Your father."

LEVI STOOD next to the driver's door of his car, clutching his keys in his fist. After all of the bombs that had been dropped on him, he'd been sent away with two unwanted things. First, a mission to obtain strands of his father's hair for some Spell of Recognition, in order to start the search for his soul. Second was Jeb.

"You're not driving my car." Levi wrapped his arms tight around his chest, hiding the keys in his fist under his armpit.

Jeb stood about two feet away from Levi. Holding his hand out, Jeb waited with that calm, annoying demeanor for Levi to hand over the keys. He would be waiting a long time. Levi could be stubborn too.

"Let's go, kitten."

"What the hell?" Levi sneered. "Don't call me *that*!"

Jeb smirked. The gesture was both unnerving and alluring. Gods, Levi wanted to punch him and kiss him at the same time.

"You remind me of a kitten. Curious and wary. Full of spit and fire and energy. I can feel it coming off of you in waves," Jeb whispered.

Jeb dropped his hand. Levi took that as a sign of victory until Jeb moved closer. Levi backed up against the driver's door as their chests nearly touched. Levi had to strain his neck to look up into Jeb's face.

Jeb leaned forward, resting his hand on the driver's window behind Levi. "You're ready to attack at any moment, aren't you? You look like you want to scratch my eyes out right now or… maybe crawl into my lap and purr."

Levi gritted his teeth, forcing away the need to touch the solid chest before him. He couldn't let Jeb get the better of him. The untrustworthy man was playing Levi to get his way. "Have you ever heard of personal space?" The words, which he'd meant to come out with more force, were merely a whisper.

Jeb fixed his gaze on Levi. Other than the slight movement of his eyes, not a muscle twitched, as if he were carved from stone. Those deep brown eyes with the light brown flecks could see right through Levi. The heat pooling in his groin messed with his head. What the hell? Was he getting turned on?

"You're afraid of me." Jeb's voice was raspy and his tone self-assured.

Levi stiffened his spine and pulled up his chin. "No, I'm not." Hard to sound convincing with a shaky voice, and yes, he was frightened by the man… and definitely turned on. That was twice today he'd felt something mirroring lust.

Jeb leaned closer. His cheek brushed across Levi's causing him to shudder. Jeb whispered in his ear. "You should be."

Levi suppressed a gasp. Jeb straightened and stepped back. His arrogance was incredible.

"Even if I was, I still wouldn't let you drive my car."

"So you admit that you're afraid of me."

"No."

"You do know that if I wanted to, I could get those keys from your weak little hand without a struggle."

"Then why don't you?" Levi would make him pry them out of his fist.

Jeez, Levi, don't taunt the large, scary man.

Jeb continued that annoying leer, his stare unwavering, slicing through Levi. Struggling to maintain the standoff, Levi finally averted his eyes. Jeb held his hand out again. Levi exhaled noisily and slapped the keys onto the palm of the infuriating man. With that went any stirrings in his groin.

"See? No struggle." Jeb grinned.

"Whatever. I don't have time for this." Levi circled around and climbed into the passenger seat of his own car, a first for him.

Jeb hopped in the driver's seat, needing to push the seat back to fit his legs. "Jesus you're short." Jeb started the car.

"Just try not to scratch it or crash into anything."

"Yeah, because it's such a classic." Jeb revved the sick-sounding engine to prove his point.

Levi closed his eyes, took a few deep breaths, and cracked the window.

"Getting a little hot?"

"Just exactly why are you coming back with me? Don't you have a car?"

"A Jeep, but it's in the shop. Had to find another way to get here."

"Carjack someone?"

Jeb let a low chuckle escape. "You're a feisty one, kitten."

"Stop calling me that!"

An hour and a half trapped in the car with Jeb. If the cocky man kept it up, one of them wouldn't make it back alive.

Levi's phone chimed. Hoping it was Logan, he pulled his phone from his jacket pocket. Just Gia.

Hey, hope ur feelng bttr. School sucks. Call me 4 the 411 on Noah.

Oh shit. If Noah had spilled to Gia about Levi attacking him, he might have to kill the man after all. Levi wasn't calling Gia with his stalker in his car. He checked his message to Logan. No response. He slid the phone back into his pocket.

"Bad news?"

Feigning interest in his life wouldn't get Levi to trust Jeb, if that's what he thought. "How about we make a deal? I won't butt into your business, and you don't butt into mine." Levi narrowed his eyes and pursed his lips.

Jeb held up his hand. "Hey, no problem," Jeb said then mumbled, "Touchy."

Levi rubbed his hands over his face. Another headache was creeping in. Or maybe the last one never left.

"You know if you don't trust me, it's gonna be really hard for me to help you." Jeb's earnest expression was unexpected.

Trusting Jeb would never happen.

"I don't recall asking for your help."

"No, you didn't. Is this how you treated your brother when he tried to help you?" Jeb looked back to the road as if he didn't expect Levi to respond.

Levi spent every ounce of energy curtailing the desire to hit Jeb, but only because he might wreck his own car. Biting hard on his lip,

Levi looked out his window, rubbing at his left temple. Hearing he didn't have a soul should have given him more than a headache. What about this missing guardian who should have been guiding him all along? And what damage did his soul have that necessitated its removal for Levi's own good or the good of others?

Evil.

Even though Dr. Winston had said innate evil was rare, Levi could have been that lucky one in six billion people to draw the evil card. An inability to feel emotion like a robot, a killing machine was the definition of evil, right? What if the evil in Levi was unlike any the world had ever seen? Like a mass murderer, serial killer, and Hitler all rolled into one or....

Psychopath.

And what about his father? Levi had argued in vain with Dr. Winston that Art Reed couldn't have agreed to remove his soul, much less known a Seer. He was way too practical to believe in anything mystical. Could it have been his mother? But Dr. Winston had said only the father—the rules and everything. Even though the father's and mother's soul combined to create an infant's soul, the father was more detached. A mother's judgment was clouded from spending nine months with the new soul. So it had to be Art, straight as an arrow, no-nonsense Art Reed.

No way.

And Jeb, who'd stalked Levi for months, had an eerie familiarity about him that had increased since Levi's first terrifying glance of him in the office. Fleeting moments beneath the surface of his consciousness vied for recognition, like a movie he'd seen years ago. The familiarity was scary and comforting at the same time. Sitting next to Jeb in the confines of the car only increased the sensation. More than a feeling of déjà vu. Why did Levi feel as if he'd been with Jeb before? And why did he feel a growing attraction to the prickly man, a kind of pull on his body, like the opposite poles of two magnets?

The throbbing in Levi's head dulled slightly. He thought about turning the radio on to quell the silence but resisted reaching anywhere near Jeb, who still played with that damned crystal. Must be the newness of wearing it.

"Why did the crystal stop working when it was in the box?" Levi asked.

Jeb grunted. "Oh, so now you're going to talk?"

Levi rolled his eyes.

"The box was lined with iron ore. Blocks energy."

"So do you go around messing with people's energy often? What about electronics? Maybe screw up TV signals, radios, pacemakers?"

A smile tugged at Jeb's lips. "Never happened before."

"So what's wrong with you, then?"

"What makes you think the problem lies with me?"

It was more of a hope. Levi was so tired of being the one with all of the problems.

"What exactly do you do? I mean besides stalk younger men?" He baited Jeb for a hint to his age. At first, he'd thought Jeb was close to Logan's age of twenty-one, yet his eyes had an aged wisdom to them.

"I work for the Seers Council." He'd said it matter-of-factly, as if he'd said he was a construction worker or a lawyer.

"There's a council?"

Jeb nodded. "Bunch of old Seers and Keepers making sure other Seers and Keepers follow the *rules*." A trace of disgust flashed with the word "rules." Jeb was definitely a rule breaker, which only increased his aura of dangerousness.

"Big on rules, huh?" Dr. Winston had given Levi the long-winded speech on the rules when Levi had questioned the need for his father's hair. Why couldn't they just ask his father where his soul was? Because there are rules and procedures to follow, and failing to follow them had consequences, whatever those were.

"That's me, the rule follower."

Levi decided to leave that comment alone. "And what exactly do you do for this council?"

He shrugged. "Whatever they ask. Mostly investigate, bring in a rogue Seer or Keeper." He turned to Levi. "Stalk *younger* men."

Jeb hadn't taken the bait and revealed his age.

"So you're like a PI-slash-bounty hunter. And they pay you for this?"

Jeb grinned. "Oh yeah."

"Huh. And how does one go about getting a job like that? Recruit from juvie?"

Jeb tensed, his grip visibly tightening on the steering wheel. He shot Levi a look that said he wasn't going there. "You ask a lot of questions, kitten."

"Do I look like a small furry mammal with a tail?" He resented Jeb's audacity greatly, and if Levi did have claws, he would have sunk them into Jeb.

Levi's phone chimed. He fished it out of his pocket. Finally, a message from Logan.

It's all good Crash :-)

Levi's relief was measurable. His thoughts went back to the bathroom, the crying and the heaviness in his chest. Real emotion for hurting Logan—remorse. Unpleasant as it had been at the time, the experience had been cathartic.

"Good news?"

Levi nodded. When he saw Logan, he was going to apologize again for good measure.

The rest of the ride was mostly silent, and Levi was grateful for that. As they entered Ticonderoga, Levi was hit by the realization that his anxiety and panic had been absent during the ride home. Too much on his mind, he guessed.

Jeb glanced at Levi. Was that agitation or maybe nervousness in his expression? "There's something I need to tell you… about the crystal. I—"

Before he could finish, Jeb pulled his phone from his pocket and studied the screen.

"Bad news?" Levi chuckled, echoing Jeb's earlier comment.

Jeb was too preoccupied to notice. "We have to step up our plans. Dr. Winston is coming tonight. She needs the hair now."

"Tonight? But weren't we supposed to meet tomorrow night?" Talk about pressure.

Jeb shrugged. "That was just pushed up to seven tonight."

"What's with the change?" Levi hated being pressured. It ratcheted his anxiety up a few notches.

"Guess we'll find out soon. We'll be meeting at my place," Jeb said.

"You have a place? Here in Ti?" Jeb actually lived in Ticonderoga. Why did that make Levi's stomach all jumpy?

"Yes."

"Where?"

"South end of town. Miller's Road."

"Really?" Miller's Road was on the east side of Lake George and not one of the houses there was worth less than half a million dollars. His interest in Jeb's place increased exponentially.

Jeb merely snorted. "My Jeep's at Leroy's. Should be fixed by now. I'll get out at the garage. Be ready at six forty-five sharp. I'll pick you up," Jeb said.

Levi shook his head. He didn't need Jeb adding to the pressure. "I can drive. Just tell me the house number."

"I'll pick you up."

"But…."

Jeb turned to Levi, his resolve evident. "I will *pick* you up. Be ready."

Apparently that was the end of the argument.

IT WAS four-thirty when Levi pulled into his driveway, just fifteen minutes late. Neither his mother nor his father, who were parked in front of the TV, noticed Levi's tardiness.

His mother noticed him first, looking up from the home magazine she read and smiling. "How was school?"

Levi's father reclined in his chair, holding the newspaper before him. Levi couldn't help but stare at him. He tried to see the man he thought he'd known, not the man who had authorized the removal of his own son's soul.

"School was good." Levi lied without hesitation. "Hi, Dad."

He wanted his father to look him in the eye, to prove that he wasn't the cause of his years of torment. But his father continued reading the paper.

"Hi, Levi." His gaze didn't leave the paper.

Any other time the snub would have caused only a moment of anguish. Now Levi felt jilted, unseen. They'd never been particularly close. He knew his father loved him, but distance separated them. That was so unlike Gia's father who was constantly hugging his daughter, talking to her, spending time with her. Ironically, Levi hadn't wanted that from anyone. Certainly, he was the one to blame for the distance.

"I'm going to the library tonight with Gia. She's picking me up a little before seven."

Lying like a pro now, Levi.

"Okay. Your father and I have a Chamber of Commerce meeting at six, so dinner is whatever you fix yourself. Not sure where Logan is." She went back to perusing her magazine.

"Okay."

Levi went up the stairs and paused at the top and listened. When no one stirred downstairs, he crept into his parent's room, feeling silly for sneaking about his own house. In the master bathroom, he opened the top drawer where his father kept his old wooden hairbrush. Levi was quite sure he'd been using the same brush for at least twenty years. If something worked, Art Reed didn't get rid of it, just like the 1985 Ford truck he continued to drive daily. Levi worked his finger into the bristles and retrieved a clump of black and gray hairs. He rolled them into a piece of tissue and exited the bathroom. Stepping into the hall, he ran right into his father.

Levi jumped back, clasping his hands over his chest. Fuck, he'd been caught. "You scared me, Dad."

His father's brow lowered. His lips became a thin line. "What're you doing in my room?"

What was he doing? "I… umm… I needed a tissue." He held up the wad of tissue containing the hair. *Real smooth, Levi.* "Have fun at your meeting." Levi passed his father and rushed to the safety of his room.

"Wow, that was close."

He tucked the tissue-wrapped hair into the front pocket of his bag and then dropped it on the floor. He just had to wait another two hours for Jeb to show up. In the meantime, he checked his e-mail and then Facebook. No messages. Nothing important. Taking a chance, he typed Noah's name into the search box, pulling up his wall. Well, Noah hadn't defriended Levi—yet. He recalled Gia's text earlier, wondering what news she had of Noah. Probably nothing Levi wanted to hear. Most likely Noah had told Gia what a freak Levi had been. After dialing Gia's number, Levi got her voice mail and left her a message to call him.

I wonder if Jeb has a Facebook page? Levi didn't even know his former stalker's last name. Typing the name *Jeb* into the search box, there were some local people with Jeb as a first name and some with Jeb as a last name. Jeb probably wasn't even his real name. Besides, the mysterious, uptight man didn't seem the type to advertise his identity on a social network. Probably didn't even own a computer.

At six thirty, Levi got a text message.

Be at the end of your driveway at six forty-five. Jeb.

How the hell did Jeb get Levi's cell number?

Jeb's number wasn't local. Pulling out his computer, Levi typed the area code into the search engine. Maine. Trying to get a more specific area within the state, he clicked on a small map on the same page.

"Great." The entire state had the same area code.

Glancing at the clock, he jumped up. Six forty-three. Grabbing his coat and bag, Levi ran out of the house and to the end of the driveway. And waited.

Taking his phone out, Levi checked the time. Six-fifty. What happened to six forty-five sharp? A light breeze blew a chill across his skin. Finally, at six fifty-five a black, soft-top Jeep Wrangler with a winch bolted to the front and oversized tires rolled to a stop in front of Levi. If he'd tried imaging the vehicle Jeb would drive, that would be it.

Climbing into the passenger seat, Levi barely had the door closed when Jeb took off. "You're late."

"I believe I told you to be ready at six forty-five. Never said I'd be here at that time."

"Do you always have to be so difficult?" Levi didn't try to mask his annoyance.

Jeb smirked without replying.

Miller's Road was only ten minutes from Levi's house. Jeb pulled into a driveway that curved through a wooded area that opened to a large two-story house. Manicured lawns and gardens surrounded the modern house. Jeb pulled around to the back and down another short drive to a small, secluded white house, close to the water.

"You rent here?" Levi asked as they walked to the front door. Even renting there had to cost a fortune.

Jeb pushed a key into the lock. "Belongs to a friend of the council."

That didn't exactly answer Levi's question.

Dr. Winston was already inside. She arranged items on the coffee table in front of a brown leather sofa. The large living area opened into a small kitchen with a set of sliding-glass doors. Beyond the doors was a deck illuminated by soft lighting. Levi imagined it overlooked the water.

Dr. Winston gave them a cursory glance. "Good, you're here. Did you get it?"

Levi retrieved the wad of tissue from his bag and handed it to Dr. Winston. He dropped his bag and stood before the coffee table. Assorted glass bottles and crystals covered the table. An ornate silver bowl sat in the middle.

"Okay, let's get started." She knelt.

Jeb circled around the sofa, pulled a chair from the kitchen table, and placed it a few feet from them. Sitting, he stretched his legs out and locked his hands behind his head. Levi continued to stand, watching as Dr. Winston added powder and blue liquid into the metal bowl.

"Why did we have to meet tonight?" Levi asked.

Dr. Winston continued her work. "Because the council asked me to put a rush on this."

A rush? That didn't sound good. "Why?"

"There's no record of the removal of your soul. Nothing in the database or archives. When I first met you, I made an inquiry to the council for info about you, but they found nothing. It's not unheard of for records to be misplaced. If a record had been found, we would know who your guardian and Keeper are. But the paperwork can't be located."

"There's paperwork to remove a soul?" Levi imagined poring over piles of paperwork much like his financial aid forms for college. Those had been a pain in the ass. He imagined a mountain of papers was needed for removing a soul. Probably deterred some people right there.

Dr. Winston glanced up. "Removing someone's soul is serious business. The procedure needs approval from all members of the council. Safeguards are in place to assure that the reasons are valid."

"If removing a person's soul can be so 'beneficial,' then why have I never heard of it?" Levi still wondered about the validity of that whole reality.

Dr. Winston stopped. "It's like any radical idea. First, it's highly protected within the Seer society. Just imagine the implications of being able to remove a soul and have control over it. Second, how do you prove that someone's soul has been removed if only Seers can see it? Anyone could proclaim a soul is corrupt and say they've removed the entity. It's a slippery slope and historically, when this craft was first developed in ancient civilizations, there was no oversight. Those who could see and remove souls did so for profit and without regard to ethics. That went on for hundreds of years before the Seers Council was developed."

Levi swallowed. His gut knotted. "How did my father know to do this? We don't even know anyone who can do something like this. I mean wouldn't I know if…." Levi trailed off. But he hadn't known that

Dr. Winston was anything more than a college professor, even with the strange items in her office. What were other people he knew hiding?

Dr. Winston's pitiful expression was something Levi didn't need. "We'll get this all straightened out. I promise."

Levi merely nodded, unsure of her claim. He glanced at Jeb who still reclined in the chair. His relaxed frame and slack expression made Levi think he might actually fall asleep.

Levi sighed. "So no paperwork? But you knew that." Maybe his paperwork had been misfiled or misplaced, ending up in that black hole where all missing paperwork ended up. Hopefully his soul hadn't been misplaced as well.

"Yes, and when none was found, the council began an inquiry into the Seer and Keeper communities looking for those responsible for the removal. After three months, they've come up empty. Now that we're sure you have no guardian… well, let's just say something's fishy. The council wants this cleared up immediately."

"So what's the rush now? I mean, it's been nineteen years. What's another day?" Levi shrugged despite wanting his soul.

"Removal of a soul without council permission is a very serious crime with dire consequences to the person or persons involved—even if it was nineteen years ago. Equate the seriousness of the charge with that of murder."

That was serious.

Opening the wad of tissue, Dr. Winston picked up a few strands of his father's hair, handling them as if they were extremely valuable. She placed the strands into the silver bowl, then added a blunt clear crystal. She lit a match, tossed it into the bowl, and a blue flame ignited, shooting about six inches into the air. Levi sneezed as the sulfur irritated his nose.

"What's this supposed to prove, and what exactly is supposed to happen?" Levi was mesmerized by the blue flame dancing in the bowl.

"When someone requests a soul be removed, the Seer places a spell over the one requesting the soul to be removed, which allows other Seers to identify that person as a sanctioned requestor. When the flame dies down, I'll retrieve the crystal, put it into the blue solution, and we'll have our proof."

"Seriously?" Levi shook his head. It was all too strange.

The blue flame burned down and then there was only a stream of smoke. Using a pair of metal tongs, Dr. Winston pulled the blackened crystal from the bowl. Steam rose as the heated crystal hit the cool liquid. Levi watched Dr. Winston intently for any indication of what was happening. She frowned.

"Did it work?" He bent and looked at the submerged crystal.

"Something must have gone wrong. I'll have to start again."

"Might as well sit and get comfortable. This could take a while," Jeb said, his position unchanged, as if he'd expected this.

Levi sat in the brown leather chair across from Dr. Winston. The only noise in the room was the clanking of her bangles against the bowl. More strands of hair went into the bowl, another crystal, more fire (another sneeze), and the crystal. After a few minutes, she wore the same bewildered frown.

"What's supposed to happen?"

"The crystal should glow red." Dr. Winston sat back on her heels, staring at the unchanged crystal as if that would garner more favorable results.

Again, Jeb appeared unaffected by the failure. Levi thought Jeb's eyes were closed, but a wry smile crossed his face. Jeb was looking right at him inciting a funny feeling in his gut. Levi quickly returned his attention to Dr. Winston, who fished around in a large black leather bag. Out came more glass containers. She cleaned the bowl with a cloth, then added powders, what looked to be dried leaves, and a few hairs. Good thing Levi had grabbed a clump of it.

"Levi, I need some of your hair."

"What? Why?" Levi touched his hair.

Dr. Winston silently held out the bowl. Levi reluctantly raked his fingers through his curls. A few strands clung to his fingers. He wiggled them above the bowl, and the strands floated down, joining his father's.

Dr. Winston lit another match. Levi sneezed. This time two separate flames filled the bowl. One green and one red engaged in an erotic dance until they flared up against one another, each trying to consume the other but constantly repelled. Jeb abruptly sat up in the chair, staring at the flames with wide eyes. Dr. Winston leaned back as the dance intensified, climbing higher, the flames joining. Levi shielded his eyes, watching through a gap in his fingers. He gasped as the bowl flipped into the air and then slammed onto the coffee table, the flames extinguished. Levi slowly moved his hand from his eyes. Black smoke trailed from the bowl. They all stared.

"Levi, where did you get that hair from?" Dr. Winston asked.

"My father's brush."

"Does anyone else use it?"

When Levi looked to Jeb, he averted his eyes. Levi furrowed his brow. "No one would want to."

"Are you absolutely one hundred percent sure no one else used it?"

Levi looked to his professor annoyed by her questions. "Yeah. It's like twenty years old and gross."

Dr. Winston rubbed her hands over her face while Jeb continued avoiding Levi's gaze.

"Would someone like to tell me what's going on?" Levi knew whatever it was wouldn't be some little thing. *Again.*

Dr. Winston stood. His gaze followed her pinched face. "The man that hair came from is not your biological father."

CHAPTER 13

LEVI JUMPED to his feet, a surge of anger taking over. "Okay, I've had enough of this crap. First, you tell me my soul is missing, and now you're telling me that my father is not my real father. Do you realize how insane all of this sounds?" Levi couldn't listen anymore. The never-ending proclamations concerning his life were rubbing him raw.

Dr. Winston remained calm. "I'm sorry, Levi, but it's true. That never would have happened if the hair had come from your biological father." She pointed to the toppled bowl.

"Well, maybe you did it wrong like the other ones."

She shook her head. "I didn't do them wrong. They didn't work because the person that hair came from didn't agree to have a soul removed. That's why I asked for your hair. Hair from two people with a first-generation connection would have burned bright purple." Dr. Winston turned to Jeb, who still sat on the edge of the chair. "You know what needs to be done."

Jeb nodded with dazed agreement while Dr. Winston looked nonplussed. Levi was sure his own face held his utter disbelief.

Dr. Winston quickly gathered what she had on the coffee table, placed them into her black bag, and zipped it. "I have to inform the council of this. Our search just got a lot harder." She headed for the door and was gone before Levi could form a sentence.

He sat back on the chair, staring at the sooty spot marring the pine surface of the table. Art Reed wasn't his biological father? Despite the utter absurdity of the idea, he let it sink in, studied it, and surveyed it from all angles. Deep down, way down, maybe in the small remaining part of his soul, that truth felt right, *too right*, as if it had been on the tip of his tongue waiting to be spoken. Art was his dad, had raised him, provided for him, but did he know another man had fathered Levi? Could Levi even be sure any of it was true?

Jeb stepped before him, holding out a glass of water. Levi hadn't even heard him moving.

Levi looked up. "No thanks."

Jeb sat on the coffee table and set the glass next to him. His knees invaded Levi's space, resting on either side of his legs. Jeb's lazy demeanor was gone. Levi bit on the inside of his cheek.

Too close.

Thoughts were difficult to hold on to as he looked at Jeb. Something stirred in Levi's gut, a trace of something warm, something unacceptable. Levi pulled his knees to his chest and leaned against the back of the chair. When exactly had his life taken such a detour into bizarro-land?

"Do you want me to drive you home?" Jeb asked, his face bearing his standard stonelike expression.

Levi dared to peer into Jeb's deep, brown eyes. There was a deceptiveness to Jeb's steely exterior, his rugged appearance, his harsh tone, his forbidding body language. Levi's gaze locked with Jeb's. Instead of discomfort, his curiosity grew. Who was this person? What experiences and heartaches had melded to craft such a seemingly impenetrable barrier? It reminded him of his own inability to connect with anyone beyond his own skin.

The slight softening of Jeb's jaw was barely noticeable but hinted to a miniscule drop in his defenses.

Levi broke out of his trance. "I'm sorry. Did you say something?"

"Just wondering if you wanted me to take you home?"

Home was where Levi's nonbiological father and lying mother were. Of course his mother had lied. You can't get pregnant and not know who the father was, unless you were very drunk. Had his mother had an affair? It was the only logical answer.

"Kitten? You're gone again."

That brought Levi back quickly. He blew out a sharp breath. "Yeah, whatever. What does it matter anyway?" Bleak weariness coated the itty-bitty remaining part of his soul.

"I've got an idea. How 'bout you just sit there until you can stop feeling sorry for yourself?" Jeb had pushed each word out between clenched teeth.

"What's your major problem?"

"Me? I've got no problem."

"Apparently you've got a problem with me."

Jeb leaned forward, mouth open as if he were going to say something. He stopped and sat back, glowering. He grabbed at that damned crystal. Levi wanted to stuff it down his throat.

"Oh, please, don't hold back. Enlighten me." His irritation with the sanctimonious man reached an all-time high.

"Sure. You've got this problem, with a possible solution, but instead of holding on to that, you're wallowing in self-pity. It's all over your face. Some people would give anything for the ability to change what has happened. Instead you're taking it for granted." Jeb sat back, returning to that impenetrable poker face.

Levi stood and glared down at him. "I think that lacking a soul can be classified as a bit more than a problem. It's not like I lost my cell phone or something easily replaced. My soul is *missing*, stolen and possibly lost by some mystery person who's supposed to be my real father. The last nineteen years of my life are one big, fat, fear-filled lie, and you're giving me shit about it. You just need to shut up about things that have nothing to do with you."

Jeb rose from the table, a good head taller than Levi. Levi was trapped between the chair pushing into his calves and the solid mass before him. His heart sped when Jeb turned up a lopsided smile.

"Feel better?"

Levi clenched his fists at his sides. "What the hell is that supposed to mean? Do you get off on seeing me feel like crap?" Jeb had to be the most annoying man alive. And Levi still wanted to kiss him.

Ugh!

Jeb leaned down inches from Levi's face. Levi's heart skipped a beat as a jolt passed through him. "Believe me, that's not what gets me off." A salacious smile split Jeb's face.

Levi stifled a gasp, then pushed his hands hard against Jeb's chest. It was like trying to move a brick wall, but Jeb lost his balance and fell back, sitting on the coffee table. Rushing for the front door, Levi reached for the knob, but before he could obtain freedom, two hands grabbed his upper arms. He was turned and his back shoved hard against the door.

Jeb slammed his palms onto the wood next to Levi's shoulders, trapping Levi between two beefy arms. "We're not done yet, kitten."

"Let me out, now. And quit calling me that!"

Jeb barely moved as Levi pulled on his arms and pushed on his chest. It was an exercise in futility, but Levi wouldn't stop fighting Jeb—or chasing his growing attraction. With Jeb, Levi's emotions were his, only his, not the fake lust he'd felt for Noah, and that irritated him, angered him—and excited him. A man who had to be straight. Of course, what else would Levi be attracted to? Might as well complicate his life a thousand times more. Fierce anger burst forth, rage for years of emptiness and fear, the lies, the betrayal. How could life have handed Levi such a lousy lot?

"Get it all out of your system. Then we move on."

Jeb's well-honed composure, his absolute control, enraged Levi even more.

"Get the hell away from me!" Levi got right in Jeb's face, but the stoic man didn't even flinch. What the hell was wrong with him?

"If you want any chance of getting your soul back, you've got to let it go. The anger and the self-pity serve no purpose."

"Why the hell do you care?" Why would anyone care about what happened to him?

"It's what I do. Whatever the council needs done, I get it done."

"So, I'm just a job?" Levi had no clue why those words felt like a knife to the heart.

"Yeah. Just a job." Jeb paused. His gaze ran down the length of Levi's body and back up. "And I don't need anything getting in the way."

"Are you as cold on the inside as you are on the outside?"

"Interested in finding out?" A flash of amusement crossed Jeb's face.

Fuck, was the asshole picking on Levi? Did Jeb suspect he was gay, and this was some subtle form of bashing?

"You—you're way too cocky." Levi's body shook as the anger seeped away, and his breathing steadied.

A few moments of silence passed between them.

"If I move are you going to play nice?" Levi shook his head and a hearty laugh rolled from Jeb's lips. "There's a spitfire in you waiting to come out. I'd bet on you in a fight any day."

Levi glared. "You don't know anything about me." Even as Levi said it the accusation had felt wrong. Again with the déjà-vu. Why did he feel Jeb knew way more about him than he should?

Jeb dropped his arms to his sides but maintained his intimate distance. God, was that Jeb's heat radiating on his skin?

"Now, why don't you be good and sit down? We've got things to talk about, and we might as well get it over with."

Levi gave him a foul look and folded his arms over his chest. "I'd rather stand."

Jeb tilted his head, half frowning, half smirking. "You are—"

"What? Stubborn? Get used to it."

Back to that expressionless mask, but not as hard as it had been. Were his eyes softer? "Not what I expected."

"And exactly what did you expect?"

"Boring."

Levi snorted. "Did you just call me boring?"

"If you recall, I've been following you around on and off for about four months. Never been so bored in my entire life." Jeb faked a yawn.

A bolt of heat exploded in the pit of Levi's stomach thinking of Jeb secretly watching him. A strange mixture of danger and excitement. "So where were you when I was in the freezing lake? Could have actually used you then."

Jeb looked away from Levi. "After your reaction at the school, I thought I'd better back off. Actually, I thought you'd spotted me and were freaking out. Turns out you didn't have to see me to react." His tone of guilt betrayed his straight-faced façade. He returned a harsh gaze to Levi, who swallowed hard. "And by the way, hanging out at the college I've heard a lot of gossip. Worse than a fucking high school." He narrowed his eyes. "Stay away from Noah Macy. He's only after one thing."

"And what's that?" The words were out of Levi's mouth before he realized what he'd asked.

"If I have to tell you that, then you're way more boring than I thought. He's gay. You're gay. You figure it out."

Levi's mouth opened and closed, like a beached fish. "Who…. How…. What…?"

Levi could feel the blood drain from his face. Thoughts ran into one another, none making enough sense to speak a coherent sentence. All the while Jeb leered at Levi with his lips clamped tight, as if anything else he'd wanted to speak was best left unsaid.

Levi snatched the first intelligible thought. "It's none of your business who I date even if they only want one thing." Shoot, he'd wanted to deny he was gay so he tacked on, "guy or girl."

Jeb snorted. "There hasn't been, nor will there ever be any girls for you. And I've made it my business, so like *you* said, get used to it."

Levi fumed at Jeb's arrogance. His relationship status wasn't Jeb's concern. "That doesn't make me gay!" God, if you weren't a horny, raging pile of teenage hormones who couldn't keep your hands off the girls, then you were labeled gay. Even if he was.

"Doesn't make you straight either, Pinocchio."

"You're calling me a liar? I wasn't the one who stalked someone for four months all covert ops and shit. I don't trust you."

"Well, then you really aren't going to trust me after what I have to tell you." Jeb's stance changed from overbearing macho to one of hair-raking nervousness. The change unnerved Levi.

"Tell me what?" He wanted to know, but it was probably something disturbing. And he still wanted Jeb to tell him, like some morbid curiosity.

Jeb exhaled, running his fingers through his hair, as if searching for courage. What could possibly scare him? "Can we just sit?"

"Stalling?"

"No. This crystal does more than block energy. It can send it as well."

"What does that mean?"

"I wasn't sure at first. But it didn't take me long to figure it out that I can send out energy. Since you're a sucking black vortex of energy, you pick it up."

"What do you mean by energy?" Levi narrowed his eyes.

Jeb shifted nervously from foot to foot. "Emotions. Feelings." He reached up and swiped his fingertip across the crystal.

Visions of Jeb touching and gripping the crystal came to Levi. "Are you telling me that every time you're playing with that thing you're sending energy out and doing something else to me?" Violated wasn't even close to how he felt.

"Well not *to* you, *for* you."

"For me? It wasn't enough that your energy almost killed me. Now you've found another way to invade my mind? Do you have boundary issues or something?" Levi gasped. "Did you drive me into the lake, to almost kill myself, to feel...." He stopped with the thought of the desire.

Jeb's dark eyes widened. "No! Dr. Winston gave me the crystal yesterday. Today was the first time I realized how it worked. But I didn't do it to... I wasn't trying to...." He appeared mortified by the accusation. "I know what it's like not to feel anything. To feel dead inside. Stuck where you are because of it."

Levi's ire dissipated as the shuttered man tried to say something real, to open up a tightly closed door.

Levi hazarded a guess. "So the anger, sadness? That was you?"

"At first, yes, but it's changing. In the office, when I'd stopped concentrating on the emotion, when I dropped the crystal, I could see that emotion quit in you. But the last few times, it didn't end. The anger just now lasted quite a long time."

"Why would you even do that?" Levi struggled to understand first and strike later.

"To help you to move forward. I need your help to find your soul and take down the person who did this, and you need to be levelheaded. Working through emotions is how most people do that. I could have kept this from you, but it just seems wrong to do this without your knowing. I'm also telling you about it before something goes wrong."

"Like what?"

Jeb turned away from Levi, rubbing the back of his neck. The muscles beneath his T-shirt rippled, giving the impression of easy strength. When he turned back, the vulnerability in his eyes melted Levi's anger.

"A few times when I was sending you energy with a specific emotion, that's what you felt. A few times when you were freaking out, I think I was able to calm you. But sometimes the emotion I tried to send wasn't what you felt. Earlier at Dr. Winston's office when you went into the bathroom, you didn't get all happy, did you?"

Levi recalled the sadness, the tears, and the feelings had been so real. No echoes or faint fleeting wisps of emotion. Nothing had ever felt so true, as if it belonged to him, as if something he'd been missing for years had been returned.

"I didn't think so."

Levi squared his shoulder with Jeb's. "Do it now. Make me feel something." He hated how anxious and needy his voice sounded.

Jeb eyed Levi suspiciously. "No," he said resolutely. "It's too unpredictable."

"Somehow I've been having genuine feelings. So real, like I own them. Not echoes of what they should be. That crystal can help me."

"I can't. Not right now. Not with you here. Alone." Levi could see the hesitancy in his face and… fear?

Levi furrowed his brow. "Can't or won't?"

Jeb stepped toward Levi. Again, Jeb was mere inches away, his face contorted, as if trying to maintain rigid control but losing. Faint stirrings of warmth within Levi gave him a clue as to Jeb's feelings. God help Levi if he was wrong about this. He might end up with a broken jaw. Taking a deep breath, he steeled his cowardly spine.

He reached for Jeb's hand, waiting for him to snatch it away, but Jeb didn't resist. Levi raised Jeb's large hand toward the crystal, while longing and trepidation warred on Jeb's face. "I can't... what I'm feeling... don't."

"Whatever it is, let me feel it, please." Levi softened his gaze and tried to convey trust he'd denied Jeb earlier.

As Jeb's hand rested over the crystal, the tormented man's eyes slowly closed.

Surging heat rippled through Levi's body, pushing him back against the door. Closing his eyes, the feeling instantly swamped his mind, swirling and pulsing—living. Levi rubbed his hands over his stomach, reveling in the feel as his skin tingled. When he opened his eyes, Jeb looked down on him, clutching the crystal so tightly his knuckles were white. A sultry aura colored his eyes, but he remained where he stood. He didn't want to trust Jeb, yet right then he did. The logical part of Levi's brain debated the duality while the illogical side soaked in every ounce of desire.

You can't do this. You've never done this before. You can't be feeling this.

"Stop it." Levi panted, closing his eyes. Electric heat permeated the air between them, crackling with an insane intensity.

"Stop what?" Jeb whispered. "Stop this?"

A light touch on Levi's jaw caused him to flinch. The fingertip traced the line of his jaw and ran down his neck. He shivered hard. The first touch was new, exciting, and oh, how he wanted more. That sensual caress shot into Levi's chest, down his spine, and lower south. Jeb's fingertip continued slowly down the nape of his neck and across his collarbone.

"Stop touching...." Levi huffed as a painful yet pleasurable tingle appeared in his groin, his cock swelling, fighting painfully against the zipper of his jeans. His thoughts faded, swirling about his head amidst the pleasure.

"Stop touching this?" Jeb's lips brushed Levi's, then found their way to the side of Levi's neck. Levi automatically tilted his head. Jeb's lips caressed Levi's tender flesh. Chills rocked Levi's body, releasing a shudder. Jeb's hot breath sent a warm rush chasing after the chill. A moment longer, and Levi wouldn't have any self-control to speak of. Levi had masturbated to porn, but his reactions had been purely physical in nature with a hollow release. This was, *fuck*, he felt like he was flying as Jeb sucked and nibbled over his neck. Heat and shivers and moans and the pressure—the exquisite pressure. If Levi didn't stop now, he never would.

"Stop... t-touching the... crystal," Levi said halfheartedly as his throbbing cock screamed at him to shut up.

"Kitten, the only thing I'm touching is you." Jeb truly wasn't touching the crystal. One hand was splayed across the small of Levi's back, and the other lifted the hem of Levi's shirt. A bare knuckle swept across Levi's stomach just below his navel. A soft whimper escaped before Levi could quell the reaction.

"Don't call me that," Levi whispered.

Jeb closed the distance between them, pressing thighs and hips and bulges together. Jeb's lips came back to Levi's and teased him with light caresses. Unable to hold back anymore, Levi pushed his mouth onto Jeb's, wrapping his hands around his neck, pulling him closer. Nothing else mattered, not reason, not logic, not doubts of trust. Nothing felt more right than that moment. Familiarity flooded Levi's senses—a déjà vu with such intensity Levi would have sworn this had happened before.

Electricity prickled and sparked and passed in the small gap between them, fueling Levi's craving. He pulled Jeb tighter against him, rising and falling against his mouth. A throaty growl escaped from Jeb as he kept up with the frantic nature of the kiss. Levi had already kissed him longer than he had Noah, yet Levi detected no murderous thoughts—just pure unfettered, spine-tingling need. Levi ran his palms over Jeb's hard back. Jeb moaned again, sending tidal waves of pleasure through Levi, relentlessly yanking him into the glorious undertow. His heart raced. A current danced in his chest, bringing an edge of pain to the pleasure.

Jeb pulled back, ending their sustained kiss. Pressing his forehead to Levi's, Jeb managed to say between labored breaths, "Kitten, what're you doing to me?"

Jeb wrapped his arms around Levi, bringing their upper bodies together. As their chests touched, a force ripped into Levi's upper body, throwing him hard against the door. Pain ripped through his side, the back of his head. A hazy vision of Jeb propelling away from him was the last thing he saw... and then darkness.

CHAPTER 14

IMAGES FLASHED behind Levi's closed eyes. Dr. Winston's class, being in her office, fleeing through the darkness, kissing Jeb in his car as sparks of electricity filled the air, with Jeb somewhere near the lake, an older man with blue eyes gazing down on him lovingly, then holding fingertips to Levi's forehead, and then darkness.

"Hey, Levi... Levi!"

A loud clap sounded near his ear.

"Hey!"

Levi's eyes fluttered open, trying to focus on the blurry figure looming over him. He frowned, disoriented. A burning agony filled his side and chest. The cold, hard floor pressed into his back. He blinked, and Jeb came into focus. The concern on his face melted into relief.

"What the hell happened?"

One minute he was in Jeb's arms in the throes of unbelievable ecstasy, and next, he was laid out on the floor. A blush warmed his cheeks with the memory of what they'd been doing.

"I don't know." Jeb shook his head and touched Levi's shoulder. Warmth flamed beneath his skin. "Are you okay? You were out for a minute. Are you hurt?"

Levi's ribs throbbed, and his chest burned and his head ached. "Just my ribs and chest. Oh, shit, it feels like someone took a bat to my chest."

Jeb rubbed at his own chest. "I know the feeling. Let me help you up."

Jeb gently placed his hand beneath Levi's shoulder and assisted him to sit. A head rush caused Levi to sway and his stomach to churn. Holding his breath, he fought the pain in his side.

"Can you stand?"

Levi nodded despite not knowing if he could or not. Slowly, Jeb eased him to his feet. Levi twisted and turned, checking his body. Not much damage despite the pain. He looked past Jeb, and saw the coffee table had been flattened.

Levi's jaw dropped. "Did you do that?"

Jeb glanced behind him and huffed. "Flew like a football and landed flat on my back." He shrugged. "Hit my head and knocked the wind right out of me." As he said it, he rubbed the back of his head and winced painfully. Pulling his hand back, he saw that blood stained his fingertips. Jeb's face faded to a sickly shade of gray as he stared at the blood.

"You're bleeding." Levi couldn't help smirking. "*And* you're really getting pale. Is the big, bad man afraid of a little blood?"

"No."

"Uh-huh. Sit on the couch, Pinocchio." Without hesitation, Jeb sat, avoiding looking at his hand.

"Ha, very funny."

Man, he was grumpy.

"Got a first-aid kit or something?" Levi hoped Jeb wouldn't pass out on him. He looked pretty shaky.

"Look under the sink in the kitchen, but I'm sure it's nothing."

"Yeah, blood is a whole lot of nothing, especially when it's coming out of your head," Levi rummaged through the cabinet. Nothing. He grabbed a towel, wet it, and returned to the sofa.

"This will have to do." Levi climbed behind Jeb and sat on the back of the sofa. Levi's legs straddled Jeb's back as he tried not to rub up against him.

"I'll do it." Jeb tried to reach around and grab the towel.

Levi swatted his hand. "Turn your head."

Jeb muttered something unintelligible, sighed, and turned, leaning his forearms on his thighs. Carefully, Levi peeled back the blood-soaked hairs. The muscles in Jeb's shoulders tensed, then relaxed repeatedly as Levi worked. The thought of rubbing the warm flesh beneath Jeb's shirt distracted Levi. Thinking with Jeb near was getting harder.

When Levi pressed the towel against Jeb's scalp, he flinched.

"Sorry." Levi continued to clean the area. Flashes of the images he'd seen as he was catapulted into the door brought tons of questions. He'd never kissed Jeb in his car or been to the lake with him, had never crept in the dark holding someone's hand, and had no clue who the older man was.

"Any theories on what happened yet?" Levi asked as he concentrated on the cut.

"Something to do with the crystal probably. It gives off and absorbs energy. Maybe a surge or something."

Levi grinned, then shivered. The energy they'd been producing could have lit an entire city block.

Levi wiped away the blood pooling in a shallow cut. "It's not bad. You don't need stitches. You'll live." Levi held the towel against the wound to stop the bleeding.

Jeb stood and turned around, yanking the towel from Levi. "I'm fine. Quit fussing with it."

Their eyes locked. Jeb folded his arms over his chest, resuming his harsh, blank expression, a wall he could erect at a moment's notice. His callousness cut across Levi.

"Did I do something wrong?" Had Jeb just realized the mistake he'd made in mauling Levi? Was the guy straight and about to kick Levi's ass?

Jeb ignored the question. "We have to find out who your father is. Do you have access to your birth certificate?"

Levi frowned. Had he ever even seen it? "My mother must have it."

"Can you get it? If not, we'll have to get a copy, which will take longer. It may have the name of your biological father, or it might not be much help at all, but we have to start somewhere." Jeb moved into the kitchen and threw the bloody towel into the sink.

Apparently, the cold façade was going to stay. Jeb had even called him Levi earlier. It seemed wrong, even if Levi didn't care to be called "kitten"—much. The crystal lay against Jeb's hard chest, unmarred by whatever had occurred. Even then, Levi's body still hummed with the electricity of Jeb's touch. It made him weak in the knees.

Levi averted his gaze to avoid Jeb recognizing the disappointment covering his face. Levi cleared his throat. "I'm not sure what I can tell my mom I need it for, but I'll think of something."

Jeb reached into his pocket, retrieving his keys. "It's getting late. I'll drive you home."

JEB WAS silent as he drove, his eyes rarely leaving the road. Levi wrapped his arms around his middle, trying to block out the invading cold that seemed to emanate from Jeb. Pulling into the end of Levi's driveway, Jeb finally looked at him. In the light of the dashboard, Jeb's eyes took on a haunting blue glow.

"Find the birth certificate. Call me in the morning. I'm going to contact Dr. Winston to see how she wants to proceed." No emotion, no hint of the passion they'd briefly shared, no nothing. Why had Jeb turned so cold, so callous?

Because even if Jeb is gay, he doesn't want you.

Maybe the crystal worked both ways and had reflected Levi's own wants and needs and desires into Jeb. Which really didn't make sense since Levi had never experienced those feelings, except for the near-homicidal encounter with Noah. Not until Jeb.

Levi grabbed his bag and exited the car. After slamming the door behind him, he walked up the driveway. The Jeep idled at the end of the drive. Levi resisted the urge to look back, wondering if Jeb watched him. When the Jeep moved and the faint hum of the motor died in the distance, so did any feelings that had lingered.

It was 10:45 p.m. when he entered the house. A light was on in the kitchen, and Levi exhaled. Someone was still up. Seated at the kitchen table and dressed in a blue terrycloth bathrobe and slippers, his mother bobbed a tea bag in a mug. Levi wondered if she'd waited up for him.

"Mom, why're you up?" Levi dropped his bag onto the floor near the door.

Without looking up, his mother asked, "How was the library?"

"Good. Got a lot of work done."

"And how is Gia?" Again, not a glance.

Intuition should have told Levi something was wrong, but he answered, "Gia's good."

A sound of exasperation escaped his mother. She pushed her mug away and wrung her hands in her lap. Levi was about to move and exit the kitchen when his mother turned toward him.

"Levi, when did you turn into such a liar?" His mother's icy tone, her hard gray eyes, her thin, tight mouth stabbed at Levi.

Stunned into silence, Levi could only stare back.

"Gia stopped by tonight to check on you. Said she hadn't seen you since Sunday and was worried. Imagine my surprise that not only were you not at the library, you weren't at school today."

Dammit. Gia never came over without calling. Levi patted his pockets searching for his phone. He groaned realizing he'd thrown his phone into his bag at Jeb's, and with the volume down, he hadn't heard it ring.

"Well, Levi?"

His mother wanted an explanation, and Levi searched for anything but came up empty.

"Are you doing drugs?"

Levi barked out a laugh. "No, Mom." First attempted suicide and now drugs. His mother watched too much Dr. Phil. Levi was too tired, too distracted, for drama.

She stood, folding her arms over her bosom. "Then tell me exactly what's going on. Did you stop your meds again? Where were you today... all night? Really, Levi, I don't know what to think. I haven't told your father any of this. He has enough to worry about without your nonsense."

"My father?" Dr. Winston's words circled his mind. *Not your biological father.*

His mother frowned. "Yes. Your father."

That switch in his brain that controlled his logic clicked off. "Where's my birth certificate?"

For a second the request seemed to unnerve his mother. "What do you want with that?"

Without thought to the consequences Levi said, "I was interested in seeing who was listed as my father."

A stare down ensued between them. Levi was resolute in his actions. He wanted answers.

"What's wrong with you? You're acting... well, crazy lately." A glint of fear shone in his mother's eyes.

"Who's listed as my biological father?"

"Your father, of course." She raised her hands, then dropped them to her sides. The pitch of her voice raised an octave. "Who else would it be?"

Levi narrowed his eyes. "You tell me."

"Levi James Reed. I don't know what you're trying to do here, but this stops now." His mother had pulled up her best mother tone, leaning forward to emphasize her threat.

Despite his mother's posturing, Levi resisted backing down. Forget the birth certificate, Levi wanted—needed—to hear the truth straight from his mother.

"It doesn't stop until you tell me the truth." He so needed the truth. "I had a test done."

She jerked her head back as if he'd slapped her. Despite her attempt to mask her horror, Levi saw the reaction.

"What do you mean a test?" His mother's voice lost its rigid tone and wavered.

"A paternity test!" Levi prayed the test Dr. Winston had performed had been correct. If not, Levi was sure his mother would have him committed.

"A what?" The deep voice roared from behind his mother.

Logan's form filled the darkness of the kitchen doorway. He wore a pair of long shorts, a Giants jersey, and was sockless. His hair was rumpled. He squinted at the bright lights.

Levi's mother spun around, grasping at her chest as Logan walked into the room.

"What's going on?" Logan looked to Levi, as if questioning what he was doing to upset their mother.

His mother remained frozen where she was.

"I was just telling Mom about the paternity test I had done."

"Excuse me?"

"You heard me," Levi said, sending him a hard look. "I'm very interested in hearing what she thinks the results were."

"Levi?" Logan's face paled. "What're you talking about? Why would you...." His voice trailed off, and he looked to his mother for answers.

"Mom, what did the test reveal? Surely, you know."

The look of distress on his mother's face, the paling of her skin, didn't halt Levi's need for the truth. Yes, he loved his mother. She'd always cared for him and Logan. She may not have been the softest or most affectionate of mothers, but she'd done her best to raise them, giving them what they needed and wanted. What he needed was her to tell the truth.

A look of reticence crossed his mother's face. Would she try to lie? Her gaze shifted to Levi and then to Logan, and then she sighed heavily.

Logan looked between them with his mouth agape. "Mom?"

"What do you want me to say?" she finally asked. "Apparently, you already know." Her tone was one of someone being unburdened.

"What're you saying?" Logan's expression took on that of a small child—wide-eyed and scared.

Levi could see Logan's Adam's apple bobbing as he swallowed repeatedly. The muscles corded in Logan's neck. Levi could tell he contemplated the true meaning of what had been said.

"She's saying that Dad's not my real father." The truth still spun wildly within Levi's head, even though he'd already known.

Logan didn't break eye contact with his mother, as if still searching for her denial or confirmation. He got the latter with a slight nod of her head. Astonishment covered his face as he turned to Levi. Confusion and sorrow swirled in his eyes along with anger.

"Mom," Logan said—half question, half lament.

Her lips thinned, her eyes narrowed as she looked to the floor. When she looked to Logan, her expression said she didn't want to answer, but did. "It's true."

Levi wanted to say something to Logan but couldn't conjure one helpful thing. Levi turned back to his mother who looked very tired.

"Who's my real father?" Levi was surprised at how soft his voice had become. This was it. Did he really want to know?

But instead of answering, his mother's eyes filled with tears. "Please." Her gaze flicked between both of them. "Please, don't tell your father."

Which one?

"Why? Did you have an affair?" Levi regained the sharpness in his voice.

"No!" Her glassy eyes widened.

"Does *Dad* know?" Logan had overcome his shock enough to demand an answer.

Holding her silence, she finally nodded. "Yes." A tear escaped down her cheek.

Levi's mouth dropped open. He'd assumed a secret affair, but his father knew Levi wasn't his. Or his mother wasn't telling the truth.

"Who did you have an affair with?" Levi asked a second time.

Her eyes flared with anger. "I told you. I didn't have an affair. I was married to another man." His mother's hand covered her mouth.

"Married? To someone other than Dad?" Logan asked. "But that means—" He stopped abruptly and stumbled back, gripping the counter as the realization must have hit him hard.

Levi stepped toward his mother. "Logan and me... we have the same father?"

She lowered her eyes and nodded, tears once again leaving wet tracks down her cheeks.

"No," Logan whispered behind Levi. "It's not true."

Levi looked to Logan, his elbows locked as he held tight to the lip of the counter. He appeared to be trying to hold himself up. The safety of the family Logan had known was gone. Levi felt more for his brother's loss than his own. Levi would go to him, but first, he turned back to his mother, who mumbled something about being sorry.

"Tell u-us who our real father is." The word *us* had caught in his throat. This was no longer only about him. "Who were you married to before Dad?"

"No. It's better that you don't know. Better for everyone. Please, promise you won't tell your father you know. It would kill him. Please."

Levi took the bargaining chip, careless of how he used it against his own mother. A voice whispered *psychopath* in his head, but Levi ignored it. "Tell me, and I won't tell Dad."

"And if I don't tell you, then you'll break the heart of the only father you've ever known? Who loves you like his own?"

Levi would never want to hurt his dad, but this was about his missing soul. "Only if you force me to. Maybe he can tell me who it is."

Logan's arm wrapped around Levi's shoulder. He looked down on Levi, the color returning to his face. Logan then looked to his mother with a resolute expression on his face. Together, he stood with his brother in solidarity, requiring an answer.

His mother stared at her children and lifted her chin. "Phillip Reed."

Levi frowned. Wait. His supposed father's last name was the same as theirs? "Who?"

"Phillip Reed. Your father's brother. He's your biological father."

CHAPTER 15

LOGAN'S FACE held the same bewilderment Levi felt. "No. Dad only had one brother, and Uncle Ray died."

Levi's mother flopped into the chair at the table. "He has another brother. Well, did."

Levi gasped. "He's dead?"

"No, but we haven't seen him since you were a baby. He was a disturbed man, and let's just leave it at that."

"What do you mean?" Levi wasn't willing to stop without all of the information.

His mother gave him a tentative look. "He had mental health issues."

Like me.

"And no one knows where he is?" Logan asked.

"No."

"But why isn't he here? Why didn't he… want us?" Despite not knowing the man, the thought that he'd abandoned them hurt.

Logan tightened his grip on Levi's shoulder.

"Like I said, he had mental health issues. He wasn't well. It started around the time I got pregnant with you, Levi." She shook her head, as if trying to shake off the painful memories.

"I have to find him."

Dread filled his mother's eyes. "Why? What for?"

"Because he's my father!"

Logan tensed beside Levi and cast him a wary glance.

She rubbed her forehead. "I can't do this anymore. Leave your father in the past, both of you. Nothing good can come from finding him."

"You can't keep him from us. You don't get to decide that. I need to know—"

Levi cut himself short. Did his mother know what his real father had done? Could she know about his soul?

She stood again, cinching the belt of her robe tighter around her waist. "When I tell you to forget about it, I'm telling you that for a good reason. Stay away from him." Her weepy expression turned hard and cold.

"Levi."

Levi ignored Logan. "And what could possibly be your reason?" He couldn't back down now.

Logan dropped his arm from Levi's shoulder. "Levi," he said in a harsher tone.

"No, Logan. I want to know why we can't contact our real father."

Her eyes flashed her anger and hurt. "Because he wanted to take you away. He kept going on about how special you were and because of that that people were going to hurt you. He wanted to take you somewhere safe. He said that if I didn't go with him that he'd take off with you, and I'd never see you again. If he didn't go, then something bad would happen to you. He was insane. Nothing bad has ever happened."

"But my soul—"

His mother rushed toward Levi, fear sparking in her gray-blue eyes. "Who told you that? Who told you about him wanting to remove your soul? Who, Levi?"

Levi stepped back. He glanced up at Logan, who looked as if he was trying to take in how crazy their real father sounded. But what Logan didn't know was that he wasn't crazy. Everything was true—all of it.

Levi could barely speak. "Did you know he actually did it? Do you know where it is?"

His mother's face twisted with disgust. "You can't remove a person's soul! He was a crazy man who needed help, but instead he ran away leaving me with two small children. If it weren't for your *father*, that man upstairs, I don't know what I would have done."

She thought Phillip Reed was a monster, but really he was just a man who'd stolen Levi's soul and caused him years of misery. How much more fucked-up could his life get?

Levi's life had been a ticking time bomb, counting down the years, the days, the hours, and seconds until the day he'd learned the truth. Any safety he'd felt in that house was gone. He bolted from the kitchen, scooping up his bag on his way out. Logan called to Levi, but Levi didn't stop. Fleeing in his car, Levi was on autopilot and soon found himself parked outside of Jeb's guesthouse. His original plan had involved going to Gia's, but he'd ended up there. He should have considered Jeb's coldness after their ill-fated moment of shared passion—or maybe just Levi's passion. He should run from Jeb like a contagious disease, but he needed to talk with someone about his fucked-up existence. Jeb was the only one who believed it.

With his father's name fresh in his mind, Levi couldn't have stayed in his parents' house of lies. Levi's guilt over leaving Logan to deal with the aftermath was sharp, but he needed answers before he involved his brother. Levi planned to stay in his car until morning, face Jeb, and hopefully move closer to some of those answers.

He rested his forehead on the cool leather of the steering wheel. Where was his real father? Where was Phillip Reed? Was he even alive? And what had his missing sperm donor meant when he'd told his wife that people would hurt Levi? Levi's mind spun with the ever-changing facts that were his life, a life he had no inkling about two weeks ago.

What had his biological father done with his soul?

A loud rap on his window startled Levi.

"You planning on staying out here all night?" Cold black eyes stared down at Levi through the partially open window.

Nothing had changed there. "I thought you were sleeping. I didn't want to wake you."

Jeb frowned as if he thought that had been a dumb idea.

Levi shrugged. His brain was wired, while his body was past tired.

Levi stared out over the hood of the car. "I know who my real father is."

"How did you find out?"

"My mother. I asked, and she told me." Levi floated in that space of shocked disbelief despite knowing the truth.

Jeb opened the door, gently placed a hand under Levi's arm, and with a tug, coaxed him from the car. Levi's eyes closed with the warmth of his touch.

"Please, don't touch me," Levi whispered. He hadn't said it to be rude.

Jeb removed his hand as if he understood. "Come inside." Without waiting, he started for the front door.

Levi averted his eyes from the way Jeb's blue jeans molded his sexy ass. God, how did normal people get through the day when constantly distracted by the utter sexiness of another person? Levi thought of the hormone-driven teens he'd watched in fascination during high school, as if they had been animals in a zoo. So this was why they acted like such single-minded creatures. It was a wonder any of them had graduated.

Inside, Levi sat on the brown leather couch. The broken coffee table was gone. Nothing hinted to the fact that Levi's life had been irrevocably changed not less than three hours earlier. And the changes kept jumping out like funhouse spooks to surprise him.

Jeb sat on the other end of the sofa, well away from Levi, and waited. Levi squashed the rising need to scream at Jeb and ask why he'd turned back into that emotionless prick. Levi needed to focus on the larger issue.

"Phillip Reed."

"Reed?" Jeb cocked a questioning eyebrow.

Levi snorted and nodded. "Supposedly an uncle I never knew. An uncle who's really my father." Levi pinched at the bridge of his nose. "And, no. No one knows where he is."

"When was the last time your mother saw him?"

"When I was a baby. Supposedly, he'd threatened to run off with me. Said something about me being in danger and that people would try to hurt me or take me or... something like that."

Jeb frowned. "Danger?"

Levi shrugged tiredly.

"And nothing since then?"

"Nothing."

Found he'd been abandoned by the man who'd stolen his soul and rejected by Jeb, who sat two feet away, all in the span of a few hours. What else could jump out and bite him? Well, the night was still young.

"At least we have a name. Maybe we can find out something about him." He'd sounded as if he'd really cared. Fat chance.

"Or maybe he changed it, or lives in a foreign country, or is dead."

"We'll find him."

Levi lay back against the couch, resisting the urge to disagree with Jeb. His energy was currently being used to fight off the fleeting visions of kissing Jeb, the touch of his hands, his hot breath against his neck, his soft, sweet lips on his.

Jeb jumped off the couch as if he'd been privy to Levi's thoughts. He paced around the living room, rubbing at the back of his neck. His brooding expression did little to quell Levi's lascivious thoughts.

Jeb stopped and faced him. Whatever had momentarily ruffled his feathers wasn't apparent in his expression. "Did your mother say what kind of danger you were in?"

Levi shook his head. "No. She claimed he was crazy. Well, she said 'mentally ill,' but that was only because of me. You know being PC and all."

Levi fought against his heavy lids and wondered how his mind could even fathom sleep right then, despite that it was almost midnight.

A car door slammed outside. Levi bolted upright, looking toward the front door, then Jeb. Jeb was motionless, listening. Slowly, he made his way to the door all stealth-like. Apparently he hadn't been expecting anyone.

There was a knock at the door.

Jeb paused and then opened it a crack.

"I'm looking for Levi," a disembodied voice said.

"Who's Levi?" *Logan?*

"I know he's here. That's his car."

Levi went to the door and pushed past Jeb. "Logan, how did you find me?"

His brother had changed from his jersey and shorts into jeans and a sweatshirt. Logan and Jeb were locked in a staring contest, neither wavering in the slightest. The testosterone was getting thick.

Without looking away from Jeb, Logan said, "GPS on your phone. After what happened at the lake, I want to know where you are at all times."

Jeb looked to Levi. Was that a green-eyed monster staring back?

"What're you doing *here* with him?" Logan surveyed Jeb with a look of disdain.

Levi figured he'd better get on with the introductions before the two men tore into one another. "Logan, this is Jeb. He's a *friend*. Jeb, my *brother*, Logan."

Cautiously, each extended their hands and shook, briefly.

"Levi, I need to talk to you." Logan motioned for him to join him outside.

"I'm not going home. Not for now, at least."

"Yeah, I get that," Logan said, indicating he felt the same way.

"Where do you want to go?" Levi was ready to get his stuff when Jeb opened the door wider.

"Listen. You might as well talk here. I'll make myself scarce."

"We can't take over your place." Really, Levi didn't want to leave.

Jeb shook his head. "It's okay. Come in, Logan."

"Thanks." Logan passed by them.

Before Levi could follow, Jeb held on to his arm and whispered, "Does he know about the soul thing?"

Blood raced to Levi's groin with the touch. He pulled away. Jeb scowled.

Levi ignored Jeb's reaction. "Just what my mother told us. Phillip Reed is his biological father too."

Jeb glanced at Logan. "Might be time to let him in on what's going on. You need someone to help you deal with this."

Which meant Jeb didn't want anything to do with Levi's messed-up shit. Message received loud and clear.

"Levi?"

Logan stood near the sofa, watching them. The perplexed expression on his face did little to hide the anguish in his eyes. Levi went to Logan, wrapping his arms around his brother and burying his head in his chest. Logan's arms enveloped him and pulled him in tight. Both of their lives had been upended, but Levi felt more for Logan. Levi's pain only echoed while Logan's must have been pulsing fresh and hot at the surface.

"I'm sorry you had to find out like that."

Logan was silent for a moment. "Dad's not our real father. How did you even know that? What made you even suspect it?"

It was such a long, convoluted, and insane story. How could he ever make Logan understand? Levi pulled away and looked to Jeb, who now stood near the kitchen table. A slight nod encouraged Levi to tell Logan everything.

"You won't believe me if I tell you."

Logan grimaced. "Believe what?"

"That I don't have a soul."

"You mean that nonsense our… biological father told Mom? Of course you have a soul. Everyone has one. You can't live without it… I think."

"What did Mom say after I left?"

Logan eyed Jeb.

"It's okay. He knows."

Logan didn't hide his loathing at that revelation. "She said that Phillip actually took off with you when you were a couple of days old. Disappeared for two days. They had the police looking for him. He brought you back, virtually unharmed except for a cut on your chest. He disappeared after that. Cops never found him."

Levi placed his palm over the center of his chest. The two-inch scar, he'd been told, had come from falling on a stick when he was one. More lies.

Jeb walked closer. "A cut?" He raised an eyebrow. "Where?"

Levi pointed to his breastbone.

"Can I see it?"

"Why do you need to see it?" Logan's protective tone soothed Levi.

Jeb didn't answer, his gaze fixed on Levi. He seemed to think it was relevant. Levi unbuttoned the top three buttons of his gray Henley and pulled it open, revealing the thin, silvery scar.

Jeb came closer in a skittish way, as if trying to get just close enough, but not too close.

A rush of heat rose from the spot where Jeb stared. Before he backed off, Jeb's eyes met Levi's and latched on to his gaze. Levi's stomach flip-flopped at the momentary heat in those dark eyes.

"That's consistent with the mark."

"Mark of what?" Logan wasn't even bothering to hide his annoyance.

"The mark where a Seer extracted his soul. A small cut over the heart opens a gateway. The blood does something to ease the extraction."

Logan sneered. "Are you kidding me? Enough with this soul stuff. Who is this guy?"

"Just sit, and I'll tell you everything, but promise you'll keep an open mind."

Logan stiffened, as if he'd already decided to discount everything. "Please." Levi couldn't do this without his brother. He needed him to understand and believe.

Logan dropped his shoulders. "I'll listen but can't guarantee I'll buy it." He cast a surreptitious glance at Jeb who had returned to the kitchen.

They sat together on the sofa. Jeb was within earshot but didn't intrude. His presence shored up Levi's resolve.

Levi told Logan everything starting with the anxiety and fear, Jeb, the emotions, the attacks when Jeb was near without the crystal. Levi told him of Dr. Winston, the flame indicating that Art Reed couldn't possibly be his biological father, and why the search for their real father was imperative—to find Levi's missing soul.

Logan listened with facial expressions ranging from disbelief, shock, dismay, anger complete with clenched teeth, quiet reflection, and sorrow. When Levi finished, he sat quietly, letting Logan process the entire pile of information. Jeb hadn't moved from the kitchen. Levi couldn't see him, but he could feel him. An unsettling but exciting tension filled the air between them.

Logan wrapped his arm around Levi's shoulder. Levi rested his head against Logan's chest. There he stayed in the silence, under the protection of his big brother. Behind them, Levi heard Jeb leave the room, taking his overwhelming energy with him.

"I'm sorry." Logan's words had come out as an exaggerated sigh. He didn't indicate if he believed any of what Levi had said, and Levi didn't ask.

Slowly, the muscles in Logan's body relaxed, his breathing deepened and steadied. Levi fought against the weights dragging down his eyelids, but eventually they won out. He slipped into the safety of sleep with Logan.

LEVI OPENED his eyes to sunlight streaming through the closed curtains of Jeb's living room. Logan was still fast asleep. During the night, Levi had moved onto the chair. At some point while they'd slept, blankets had been draped over both of them. Logan's head was cocked off to the side against the back of the couch. Levi feared he'd have a horribly stiff neck but refused to wake him.

He set out in search of a bathroom. Warily, he crept down the hallway next to the kitchen, praying Jeb wasn't up yet.

Yes! The first door on the left was a half bath. Levi tried to be as quiet as he could. He relieved himself and washed his hands. When he opened the door, Jeb stood outside waiting. Levi stopped in his tracks.

He scowled. "Follow me." He sure wasn't a morning person. Jeb still wore the same clothes from last night, and Levi wondered if he'd even slept. "I want to show you something." He turned and went farther down the hall, entering the last door on the left.

Levi followed him into a bedroom, with large ceiling-to-floor windows overlooking the lake. A set of french doors led to a small patio. The bed hadn't been slept in. Levi quickly blocked out thoughts of Jeb in bed.

Jeb went to a small desk opposite the bed, which held a desktop computer. He motioned for Levi to sit in the chair in front of the computer. After hesitating, Levi lowered himself into the seat.

"I've done a computer search for the name Phillip Reed. Quite a common name. I've come up with some possibilities that I want you to look at. Narrowed them down by age."

Levi looked at Jeb, confused by his request. "I have no clue what my father looks like. How can I help?"

Jeb moved behind the chair and reached over Levi's shoulder to the mouse. He gave it a quick jiggle, and the computer screen came to life. Jeb's arm was inches from Levi's skin, and the hairs on Levi's arms rose. He suppressed a shudder.

"Just look. Maybe someone will be familiar, like a family resemblance or something." Jeb's body lightly touched Levi's hair, and the shudder Levi had suppressed ran through him.

Jeb had minimized a dozen or so web pages. He pointed the cursor to the first box at the bottom of the screen and clicked the mouse. The web page opened to a photo of a man with gray hair and green eyes. A "Phillip Reed" but looking nothing like anyone from his father's family. They all had blue eyes.

Levi shook his head. Several more web pages with images, and no one stood out to him, but what guarantee did he have that he was right? Just as he was about to protest to further wasting time, Jeb clicked a page and moved around to the side of the chair.

Across the top of the page was *Thornton, Ivey, and Reed. Attorneys at Law.*

"Scroll down the page." Jeb was way too close.

Levi did as Jeb asked. First, there was a picture of Ira Thornton and a brief paragraph about the man. Next a photo of Stanley Ivey and more writing. Another picture rose up the page. Those blue eyes. Levi leaped to his feet and nearly tumbled back over the chair.

That blue-eyed man. The one Levi had seen after he'd blacked out. The one who had touched his forehead and brought on the darkness.

His *real* father.

Jeb grabbed Levi's arm. "Does he look familiar?"

The urgency in Jeb's voice wasn't enough to pull Levi's stare away from those very blue eyes. So familiar and strange to him at the same time. How could he have seen this man in his memories? Had Levi seen a photo of the man at one time and the memory surfaced from some hidden recess of his mind?

"Hey." Jeb shook Levi's arm. "Where have you seen that man before? Tell me."

Jeb's eyes burned with an intensity Levi had never seen before. His strong fingers dug into Levi's arm with alarming strength. The action spiked the fear in Levi.

"I-I… yesterday when I was unconscious. I saw that man touch my forehead—"

"And then everything went black." Jeb loosened his grip slightly.

Levi couldn't contain his gasp. "How did you know?

"Because I saw the same thing."

CHAPTER 16

LEVI HELD Jeb's stare, unable to look away. A tinge of fear colored the fearless man's eyes. Subtle, but Levi could see it.

"You saw *them* too?" Levi asked, barely a whisper.

Jeb nodded. "With you by a lake… sitting in Dr. Winston's office… in the car… with you… that man touching my forehead."

"Your forehead? He did the same to me. What the hell's going on?" Levi couldn't fathom the weirdness.

"I would've guessed that the connection with the crystal had allowed me to see what you were thinking, but my images were from my point of view. Yours?"

"Same. From my point of view." Levi paused. "Nothing I saw has happened, except for being in Dr. Winston's office, so they can't be memories. It's like we saw something…. Do you think we saw the future?"

Jeb ran his hand over his mouth "Only certain Seers can see the future, and even that is flawed. Their visions aren't always clear or are out of context. More like pieces of a larger puzzle. Besides, their abilities are highly coveted, so most never reveal what they are to anyone. Nostradamus was said to have been a Seer with that ability. He recorded such vague visions that they could have fit dozens of different events."

"Can Dr. Winston see the future?"

Jeb shook his head.

"You and I saw the same thing, and I've never seen that man before yesterday." Levi pointed to the computer screen. "Have you?"

"No." Jeb raked his hand through his hair. He was totally unnerved. Levi didn't just know it, dammit, he felt it. If not for the fear of rejection, Levi would have wrapped his arms around Jeb.

"This scares you."

Immediately, Jeb said, "No." His lips hardened to a thin line.

"I can feel it. Here." Levi raised his hand and rubbed at his sternum.

Jeb regarded him for a second. "That's *your* fear." Jeb crossed his arms, reestablishing that wall of ice around him.

"My fear is in here." Levi pointed to his head. "If you've forgotten already, I don't have much of a soul. You're the only one who makes me *feel* anything here." Levi patted his chest.

Jeb shifted, a sneer curling his lip. "It's not me. It's the crystal." Jeb seemed to withdraw into himself even further, but something was evolving, changing where the crystal was concerned. It was the only explanation. Without Jeb's touch on the crystal, emotions were still reaching out like tendrils to Levi. Excitement and fear and lust and confusion all rolled into a tight ball.

"Levi?"

Levi jumped at the sound of Logan calling out his name. He broke from Jeb's chilly stare and went into the hallway.

"Down here." Levi motioned his brother into the room.

Levi swore he saw a hint of disgust on his brother's face when he found that Levi was in Jeb's bedroom. Levi had no clue if his brother thought he was gay. Even if he did, Logan wasn't going to come right out and say anything. Levi would have to tell him and had no clue how to say the words. What if Logan couldn't deal? Add that to the list of shit that would irrevocably change his life.

"I have to go to work." Logan scrubbed his hands over his face. Dark circles were the evidence of his fatigue.

"Can't you take the day off?"

He shook his head. "Da-ad…. We have a survey that has to be completed today. I can't leave him hanging, no matter what."

Logan was going to have to see their father. The idea set butterflies lose in Levi's stomach. Never again would they look at their father-slash-uncle the same way again.

Levi grabbed Logan's hand, yanking him to the computer. "I think we found Phillip."

Logan grimaced but didn't speak.

Levi jiggled the mouse, and the photo popped onto the screen. Logan glowered, continuing with his stone-like stance. Only the muscles in his jaw moved. "He looks like me."

Levi had to agree. The same eyes, sharp jaw, slim face. There was no denying now that this man was their father.

"What do we do now?" Logan tore his gaze from the image of the man who had abandoned them. A new fire burned in his eyes.

Jeb motioned to the screen. "I go and bring him in. He's in Troy, just outside of Albany."

"Into where?" Logan's tone was sharp.

"To the council. They've got questions they want answered. First off, where's your brother's soul? And second, who sanctioned its removal?"

Logan moved past Levi toward Jeb. Logan was a couple of inches taller, but Jeb was wider, his body thicker with corded muscles. "Why're you feeding Levi this bullshit? What do you want?"

Jeb sneered. "I don't want anything. I work for the council, and I do what they tell me. They sent me here to look after Levi. And this morning they told me to bring Phillip Reed in. That's what I'm going to do. What you choose to believe about your brother is your own business."

A standoff turned into a stare-off. Logan's fists were balled against his thighs. Jeb's jaw clenched tight. "Oh my God, will you two give it a rest!" Levi stepped between them. "Enough with the testosterone contest."

While the scowls didn't leave their faces, there was a sense of backing down between them.

"Logan, I'm sorry if you can't believe all of this, but it's real. I had the same reaction, but things just keep getting weirder, and this is what makes sense right now." Levi turned to Jeb. "This may just be a *job* to you, but this is *our* lives, and they've just been turned upside down. While I appreciate your help, a little understanding would go a long way here."

With that, Levi left them to either kill one another or learn to deal with the fact that they were on the same side. He hoped for the latter.

In the living room, he sat on the sofa and waited. Jeb and Logan returned about twenty minutes later. Both were unmarked, and there was a visible decrease in the tension between them. Levi wondered what they'd said but remained silent.

Logan stopped next to the couch but didn't sit. "I'm heading to the site and should be done by noon, and then I'm going with Jeb to bring Phillip in."

Levi bolted off the couch. "Excuse me?" Logan didn't even flinch. Apparently he'd been expecting the overreaction. Levi didn't wait for any type of response. "No, you're not."

Logan shifted and stuffed his hands into his vest pockets. "I'm going. I have to do this. Maybe Phillip will come without a struggle if I'm there."

"Without a struggle?" Levi hadn't even fathomed a struggle. "You can't let him go." He turned to Jeb who wore his famous stoicism, completely guarded.

"He's a big boy. Besides it always helps to have more muscle—not that I really need it," he added with that cockiness that made Levi grit his teeth.

Logan grasped Levi's shoulders firmly. His face held the caring and concern he'd relentlessly expressed for Levi over the years. But Levi could also see restlessness, an aching need to do something, anything. "Don't worry about me. Just tell me you're doing okay."

"I'm good." A white lie for his big brother. Levi forced a ghost of a smile. Logan returned the favor.

Still clutching Levi's shoulders, the pads of Logan's fingers created a dull ache that Levi welcomed, wishing to feel anything. Logan glanced in Jeb's direction. "Bring him up to speed. Here? Noon?"

Jeb nodded, and Logan left.

Levi assessed his next move. His first instinct was to slug Jeb in the jaw for dragging Logan into his disaster. Only he was the one at fault for that. Levi pinched the bridge of his nose. If anything happened to Logan....

"I spoke with Dr. Winston after you left the room," Jeb said, shattering the heavy silence.

He walked toward Levi, his height definitely an advantage for intimidation. With each step, the air pulsed in waves, swirling and rushing around Levi, caressing his skin. His breath caught in his throat. Quickly, Levi retreated several steps. Jeb halted. If Jeb hadn't grimaced, Levi might believe he hadn't felt the surge of energy, but he'd felt it too.

"I've been authorized to bring your father in by any means necessary."

"Any means necessary? What're you some kind of vigilante or something?"

"It means that if I have to subdue him and then hog-tie him, then that's what I'll do." There was a bit too much amusement in his voice.

Levi narrowed his eyes. "Just love the violence, don't you? Make you feel like more of a man?"

Before he could take a breath, Jeb closed the space between them, towering over him. Jeb's warm breath was on his face.

"Don't push me." While Levi had known Jeb was speaking of metaphorical pushing, Levi took the dare to mean something else. With both hands, Levi pushed hard against Jeb's chest. The effort swayed Jeb's body but didn't move him.

"Watch it." The rough growl ripped through Levi's body.

Ignoring his warning, Levi stepped back on one foot and propelled his momentum forward, shoving Jeb hard. Jeb stumbled back a few steps. A feral grin crossed the man's face. How could he hate the man so much and be so attracted to him at the same time?

Levi repeated his action. This time Jeb captured Levi's wrists and yanked him forward, their groins touching. Jeb's dark eyes stared a path up Levi's chest and neck to his lips. Levi ceased his struggle.

"What's wrong with you?"

Levi refused to answer, testing the grip on his wrists, but Jeb held tighter. Levi's heart sped with Jeb's close proximity. The permanent sneer held fast to the powerful Jeb's lips. His masculine scent tickled Levi's nose and spread warm fingers through his body. Raw, intoxicating power.

Levi let a bark of laughter escape. The sound raised Jeb's brow. "You wanna know what's wrong with me? Have you looked in the mirror lately, buddy? I'm not the one who went all ice king after we kissed yesterday. You're as emotionally stunted as I am. I don't have a soul. What's your excuse?"

Jeb's lips parted, exposing the whites of his teeth, giving him an animal-like aura. Intense, stifling heat filled the air. Levi fought to keep from wilting like a cut flower in the sun. All he could think about was kissing those soft lips as his hard-on fought for release from his jeans.

Pull it together, Levi.

"Maybe that kiss meant nothing to me."

Levi gritted his teeth. "You're a jerk."

Jeb leaned in until only inches separated their faces. A low resonating grumble escaped from deep within his throat.

Levi leaned his head back. "Did you just growl at me?"

Jeb said nothing, maintaining the intimate distance. His eyes narrowed further.

"Are you trying to scare me?" A knot twisted in Levi's stomach.

Jeb's sneer pulled his lip further. "Is it working?"

A little.

Truthfully, Jeb had been more successful with working Levi into a frenzy of sexual frustration. He shook his head.

"Remember, I said that you *should* be?" Unsure if that was a rhetorical question, Levi nodded. Images of Jeb's mouth taking possession of his flashed in Levi's memory. He saw so much of himself in the closed-off man.

"It's best you stay away from me, kitten." Jeb's voice had taken on a low, husky rumble.

The sound forced a sharp breath into Levi's lungs. The question of why he should fear Jeb entered his mind, yet his first reaction was to lunge forward and capture Jeb's lips. Levi's action immediately caused Jeb to release his wrists as he pulled away. Without forethought, Levi grabbed at the back of Jeb's neck. Again, he slammed his lips onto Jeb's. Sucking in the sweet honey taste, making sure to avoid the crystal, Levi just needed him. Jeb's hesitation was evident in how his lips resisted. When he parted his lips inviting Levi in, Levi didn't hesitate.

Strong hands gripped Levi's hips, holding him tight. Jagged breaths and heaving chests and bucking hips... Levi went at Jeb with an abandon he'd never come close to. Tasting, feeling, wanting all of him, was all that mattered now. A filmy gauze of desire settled over his mind, making rational thought impossible. A crackling sound filled the air, pain once again licked between their expanding chests, fueling their passion.

A low, heated moan escaped Levi's throat. With that sound, Jeb yanked his head back. Cold air rushed in where there had been warmth. Stunned, Levi opened his eyes to see Jeb halfway to the kitchen.

Jeb's lack of control was evident in his pacing. His chest heaved, his hands clutched at his head. Levi's hands went to his throat where his racing pulse strummed against his palm. "What's wrong?"

Jeb averted his gaze, refusing to even glance Levi's way. Levi had gotten to him and could tell the usually in-total-control man didn't like it one bit.

"Answer me!"

Jeb spun on his heels and bolted toward him. "I'm here to get your soul back and that's all. Do you understand? Keep your hands to yourself." A war raged in Jeb's eyes, but what he was fighting Levi didn't know.

Hot tears stung Levi's eyes, but no way would he let unfamiliar emotions betray him. Not now. Not for Jeb.

Jeb frowned, and a sympathetic expression crossed his face, no doubt resulting from Levi's momentary shock and pain. A searing dagger plunged into Levi's chest repeatedly. Gasping, he worked to calm his breathing, fighting off an overwhelming wave of panic. Not from fear but from rejection.

"Yeah, no problem. You'll never have to worry about me touching you again."

Grabbing his bag near the couch, Levi strode to the door and slammed it behind him. Only when he was safe in his car and a mile from Jeb's house did he allow the pain to appear on his face. Fucking emotions sucked.

Not wanting to go home and knowing Gia was at the college, Levi decided to make his first class at ten, welcoming the distraction. He settled into his seat in sociology class and tried to focus. Unfortunately, the only distraction he found were thoughts of Jeb's blatant rejection. Having spent a great part of the last twenty-four hours near Jeb, Levi was now faced with the vacuous emptiness of his former life as the effects of the crystal slowly wore off. Levi was sure they would fade the longer he was away from Jeb.

Without the crystal, if Jeb even came near Levi he could potentially kill him. And with the crystal, the desire, which seemed as real to Levi as the air he breathed, was just a false entity, conjured by a mystical rock around the neck of a really hot guy. Hard pecs, wide shoulders, strong chin, beautiful brown eyes. Jeb wouldn't have even kissed Levi without that crystal around his neck. One downside to the ability to feel emotions? Knowing firsthand what rejection felt like. Levi forced his thoughts back to his sociology professor. A losing battle.

After class, Levi wandered into the lounge where Gia held court. When she spotted Levi, she pushed a few people out of the way to reach him.

"There you are. I'm so sorry about messing up things with your parents. Why didn't you tell me I was your alibi?"

Truthfully, Levi had always been the one who covered for Gia and not the other way around. Levi had never needed an alibi, but now he seemed to need lots of them.

"I know."

"Did Maggie freak? She tends to be a freaker."

Levi flinched, recalling the confrontation with his mother. "A little. No harm, no foul. All is good."

"So spill. Where were you?"

"I just needed to get out and think. I drove to Glens Falls and back." Lies were getting so easy.

Gia narrowed her eyes and pursed her lips. "Why would you drive there?"

"Just a random destination. I wanted to forget the whole thing with my mom."

Gia gave Levi that look that said it wasn't over, then smiled and pulled Levi down to the couch. She launched into gossip about Sarah and Matt, and Levi nodded, half listening to his friend.

Tension built up in his stomach, invading his shoulders and jaw. Rolling his neck, Levi fought it off. Something akin to a mental tap on the shoulder caused him to turn around. On the patio, groups of people sat at tables, enjoying the spring sunshine. Levi wasn't sure where the pull was coming from. Closing his eyes, he focused on the direction of the warm energy. As if trying to locate the direction of a sound, Levi turned his head slowly.

There it was.

Opening his eyes, it took less than ten seconds to lock eyes with Jeb, who sat at one of the tables. A raised eyebrow indicated he knew Levi had seen him.

"What the hell is he doing here?" Levi mumbled, catching Gia's attention.

Gia glanced in the direction Levi glared.

"What are you...?" Gia trailed off as she strained to see, and then a wide, toothy grin crossed her face. "Oooh, eye candy."

Levi spun around, warmth filling his cheeks. "What?"

Gia got all cocky. "I see you ogling the eye candy. I knew you couldn't resist him."

Levi sucked in a breath. How did she know about Jeb?

"Oh yes. He's a nice specimen of man. And he wants you bad," Gia said with a self-satisfied expression.

Confused, Levi glanced back to Jeb. Gia's words tugged at his heart and twisted his stomach.

"Don't look so stunned. You're all he talks about. He's been sending you tons of messages on Facebook, but you haven't answered."

"What're you talking about?" Gia had talked to Jeb? He did say he'd spent time at the college watching him. Had he talked to Gia? Facebook? Levi found it hard to believe Jeb spoke to anyone, ever.

"*Duh*. Noah? Mr. Hottie?"

Levi spotted Noah sitting with his back to Jeb at the next table. Levi hadn't even been aware of Noah—or any of the thirty or so other people on the patio. Jeb did that to him. Twisted his insides up, brought tingles to his skin, and thoughts of naked bodies and erections. Jeb, who had told Levi, in no uncertain terms, that he was hands-off. A blush of embarrassment colored Levi's face. Clearly, Jeb had been the one who'd showed Levi those emotions first. Jeb's emotions. *Hypocrite.*

Levi continued watching Noah, hoping Jeb would notice where Levi's attention was focused. Without breaking that gaze, Levi made a devious plan.

"Does Noah really like me that much?" he asked Gia, his stare unwavering.

"Asks lots of questions about you. Sends you messages. Saved your life. I'd say that's a big yes."

"I should go talk to him, then." A smile spread across Levi's face.

Gia slapped his arm. "You go, girl!" Levi frowned at Gia's choice of terms. "You know what I mean." She waved him onward.

Levi stood and walked around the couch and through the open doors into the bright sun. Despite the sudden glare, Levi kept his eyes locked with Jeb's. Jeb shifted in his seat and looked around. Was he afraid Levi would talk to him?

Stopping next to Noah, Levi shot a sharp glare at Jeb, then to Noah, softened it with a half smile, and then spoke.

"Hey, Noah."

Until he looked at Noah, Levi had forgotten about the incident where he'd wanted to kill the man. Now his green eyes were a not-so-subtle reminder. How would Noah react? *Shit!* What had Levi been thinking?

With the sun behind Noah's back, Levi had to squint. He nervously chewed on the inside of his cheek, waiting for what could be a very embarrassing encounter.

A smile curled at the corner of Noah's lips. "Hey, Levi." Noah patted him on the shoulder in a safe, manly gesture. "How're the ribs?"

"Good." Out of the corner of his eye, Levi kept watch on Jeb, who glared. Levi stepped close enough for a small level of intimacy but stayed far enough away that others probably wouldn't notice. Levi gave Noah as much of a shy smile as he could without throwing up.

"I just wanted to thank you again for helping me last week." Levi spoke loud enough for Jeb to hear. "And I'm sorry for taking off the other day. I hope you're not too pissed off at me?" Each word was coated in a syrupy sweetness.

"Hey, what're friends for?" Noah winked.

Levi belted out a highly hideous and fake laugh. Trying to be nonchalant, he stole a look at Jeb. Levi felt waves of anger rolling off the uptight man. Fists clenched in his lap. His chest rose and fell rapidly. The steely look he returned could have frozen water. Levi knew his reaction had nothing to do with jealousy, but pissing Jeb off was the next best thing.

Levi raised an eyebrow and returned his attention to Noah, plastering on a wider fake smile. "Yeah, friends." Levi winked back and could only imagine how sickening his behavior truly was, but he kept going.

After a short discussion about classes, Noah switched to the subject Levi had hoped for. "So, how about we do something one of these nights? We could take a hike or something."

Assuring Jeb's continued audience participation, Levi nodded. "I'd love to hike with you." Levi hadn't realized how exhausting acting like a lovesick puppy could be when you were trying to fly under the radar. He needed to end this exchange quickly. "I have a lot of catching up for school, but how about next week? I can send you a text." Levi pulled a pen from his pocket. "Here, write your cell number on my hand."

"Okay." Noah took the pen and branded Levi with his number.

Behind Noah, Levi heard a chair skidding across the stone. A very angry Jeb walked past Levi, bumping hard into his arm.

"Come. Now." He'd growled the command under his breath and then stormed toward the front of the school.

"Hey! Rude much!" Noah went to go after Jeb. Levi grabbed his arm. Noah glared down at Levi. "What a dick."

"It was an accident," Levi had never understood the need to beat the crap out of anyone over small shit.

"I'll call you. Gotta go."

Levi moved away quickly before Noah could say anything anymore. Turning the corner where Jeb had disappeared, Levi stopped cold in his tracks. Jeb was more than pissed. A glowing, fiery rage in his eyes gave a clue as to what was boiling under the surface.

He looked like he was going to kill Levi.

CHAPTER 17

LEVI RECOILED from the fury on Jeb's face. Turning to hightail it out of there, Jeb grabbed Levi by the wrist and then pushed him against the hard brick of the wall. Stunned, Levi could only gape at Jeb losing control. Would Jeb hit him?

When Jeb made a move toward him, Levi turned and raised his arms in self-defense. Waiting for the inevitable blow that didn't come, Levi peered up at Jeb. His fury had been replaced by angry annoyance.

"What're you doing?" he asked in exasperation. The expression on his face was one Levi knew well.

Levi hesitantly lowered his arms. "I thought you were going to hit me. You looked *that* pissed."

With disdain, he said, "Don't doubt that I am truly pissed off, but I never lose control."

Levi stiffened and returned the contempt. "And what the hell do you have to be so pissed off about?"

"I told you to stay away from that ass. He's only after one thing." Levi could swear something wild burned in Jeb's chocolate eyes, something like jealousy.

"You told me? Who in the hell do you think you are? What gives you the right to butt in? You made your position *very* clear." Levi leaned back against the wall. "And maybe *that*'s the one thing I'm after."

Jeb raked his fingers through his hair. "What's with the fucking high-school act out there? How about acting your age?" While Jeb may not have actually lost control, Levi felt he'd pushed him pretty damn close to it.

Jeb's words were right on the mark. Levi knew what he'd done was a middle-school move, but he had no clue how to deal with the invading emotions of wanting someone. No clue how to traverse that minefield. He'd never dated in high school and probably was at about a middle-school level when it came to that knowledge.

Without warning, Jeb grabbed Levi's arm again and yanked him toward the parking lot.

"Let go of me." Levi dug his heels into the pavement.

"You're going to my house where you can stay out of trouble until I get back."

Levi turned his wrist and yanked it from Jeb's grip. When Jeb spun around, Levi cocked his arm back and punched Jeb in the mouth. Jeb's head snapped to the side, but he quickly recovered. Levi shook his hand. Fuck, he'd never punched anyone before. Terror invaded Levi as he watched every muscle in Jeb's body coil in preparation to strike back. Levi steeled himself for the ass whooping of a lifetime, but Jeb merely rubbed at his jaw. The man did have phenomenal control. Unfortunately, the maelstrom of emotions battling in Levi stole any control he might have.

"Touch me again, and I'll beat the shit out of you next time." Levi fed off the anger that pulsed from Jeb.

Jeb pursed his lips until they were thin and white.

"You have no right to tell me what to do just because you're helping me get my soul back." Levi pointed at Jeb's chest. "I'll talk to whomever I want, whenever I want. I'll go out with whomever I want and have se—" Levi cut his sentence off. "*You* lost the right to tell me anything with your 'hands-off' comment and your perpetual bad mood."

With a slow, precise movement, Jeb moved Levi's finger away from his chest. "Do whatever the fuck you want. I couldn't care less." The calm, calculated tone, Jeb's overly stiff posture and stony expression gave him a deadly air.

With that, he strode away and got into his Jeep. But when Jeb took one final glance at Levi, the anger had gone. What had replaced the anger was an expression Levi couldn't decipher, but he was slammed hard with guilt. The Jeep started, and the tires spun as if Jeb couldn't get away from Levi fast enough. Levi curled his fists, digging his knuckles into his thighs until he was sure they'd leave marks. What the hell was it with Jeb? Hot and cold, distant, totally annoying… totally hot… totally wanting nothing to do with Levi. Then that look… that mournful, aching look.

And yes, it hurt. It hurt a fucking lot because he didn't know what it meant.

Levi rubbed at the growing ache in his hand from hitting the steel wall that was Jeb's jaw. Once the shaking in his body had died down, he returned to the lounge where Gia waited on the couch. "So spill, you flirt."

Levi gathered his stuff. "Uh, you saw that, huh?" Not his finest moment. He debated telling her about Jeb but decided not to. "It's not what you think."

"It looked to be exactly what I think. Levi, I want you to be happy. Get out there and live life. I care about you."

"I know but, please, Gia, Noah isn't for me. I was…. What I just did was from guilt."

Gia chewed on her red lip, no doubt contemplating what he'd said. "You really don't like him, do you?"

Levi dropped his shoulders. "No, I don't."

"Okay, no more about Noah. I really did think you liked him, but if he's not *it* for you, there are other guys out there."

Gia's smile warmed him probably for the first time ever. Shit, and if he never got his soul back, he'd have to follow Jeb around for the rest of his life just to feel anything like that.

"Thanks." Levi relaxed only for a moment.

Ugh! What had he done? And since when did he resort to juvenile tricks like flirting to make someone jealous?

Never. Because there never had been a guy.

It was all because of that crystal. Levi was going to find his soul, and the sooner he located it, the sooner he could get away from Jeb and his endless barrage of emotions. What would it be like to have emotions of his own, feelings that came from his own soul? The emptiness in his chest weighed heavily, the hollow ache returning, fueling the need to do whatever it took to get his soul, to be a human being again. Or was it for the first time? What he was at that moment wasn't worthy to be called human. He knew what he had to do.

"You okay?" Gia's voice pulled Levi back from the distance he'd drifted.

"What time is it?"

"Umm… 11:54," Gia said with a glance at her phone. "Why?"

"I just might make it. I have to go. I need to catch Je—Logan before he takes off. I'll call you." Levi sprinted out the patio doors and to the parking lot.

Fumbling to get his keys, Levi called Logan, but his voice mail picked up. Driving from the school parking lot, Levi managed to get a text out to his brother without crashing his car.

Wait 4 me. Going w/ you. Be there in 10.

Gunning the engine, Levi barely made it through a yellow light. Praying no cops spotted him, he drove on the right-hand shoulder to pass a car signaling to turn.

His phone lit up with a text message. *Shit.* Jeb.

U will stay at my house and wait like a good little kitten.

Levi let a growl loose from his throat.

Fck U

U offering?

Levi threw the phone on the seat. What a dick! Jeb was going to get a world of fury unleashed on his ass when Levi got hold of him.

Levi barely made the corner into the driveway without taking out the mailbox. He skidded to a stop next to Jeb's Jeep and threw the car into park. He jumped from the car. After sprinting onto the porch, he threw open the unlocked door, and then bolted into the house.

"Where are you, you son of a bitch?" His voice echoed through the silence.

Nothing.

Running from room to room, Levi could picture that shitty sneer on Jeb's face and seethed with the desire to wipe it off for him. Each room was empty, including the last room he searched, Jeb's bedroom. Levi stood in the center of the room and let out a primal, gut-wrenching scream. Jeb made him *that* angry. And still he wanted more.

Closing his eyes, Levi worked to calm his racing heart, to release the tightly wound muscles, and calm the fury clawing like some wild animal to be released. How could one person tangle his insides up so painfully? Levi was the one out of control. How was he supposed to wait here in this god-forsaken silence and do nothing? Three hours round trip to Troy, and what guarantee did he have that Phillip would be there or even come with them?

Maybe Levi could do something.

Jeb's computer was still powered on. He jiggled the mouse, and Phillip Reed's picture popped up. Levi couldn't help but flinch as those blue eyes stared back at him, his father's eyes—the father who'd betrayed him and turned his life into a living hell. Quickly, he scrolled to the top of the page looking for a phone number.

When he located one, he grabbed the cordless phone from the desk, and Levi dialed before he lost his nerve. If he could talk to Phillip, tell his absent father he knew about his missing soul, then maybe he would come willingly. What parent wouldn't come when their child was in trouble?

Well, maybe one that put that child in danger in the first place.

"Thornton, Ivey, and Reed," a cheerful voice announced.

A nagging thought told him to hang up.

"Hello?"

Levi stumbled for a moment. "Umm… yes, Phillip Reed…. Please."

"One moment."

Silence, then a click. Levi sucked in his breath waiting to hear his father's voice, but the receptionist spoke. "Mr. Reed is unavailable at this moment. May I take a message?"

Damn. "It's really important that I talk to him now. Is there any way you can interrupt him?"

"Is this an emergency, sir?"

You could say that. "It's just really important I talk to him as soon as possible."

"If you give me your name and number, I can get a message to him."

Levi chewed on his bottom lip and paused, debating what to do, how far to go. "Will he be available any time soon?"

"I can't say. If you give me your name and number, I'll give the message to him immediately." She sounded like a professional broken record.

Levi had no other choice and gave her his cell phone number. "This is Levi Reed. His son."

A few seconds of silence passed. "His son?"

Great, she knew Phillip didn't have a son named Levi. He wondered if he had other children. "Yes, and it's an emergency. Tell him that Logan and I need him, now."

Before the woman could reply, Levi ended the call. He chucked the phone onto the bed as if it were on fire. His heart climbed into his throat, practically strangling him. He wiped his clammy hands on his jeans.

Back at the computer, Levi pulled up the picture of Phillip. Fixing on the man's eyes, Levi focused as his vision tunneled and darkened and the picture of his biological father grew smaller, farther away. A whooshing sound filled his ears, and he felt as if he were being transported from the room. His vision blurred, and in a blink of an eye he was sitting before Phillip Reed. How did he…?

Levi tried to speak, but he couldn't. It was as if he was inside someone's mind seeing and hearing what they did, feeling what they felt. Beneath him was the softness of the sofa, next to him the steady breaths of someone unseen, on his skin a cold draft, in his hand was another that held him in an iron grip. Daylight flooded the room, but Levi couldn't see where they were. Only visible was the knotty pine vaulted ceiling above Phillip. That could have been a million different places in the Adirondacks.

Levi focused on his biological father's eyes, hopeful yet sad, mirrored by the slight smile on his face. The man moved in slow motion as he stood above Levi. Levi saw a movement out of the corner of his eye. A hand held his in a tight grip. Jeb. Phillip reached out and touched Jeb's forehead with two fingers.

Apprehension replaced Jeb's usual sneer. Keeping his fingertip against Jeb's forehead, Phillip then placed the fingertips of his other hand on Levi's forehead. Under his breath, he muttered words Levi didn't understand. Tingling warmth expanded outward like electric fingers reaching through Levi's brain, seeking and probing. A fiery pain exploded in his chest as Levi gasped, and then darkness.

LETTING OUT a groan, Levi rolled onto his back. Hazy memories of Jeb and Phillip Reed swirled from the fogginess of his brain. He swore he could still feel the tingle in his head. Sharp pulses bit at the sides of his temples and along the base of his skull. Moaning, he squeezed his hands hard against his head and attempted to sit up. Caught halfway, Levi swayed. His hand went to the floor to keep him from falling back. He would have sworn he had one whopper of a hangover, if he'd been drinking. That might explain the blacking out and the fact that it was now dark outside.

Panic caught Levi's breath as he jumped up from the floor, grabbing the desk to steady himself. How long had he been out? The digital clock on the nightstand filled the air with an eerie green glow.

Eight seventeen.

Impossible. He'd been out for over eight hours! In his state of confusion, Levi started to doubt the day. He shook his head.

Logan…. Jeb. They should have been back. Another dose of panic jacked up his heart rate. He searched his pockets, but his cell phone wasn't there. Dammit. He'd left it in the car. What if Logan had tried to call him?

Levi burst out the front door. He hadn't even bothered to shut the door to his car when he'd arrived earlier, which meant his car battery would be dead. The old piece of crap couldn't even hold a charge to power the dome light for long.

Snatching the phone from the seat, he pressed the Home button, and the screen came to life. Shit. Twenty-seven texts and a bunch of missed calls all from Jeb and Logan. Words shouted out at him when he opened the messages. The last text from Jeb screamed at him.

Where the hell are you? Call me now! It's about Logan!

Logan? Oh God, what happened?

Without hesitation, Levi dialed Jeb's number. Before the phone had a chance to ring, someone ripped it from his hand.

"I'll take that," a deep voice said from behind him.

Levi spun around, and his eyes widened at the sight of a tall figure wearing a black full-face mask. Levi tried to back away, but the cold metal of his front fender blocked him. The man chucked Levi's phone over his shoulder. A feral grin appeared behind the slit in the mask. Narrow, dark eyes gave him a sinister appearance.

"W-what—" was all Levi got out before the man's gloved hand reached out and gripped him around the neck. Levi clawed at the leather-clad hand, but the pressure against his trachea only grew. Opening his mouth, Levi couldn't force anything out, not even a squeak. Terror flooded his mind. His lungs burned. Cold, detached eyes watched him with what looked to be sadistic pleasure. The death grip gave no inkling of loosening. Darkness feathered into the sides of Levi's vision.

I'm going to die.

Images of those in his life flashed before him. Logan, his mother and father, Gia…. Jeb.

No!

The hand on his neck slowly pushed Levi back against the hood of his car. His eyes watered, and his lungs screamed for oxygen. Levi made a last-ditch effort to move, yanking his head to the side. The jerk was enough to dislodge the hand and allow a sharp intake of breath. Within seconds, the hand was back at Levi's throat, the grip even tighter.

The man leaned over, settling his mouth next to Levi's ear. "Just give in. It'll be easier," he whispered in a sickening attempt to rush Levi's death.

CHAPTER 18

THE RINGING of Levi's phone startled both of them. The masked man jerked upright. Levi raised his knees. When he had enough room, Levi kicked him in the chest. His sneakers connected with a dull thud, and the man flew backward. The hand that clenched his throat was ripped away. Pain burst through Levi's neck and jaw, as if the man had taken half of his throat with him.

Rolling back over the hood, Levi fell off the front of the car and onto the pavement. Small rocks and dirt cut into his hands and the side of his cheek. Gasping and choking, he forced air into his lungs but took no time to pause. Crawling to stand, he booked it toward the house. Slamming the front door and locking it behind him, he didn't stop until he was back in the bedroom and had locked the door behind him.

The cordless phone was… on the bed.

In the dark, he searched blindly with shaking hands.

The crash of glass froze Levi where he knelt on the bed. Holding his breath, he heard the faint sound of glass grinding beneath someone's shoes. Fuck, the man was in the house! Past reasoning or rational thought, pure adrenaline fueled Levi. Fight or flight, and he chose flight.

Forget the phone and run!

Levi vaulted off the bed. Reaching the sliding door, he yanked on the handle. The door didn't budge. He fumbled in the dark for the lock. Damn, his hands needed to stop shaking. Finally, the lock clicked. He gained enough forethought to slide the door quietly and close it the same way. Ducking down, he made his way to the edge of the deck. Creeping along the side of the house, he kept to the shadows. He tried to slow his breathing and calm his heart, which tore up the inside of his chest. One thought broke through any calm he'd managed to hang onto.

What if there was more than one of them?

How was he going to get away? Closing his eyes, he worked to devise a plan. His car was dead, or so he thought. Possibly it would start. Maybe. Probably not, but he had to try. Logan entered his mind. He shook off the panic. Logan was okay. He had to be.

Urging his ever-weakening legs along, Levi stopped at the end of the house and peered out into the driveway. A lamp, mounted high on a pole, lit the entire area in a bluish white glow. Nothing moved. No sounds. The moon, high in the cloudless sky, illuminated the dark woods surrounding the house, allowing Levi to see if someone came from that direction. It was now or never.

Bolting from the shadows near the house, Levi crossed the driveway and leaped into his car. Praying as he turned the key didn't help. Dead!

"Shit," he said through gritted teeth.

Running was his only option. Run his ass off to the next house about a quarter of a mile down the road. Actually, the road probably wasn't the best way to go. Could be more people watching the house. After climbing out of the car, he crouched and watched for the man who he hoped was still in the house.

Levi needed his cell phone. He crawled on the ground looking in the direction the man had chucked it. The blessed ringing clued him into its location under Jeb's Jeep. Levi lay on his stomach and reached his arm under the Jeep, practically crawling underneath to reach the phone. Just as he wrapped his hand around it, the ringing stopped. Kneeling, he was about to swipe the screen to input the lock code when he heard the man screaming that he would find Levi and "make him wish he was dead."

Phone in hand, Levi bolted for the woods. He had to cross the large manicured side lawn to reach the cover of the woods. Of course, he was wearing a fucking white sweatshirt and glowed like a neon light bouncing over the lawn. The cold wind chilled the sweat pouring down the back of his neck. He looked over his shoulder and had to suppress the scream clawing from the pit of his stomach, expecting the man to grab him. Why the hell would anyone want him dead?

A shout for Levi to stop nearly froze his legs. Looking back, he saw the man in the driveway.

"Get him! She wants him tonight!"

"Fuck!"

Levi forced his legs to move faster, recalling his previous run in the woods, the fluid movements, the emotions pushing him as he ran. Reaching the trees, he had to slow down and pick through places where the shadows blocked out the moonlight. He stumbled over rocks and fallen trees but stayed upright by some miracle. What direction he was headed was up to his intuition. The only sounds were the crunch of branches and dead leaves. Anyone with ears could follow him, but he didn't have time to be quiet. He didn't have time to think of anything but escape. Logan tried to fill his head over and over, but he pushed him away. He had to focus on staying alive long enough to get to his brother. Get to Jeb.

Behind Levi, the sound of breaking sticks pressed him to go farther. Someone was coming up behind him. Adrenaline pushed him to go faster. Branches whipped at his legs and torso. A dead branch dug hard into his cheek, but the searing pain and dripping blood didn't stop him. The moonlight glinted off the phone in his hand. He tried to unlock it while moving, but it was impossible. He could hear that the person behind him was gaining. Shit, how was the man moving faster than he was?

Should he hide? His mind ran scenario after scenario—hide behind one of the outcroppings between the trees, climb a tree—but in each one he ended up dead.

The muscles in his legs burned. When a crack filled the air behind him, he stumbled and then was tackled from behind. His chest crashed against a massive tree trunk. He swore every one of his ribs shattered. Crying out, he landed on his stomach with the heavy weight of someone on his back. He jabbed his elbows, trying to cause the person pain. The man merely grunted when Levi actually connected. Strong arms wrapped around Levi's chest, constricting painfully. His mending ribs screamed, and the air trapped within Levi's lungs was forced out in a guttural groan.

"Stop fighting me," the man said.

Levi bucked and kicked his legs out, never willing to give up.

"Let… me go!"

"Shut up and calm the fuck down, Levi."

Levi froze. "Jeb?" Levi had managed to speak despite the weight compressing his chest and the pain of his rib.

His mouth was next to Levi's ear. "Yeah. Just be quiet." The heated air skated over Levi's skin. His muscles shook with overuse, and his cheek burned. He was being chased by someone he was sure wanted to kill him. Jeb on top of him didn't help to clear his thoughts. Levi shook harder. Jeb tightened his arms.

"You okay?" Jeb whispered.

Levi dropped his forehead against the scratchy leaves and shook his head. His fear ramped up as he heard the voices of men in the distance. Levi wanted to run, he needed to….

"We have to get out of here. They're coming," he managed to whisper even though he wanted to scream.

"It's better if we stay right here. What color shirt do you have on under this sweatshirt?"

"I'm not wearing anything under it."

"I'm sure that smooth skin of yours is even whiter than that sweatshirt.

"You're joking at a time like this? That man tried to kill me."

"Shhhhh!"

"Fuck, he tried to strangle me." Levi groaned, feeling the raw soreness in his throat.

A throaty growl came from Jeb, a confusing sound as Jeb's thumb rubbed Levi's chest in an almost comforting manner. Levi wondered if he even realized he was doing it. "You'll be okay. I won't let them get near you. I'm pretty sure they're moving away from us."

Levi's terror hit a new high when he remembered Logan. He tried to jump up.

"Stay down."

"Where's Logan?" Fresh panic flooded Levi along with memories of Logan's accident, the uncertainty of not knowing if he'd live, and, if he did, would he be brain damaged? Now was he even alive? "Tell me." He whispered as loud as he could.

"He's... not here," Jeb said.

"Where is he?"

Jeb's hand covered his mouth. "Quiet." After a few seconds he removed his hand. "Someone grabbed him. There was nothing I could do about it, or they would've gotten me too." *No.* Not Logan.

"But you left him.... you should have stayed and...." His breaths increased, and he was light-headed. He needed Logan. What if they hurt him? What the fuck was going on?

"Hey." Jeb rolled off Levi. He yanked him from the ground and onto his knees as if he weighed nothing. "Breathe."

Levi sat back on his heels and lowered his chin. He had to get it under control before the dam broke and he was useless to help his brother. Jeb's warm hand rubbed at the nape of his neck, and Levi concentrated on the touch.

"W-who took him? Phillip?" Levi sucked in a deep breath and held it. Falling apart wouldn't help Logan.

Jeb sighed wearily. "I don't know. It was messed up. We got separated inside the building. When I finally found Logan there were two guys and a woman holding him. I stayed out of sight. I heard them mention your name, and I knew something was wrong."

Levi looked up at Jeb. The furrow of his brow and the set of his jaw didn't match the concern coloring his eyes. They stared at one another, and Levi wanted nothing more than to fall into Jeb's arms and feel safe again. Instead, he stood and held out his hand. Jeb regarded the proffered hand without expression or an inkling as to what he might do. Levi hoped Jeb would let down enough of his wall to take something Levi offered. When Jeb took his hand, Levi exhaled. The tingling warmth as their palms rubbed together caused Levi to close his eyes. When he opened them again, Jeb gazed up at him with a curious expression. Levi tugged on his hand and Jeb rose from the ground.

Jeb didn't release his hand. Levi swallowed hard. "Let's go find Logan," he said.

Jeb nodded, his gaze unwavering. "I'm sorry. It's my fault. If I hadn't let him go… I just didn't know." He wiped at his mouth. Still he held on to Levi's hand. "I have no fucking clue what's going on. I tried to call Dr. Winston, but she isn't answering."

"Can't you contact other members of the council?"

Jeb shook his head. "Dr. Winston is my handler and communicates with the other members. Many of them don't want their identities known. The man who owns the house I've been staying in is a member of the council, but I've never met him. Don't know his name. It's one of his vacation homes, and he never comes here."

"Well, standing here isn't helping anything. Do you have Logan's truck?"

Do you think they're hurting him? Do you think I'll ever see him again? Do you think he's alive?

Jeb continued to hold Levi's hand, and that went a long way to keeping Levi from falling apart.

"I do, but it's parked just south of the house. When I drove up the road, there was a van parked by the driveway. Didn't seem right, so I left the truck farther down the road and came through the woods. Made it to the driveway when I saw you booking it across the lawn. I would have gone after the guy chasing you, but then I caught sight of another guy going down the driveway. I circled around by the water. By the way, thanks for making so much noise." Jeb finally released Levi's hand, the cold air stealing the heat. Jeb looked to his cheek and then wiped at the blood with his fingertips.

"Stick got me."

"Looks shallow." There was an ongoing annoyance in his expression, but the pissed-off demeanor was missing.

"None of our vehicles are accessible. We need someplace to figure out what we're going to do next and get cleaned up."

Levi chewed on his lip. Home was out. What would he even say to his parents? Only one person he could call. "I have a place."

WITHIN THIRTY minutes, Levi and Jeb had made their way through the woods to the boat launch farther down the lake. Jeb stopped Levi as they neared the edge of the woods and scanned the area before they emerged. Gia's car sat running by the water, right where Levi had told her to wait.

"That's Gia."

Taking Levi's hand again, Jeb led him from the woods and to the idling SUV. Jeb threw open the back door and shoved Levi inside. Gia squealed with surprise, and before she could say anything, Jeb shouted, "Go! Drive!"

Looking to Levi, Gia's eyes widened upon seeing Jeb. "Who the hell—?"

"Just go, Gia!"

"All right already." Gia quickly shifted into gear, doing a one-eighty, and headed away from the lake.

Levi sat back, wiping a shaky hand over his forehead. As they pulled onto the main road, Gia glanced back. "You're bleeding and…. And who the hell is this Neanderthal?" She pointed over her shoulder.

"Gia, Jeb. Jeb, Gia."

"Charmed," Gia said dryly. "How about a bit more?"

Levi ignored her request. "Is your father still out of town?"

Gia sputtered and then said yes.

"Can we go to your house? We need someplace to get cleaned up. I promise I will tell—"

"Wait, can you trust her?" Jeb eyed Gia with suspicion.

"Who in the fuck do you think you are?" Gia downshifted and skidded around the corner onto Main Street. Levi slid across the seat and into Jeb's side.

"Fuck, Gia!"

Jeb chuckled. "I like her."

Levi rolled his eyes. "Can we crash at your house?"

"Yeah, but the minute you cross my threshold, you spill it all."

"Yes, dear," Jeb said, his amusement clear on his face.

Levi shook his head and didn't bother moving back to his side of the car, and Jeb didn't seem to mind that they were sandwiched together.

CHAPTER 19

LEVI FOLLOWED Jeb from the car and moaned as his muscles and ribs protested his movement. He was stiff, and he knew it would only get worse. Jeb reached for his arm to help him, but then pulled back as if he'd thought better of it. Great, the wall goes up again.

As Gia led them into the house, her phone rang. She frowned at the caller ID and told Levi and Jeb, "Make yourselves at home. You know the place, Levi."

He nodded and started to move toward the kitchen but stopped when Gia said, "What's up, Noah?"

Jeb ran into the back of Levi and raised a questioning brow, but Levi was busy listening to the conversation.

"What? Why do you want to know where Levi is?" She paused. "Listen Noah, I told you Levi said he wasn't interested." Another pause. "I don't think talking to him will change his mind." Another pause, and she rolled her eyes dramatically. "Yeah, Noah, if I see him, I'll tell him you want to talk."

Seeing the scowl on Jeb's face was partially amusing and annoying at the same time.

"You told him I wasn't interested?"

"Yup, after you left today. Apparently, the squirrel in his head is taking a break. He might want to give it some nuts and get it back on the wheel."

Jeb snorted. Levi had to agree with her. He went into the kitchen with Jeb close behind. He pulled two waters from the fridge and handed one to Jeb. After cracking his open, Levi downed the cold, refreshing liquid in one take. Jeb smirked and drained half of his. The silence was heavy in the air, and Levi was about to break it when Jeb asked, "So are you?"

"Am I what?"

"Are you interested?"

Levi drew out his answering and enjoyed seeing Jeb squirm, not that it meant anything. He'd made his position where Levi was concerned very clear.

"Why should you care?" Levi tossed his empty bottle into the recycle bin.

"Because... I.... He's a jerk."

Levi frowned. "Yeah. Whatever."

He pushed past Jeb, but he grabbed Levi's arm.

"What's your damage?" Levi barked.

Jeb glared, saying nothing, showing nothing. "I care."

"Is that so?" Levi asked in a gentler tone.

In Jeb's eyes, Levi saw something that caused him to pause. Jeb's hand was still curled tightly around his bicep. The muscle in Jeb's hand twitched. Another stare off. Levi decided to wait him out, but the ringing of Jeb's phone interrupted the moment.

"Fuck." Levi went to the sink, wetting a towel to clean the blood from his face. Jeb answered and told whoever had called the sordid tale of going to get Phillip and Logan going missing.

Levi leaned over the sink, the breath stolen from his lungs upon hearing Logan's name.

"What happened to Logan?" Gia asked, rushing over to Levi. When she reached him, Levi grabbed her and wrapped her in his arms.

"Oh fuck, sweetie, what happened?" she whispered.

Levi couldn't stop shaking. "Someone took him, and someone tried to strangle me... and I had to run, and it's all fucked-up."

"Okay, I understood about five words of that. Just calm down. We'll figure it all out."

Levi nodded and pulled away from Gia, who patted his shoulder lovingly. Jeb finished his call. Levi needed to know something... anything.

"That was Dr. Winston. She thinks she's uncovered something about your father, but she's working on getting more information. For now, she wants us to stay put."

That wasn't happening. "No. We have to get Logan. We can't just wait around. What if they're hurting him?" Levi stepped back when Jeb tried to reach for him. "I can't just sit around and do nothing."

"Levi, what the hell is going on?" Gia asked, but they both ignored her.

Jeb's eyes narrowed. "And what do you plan to do?"

"Something! Anything!"

"Where is he?" Jeb raised his brow. "Who has him and why? If you can't answer those questions, then you can't do anything but head off and probably get caught or killed."

Levi inhaled sharply. "What if the men who went after me have something to do with Logan missing? They were trying to kill me too? What if they hurt him or killed him?"

The room spun. Levi fought the weakness in his knees, but he wasn't going to let his fucking dam crumble now. Logan was okay. If he believed that, then he could keep going, keep it together.

"If they'd wanted him dead, they would have done it when they caught him. Logan was taken for a reason."

Levi knew the reason but couldn't speak the words.

"Why?" Gia asked.

Jeb and Levi stared at one another. Levi had no clue how to even begin to tell her what had happened and that he had no soul. He opted for the believable version. "I found out that my dad, that Art Reed isn't our real father. My dad has another brother I didn't know about, Phillip. When Logan found out he went to see Phillip, to meet him, and didn't come back. Then a bunch of guys tried to grab me at Jeb's. It's all kinds of fucked-up."

"Levi, why in the name of all that is holy do they want you? You're kind of boring."

Levi shook his head. "I don't know. It must have something to do with finding out Phillip is our father." He sagged back against the table, exhausted physically and mentally, wishing to wake up in his bed before all of this shit had rained down on him.

Gia's eyes rounded. "Do you think he's in with the mafia or something?"

Levi gave Gia that are-you-kidding-me look.

"It's possible. Have you ever heard of the Italian Mafia? They're some crazy fuckers. What does this Phillip do for a living?"

Jeb snorted. "Lawyer."

Gia nodded knowingly. "Lawyer for the mob."

Levi rubbed his gritty eyes.

Jeb stepped closer until he was only a few inches away. "It's been a really long day, and you look like you're about two minutes away from collapsing. We need to clean up, get some food and sleep, and tackle this once we can think rationally."

"Why aren't you calling the police? Do your parents know? We can't just sit around here." Gia narrowed her eyes at Jeb. "Maybe he has something to do with this. I mean, who is he? How do you even know him?"

Levi locked eyes with Jeb, who raised an eyebrow as if interested in how Levi was going to answer that one.

Levi rubbed his gritty eyes. Anything was possible at that point. "He doesn't have anything to do with this, and he's helping me to find out what happened, what these people want. I can't…. They said no cops or they'd kill Logan. Just let us deal with this, Gia, please. I trust Jeb."

Gia frowned, glaring down Jeb, then seemed to relent. "Okay, but I need more info. First, though, I'll whip up some sandwiches," Gia touched Levi's arm. "You're dirty and need a shower. There are towels in your room. Show Jeb the bathroom in the guest room. I'm sure my father has some clothes that will fit you, Jeb."

Levi thanked her and then led Jeb to the stairs. Going up Jeb asked, "Your room?"

"I've stayed here so much that I have a room. I have clothes here too."

"Lucky." At the top of the stairs, Levi pointed Jeb to the door on the right. "There's an attached bath that should have everything you need."

Jeb nodded and hesitated as if he wanted to say something. Again, Levi waited, but Jeb lowered his eyes and disappeared into the room. Levi was pretty sure the stoic, walled-off man was going to be the death of him. Somewhere in there Levi was sure there was someone who could laugh, feel deeply, possibly even love. The real Jeb that had been closed away by something. Someone had to break through the façade to get to him. Apparently, he wasn't the one with the power to do that.

After they'd showered, Levi and Jeb had joined Gia in the living room. The convoluted and partially fictitious story about Phillip, Logan's disappearance, and imaginary contact from the kidnappers. Levi only wished he had heard from whoever held Logan. Gia had been speechless, which was a state of being Levi was sure his friend had never experienced. That had ended when she told Jeb that if he was going to drool over Levi like an ice cream cone he might as well take a lick. Levi had choked on his soda and practically hacked up a lung. For the rest of the meal, Jeb had stared resolutely at his plate, which amused Gia to no end. She even had the big, bad man blushing. Levi had almost felt sorry for him.

Now, Levi eyed his bed as he stripped off his T-shirt and pants. His ribs ached, and the cut on his cheek pulled whenever he spoke, smiled, or frowned. He checked out his neck in the mirror. Faint finger-shaped bruises that had previously been red were forming.

Levi didn't give a shit about any of his injuries. Somewhere Logan was being held and possibly tied up and beaten and who knew what else. Maybe they were treating him well? Yeah, because kidnappers were compassionate. Images of Logan tied up, bruised, bleeding, pleading for his captors to stop, to be set free, to not be killed were numerous. Levi leaned forward, lowered his head, and rested his hand on the wall for support. Levi needed to feel something, anything, even if it was partial rejection from Jeb.

He exited the bathroom without stopping to think if going to Jeb was a good idea or not. Opening the bedroom door, he was surprised to find Jeb standing there. The flabbergasted look on Jeb's face was that of someone being caught.

"Did you knock?"

Jeb shifted, then looked down the hall. "Umm, no."

"What're you doing?"

Jeb wiped his hands over the front of his shirt and then looked to Levi. When his gaze fell on Levi's bare chest, he visibly swallowed hard. His milk-chocolate eyes picked up the light from Levi's room. Levi could see the hesitation, but also an openness he'd never seen in Jeb.

"Jeb?"

"I... um... was just...."

"Lurking outside of my door?" Levi smirked seeing at how flustered Jeb appeared.

"No. No." He shook his head.

Damn, he was a basket case when it came to interpersonal crap.

"Well, I was coming to knock on your door."

That raised Jeb's brow.

Levi felt self-conscious. He hadn't totally thought through the consequences of going to Jeb's room. Despite the need to be with Jeb minutes ago, Levi was now terrified of further rejection from Jeb. Despite that, he decided to be truthful.

"I didn't want to be alone."

The muscles in Jeb's jaw twitched, otherwise he remained still. He seemed to relax. "I could sleep on the floor."

The floor? Well, what did he expect? Jeb to sweep him off his feet, carry him to the bed, and make love to him? But Jeb on the floor was better than Jeb in his own bed.

"There are blankets and pillows in my closet." Levi stepped back to allow Jeb to enter. As he walked past, Levi could smell the soap he'd used, mixed with that earthy smell of Jeb. Levi closed the door. Going to the closet, he opened that door. He shuddered hard when Jeb's fingertips ran over his back.

"Your skin is so perfect. So soft. Not a scar or a blemish." A shudder rushed through Levi as the tips of Jeb's fingers ran over his shoulder.

"Thanks." Levi immediately regretted the lame word.

He remained facing the closet, unwilling to believe Jeb's intentions were anything but platonic. No matter, Levi wanted more and got his wish when Jeb's other hand joined the first, running over Levi's shoulders, down his arms and were gone. Before Levi could protest, Jeb's arms wrapped around his chest and pulled Levi back against him. Jeb was hard and warm, and Levi melted like an ice cube in the hot sun. When Jeb nuzzled at his neck, Levi moaned so wantonly he was sure Jeb would push him away. Instead, he kissed behind his ear.

"Love the sounds you make, kitten. You turn me on so fucking bad. I can't think straight."

The words stunned Levi. Perplexed, he tried to react but feared closing Jeb off again. When Jeb laid kisses across Levi's shoulder, he rubbed his cheek against Jeb's hair. Levi's cock was hard and tenting his boxers. At the small of his back, the evidence of Jeb's arousal jutted against him.

Levi reached back and rubbed Jeb's hip. "I didn't think you even liked me."

"Fuck, kitten, you're all I can think about. Been jacking off like a thirteen-year-old over you for months. I just… I don't know how to do this."

Levi froze. "Are you saying you don't know how to have sex with a guy? You aren't gay?"

Jeb snorted. "I'm definitely into guys, and I've had plenty of sex but never with someone who made me feel like this."

Levi chewed on his lip. "Like what?"

Jeb's hand wandered down his stomach. God, Levi's cock was going to explode just from Jeb touching him.

"Like all twisted up inside. Like I've gotta have you, not just for sex. I don't get it, but I love to hear you laugh, see your face when you're totally pissed off at me. I've never…."

Levi turned in his arms and rested his palm against Jeb's cheek. "I know."

The crystal lay against Jeb's chest. Levi eyed the shocking piece of jewelry warily. He wasn't anxious to get thrown into a door again. Jeb, seeing where Levi's gaze had settled, pulled the necklace over his head and threw it onto the dresser. Levi waited for any kind of reaction, but nothing happened.

"Maybe it just needs to be close by?" Levi forced a shaky laugh.

"Good." Jeb leaned down and brushed their lips together. Levi moved his hand to the nape of Jeb's neck and pulled him closer. The kiss was languorous but filled with a greater passion than their previous kisses, which had burned too bright and hot. Their hands explored skin, breaths increased, groins ground together. When Levi pulled back, Jeb frowned. His lips were red, his face flushed, and the lust-filled panting gave Levi a boost.

"*I've* never done this before."

Jeb flashed Levi a cocky smirk. "I suspected as much."

Levi should have been embarrassed. "I just. I've never been able to feel this, here." He covered his heart with his hand. "It's always been sort of dead, but you've done something to changed that. It's…."

He choked on the words. It was the fucking crystal. Probably making both of them want and need. Once it wasn't needed anymore, those intense feelings, Jeb's need for Levi would fade.

"Hey, I get it." Jeb gently covered Levi's hand, which still rested on his chest.

He didn't think Jeb understood, but Levi smiled anyway. He wanted to ask what Jeb wanted, what he was thinking, where this was going, but he knew the answers would ruin the moment.

Jeb kissed Levi, tentatively, as if asking permission this time, and then deepening the kiss as Levi responded. Warmth rushed Levi's gut and filled the hollow in his chest. Whatever the reason, Jeb wanted him right then, and Levi needed this, needed to feel the lust and heat and the yearning to devour another person. Jeb licked at Levi's lips and then across his jaw. Still holding Levi's hand between them, Jeb grasped Levi's hip and ground their erections together.

When Jeb bit on his neck, a rush of air left Levi's lips. He needed Jeb closer, needed the contact and tangled his fingers in Jeb's hair. He pushed his hips forward, feeling Jeb's hard cock. Jeb groaned. If he weren't already plastered to Jeb, he'd get even closer, crawl inside of him. Levi jumped as Jeb's hand landed on his ass and rubbed his crack through his boxers. Passion warred with nervousness. This was Levi's first time, which he'd heard described as fumbling, awkward, and painful. But Levi had gone too far to turn back. If this was his only chance with Jeb when his walls were down, when his need for Levi showed in every movement, every touch, Levi would be a fucking fool to throw it away. And Levi so wanted Jeb to be his first.

Levi tested Jeb's willingness by guiding him toward the bed as he worked at Levi's neck, licking and nipping and… *oh, fuck*… biting hard. Who knew Levi's dick would love the attention paid to his neck, but there seemed to be a direct connection between the two. And still Jeb held Levi's hand. The tender action, whether intended or not, allowed Levi to believe this wasn't just sex, this wasn't just Jeb needing to fuck. Right then, Levi could believe that Jeb wanted him, wanted to make love to him, and that thought fed what little part of Levi's soul remained.

As they reached the bed, Levi easily pushed them down, falling onto Jeb. As their groins met and their cocks rubbed together, more moans escaped Jeb's mouth and this time Levi initiated the kiss, their tongues tangling. Their free hands roamed each other's bodies, learning and exploring. Their hands remained entwined as if they'd found the missing part of themselves. Levi knew they had to let go to move on; however, that had a different meaning to Levi than just releasing hands.

Levi surveyed Jeb's heavy-lidded eyes. Without thought, he ran his fingertips over Jeb's forehead, his brow, over his cheeks and lips, soaking in the beauty of the man beneath him.

"Perfect," Levi whispered, straddling Jeb's hips, finally releasing his hand.

Jeb growled deep as Levi ground his ass against his bulge. Levi grasped the hem of Jeb's shirt, ready to expose his hard stomach, when Jeb grabbed his wrist, stopping him.

"Don't."

CHAPTER 20

THE DEFINITIVE tone puzzled Levi. Was Jeb embarrassed to be seen naked?

"What's wrong?" Levi ran his fingertips over the dark hair peeking from beneath the shirt. The muscles in Jeb's stomach jumped. Pushing the material with his finger, Levi caught sight of a deep white line crossing Jeb's belly. Another few inches, and there were more lines. More scars. *Shit.* Jeb's expression was pained as he shook his head, but Levi needed him to know that he wanted all of him.

"It's okay. I don't care. Just want to feel your skin against mine."

Jeb's grip on Levi's wrist relaxed but still held him loosely. Levi pulled Jeb's shirt higher, exposing a lightly furred belly crisscrossed with a multitude of scars. Leaning down, Levi ignored the questions whirling around his mind as to the origins of such devastation on Jeb's skin. He licked at the grooves between the muscles, dipped into his belly button, concentrating on making this good for him. Jeb's stomach flinched. His breaths were shallow, his body tense, as if he waited for something unpleasant to come. That wouldn't happen, because Levi intended to give Jeb all of the pleasure he could.

Bunching the shirt up over Jeb's pecs, Levi suppressed any reaction to the deeper red scars he'd uncovered. Lying against Jeb's chest were three gold crosses hanging from a chain. Jeb grasped the crosses in his hand and slid them until they rested on his shoulder.

The solemn look in Jeb's eyes forced Levi back to his ministrations and the taut skin of Jeb's pecs. Levi licked and kissed, stopping to suck up a mark every so often. Just the act of worshipping Jeb's skin had him leaking in his boxers. Jeb ran his hands over Levi's back, his neck, through his hair, and Levi moaned as waves of shivers cascaded through him.

Adjusting his hips, Levi lined up their erections, applying pressure while rubbing a hard nipple with his tongue. Being who he was, he'd never fantasized about sex with another person, had never felt the swirling passion in every inch of his body, never had someone be the focus of every thought. So this was why the teenage boys were always so horny. Hell, he'd missed out. He'd have to make up for it. And he couldn't believe how forward he was acting, but somehow, being with Jeb increased his boldness.

Biting down on the pebbled flesh of Jeb's nipple drew a hiss from his lips. Jeb guided Levi's head, gently encouraging him to work the nub longer, showing Levi what he liked. When Levi had finished with that nipple, he moved to the other one, giving the hard nub the attention it deserved. In between, Levi licked the salty skin and bathed the scars, loving every inch of Jeb.

"Feels so good." Jeb bucked his hips, and the delicious pressure pushed the air from Levi's lungs. He slid back onto Jeb's thigh, grinding his balls against the muscle, wondering if his head would explode if he had an orgasm this turned on.

"Come here." Jeb held his arms out. "Kiss me."

Levi dove for his lips. Jeb wrapped his arms around Levi, flipping him effortlessly onto his back without parting their lips. While he plundered Levi's mouth, Jeb worked his own sweats and underwear off, then pushed Levi's boxers down. When the heated skin of their erections met, they groaned simultaneously and thrust frantically against one another.

"That's it, kitten. I want you to come all over me."

The gruffness of Jeb's voice, those words, had Levi grinding harder, frantically seeking release. Levi wrapped his arms around Jeb's neck, pulling him close, needing to come. He'd never felt such unmitigated pleasure. When he'd come in the past, he'd experienced pleasure in his groin, his balls, but not through his entire body. This built like a maelstrom churning in his arms and legs, in his toes and fingers, in every nerve and cell. He panted until he was sure he'd pass out and clung tight to Jeb, fearing when he finally found his release he'd fly off the planet.

"Oh… God… J-Jeb."

"Do it. Come for me."

Every muscle in Levi's body seized. He threw his head back, thrashing on the pillow. "Oh fuck!" High-pitched moans spilled out as Levi's balls tightened painfully and then shot warm cum between them.

"Fuck yeah." Jeb chanted the words over and over, still humping against Levi, his dick scraping over the sensitive skin of Levi's cock.

Levi gasped for air, still clutching Jeb, while tears stung and filled his eyes. An overwhelming rush of emotions clouded his head and pained his chest, and dammit, he wasn't going to cry. He couldn't stop, though, and the tears ran down the sides of his face and into his hair.

Jeb groaned, his face buried in Levi's neck. Levi closed his eyes, petting the back of Jeb's head, his other arm wrapped tight around his back. Their exaggerated breaths filled the air, and the emotional overload began to fade away.

Jeb traced his finger over the side of Levi's face and jaw. When he stirred, Levi tightened his grip, wanting to stay as they were for just a few more minutes. Jeb seemed to understand and rolled them onto their sides. Levi laid his head on Jeb's shoulder, burying his face beneath his chin. He needed time to get his emotions together and hoped Jeb didn't notice the shakiness in his breath. Jeb pulled him against his chest and threw a leg over Levi's hip.

"I do get it," Jeb whispered, and Levi noticed the same shakiness in his voice, the same hitch in his breath.

When he leaned back, he saw the glassiness in Jeb's eyes. Levi thought maybe you didn't have to be missing a soul to feel hollow and dead inside. Levi kissed Jeb, trying to convey how much the momentary lowering of his defenses meant to him. When they parted, Jeb grinned. "If we don't clean up soon, we'll be stuck together." The playful glint in Jeb's eyes brought a smile to Levi's face.

"Yeah, this stuff is like superglue."

Jeb chuckled. Levi waited for Jeb's inevitable retreat behind his barricade.

"Maybe we should sell it. No lack of suppliers." Jeb brushed his hand over Levi's softening cock.

Levi gasped out a laugh. "Super Sperm Glue. Bet it sells like crazy."

Jeb leaned up on his elbow, gazing down on him. "We'd be millionaires. Could lay on a beach somewhere, naked, and not have to worry about anything."

Picturing Jeb naked on a beach had Levi's cock stirring again. Damn, when he got his soul back he'd probably be hard twenty-four seven. "Anywhere with you sounds like heaven." Levi quickly regretted the words. He looked away because Jeb had only said "we." He could have been thinking of someone else.

"Hey," Jeb said softly. Levi couldn't ignore that throaty request and looked to him. He never failed to melt Levi's heart with that rare caring expression. "Let's get cleaned up and get some sleep."

Levi nodded, and they separated, rising from the bed. Levi kicked off his boxers and carried them into the bathroom, surprised when Jeb followed, his sweats in hand. Levi grabbed a washcloth and wet it with warm water. He started to clean himself when Jeb took the cloth from his hand. Levi watched as Jeb gently wiped his chest and stomach, working his way down to Levi's semihard cock, and if he kept going, Levi would definitely be hard again.

"Thanks." Levi took the cloth from Jeb to avoid the embarrassment of getting rock-hard.

When Jeb gave him a questioning look, Levi turned away, rinsed the cloth, and then returned the favor, wiping cum from Jeb's chest. For some odd reason, Levi had an urge to lick it off. He shook his head slightly and continued cleaning the drying cum from the dark hairs. The work was more tedious than he'd thought, but he had more time to study Jeb's scars, which crisscrossed and circled Jeb's chest and stomach. Most were thin silver lines while a few were red and wide and definitely had required stitches. If he had to guess what caused them, he'd have said a very large, sharp knife. Levi couldn't imagine the horrifying pain of skin being carved. Who was that sick? Unless… unless Jeb had done it to himself.

Jeb stopped Levi when he moved lower toward his groin. Levi's cheeks pinked as Jeb took the cloth from his hand. "If you clean that, we won't be sleeping any time soon."

Levi's face heated. He pulled on his boxers and avoided watching Jeb finish cleaning himself.

Jeb threw the cloth into the sink and then pulled on his sweats. Instead of leaving the bathroom, he ran his fingers through his hair. He was tense. His eyes looked to the floor. "I'm sorry for… for being so… I'm not good at people, at showing people who I am." He paused and several emotions crossed his face. The muscles in his jaw bulged. Levi waited.

"Something happened to me about two years ago, and I was cut up pretty bad. You're the first person to really see them. I don't show them to *anyone*. But after driving back from Troy and thinking something happened to you… I was scared."

"That I was hurt?"

Jeb nodded.

That shouldn't have made Levi feel so special because Jeb's attraction had to be the work of that damned crystal. But what if—He cut that thought off quickly.

"How did it happen?" Levi traced one of the shorter scars with his fingertip.

Jeb paused as if he were deciding if he should reveal something so personal. He crossed his arms and looked directly at Levi. "You asked how I came to work for the council. Well, I was a guardian for my nephew, Connor."

"Your nephew had his soul removed?" Levi thought he should meet someone else who didn't have a soul. There should be a support group, although, he'd be a group of one if it was for those whose souls were currently missing.

Jeb nodded. "Yeah. I'd never heard of such a thing, but my brother Brian's wife Danica was part of the community. After Connor was born, she took him to a Seer, which I guess is what they do when a baby is born. They told her the same thing that Dr. Winston said about discordant energy and such. At first, I didn't believe it. I mean the idea of removing a soul is like something you'd see in a movie or read in a story. Even after all of the education and crap I had to go through to be his guardian, I wondered if they were some kind of cult. But even if I didn't agree, they were going to remove his soul anyway, and I wanted to protect him. I loved that little guy, and I figured he was the closest thing I'd ever have to a child, so I agreed."

"Wow, that's a huge responsibility. You were so young." Would Levi ever be ready for something so huge? Probably not.

Jeb shrugged. "I did it. There was a ceremony were the Seer cut the short line down his chest like yours, didn't really hurt him, and did some chanting and then said his soul had been removed. I couldn't prove if it was or wasn't. After that, I was responsible for helping to raise him, for his moral development and helping him to be a good person. It's like a step up from a godparent, and I loved it."

The glint of joy in Jeb's eye couldn't compete with the pall of sadness that covered his body, and Levi knew this story didn't have a happy ending.

"What happened?"

Jeb cleared his throat, and when he spoke his voice was choked. "I moved in with Brian and Danica. We lived in Portland, and the neighborhood wasn't the greatest, but it wasn't anywhere that you worried about being safe in your own home. I mean there were some local 'gangs,' but mostly they were young kids who were into mischief." Jeb stood taller, as if looking for the strength to continue. "One night, I heard popping noises, like gunshots."

Levi wrapped his arms tight around his stomach, ready to stop Jeb because the pain of his words had grabbed Levi in an icy grip.

"Connor was about six months old. He was teething and not sleeping through the night. Danica and Brian were exhausted since they both worked during the day. I was a part-time college student, and when I wasn't in class, I was with Connor. So that night I took him to my room."

He stopped and blew out a breath, his eyes looking off into the past. "They shot Danica and Brian in their sleep." He paused, and Levi could see him swallowing repeatedly before he cleared his throat again. "I slept in a room in the basement, and there wasn't a way to get out without going to the first floor. Whoever was in the house was moving around upstairs. I figured they were robbing the place, so I hid Connor in the crawlspace behind my closet, hoping they'd leave. The space was too small for me, so I hid behind the door."

Jeb's eyes showed the agony of the memory, the helplessness he must have felt. "I tackled the first guy who came through the door, but there were three of them, and they pinned me to the floor. I told them to take what they wanted, prayed they would leave, but…" His eyes widened. "I knew they'd shot my brother and Danica. They weren't going to leave me alive. All I wanted was for them to get it over with and leave. Someone would find Connor. But… but they asked me specifically where Connor was."

Levi's hand unconsciously covered his mouth.

"For some reason, they wanted him, but I didn't tell them where he was… I didn't," he said as if to reassure himself. "I didn't tell them even when they cut me over and over. I didn't tell." Jeb's lip quivered. "But Connor was probably scared, and his mouth hurt, and he cried. They found him. I watched as one of them left the room with him." Jeb's expression turned hard and cold. "I told them I would gut them if they hurt my nephew. If they harmed one hair on his head, I would hunt them down and kill them. They only laughed as they stabbed me in the chest and shot me in the gut, left me for dead. I tried to get to my phone, but I blacked out."

Holy shit. "What happened? Did they ever find him?"

Jeb shook his head. "No. I spent two weeks in the hospital, was questioned by the police, even by a liaison for the council since Connor had been taken specifically. The police said it was a robbery gone bad, probably by one of the gangs because of what was carved into my chest. They couldn't tell me why these guys asked for the baby or what they did with him. They said I'd probably been so out of it I heard wrong. But I didn't. I don't even know what they did with Connor or if he's even alive."

Levi wondered how he'd deal with his entire family being murdered. Even now, Logan was somewhere, probably scared and wondering if he'd ever see his own family again. A black, caustic pit of despair welled in his gut.

"I'm so sorry, Jeb."

Jeb ignored the platitude. "Anyway, I ended up working for the council after that, hoping someday…."

Levi was hesitant to comfort Jeb as he watched those walls start to build back up. He wasn't going to allow it. He wrapped his arms around Jeb who was stiff, unmoving. Levi waited, hoping to God he hadn't shoved Jeb back into his self-made prison. Three crosses on his chain. Three dead members of his family or two dead and one presumed dead. Fuck, Levi had no clue about the depths of sorrow life could serve someone until then.

Slowly, Jeb relaxed against Levi and accepted his comfort. Levi considered it his mission to bust all of those walls down permanently, even if Jeb ended up leaving when this disaster played out.

"Let's go to bed," Jeb whispered. "It's late, and we need sleep before we have to meet with Dr. Winston tomorrow. Hopefully, she'll have some information for us."

Levi released Jeb, and they exited the bathroom. When Jeb headed toward the door, Levi's disappointment flared. He wasn't going to stay, so Levi asked him to shut off the light on his way out. He yearned to have Jeb close all night. One step at a time, he reminded himself, or Jeb would run from him. The light went off, and Levi crawled under the covers relishing the cool softness when he felt the bed dip. Jeb settled in behind him. Levi was almost afraid to breathe as Jeb fluffed his pillow and pulled the blanket over them. When Jeb spooned him, Levi's heart jumped into his throat.

"Is this okay?" Jeb whispered into Levi's ear.

"Yeah." It was more than okay. Levi pulled Jeb's arm across his chest and threaded their fingers together.

"I've never told anyone about my family before."

Levi turned his head and rubbed his cheek against Jeb's scruffy one. "Thank you." Levi placed a gentle kiss on Jeb's lips, reveling in the fact that Jeb trusted him enough to reveal the most horrible moment in his life. Levi settled back in, wiggling his butt against Jeb.

Jeb sighed contentedly behind him. With Jeb holding him close, Levi was able to drift off to sleep.

CHAPTER 21

MORNING CAME too quickly for Levi. During the night, Jeb had stayed close, pulling Levi back if he wandered too far. When he woke, Levi's head was on Jeb's chest. Jeb's mouth was open, and he snored softly in a deep sleep. Relaxed and unguarded, he was beautiful to Levi. Jeb had been through hell for the past two years. No wonder he'd closed himself off. You couldn't experience that level of loss and not have it affect you horribly. Jeb had chosen to deal with his pain by cutting himself off from his heart. Seems he did have some idea of what it was like to be an emotionless husk—although Jeb did *have* emotions, he'd just chosen to turn them off. Even so, Jeb had opened up to Levi, and they were now in the same bed after mind-blowing sex. And didn't that just slam Levi with a truckload of guilt. He was busy having fun with Jeb, and Logan had been kidn—Shit, he couldn't even finish the word in his head. They would get him back soon. Levi had to believe it.

He wished Jeb were awake, wished he would—Levi bolted upright, his mind frantic. What reaction would Jeb have when he woke? Would he be back to Mr. Ice and freeze Levi out? That thought was like a fist around Levi's heart. Guilt and grief and pain and panic had Levi crawling over Jeb for a quick escape. He had wanted emotions. Well, there they were, filling him, overflowing and seeping through the pores of his skin. Luckily, he didn't disturb Jeb, who only rolled over in his sleep.

Levi dressed quietly, fled the room, went down the stairs, passed through the kitchen and out onto the deck behind the house. The sun was rising over the mountains of Vermont. The crisp spring air brought clarity to his emotion-riddled mind. In the distance, the birds chirped all happy and fucking carefree, unaware of the shit raining down on him, and for a moment, he hated them. He hated them as if they were the cause of every single one of his problems. His father and mother, Logan—he sucked in a deep breath—and Jeb who would no doubt wake with regrets and shut Levi out with those cold eyes. And when the crystal was no longer needed, Jeb would disappear from his life. Not that he owed Levi anything or had to stick around just because they'd had an awesome orgasm together.

Even if they'd held one another all night, and Jeb was already in Levi's heart, that didn't mean Levi was in his.

Levi had been a one-night stand.

"Fuck." He pulled at his hair, knowing he was being irrational.

"That causes premature balding I hear."

Levi turned to see Gia standing in the doorway, holding a steaming cup of coffee. Levi gazed down at his hands and the strands of hair twined around his fingers. Pulled a little too hard. He dropped his hands and groaned.

Gia stepped onto the deck, leaving the door open. "You don't look like someone who got lucky last night. I mean, I wasn't the one moaning, so it had to be someone else in the house." She smirked, but her usual mirth was missing from her dark eyes. "Was your trip here to this deck your walk of shame?"

"Pre–walk of shame."

She leaned her hip against the railing, sipping her coffee. Unlike Levi, she was dressed for a cool morning with a bright blue fleece pullover, jeans, and those god-awful fuzzy pink leopard-print slippers. "So nothing has happened yet, but you're expecting the worst. Typical."

The knowing tone made Levi want to step on her fuzzy slipper—hard. He was going to ask what she'd meant, but silence was always a prompt for Gia to talk, so he waited.

"I'm sure you have gloomed and doomed it to death already. It's all over but that fat lady and singing. Did you use your crystal ball or your powers of reading the future to figure this one out, swami?"

Levi lowered his head, and even though he found her forthright sarcasm amusing, he couldn't laugh. "I'm not stupid, Gia. Look at him. He's gorgeous and perfect and totally closed off. Emotionally unreachable."

Gia's snort was so loud that a few birds took flight from the nearby tree. "You just described yourself. You're perfect for one another."

Levi shook his head and looked out over the mountains. A hawk soared on the wind, dipping and diving erratically, then shooting up into the sky. Levi closed his eyes, trying to imagine the freedom to soar on the breeze. When Gia touched his arm, Levi looked over his shoulder.

"I can't focus on this now anyway. I have to get Logan back."

Gia touched his arm. "I get that Jeb is all superhero, and this has something to do with your real father, but I ask you again, shouldn't you be calling the cops?"

"No." Jeb stood in the doorway, hair tussled from sleep. He'd dressed in the jeans and T-shirt Gia had given him. When Levi met Jeb's gaze, he wasn't sure how to react. Jeb wore that neutral expression that gave absolutely nothing away and would win every game of poker he played. This was it. That morning-after moment was there. Taking a chance, he smiled—wide.

Jeb's moment of hesitation was the longest couple of seconds in Levi's life. When the rigidity in Jeb's stance relaxed and his eyes lightened, Levi hoped his decision had been the right one.

Jeb stepped onto the deck, large feet bare and sexy as hell, his stride full of his undeniable confidence. The early sun lightened his eyes and shone on his wavy hair. Levi could look at him forever. Jeb walked toward Levi but didn't stop or halt his progress until he'd wrapped an arm around Levi's shoulder, pulled him against his side, and laid a scorching, I-own-you kiss on him. When Jeb finally released his lips, Levi wasn't sure if his feet still touched the deck. Jeb rubbed his scruffy cheek against Levi's and in a low, rumbly growl said, "Good morning, kitten. I missed waking up with you."

Levi swallowed hard, and then again. The wide-eyed look on Gia's face and her lack of any sarcastic comeback made the moment even more surreal.

"Sorry… I… I needed…."

Smooth talking, Levi.

Levi could feel his face flaming, but he leaned into Jeb's heat.

"I can see that you two want to suck face, and while I'm all for the show, I'm going to take a shower, and then you're both filling me in on what superhero here is gonna do to save the day. Seriously, it had better be good, or I'm calling someone myself." Gia flipped her hair dramatically and entered the house.

Levi's gut churned. He'd never had a morning after. God, if everyone's morning afters were like this, it was a wonder anyone had more than one.

"She's quite a spitfire, isn't she?" Jeb chuckled.

Levi smirked. "Yeah, she's something else." He unconsciously snuggled closer to Jeb. When he realized what he was doing, he stiffened. If Jeb noticed, he didn't comment on it.

"I spoke with Dr. Winston. That's why I came looking for you. She may have tracked down Phillip through some member of the council. She wants us to meet her tomorrow morning. She gave me an address in Crown Point by the bridge to Vermont."

"Does she know where Logan is?" Levi rested his forehead against Jeb's shoulder. He stayed well away from the crystal, which Jeb had put back around his neck.

"No, but if we can find Phillip, I'm betting Logan isn't far away." Jeb's reassurance was appreciated.

Levi prayed that was true. What he didn't understand was why Phillip would want Logan unless…. Of course, to get to Levi. Duh. He'd make a lousy detective.

"Oh, I also came out here to give you this." Jeb handed Levi his phone. "Been ringing like crazy."

Levi took the phone and unlocked it. Five calls from home. Five messages. Had to be his mother, probably calling to see what he was going to do about his father—the nonbiological one. He couldn't deal with her right now. What if she asked about Logan? Levi couldn't handle the question.

"Who called?" Jeb asked.

Before Levi could answer, the sliding door opened. Gia stood in the doorway. Levi couldn't recall ever seeing her so pissed off. The irate scowl on her face would have been comical if it didn't scare Levi. Shit, what had he done?

Before he could ask, Gia stumbled onto the deck.

Levi snorted. "What're you, drunk?"

His laughter was cut short when he saw Noah behind Gia. His usual jovial, laid-back expression had been replaced by fierce determination. Levi actually quirked his head to the side, about to ask what he was doing there, when Jeb growled and stepped in front of him. Was he jealous?

Levi tried to get around Jeb, but Jeb pushed him back into the railing.

"What the fuck are you doing?" Jeb asked.

Gia pointed her finger at Noah. "You've lost your fucking mind. When I get that thing away from you, I'm going to beat the shit out of you with it!"

Levi saw the gun Noah held and slipped out from behind Jeb, who grabbed his arm.

Noah had a rifle, and it wasn't because he'd just come in from hunting. He had it pointed right at Jeb.

"Levi, if you want to see Logan again you need to come with me." Noah's eyes never wavered from Jeb.

Levi's heart went from zero to a hundred in seconds. Flashes of Jeb collapsing with a hole in his chest had Levi stepping in front of him.

"Noah." Levi hated how shaky his voice sounded. "W-what do you know about Logan?"

Jeb tried to move Levi behind him, but Levi stepped toward Noah, putting more of his body in front of the gun. Fuck, it was stupid and dangerous, but he couldn't let Jeb get hurt.

"You'll find out when we get there."

"But why the gun, and what the fuck did you do with my brother?" Levi didn't care that Noah could kill him. He was tired of being pushed around, of being at the mercy of everyone else. Damn, when would it all stop?

Noah shifted nervously, his steely façade slipping to show a minute trace of something like fear.

"Why the gun?" A thought had Levi frowning. "Is this because of what happened the other day?" What if the result of Levi trying to hurt Noah and then flirting with him only to pass him over for Jeb had pushed him to react? Would something like that warrant kidnapping someone's brother? Was Noah a psychopath?

Noah looked confused and then shook his head. "No. Don't... I have to make sure you come, and I don't know who *he* is." He waved his gun at Jeb.

"Pointing a gun in my face isn't the way to get on my good side. Why don't you put that gun down before someone gets hurt?" Yeah, that menacing tone wasn't going to get Noah to comply anytime soon.

Noah ignored his comment. "Let's go.... Now."

Jeb stepped closer to Noah, who took a step back. "Will Phillip be gracing us with his presence, because I have some choice words for him."

Levi frowned. Phillip? Why would Phillip be there? Levi rolled his eyes at his stupidity. Phillip had Logan, which meant Noah was there on Phillip's behalf. Jesus, the surprises never stopped. Levi shuddered. He was going to meet the evil who had spawned him. What the hell did the man want?

"Just move it."

"If this has to do with Logan, then I'll come," Levi assured him. "You don't need a gun." Those things went off accidentally all of the time.

Apparently, not planning to lose the gun, Noah waved the weapon toward the door. "Time's wasting."

Levi knew he didn't like Noah for a reason. This shit solidified his dislike into something bordering on hate.

"I'm not going anywhere with you, you stupid fuckhead." Gia crossed her arms.

Noah shrugged. "Don't need you. Just these two."

Gia's mouth gaped, and she seemed to have changed her mind. "Like hell you're taking off with my best friend and his boyfriend at gunpoint."

Noah narrowed his eyes at the word "boyfriend," and his jaw clenched repeatedly.

Fuck, Gia, don't piss off the guy with the gun.

"It's okay. Just stay here. I'll call you later." Levi didn't wait for her reply. "Noah, please, tell me, is Logan okay?"

Noah flinched, and Levi wondered what that was about. "Just… I need you to come with me."

Stepping even closer to Noah, Jeb ignored the threat of being shot. "We'll come with you, but I swear to God, if you harm one hair on Levi or Logan, that gun won't protect you."

Jeb's piercing glare, his muscles bunched like a tiger ready to pounce, had Noah nodding in agreement. Jeb herded Levi into the house where they put their shoes on. Out in the driveway was a car complete with a tall, burly dude—obviously the muscle—who Levi had never seen before, cementing the seriousness of the situation.

Jeb was forced to sit in the front with the mystery man who didn't speak at all. Levi sat in the back with Noah, eyeing the rifle pointed at Jeb. He hoped Noah's finger didn't slip and accidently shoot Jeb.

"Just tell me if Logan's okay?" What Levi really wanted to ask was what the fuck did Noah want with Logan, and who was the guy driving the car, and where the hell were they going? But he held back.

Noah remained silent. Levi was ready to plead, but Jeb glanced over his shoulder and gave him a ghost of a smile, some reassurance when there was little to be had.

Fear ate a hole in his stomach. When they headed toward the lake, Levi knew exactly where they were going—the camp where Noah had saved him. Not much of a hero now.

For a second time, he sat in the boat, heading back to the camp. During the ride, they kept Jeb and Levi separated. Levi had visions of tipping the boat and their captors falling into the icy water, but he and Jeb would go in as well. The air was warm, but Levi knew all too well how cold that water was. That brought attention to his aching ribs, the cut on his face, and the dull ache in his muscles. He could have used some cold right about then.

Hopefully, all of this would be over soon, but there was no guarantee that Phillip would know where his soul was. When had Noah hooked up with Phillip? Of course, Phillip was the lawyer that owned the cabin. Another duh. Levi sucked at this shit big time.

When Noah docked the boat, they all climbed out. Jeb stepped in front of Levi, shielding him from Noah who rolled his eyes. He told them to head toward the cabin. They walked up the worn path, and Levi's stomach pushed up into his throat. He feared he couldn't speak if he had to. He was about to come face-to-face with his biological father, and while that terrified him, his anger was quickly eating up the fear.

Following the large man inside, Levi instantly spotted Phillip across the room, standing all evil dictator-like, his blue eyes glinting in the sun streaming through the window. Shit, he really looked like Logan. "Welcome, Levi."

Just as Levi was about to let lose a string of obscenities on his biological father, a sound to the left caught his attention. Levi gasped, his eyes widened, and he actually stumbled back into Jeb, who steadied him.

"Dad?"

Art Reed stood before the fireplace. Had they brought Art there as well with threats of never seeing Logan alive again?

"What're you doing?" Levi looked to Phillip. "Where's Logan?"

Phillip didn't speak but looked to Art, eyebrows raised, as if he were deferring to his brother. Mouth gaping, Levi looked back to his "father."

"Logan isn't here."

"What do you mean? Noah said—"

"*We* don't have him, but we're going to get him back. Sit down. We have a lot to talk about," Art said in his usual no-nonsense tone.

A stiff wind could knock Levi over at that point. His dad was part of the craziness, and Logan was still missing.

CHAPTER 22

LEVI'S SHOCK rendered him mute, rooted where he stood, staring at the man he'd called "Dad" his entire life. Levi couldn't even fathom he had any part in his fucked-up reality.

Jeb didn't have any trouble moving closer to Phillip, who tensed. "What the fuck is going on here? Where's Logan?"

Jeb moved toward Phillip, and Noah stepped between them, gun still in hand. "Back off." He must have sensed Jeb was a threat, which was smart.

Jeb's hands were fisted at his side as he sneered at Noah.

"Who are you?" Phillip eyed Jeb with contempt as if he had the right. "What do you want with my son?"

That snapped Levi to attention. "I'm not your son!" He didn't give a shit about the wince on Phillip's face.

"Levi, come over here," Art motioned for Levi to join him, his gaze unyielding on Jeb.

"No." Levi's refusal caused his dad's eyes to widened. "I want to know what's going on."

Phillip apparently didn't care what Levi wanted. "You don't know him. He could be dangerous. Step away until we can figure out if he's a threat."

Levi barked out a laugh that forced all eyes on him. "A threat? Out of everyone in this room, he's the person I trust the most. Noah brings us here at gunpoint. Dad, you lied to me all of these years, and you're here with the person who abandoned me and Logan and had my soul removed. Yeah, I think not."

"I want to know exactly who you are." Phillip wasn't letting that go.

"It's none of your fucking business who I am." Jeb wasn't backing down. "You only need to know that I'll be your worst nightmare if you even try to touch Levi." Jeb grasped Levi's hand and laced their fingers together.

Levi tried not to react to the gesture, but his insides tingled, ramped up by the adrenaline of the situation. He leaned into Jeb. Art looked to their hands and then to Levi. The corner of his lip raised. Phillip was frowning.

"What?" Levi challenged his biological father, not giving a shit what he thought about anything.

Levi looked to Art. The tension had left his face. He almost looked... happy. "It seems you trust this man, Levi. I've never known you to be a poor judge of character. So why don't we relax. This is getting us nowhere. Sit and we'll work all of this out."

Phillip tried to protest, but Art stopped him. "We have to trust Levi on this." He leveled a pointed stare at his brother. "This is one time when *you* need to trust me, Phillip. I know Levi." The *you don't* was unspoken. Phillip scowled but nodded his assent, albeit reluctantly.

Art moved to one of a pair of wooden rocking chairs near the fireplace. He gestured everyone to join him. Grudgingly, Phillip sat in the other rocking chair near his brother. Levi waited, and when Jeb didn't move, he prompted him to sit on the couch, which Jeb did with great care. His wary gaze shifted between everyone in the room. He was ready to strike if anyone tried anything.

"Who's that?" Jeb stared at the mystery man who stood off to the side having yet to speak.

"Hank is employed by my firm for when we need some extra assistance," Phillip said. "Don't worry about him. He only does what I tell him to."

Levi didn't care who he was. "Where's Logan?" Levi wanted his dad and Phillip to know, needed them to know.

Phillip leaned forward elbows on his knees. "We don't know where his is."

"Fuck," Levi whispered.

"Why should we believe you? He was taken when we were headed to get you." Jeb's stare was filled with accusation.

"Because he's telling the truth," Art stated succinctly. "We're not sure who has him. We're working on getting information as to the who and why at this point." Art's momentary glance to Phillip was that of trepidation and sorrow, and Levi knew they were telling the truth. His brother was still missing.

Levi rubbed his face. He pressed his palms against the sting in his eyes. Jeb leaned into him and wrapped an arm around his shoulder. "We'll find him," he whispered and kissed Levi on the temple, his lips remaining on his skin, so reassuring. He relaxed into Jeb. And then he remembered that his father—make that fathers—were in the room watching the display of affection. When his anger had been in control, he hadn't cared. Now, he wasn't so sure. What if his dad rejected him? Levi still didn't want to disappoint him.

When Levi looked at Art, his expression wasn't one of disappointment. So not what Levi had expected.

"Dad... I... um...."

"I always wondered when you'd figure out you liked boys. I mean, you'd never seemed to be interested in dating, so I couldn't be totally sure if you leaned that way."

Levi's mouth dropped open. His father had known. But how?

"You're probably wondering how?"

Levi could only nod.

"Remember when you used to come to the survey sites with me when you were around thirteen?"

Levi had forgotten, and when he remembered, his cheeks flushed. "Yeah, so?"

Art smiled wide. "You were like a puppy following my intern, Brett, around. It wasn't sexual or anything and kind of looked like hero worship, but I knew it meant more for your future."

Levi sat forward, the anger swelling to replace the shock. "Yeah, well, until recently, I never felt anything for anyone. No emotions, no desire for sex, no sex at all for that matter until last night."

Oh fucking hell.

Levi lowered his head, a flush of heat covering every inch of his skin. He'd revealed to not one but two fathers, Noah, and a stranger, that he'd had sex with his—with Jeb, who chuckled. He released Levi's hand and then rubbed the back of Levi's neck. Levi leaned into the touch, which sent a shiver over his skin.

Art cleared his throat. "Okay.... Well... congratulations on that."

Levi glared at him and then Phillip, who was quiet. Wasn't he the ringleader? Didn't he have Levi's soul?

"Where's my soul, *Dad*?" Levi spat at Phillip. "Because I'd like to have it back now. Been a bitch not having it all of these years. Pretty much made me a basket case. A fucking nut job. Did you think of that when you had it removed?"

The paleness creeping into Phillip's face was disconcerting, but Levi pushed on. His body tightened with each second, his head pounded, and he felt as if he was going to fly into pieces.

Jeb's grip on Levi's neck tightened. "Hey," Jeb said, but Levi ignored him.

"Oh, and thanks for abandoning me and Logan and"—he looked to Art—"for lying to us for all of these years."

A wave of electricity sparked through Levi. He jolted, but that shock spurred him on.

"Levi." Phillip stood and moved toward him.

"Is Mom in on all of this too, because that would just ice my fucking cake!"

Jeb cried out and his hips came off the couch. A crackle of energy arched visibly between Levi and the crystal on Jeb's chest. Jeb's head fell back, and his hand clamped hard around the nape of Levi's neck.

"Jeb!" Levi reached for him, but Phillip pulled him away.

Once Phillip had him a good distance from the couch, Jeb's body relaxed, but the muscles in his arms and legs twitched. He panted hard, eyes glazed over.

"Jeb, are you okay? What happened?" Levi tried to go to Jeb, but Phillip still held him.

"Wait," Phillip said softly.

Art sat on the coffee table facing Jeb. "You okay, boy?"

Jeb's eyes were unfocused, but he licked at his lips and nodded. He didn't look okay, but he didn't appear to be hurt too badly. Art studied the crystal on his chest and then lifted his shirt. There was a small scorch mark on his skin. Phillip released Levi and moved quickly to Jeb.

"Where did you get this?" Phillip's tone demanded an answer as he surveyed the scars on Jeb's chest. Jeb blinked and frowned. When Jeb didn't answer, Phillip grabbed him by the biceps and shook him. "Where?"

"None of your fucking business." Jeb narrowed his eyes.

"Stop." Levi pulled on Phillip's arm. "It's just a bunch of scars. He was attacked."

Phillip didn't release Jeb. "It's not just a random bunch of scars. It's a symbol for a radical religious hate group who believes those without souls are evil. Their goal is to exterminate that evil. It's the same group we think has Logan."

Jeb's eyes, which had been hazy, were now crystal clear and tinged with aged anger. A hate group had Logan. A group that hated the soulless.

"How did you get this?" Phillip asked again.

"Some men broke into our home. They killed my brother and sister-in-law and… my… and Connor." Jeb's voice shook.

Phillip and Art's eyes both widened.

"You're Jebediah Monroe," Art whispered.

Jeb scowled. "Yeah, so?"

Phillip released Jeb. His newly found father's determined anger was replaced with an expression of pity. "I'm sorry about your brother, his wife, and your son."

Jeb sucked in a lungful of air. When he didn't correct the mistake Levi said, "Son? No, it was his nephew."

Jeb lowered his gaze. The small hitches in his breath scared Levi.

"Jeb?" Levi sat next to him. When he rested a hand on Jeb's thigh, he flinched.

"Connor was my biological son," Jeb confessed breathlessly.

"But you said he was your nephew." Why would he lie? Did he have an affair with his sister-in-law? That just didn't seem like Jeb.

Jeb pursed his lips, visibly swallowing. "My brother couldn't have children. He had leukemia when he was a kid, and the chemo made him sterile. My brother didn't want to use the sperm of some stranger who'd jacked off into a cup. And they were going to adopt, but I offered to donate. That way his kid would be biologically related to him. I didn't think of him as mine. Connor was my brother's son and I was his uncle."

Levi reeled from the information. Jeb had a son. A piece of him in another human being, and Levi couldn't explain why that idea warmed his heart. But when he remembered what had happened to the infant, that feeling turned cold.

Jeb looked to Phillip and Art. "I didn't know the symbol belonged to the group you're talking about. No one who looked at it knew what it was. The police had said it could be some secret gang symbol or possibly done to throw off the police. Does this group have Connor?" Any sorrow or self-pity Jeb had shown a moment ago faded, and he looked hopeful. If this group had Connor, Jeb could possibly get his son back, even if it had been two years.

Phillip gave Art a sideways glance. Art shook his head as if to say he wasn't going to help him.

"Well, shit." Phillip raked his fingers through his graying hair. "This group, the Righteous, they're extremist, purists. They believe those without souls are evil and that evil will infect others who have souls, those who are good, kind of like a plague. They believe the only way to eliminate the threat is to *eliminate* the threats."

Jeb stared at Phillip, not moving, not breathing. Levi saw the moment the knowledge sunk in. "No," Jeb said emphatically.

"I'm sorry, Jeb. They… they kill anyone they find without a soul. Their goal in taking Connor was to kill him."

Jeb stood defiantly. "No, they didn't kill him. I saw them take him from the room. I saw them. They didn't kill him."

Art spoke when Phillip failed to. "There's a ritual. They would have taken him to another location. But I'm sure that… I've heard the deaths are humane, without pain. I know that doesn't help right now, but…."

God, what else could a person say about that? A humane death at the hands of a group of murderers. They killed an infant, for Christ's sake. Jeb's innocent son.

The mournful wail that came from Jeb was nothing compared to what happened next. A volley of growls and screeches erupted from him. He lifted the twig coffee table and flung it at the wall, the remnants a pile of kindling on the floor.

Levi couldn't stand to see him so destroyed. "Jeb. Stop."

Jeb was past hearing anything. Hank tried to charge Jeb, who clotheslined him. A lamp, another table, anything he could get his hands on. Jeb tore up the place with mournful wails that stung Levi's eyes with tears.

Art tackled Jeb, getting him to the floor. Phillip, Noah, and Hank joined in trying to subdue Jeb. Fueled by the adrenaline of his rage, Jeb continually broke free of their grip. He was so strong. They wrestled him to the ground, but over and over he broke free.

Noah grunted after Jeb punched him in the face. "Stop fighting." Jeb got in some good punches and kicks. Everyone except Hank pleaded with Jeb to stop.

"Hank, get his other arm." Art had managed to gain control of his right arm. Hank struggled to pin the thrashing limb.

"Let me go!" Jeb twisted and tried to get his foot under himself. When he pushed his lower body off the floor, they flipped him onto his stomach and pinned his arms behind him. Phillip practically sat on his legs. "Don't hurt him." Levi wanted to say anything to help but was at a loss.

"I don't think he's the one you should be worried about," Phillip said through clenched teeth. He wiped blood from the corner of his mouth.

Jeb still fought weakly, but his movements were halfhearted, and he appeared to be exhausted. The wails had turned to moans and pleas of "no" and "Connor." Levi pushed past Noah, who held Jeb's shoulder down.

"Jeb." He was facedown, his forehead rocking on the wood floor. Levi cupped his cheeks and turned his head. "I'm so sorry." Levi wiped the wetness on Jeb's cheeks with his thumbs.

"I can't believe it," Jeb whispered, a gut-wrenching plea as if Levi could tell him they were wrong.

"I'm sorry. Let him go, please."

They hesitated, looking to one another, and then Art and Noah released Jeb's shoulders. Phillip got off Jeb's legs, and Noah and Hank backed off. Levi sat, crossing his legs and running his finger through Jeb's hair. Jeb lifted his head and then wrapped his arms around Levi's waist. Levi closed his eyes, ignoring the whispers of those around him. Jeb, and how he was going to survive this, was all that Levi cared about.

LEVI SPOONED Jeb on a bed. After ten minutes on the floor, Levi had coaxed Jeb to move into one of the bedrooms. Jeb had stopped crying as soon as he'd been released. Since then he'd been quiet. Very quiet. Levi cradled Jeb to his chest. The sun had moved over the cabin, setting behind the mountains, and the room darkened. Levi had no clue what to say but "sorry," and he'd said that too many times already.

With a deep sigh, Jeb finally spoke softly. "All these years, I'd prayed he was alive somewhere. Hoped I'd find him. Turned it into a fantasy that someday, when I found him, I would raise him and tell him about his father and mother."

Jeb stopped speaking, and Levi hugged him closer as he shuddered. But it wasn't sobbing that had caused the movement. Jeb sat up. A fire burned in his bloodshot eyes, a steely determination that made Levi actually sorry for whoever had killed Jeb's beautiful son. Levi didn't believe in vigilantism, but he wanted to rip those who'd killed Jeb's family into hundreds of pieces. The problem with revenge, Levi thought, was that it rarely took away the pain, and it left a mark on a person's soul—if they had one. Since he didn't, maybe he could be the one to exact revenge. Get a free pass and all.

Jeb rubbed his face, as if he could erase all traces of pain and sorrow. He was quite successful. His brow dipped low, and his lips thinned. He stalked to the door and threw it open with a bang. Levi scrambled after him. Jeb surprised Phillip by grabbing him by the shirt and pushing him against the wall with a thud.

"I want to know how you knew about the symbol on my chest, how you knew my name, how you know this radical group, and where the *fuck* your son's soul is."

The growl, the crazed look in Jeb's eyes, paled not only Phillip's face, but Art's as well. "No need to rough him up to get your answers." Art motioned to the chairs around the table.

"I'd better get the answers I want." Jeb hesitated, then released Phillip, yanked out a chair, and sat, scowling at Art and Phillip. Levi took the chair next to Jeb. The anger flowing from Jeb barely competed with the sorrow he tried to mask.

Art and Phillip sat as well. Levi looked around the room, but Noah and Hank weren't anywhere to be seen, which was good with him. Hank gave him the willies with his silence, and Noah, well, they didn't have the best history.

"Okay," Art said. "First, we know about you and Connor because we're members of the council." That raised Levi's and Jeb's eyebrows. "At the time of the incident, we were assured by the police that this was a home invasion gone wrong. In their reports, Connor was kidnapped, and a baby matching his description.... Well, he was found a few days later in a Dumpster."

Shit. Connor really is dead.

Jeb didn't react except for a quiver in his jaw.

"Since you thought he might still be alive, then I'm guessing they never contacted you?" Phillip asked.

Jeb shook his head. His fists tightened where he had them on the table. "A fucking Dumpster!" Jeb pounded on the table, but with a few deep breaths, he was back to staring at Art and Phillip. "Why didn't the council tell me any of this? I was questioned by two of them."

Art and Phillip looked at one another, each frowning, and then back to Jeb. Phillip leaned forward. "The council never sent anyone to speak with you. Once we had the police report, our involvement was done."

"Maybe someone else from the council sent them." Jeb was insistent.

"I'm the head of the council," Phillip said. "That order needs to come from me."

"Maybe someone did, but you didn't know it?" Levi asked.

They both shook their heads.

"Milo Covington and Devon Adessi from the council. They asked me tons of questions, and then Milo asked me to work for the council."

"Milo?" Levi asked. "Are you talking about Dr. Winston's teaching assistant?" Dr. Winston had never indicated to Levi that Milo was a council member.

Jeb frowned. "Yeah. I started working with Dr. Winston immediately, and I haven't had much contact with either of them."

Art ran his hand over his stubble-covered chin with a perplexed expression. "We've never heard of them before, and *you* don't work for the council."

"Of course I work for the council. For two years, I've been bringing in rogue Seers and Keepers and whatever the hell else you fuckers want!"

Phillip kept his expression neutral. "I don't know who you're working for, but it's not the Seers Council. If you worked for the council, you would have known who the Righteous are, since they're the number one enemy we fight against. They've killed several Seers and Keepers over the years."

Jeb was quiet. Levi wanted to touch him but refrained. "Jeb works for Dr. Winston, who's on the council. She's the one who told me my soul is missing and that Dad wasn't my real father, and she's helping me to get my soul back."

Phillip rested his elbows on the table. "Levi, your soul isn't missing."

"What?"

"I masked it with a powerful spell so other Seers couldn't read it."

Levi gaped like a fish. "No, Dr. Winston is a Seer on the council and told me it's missing. I mean, it all makes sense. I've been so lost all these years, so empty and unfeeling and emotionless, but now something has happened and that's changing. It has something to do with Jeb and the crystal—"

Art pointed to the crystal. "What's it for? Where did you get it?"

"Lorna—Dr. Winston, gave it to me after Levi had some weird reaction to my presence." Jeb lifted the crystal, rolling it between his fingers.

"Weird reaction?"

Levi told them about stopping his meds, the physical attacks when Jeb was around, the test on Art's hair that revealed Levi's paternity.

"You let him stop taking those meds?" Phillip's angry tone matched his accusing gaze.

"Of course I didn't let him stop. I found out about it from his mother, but when I asked Maggie and Logan, they assured me he'd started taking them again." He glared at his older brother. "And don't be accusing me of anything. I've done every single thing you've asked of me over the years. Every rune and sigil and bag of herbs you sent me, I placed in his room. I made sure he went to see that practitioner who helped him under the guise of therapy to strengthen the spell you cast. I gave him the concocted meds you sent and put them into the prescription bottles. I didn't get too close to him because of your fear that our biological connection could weaken the spell. I did it all for *our* son. So don't you turn any of this onto me. You're the one who set this up twenty years ago."

"If I didn't, they would have found out what he was and taken him!" Phillip banged his fist against the table, rattling the glasses scattered across the top.

Levi couldn't look away from his dad, Art Reed, who he'd always thought loved Logan more than him, who'd never shown Levi the love he'd so freely given his other son. And it had been to protect him. Well, shit.

"Whoa," Jeb said, actually the calmer one in the room now.

Levi was speechless. If the room spun any faster, it might catch up with his dizzying thoughts. "W-what am I?" Levi held tight to the edge of the table. No doubt seeing how off-kilter he was, Jeb placed a hand on his shoulder. Levi was sure any second he was going to throw up.

When Phillip paused, Jeb growled. "Tell him."

"A combination of a Seer and a Keeper.... Just like me."

CHAPTER 23

THE PRIDE that tinged Phillip's tone increased Levi's nausea.

Jeb looked as stunned as Levi felt. "And what does that mean?"

"It means that you can see souls and keep them and in some capacity see future events and fates. Only about 5 percent of the community is born as both a Seer and a Keeper."

Okay. He was both, but what had he meant by "future" and "fates"? Levi decided to go with the less scary of the two. "I can see the future?"

"Your own future. Vague representations of what's going to happen. Pieces here and there." Phillip shrugged. "It's never meant anything to me. It's more like déjà vu."

"I've had that feeling, but recently I've seen some things that haven't happened yet." Levi rubbed his palms on his thighs. Would be nice if he could see something useful. He was pretty sure seeing fates wouldn't be as innocuous. "What did you mean by fates?"

"Deaths," Phillips said.

Of course.

"Not only did I save you from being taken by others who would have used you for profit and their own agendas, I kept you from having to live with that agony." Phillip's gaze was intense, unyielding, and Levi knew he'd made a sacrifice.

If he could see deaths, then Logan was still alive, right? "I would know if Logan was dead or going to die?" He so didn't want to see that ever.

"Maybe. I've only ever seen the deaths of those close to me, like family and some friends. But this power, at least for me, has been highly unreliable. There's no rhyme nor reason to the visions. They come when they come. I can't bring them on. Family members, people that I've known died, and I didn't see it." He chuckled morosely. "One constant fact of the visions is that the death will happen soon, within days. It could be longer, but most likely sooner.

"It's horrible seeing someone you love die before it happens. I knew a day before your Uncle Ray died." Phillip's voice shook, and he looked away, his long-held suffering visible on his face. "I tried to reach him, left messages to call me, called Art, tried everything, but he'd gone away with his wife and was unreachable. Sometimes I wonder...."

When he didn't continue, Art said, "If Helen didn't give him the message."

The crestfallen look on Phillip and Art's faces was telling.

"But why?" Levi barely remembered the woman from his childhood but didn't recall her as being nasty.

"That's just something she would have done." Art's eyes flared with rage. "She was a gold-digging whore, and that's being nice. She slept around, used Ray, and he was too blinded by her, why I have no clue, to see the truth. He was an idiot, and he told her what Phillip was and what he could do. She tried to convince Ray, all of us really, that we could get rich using Phillip and that we should find him. Luckily, Ray never told her that we knew where Phillip had been all along. At times, her antics nearly tore the family apart. In the end, she got what she deserved, nothing. All of his money and his property went to Phillip and me. After that, she took off, and it was good riddance to rubbish."

Phillip nodded, and for the first time, Levi felt something for his biological father. He'd suffered with his "gift." What would happen to Levi when he was hit with those visions?

"I'm really going to see deaths?" Levi's heart kicked into overdrive. If he could have run away from the danger, he would have, but it was inside of him, had always been inside of him.

"It's a possibility if I release your soul."

"*If?*"

Art waved his hand. "This isn't your decision, Phillip. Levi's the one who has to decide. He's a man, an adult, and you've done your part in protecting him, but like he said, he's suffered all of these years."

Phillip crossed his arms. "You can't leave this decision to him. He doesn't understand the risk, the danger to him, the Righteous, being a part of this community, seeing people you love die, the danger!"

Art didn't appear moved by Phillip's outburst. "Then tell him and let him decide, unless there's something else you're not telling us."

Phillip clamped his lips. His blue eyes held his sorrow. "Isn't all of that enough?" He leaned over the table, reaching for Levi's hand. "I just want you to be safe. I'd die before I let anyone hurt you. I'm so sorry for how you've suffered. If I'd known... I wish I had known."

"Dr. Winston said I was supposed to have a guardian. A person would have guided me without a soul. Why didn't I have one?"

Art shifted in his seat. "You did. It was me, Levi."

"Oh," Levi said. "Why didn't I know? Why didn't I know any of this?"

"This wasn't a normal soul removal. As I said, yours is hidden, and no one but Art and I knew about it. Apparently the spell I used affected your energy, created what looked to be anxiety and depression when you were just a toddler. It took us a while to get it under control with the right combination of roots and herbs in your pills. Art kept me up-to-date on how you were doing, and Dr. Ross helped to regulate your meds. We really thought once that formula was stable you were doing better."

"It was better, but better is a relative term. I could function, but I still had panic attacks and felt empty, and I wasn't living." Levi bit his lip hard. "Listen, you both tried to help, and I'm sure whatever you did prevented what I was going through from being really bad. I just kept a lot of it to myself."

Art pursed his lips but didn't speak, as did Phillip.

Levi had a decision to make, but to him it was a no-brainer. What he'd been able to feel since the hollow had been filled was amazing, like going from black-and-white to color. But to make that a permanent part of his reality, he had to bring his soul out of hiding, making him a target of the same group that probably had Logan. And he'd be haunted by death scenes of those he cared about. But then again, he could possibly save someone, stop their accidental death. That would make it all worth it, right? But Phillip shook his head when Levi mentioned the bonus.

"If someone is dying of cancer or another illness, you can't change that. With accidents, there's a chance to change what's going to happen, but the visions can be vague and usually don't give information about where or the date and time. The vision can be moments before the death. It's devastating when you fail. And if you don't fail, there's still that unshakable image of seeing someone you care for die. Some of the visions can be horrific, graphic, and...." Phillip trailed off, his eyes looking somewhere far off outside of the cabin.

Art patted his brother on the shoulder. "Phillip learned to block them, and he'll teach you how to do it as well."

Phillip sighed heavily. "It'll take some time before you can really block them out, practice."

"So you don't have the visions anymore?" Jeb asked.

"Not of people's fates, and it's worked for the most part over the years. But when I'm stressed or upset, it's harder to block."

The weariness in his father's eyes looked more like exhaustion and told Levi he hadn't had an easy life.

"So, you can unmask my soul, and I'll be normal… well not normal, but I'll keep feeling the way I do near Jeb and the crystal?"

"I can and yes."

Levi smiled, forcing himself to relax. "I want to do it."

"Levi, you have to really think about this. Once I unmask your soul, I can't hide it again. It's a powerful spell that only works on young souls. Once I remove the spell, there's no going back."

Jeb squeezed Levi's leg, and Levi took his hand, grateful for his support.

Art faced Phillip. "You promised you'd let him decide and abide by his decision."

Phillip grimaced, but his face showed his defeat. "I won't do it until you've had some time to think about it. We have to deal with this Dr. Winston and Milo. Jeb, have you had contact with the other person you mentioned?"

"Devon Adessi? No, I only saw him that one time in the hospital. Haven't seen or heard from him since."

"Well, Dr. Winston isn't a member of the council, and she sent you to watch Levi. Apparently, this Milo person is in on whatever she's doing. They might be working for the Righteous or have their own agenda. There have been Seers and Keepers in the past who've tried to steal the powers of others, but the spells needed were banned by the council over thirty years ago. The information is protected in vaults in different locations only known to upper council members. It doesn't mean someone couldn't get them, but they are very well protected."

Art stood. "I'd also like to know why Levi had such an adverse effect on Jeb's energy. It doesn't make sense unless it has to do with your son and why his soul was removed." Art pointed to the kitchen. "I'm going to make us some food, and then we'll try to untangle this mess." He headed to the kitchen.

Phillip stood and stretched. "I need a drink." He disappeared into the kitchen as well.

Levi stared at the dark tabletop, his eyes tracing the scratches in the wood. The information overload was filling the spaces between his synapses, and nothing else was getting through. He was a Seer and a Keeper, and fuck, could see people's fates? What a crappy thing to be able to see. Could he see his own? Some people would want to know when and where and how they would die. Levi preferred that to be kept a secret. So he'd definitely have to learn to block the gruesome power, because he was definitely getting his soul back.

"Levi?" Jeb's voice pulled Levi from inside of his head. Jeb shook his shoulder, and the concern on his face for Levi was endearing.

"Huh?"

"Are you hungry?"

On the table was an assortment of sandwiches, soup, and what looked like macaroni salad. How long had he been sitting there stuck in his mind?

Levi nodded. Jeb gazed at him warily before settling in to eat. Levi put food in his mouth and chewed. He couldn't say what he ate or how it tasted, but he managed to put enough away to satisfy two fathers and a boyfriend or lover or whatever Jeb was.

After dinner, they were outside on the porch as a light breeze blew off the lake. Levi sat on the porch swing beside Jeb, who threw an arm across the back of the seat and over Levi's shoulder. Jeb tucked him under his arm, and it surprised Levi how right that felt. Jeb might have been closed off and afraid to love, but Levi was finding he had ways to show he cared.

Art sat in the rocking chair on the other side of the porch, while Phillip leaned against a porch post and told them about the Righteous. The group had sprung up about twenty years ago. Phillip was convinced the founder had to be a Seer or someone who had control over a Seer. The deaths of people known to have had their souls removed had been sporadic, most likely the result of the Seer getting lucky and coming across some who'd had their soul removed. Someone could have given them the information as well.

"The appearance of the Righteous also caused Seers and Keepers to go underground or hide who they are for fear they'd be found by the Righteous and killed. About six years ago, they kidnapped a Seer and Keeper right from their homes and killed them. That was a message to the community that you can't hide. Those who went into hiding have taken great pains not to be found, but the Righteous have killed enough of us over the years to be a threat."

"But they still remove and keep souls despite the danger?" Levi asked, his feeling of being safe in the world slowly being undermined.

Art rocked in his chair. "They believe in what they're doing and don't want to stop helping people. If we could just get to the higher-ups in the Righteous, break down their network, we could eliminate that threat, but they're good at what they do."

"Yes." Phillip nodded his agreement. "Like us, they're just normal people who have another purpose, and they guard themselves against outsiders. It's hard to pin down exactly who and where they are."

A phone rang, and everyone patted their pockets. Phillip pulled out his phone and looked at the screen. "I have to take this. I called a friend who's gathering information we're going to need. Hopefully, he's found something." He went into the house and closed the door behind him.

Levi's thoughts went to the phone calls he'd ignored earlier from home. "Dad, what about Mom?"

Art sat forward, elbows on his knees. "What about her?"

"Does she know about all of this?"

His dad rubbed at his lined forehead. "No. I never told her. Phillip and I didn't think she needed any of this on her."

"But she thinks Phillip was crazy, that all of the talk about souls was his delusion. Wouldn't it have been easier to tell her?" Maybe Phillip could have stayed instead of hiding. But that would have put them in danger.

"It was for her protection. The less she knew the better. Maybe we should have told her. I don't know. Keeping it a secret has been stressful." Art looked out over the lake.

Levi could only imagine. "Does she know what's happening now, with Logan? Does she know he's been kidnapped?"

"No. When she told me you knew about Phillip, she was so upset. Like she'd failed you as a mother, which is nonsense. I know you were upset, Levi, but the way you confronted her was harsh. Your mother loves you both more than anything in this world."

Levi closed his eyes. "I'm sorry. I wasn't thinking."

"You can tell your mother when you see her again. I didn't tell her about Logan. She thinks that the three of us have gone away to work all of this out between us. She was relieved when I said you'd agreed to go. Hopefully I won't regret not telling her."

If Logan didn't come home, if he was dead, that regret would probably triple.

"He'll be okay, Dad." There was no other acceptable outcome.

"I know we will too." His dad looked him right in the eye, and Levi couldn't remember his gaze ever being so poignant. A gentle smile crossed his face, and then his dad stood and stretched. "I'm stiff from sitting for so long. I'm going to take a walk. I'll be back soon."

Levi watched his father descend the stairs. Logan had to be alive, and Levi wouldn't believe otherwise. When Art disappeared into the woods, Jeb turned his head and rubbed his lips over Levi's forehead. Levi shuddered.

"You cold?" Jeb asked in that low rumbly voice Levi felt in his bones.

Levi chuckled. "No, you're like an oven with the heat you give off."

"Well, I am *hot*." Jeb quirked his lip.

"And very self-confident as well."

Jeb nuzzled Levi's neck, and Levi suppressed his moan. He put his hands under Jeb's shirt, the skin so soft and warm. He wanted to strip them both and drape himself over Jeb so every part of their bodies touched.

"You know you love it, kitten."

And he did. Jeb's haughty self-confidence, his strength, and that annoying self-control, all of it. He also didn't mind being called "kitten." He was falling headlong into having deep feelings for Jeb, such a dangerous place for his heart to be. Jeb was his first, but he was pretty sure he wanted him to be his last.

"Tell me." Jeb gave him a coy smile. "Tell me you love it."

What was he looking for? Was this his way of asking for confirmation of something, because if it was….

Levi pulled back and looked into Jeb's eyes. The brown was so dark, so deep and endless, that Levi felt he could get lost in there forever.

"Yes, I love it." The words seemed like a vow.

Jeb grasped Levi's hand. His coy smile had faded. He appeared deeply moved by those words. He didn't speak, so Levi ventured a guess at what he really needed to hear.

"I'm here, with you, and I'm not going anywhere."

Jeb swallowed hard, then pulled Levi against him again. Levi was okay with the fact that Jeb didn't say anything. For Levi, Jeb's actions had spoken louder than words. But when Jeb whispered, "Me neither," Levi's heart skipped a beat.

Several minutes passed, and Levi's attempt to ignore his burgeoning bladder failed. He was so comfortable against Jeb, he didn't want to move from the quiet, intimate moment they'd created. When his gut cramped, he excused himself, and Jeb playfully asked him to return quickly. "Well, the swing is off-balance now" was Jeb's excuse for his request. Levi snorted, then ran into the bathroom, quickly relieving himself, and was ready to bolt back to Jeb when he heard Phillip shout.

He crept down the hall toward the bedroom his father occupied. "We have to stop this now."

Levi knew he shouldn't eavesdrop, but he couldn't make himself leave.

"I can't just let this play out. I thought I could, but I can't." Silence. "But Levi…. Yes, I'm listening."

What did he have to let play out? Levi wished he could hear the person on the other end. Phillip paced frantically in the small room. His fingers ran continuously through his hair.

"Yes, I know all of that, but now that it's so close, I want to protect him…. I don't want to hurt him. He already resents me for what I've done." Phillip sounded so defeated and hopeless.

More pacing and silence.

"I just feel so helpless. I've spent the last nineteen years trying to stop this, trying to change the outcome… trying to… ugh!" Phillip yelled to the ceiling, then sighed. "Of course I trust you." He sat on the edge of the bed. "I just wish…."

Levi wanted to know what he wished. Did he wish Levi would choose not to get his soul back?

"Tomorrow. Yeah, I'll let you know when." Phillip chuckled. "That's right. *Ho perso la camicia a Freni e Frizioni, amico mio.*"

Was that Italian? Levi didn't know anything about his biological father, and that bothered him. He had to trust this man with his life, with Logan's life. Levi's dad trusted him, so shouldn't that be enough?

Levi backed away from the door and returned to the living room, which was now full. Noah and Hank were back, and Art and Jeb had come inside. Levi needed to be alone for a minute to think. As he walked toward Jeb, Noah's gaze followed him, unyielding and just creepy.

Jeb stood and went to Levi, resting his hand on Levi's hip. "Hey, you okay?" Jeb studied his face so intently Levi had to look down, because he wasn't okay, and he didn't want to look at Jeb when he lied.

"Yeah." He looked at Jeb and couldn't read his expression.

Phillip returned to the living room. Levi watched as he went to Hank and Noah. They whispered urgent words among themselves, and then with a nod Hank left. Phillip looked to Levi as if he intended to speak with him.

Levi didn't want to be near him. "I'm good. I just need some air. I'm gonna go outside for a minute."

Levi hoped Jeb didn't ask if he wanted company. "Okay, I want to talk with Phillip about Lorna and Milo, see if he found out anything on his call."

Levi didn't want to stick around for that. He excused himself and went outside and down to the dock. He noticed the boat missing. Hank must have taken their only transportation from the cabin. Levi shuddered, feeling as if he was trapped there. He needed to relax. He closed his eyes, listening to the birds, the water lapping at the shore, the incessant sounds of insects. He recalled his doomed jog through the woods and the freedom and extreme happiness he'd felt for that short amount of time. That happiness was present when he was with Jeb. Levi wanted more of him, and Jeb seemed to want more, but Levi couldn't be sure. They were too screwed up to talk about feelings and what they wanted. Levi only hoped Jeb felt the same—especially after they no longer needed the crystal.

While the good news was that his soul wasn't missing, just masked somehow, Phillip seemed to be dead set against restoring what he'd taken away. He was grateful to Phillip for what he'd done, what he'd sacrificed, but Levi felt resentment building toward the father who'd left him and wanted to deny him what was his. The snapping of a twig startled Levi, and he turned to find Noah standing on the path behind him.

"Hey." Noah had stuffed his hands deep into the pockets of his khakis. "Can we talk for a moment?"

Levi bristled but nodded, dreading what Noah could possibly want to say.

Noah stepped up next to Levi, who focused on the waves shimmering in the afternoon sun. After a moment of silence, Noah spoke. "Things are kind of crazy, right?"

Levi snorted. "Understatement."

Noah shifted nervously. His hair was pulled back on the sides, and Levi remembered that day in the hospital when he'd lusted after the guy. Seeing Noah's discomfort, Levi couldn't help but feel crappy. He'd led Noah on several times, and that hadn't been fair.

"I'm sorry for all of the crap… you know… well, over the past few weeks. I hope we can focus on what's important here. I have to get Logan back. We need your help to do that."

Noah smiled wide. "I really liked you Levi, but hey, it didn't work out." He shrugged. "Plenty of fish in the sea as they say."

Well, jeez, he could have felt some kind of loss, Levi thought, but then again that wasn't the point.

"I'm here for whatever it takes to clean up this mess. I've been working for your father for a couple of years, and I've thought very highly of him. I had no clue about his soul Seer Keeper thing until recently… yours too… and I have to say it blew my mind." He laughed dryly. "I mean who knew *you* were so special, Levi."

There was something about the way Noah had said those last words. When Levi looked at Noah, though, he was all smiles and relaxed, nothing to support what Levi thought he'd heard.

"Nothing special about me."

"Ah, but there is. Phillip can't stop talking about his son, about how special you are and how you need to be protected."

Levi surveyed Noah and wondered if he caught a hint of jealousy there.

"I don't need to be protected." Levi let his harshness shine through.

A flash of anger and possibly disgust crossed Noah's face, but then he smiled. "Maybe you do and you should listen to Phillip. Although, I don't agree with him about not returning your soul."

That wasn't what Levi had expected to hear. "You don't?"

"No. I definitely think you should get it back. Might melt that ice you have around your heart."

Before Levi could respond, Phillip approached the dock.

"Noah, can I speak with Levi for a moment?"

Gaze still on Levi, Noah tilted his head. "Sure, Phillip. Talk to you later, Levi."

As Noah passed, Phillip patted him on the shoulder. Noah smiled wide, almost too wide, nodded, and made his way up to the cabin. Did Noah feel threatened that Levi would take some coveted place he held with Phillip? What place that would be Levi hadn't a clue.

Phillip took Noah's spot next to him, and all hope of relaxing was gone. Levi had questions. Foremost why Phillip had chosen to take off when he had a toddler, a wife, and a baby, and why he thought Levi didn't deserve his soul back.

"I didn't want to leave," Phillip said as if he'd read Levi's mind. Maybe he could do that as well.

"Then why did you?"

"Because someone found out what I was. I don't know how since I'd blocked my soul from other Seers. Anyway, I started to get threats, maybe from the Righteous, I don't know. I thought if I had to I could leave, but when I found out that you also were a Seer and a Keeper it wasn't just me in danger. But your mother wouldn't believe what I told her and wouldn't leave with me, so I hid your soul and went alone."

He left because Levi's mother wouldn't. That was a huge sacrifice. Damn.

"I'm guessing Logan doesn't have these abilities?"

"No. He doesn't. The abilities aren't passed on to every child. Art and Ray didn't get them, but I did from your grandmother. When I first left, I changed my name and moved to the West Coast. I didn't stay in one place for very long. I was in Nevada, New Mexico, Oregon, even Alaska. It was only a couple of years ago that I returned to New York. I started using my old name in case you boys needed to find me you could—which you did." He looked out over the water. He appeared older in the daylight, more haggard. "The Righteous located me somehow. Lousy timing with Logan coming to find me and all. My secretary gave me your message, and I asked Noah to check on you. I should probably tell you, I had him keeping tabs on you this past year. Just so I knew you were doing okay in school. When I got your call, I had to let him know the danger. But he couldn't find you that day, and I'm glad you weren't the one who came after me."

"Well, Logan did, and they got him because they thought he was me." *Shit!* "And what the hell, Jeb has been watching me since I left

Plattsburgh, and now you're telling me Noah was spying as well. Who the hell else is watching?" Levi shuddered at that thought. "Are the Righteous watching me?"

What he really wanted to ask was if he could trust Phillip. Did he really have Levi's best interests at heart?

Phillip swallowed hard. "Until Logan was taken, I thought they didn't know who you were. Hearing about these fake council members and this teacher of yours, though, I'm not sure. They may have been watching you through Dr. Winston and this Milo person. I thought Jeb too, but it appears they've used him as well for some reason."

"But Dr. Winston was nice to me. She wanted to help me get my soul back, wanted to know who my guardian was and…. She was too interested, wasn't she?"

Phillip shrugged. "Maybe."

"I'm sorry I screwed up. I thought I could trust her."

Phillip gripped Levi's biceps and turned him. His determined gaze cut into Levi. "Listen to me. You didn't do anything wrong. You didn't know about any of this. I'm very proud of you. Art sent me pictures and kept me up-to-date on everything you and Logan were doing. I couldn't be prouder of both of you." Levi watched Phillip's eyes fill with tears, and even though his father blinked rapidly, they still fell.

Levi bit down on his bottom lip, hoping the pain would stop the tremble there. No luck. He soothed his lip with his tongue and then said, "Even if I'm gay?"

Phillip chuckled and wiped at his cheeks. "I don't care who you love, as long as you get the chance."

"Did you love Mom?"

Phillip appeared to be flustered, his gaze darting around. "I loved her as a friend. I married her because back then it was expected. It was the only way to keep people from finding out the truth about me."

"The truth?" How did marriage keep someone from finding out about his Seer abilities?

Phillip grinned, and his eyes softened. "Once this is over, I'll introduce you to my partner, Rene. He can't wait to meet you and Logan."

"*He?* You're gay?"

The shock on Levi's face must have amused Phillip, because he laughed heartily.

"Guess we're more alike than you thought? Right now, though, we have to find Logan. I have a sinking suspicion your professor has a hand in this. She may be part of the Righteous, and I'm terrified knowing she was so close to you."

Levi wanted to shake his head. Dr. Winston? But there were too many facts including that she'd lied about being a part of the council.

"Who was on the phone? Did you get any information?"

Phillip blanched, and Levi knew he didn't want to tell. "An old friend. Someone I trust more than anyone. He's checking on your teacher and trying to get information on any plans the Righteous may have brewing. He has a contact on the inside—"

"He knows someone in the Righteous? Then why doesn't he know where Logan is? He's been missing for days." What the hell?

Phillip rested his hand on Levi's shoulder. "He hasn't been able to contact his informant. He didn't say as much, but I can tell he's concerned that he might have been found out. He's doing everything he can. We all are. I promise."

Levi wished he'd had enough trust in the man. Maybe he didn't totally trust him because he'd abandoned him and Logan. Levi's inner child wanted to hate him, scream at him for leaving, and blame him for every miserable thing that had happened. He reminded himself that Phillip left to keep them safe. Even so, it still hurt.

"What do we do next?"

Phillip dropped his hand. "Jeb meets with Dr. Winston as planned, and then we find out exactly what she wants. We find out if she's part of the Righteous and if she has Logan. There's a chance we're wrong, but I hope not, because this is the only lead we have at the moment."

Levi rubbed the toe of his sneaker against the worn wood of the deck, and then a chill ran up his spine. "Will they hurt him?"

"I think they want something, and if they do... hurt him, they wouldn't get it."

"They want me, don't they?"

"I'm not sure." Phillip's tone was less than convincing.

Again, more questions and no answers.

"Come on." Phillip slapped him on the shoulder. "Let's make some plans to kick some ass."

Levi grinned, liking that they weren't just going to sit back and wait. They walked toward the cabin, and even though he hadn't spent any time alone, Levi did feel better.

"So, this was Uncle Ray's cabin?"

Phillip nodded. "Yeah, it was. I heard you came here a lot as a kid."

Levi was about to answer when Noah stepped out onto the porch. He watched them silently.

"What's up, son?"

The endearment struck Levi hard. He wondered about the less-than-thrilled expression on Noah's face.

"Art needs you in here."

They followed Noah inside and into the living room. Jeb sat on the couch, his shirt missing. The scars on his chest were highlighted with black, the symbols standing out in stark contrast against his white skin.

Phillip's eyes rounded. "What the fuck? How did I miss that?"

"You didn't get a good look at the entire symbol. Part of it wraps around his side," Art said smugly. His father did always love pointing out what others failed to see.

"Missed what?" Levi sat next to Jeb. Jeb placed his hand on the small of Levi's back and a smile tugged at his lips. Levi gave him a reassuring smile back. Taking a good look at the symbol, he inhaled sharply and tensed. "I've seen this before."

Art grimaced. "Where?"

"When I was in Dr. Winston's class doodling in my notebook, and I drew it exactly like this. It wasn't until I was looking back through my notes recently that I saw it again." Yup, the angles, the intersecting lines were exactly what he'd drawn. "What is it?" And how had he known to draw it?

"I'm guessing your abilities were ramping up in the last few months if you subconsciously drew this." Thankfully, his dad didn't look as freaked as Levi felt.

"What do you mean?" Jeb asked.

"Seeing the future. It's probably why you drew this symbol. As I said, seeing the future is like trying to see through fog that clears only long enough to give you bits and pieces of a scene. Without context, the information can be useless." Phillip continued to stare at the symbol, hands on his hips, a look of disgust on his face. "It's the symbol to unmask a soul. It's similar to the one the Righteous use as their calling

card. They use the Symbol of Orion with the Mark of Rasa added in."
He pointed each one out. "I'd always hoped their use of that symbol was
a lame attempt to mock the council, but apparently they know what it's
for." Phillip looked poignantly at Levi. "This is the reason you had such
a negative reaction to Jeb."

Jeb wrapped an arm around Levi's shoulder as if to tell everyone
he wouldn't hurt him.

"Whenever Jeb got close, he was negating the spell I used to mask
your soul and was essentially pulling it out of hiding."

Levi swallowed hard. "I felt like I was dying."

Jeb's hand on Levi's back tensed. Levi ran his hand in a soothing
motion over Jeb's thigh.

Phillip looked to Levi. "You said that the effects started to occur when
you stopped taking your medications. Most of what you were taking was a
mixture of ingredients to keep the spell stable. You stopped taking the pills,
and the spell came under the influence of the symbol." Phillip looked to Jeb.
"Call Dr. Winston. Set up a meeting tomorrow."

"We need to restore his soul," Art said.

Phillip balked. "Why in the hell should we do that? It's probably
what they want."

Art narrowed his eyes. "What do you mean 'what they want'?"

Phillip shifted his gaze to Levi and then back to Art. "Because without
his soul he doesn't have his power. They want him for something. We talked
about this. It's too dangerous to send him in there with his soul."

"Not if we're there as backup. And your contact hopefully can
get us some information before then. Also, if this woman is a Seer,
she'll know he's had his soul restored. Then we'll hopefully know
what she wants. She's been helping Levi get his soul back. There's a
reason for that."

"Why are you so anxious to put my son in danger?" Phillip faced
his brother, anger marring his features. His posture rigid.

"Your son?" Art squared off with his brother. "I raised him for the
last nineteen years, made sure he was safe while you were gone. I've
been his father."

Phillip's face reddened. "I was out trying to stop this from
happening, trying to find an answer to keep him from being a target for
others to use." Phillip had forced the words out between his clenched
teeth. "And you want to do just what I've been trying to prevent."

Levi stood, hating being talked about as if he weren't even there. "Stop it. I want my soul back no matter what. It's my decision." He pointed to Phillip. "Not yours." He pointed to Art. "Or yours."

Jeb stood as if in solidarity with Levi. At least he had someone who would let him make the decision.

Phillip grasped Levi's shoulders, leveling his widened blue eyes with Levi's. "You don't know how dangerous this is. You don't know what these people are capable of. I've spent my entire life trying to protect you, trying to save you from this. Please, Levi, I can get Logan back without doing this. Then we can talk about restoring your soul, have a plan."

The absolute sincerity in his father's eyes was overwhelming. But choosing to wait to get his soul wouldn't change their current situation. "They won't stop. They know who I am, and I'm not any safer without my soul than I am with it."

"Levi has suffered enough without it," Jeb said. "And I'll protect him with my life."

Jeb's expression was determined, confident. He met Levi's gaze, and for a moment they were joined in one goal. He squeezed Jeb's hand to acknowledge the sentiment. "You can protect me all you want. But I need to do this." Levi paused, unsure if he should say anything about the phone call he'd overheard, but he needed to know what his father was talking about. "I heard you on the phone when you were in the bedroom. You were talking to that friend of yours?"

Phillip dropped his arms. His caring concern was quickly replaced by something bordering on annoyance "You were listening?"

Levi felt a rush of guilt. "I didn't mean to. I was coming out of the bathroom when I heard you yell. Who were you talking to?"

Phillip pursed his lips, and Levi wondered if he would answer. "I told you, he's an old friend and a Keeper. His family's line of Seers and Keepers goes back hundreds of years."

"Keepers hold the extracted soul, right?" Again, the image of jars of souls filled Levi's mind, whatever a soul looked like.

"Yes. They have the ability to take on the souls of others." Art returned to his seat. Jeb coaxed Levi to sit on the couch, and he complied. Phillip was last to sit.

Jeb rested his hand on Levi's thigh, swirling his finger over the denim material and sending chills through Levi. "What do you mean take them on?"

"They can harbor souls in their bodies, carry them until they're needed again," Phillip said as if it was an everyday thing. In his world, it was.

Levi frowned. So not jars. "In their bodies? Just stuff them in there until it's full?"

He rubbed his chest, wondering what holding souls felt like.

Phillip actually chuckled, and much of the tension in the room broke. "There's a limit depending on the Keeper, on how strong they are."

Jeb sat forward with apparent renewed interest. "What if a person who's had their soul removed dies? Does the soul stay with the Keeper? Connor had his soul removed. Does someone still hold it?"

Art shook his head. "The soul needs the connection to the body, the small part of the soul remaining. When that life ends, the soul leaves the Keeper. I hear it can be quite jarring to the person holding the soul."

Art looked to Phillip as if for confirmation. "For me it's kind of like a part of me is suddenly missing."

Jeb sat back slowly, and Levi knew he was disappointed.

"There are ways to keep a soul from moving on when the body connection is severed, but as I said before those higher-level spells have been banned. There's no reason to hold on to a soul except for nefarious reasons such as blackmail, revenge, or power."

"Wait, what if the Keeper dies?" Levi asked. Would the people die as well?

"Every Keeper who holds souls is connected to other upper-level Keepers to safeguard against such instances. Using a connection spell and a specific symbol that each Keeper wears, the souls travel that connection and move to the other Keeper."

Jeb guffawed. "What if they're thousands of miles from one another?"

"Doesn't matter. The connection exceeds space and time."

"Wow." Levi wasn't sure he wanted others inside of him, even if only their souls. Seemed like an enormous responsibility. He assessed Phillip, who looked like a normal man, but... "Do you have souls in there... right now?"

"A few dozen."

"Shit," Jeb said. "Is that amount normal?"

Phillip straightened in his seat. "No. It's definitely a higher-level Keeper ability. Most Keepers can only hold around eight to ten. It's difficult until you learn to control the extra energy. That takes time and practice."

"What happens if you can't control it?" Jeb asked.

"Keepers have a special ability to take on the extra souls," Art said. "They don't allow souls to take over and influence them. It's essentially like having another person inside of you, and while they can't take over and control their Keeper's mind, they can affect thoughts and feelings. Technically, the soul is still connected to its body. Without training, someone holding too many souls can run into some serious issues."

"Such as?" Jeb asked.

"The souls carry discordant energy, essentially flaws, which is the reason they were removed in the first place. There's also myths of dark energy, something innate triggered by the loss of control. There are some old stories of Keepers overcome by the darkness and, well, let's say they weren't very nice after that. No one really knows since the craft is now highly regulated."

Phillip jumped up from his chair, paced across the room, and then turned. "That all happened before the formation of the council and the strict rules. But if you don't have your soul unmasked, then you won't have to worry about it."

Levi had already made up his mind. He ignored Phillip's comment. "When you were on the phone you also said that this had to play out, but you didn't like it. What did you mean?"

Phillip sighed. "My friend agrees with Art. He says we need to restore your soul to get information about why they're after you. But... I don't want you to have to do this. I hate it all, and I just want you to live a normal life."

Levi laughed morosely. "Nothing about my life has ever been normal. And I don't think keeping my soul hidden will help anyone. Maybe we can stop at least one person who wants to harm others. Maybe we can fight back instead of running." Even though that thought made Levi want to puke.

Phillip shook his head and actually chuckled, despite looking as solemn as a mourner at a funeral. "You did raise a great kid, Art. I guess my vote is overruled. If you won't take my advice, I'll unmask your soul."

Why did the tone of Phillip's voice make the choice sound like a death sentence?

"How do you put it back?" Levi burrowed closer to Jeb, needing that feeling of safety again.

The silence in the room was more telling than words.

"We'll block the energy of the crystal."

Levi sat up, truly hoping he'd heard incorrectly. "But when Jeb wasn't wearing the crystal it nearly killed me!"

Phillip's body sagged, his mouth drooped, but his gaze never left Levi. "It won't kill you, but you'll wish it had before it's over."

They decided not to waste any time trying to kill Levi. Art had wanted to start immediately, but Levi needed time to process everything. He wasn't looking forward to his head exploding, because that's exactly what had nearly happened the last time he'd encountered Jeb without the crystal. They'd commence first thing in the morning.

LEVI SAT on the edge of the bed, rubbing his hands over his arms, trying to get warm. Why did it feel like his bones were made of ice?

Jeb was in the shower, no doubt scrubbing the marker off his chest. He had to live with that daily reminder of the most horrible time of his life. Levi rubbed faster needing to get warm. Jeb had a son, and he was dead. Levi should be more grateful only missing his soul, he thought. He couldn't imagine losing a child, and Jeb had been forced to relive that horror. During dinner, he'd been quiet, heck they'd all had been quiet, processing the fucked-up situation for what it was. Then they'd pulled out of their funks and started planning their attack.

Jeb had placed a call to Dr. Winston. On speakerphone, she stated she knew where Logan was being held. Levi wanted to scream for her to return his brother and accuse her of being a lying bitch. Did she have Jeb's son killed? Did she know who Jeb was? Was she some powerful Seer who was out to destroy other Seers and, if so, what the heck for? If Levi didn't stop thinking, his head would explode before tomorrow.

He pulled back the covers on the bed when the bathroom door opened. Jeb stepped out surrounded by a cloud of steam. His chest had been scrubbed raw and was close to bleeding in some spots. He stopped in the doorway, and his gaze roamed over Levi's body, surveying every inch, then settling on his groin.

Levi stood and planted his feet as Jeb prowled across the room. The towel around his waist hung low on his hips and seemed to defy gravity. Water drops flowed over his skin, hugging the contours of his body as they ran down his toned torso. When Jeb stopped before him, Levi wanted to say something profound, something that would make everything better for the moment. But when he opened his mouth to speak, all that came out was "Kiss me."

CHAPTER 24

THOSE MUST have been the right words. Jeb wrapped an arm around Levi's waist and slammed their bodies together, taking possession of Levi's mouth. More than a claiming, Jeb owned Levi, even if only for that moment. When Jeb came up for air, the feral look in his eyes nearly buckled Levi's knees. Jeb took care of that by cupping Levi's butt and lifting him from the floor. Levi squeaked and wrapped his legs around Jeb's waist. His cock was trapped between their bodies, hardening as Jeb spread his cheeks and massaged Levi's hole. Levi groaned when the tip of Jeb's finger pushed inside, teasing, but not going any farther. He wanted it. Needed it. Relaxing his grip around Jeb's neck, Levi dropped and forced the finger inside. He hissed at the burn but pushed down farther.

"Careful." Jeb's voice was a rough whisper. So fucking sexy.

"Feels good." Levi panted. "More."

Jeb slowly pulled his finger out and began a torturous slide in and out, driving Levi crazy. Levi kissed and sucked his neck, licking at his pulse point, his fingertips kneading the back of Jeb's neck. Running his lips over Levi's pec, Jeb stopped to suck a nipple. Levi bucked, the sensation of Jeb's mouth as good as being on his cock, not that he'd ever had his cock sucked before.

"Put me down." Levi tried to unwrap his legs.

"I kind of like you up there." Jeb rammed that finger back into Levi.

"Fuuuuck." All of the air left Levi's lungs. His cock leaked copious amounts of precum onto Jeb's stomach. Levi wriggled, and Jeb didn't have any choice but to remove his finger and lower him to the ground.

"Not enjoying what I was doing?" An evil grin split Jeb's face.

Levi smacked his chest playfully. "You know I was." In one motion, Levi fell onto his knees, yanked the towel from Jeb's hips, and had Jeb's cock in his sights. He grasped the hard shaft, larger around than his own but shorter in length. Beneath his palm, the throbbing excited Levi, knowing he was the reason Jeb was hard.

"Fuck, kitten, you look good down there."

Levi eyed the head where a bead of precum pooled. It was do-or-die time. Levi wanted to suck Jeb's cock, needed to taste him. God, what would Jeb's mouth feel like stretched around his own shaft, the wet heat moving over his sensitive skin? His cock hardened with that vision.

"Suck it."

Levi prayed Jeb didn't shove him away in disgust. Taking the plunge, he engulfed the head, the salty, bitter precum exploding on his tongue. He experimented, running his tongue over the head, drawing a moan from Jeb, who clutched his fists at his sides. At least he wasn't shoving it down Levi's throat and gagging him. Taking more of the cock into his mouth, Levi's excitement grew as his nose practically touched Jeb's groin before he had to stop. The musky smell of Jeb, mixed with how he tasted, notched up Levi's arousal. He grabbed his own cock and stroked it several times.

"No cumming yet." Jeb's command caused Levi to release his rigid shaft, dying for friction.

Levi started to suck Jeb's cock with great enthusiasm. He hollowed his cheeks, increasing the suction until the head popped out of his mouth. He worked his tongue over the large vein, moving down until he was sucking Jeb's furred balls. Driven by Jeb's groans, he took the bulbous head back into his mouth. He tongued the slit and then slowly took more in. Jeb's hands settled on Levi's head, gently guiding him forward, not rough or demanding. Levi's plan was to stay there until Jeb filled his mouth, but Jeb had other plans. He pulled his dick from Levi's mouth with a pop.

Levi gazed up at Jeb's flushed skin, his pupils wide, tongue trailing over his lips. Jeb smoothed his palm over Levi's cheek, and when his thumb came near Levi's mouth, without thought he sucked it in, swirling his tongue over the digit as he had Jeb's cock.

"You're the sexiest man I've ever met." Jeb's voice was raspy.

Levi wasn't sure what to say to that. Him, sexy? Jeb reached down, pulled Levi to his feet, and attacked his mouth before Levi could deny his words. While it might not be true, with Jeb, Levi did feel sexy and desired and safe. While all of those were important, it was the safety that meant the most to Levi. His trust with his dad and mom had taken a major hit, and he knew nothing about Phillip. Even Noah was definitely out. Levi needed Jeb more than he could let him know.

By the time Jeb released his mouth, Levi was gasping, his nerves afire. Jeb ran his finger over Levi's nipple, then pinched hard.

"Shhhhit." Levi went up on his toes.

Jeb, the bastard, chuckled. "Like that, huh?" Then he pinched his other nipple.

Levi moaned, the sound swallowed by Jeb who dove in for another mauling of Levi's mouth. Levi tried to be quiet because he had not one, but two dads sleeping in the cabin. That should have terrified him, but he couldn't stop, couldn't halt the burning heat building in his gut. The heat that told him what he wanted, forced him to utter the words, "I want you to fuck me."

Those words seemed to drive Jeb harder. He didn't stop kissing Levi, didn't halt to question his decision, hopefully wanting it as badly as Levi did. And while the thought of getting that large cock up his ass scared him, he buried that fear. To lose his virginity to someone he cared deeply for, even if that someone didn't feel the same for him, was right. Levi wasn't going to back down now.

"I saw something we can use in the bathroom. Luckily, I have a condom in my wallet." Jeb moved away to get the stuff.

Fuck, Levi hadn't even thought of any of that. He would have let Jeb fuck him into next week without a condom. Stupid.

Levi lay back on the bed and grasped his cock, which had been desperate to be touched. He licked his palm and stroked his shaft several times.

"Fuck, that's hot." Jeb crawled onto the bed. "Gotta have some of that." He smirked. "I also found a stash of condoms in the bathroom."

Levi wondered for a second who they belonged to and then decided he didn't care.

Jeb turned around and placed his knees on either side of Levi's head, his cock hanging over Levi's mouth. He would have sucked on that luscious shaft; however, his brain short-circuited with the wet heat of Jeb's mouth on his dick.

"Oh shhhhhit, J-Jeb." Levi's hips bucked of their own volition. He clamped his eyes shut, caught in the overwhelming sensation flooding his groin, curling into his belly, and tightening his balls. Blindly reaching up, he grasped Jeb's cock and stroked it, while he rolled Jeb's balls in his other hand. When he opened his eyes, the pleasure in his groin had evened out enough so he could think.

He ran his hands over Jeb's ass, squeezing the round globes. Jeb jerked when Levi's thumb lightly crossed his hole. Levi wondered if Jeb would ever allow Levi to venture there. For now, he concentrated on sucking Jeb's cock and fondling his balls, loving the smell of Jeb surrounding him, reveling in the weight of his body on him.

Levi was lost in the pleasure when Jeb's wet finger pushed into him. Levi's body tensed automatically. Jeb released his cock. "Just relax." Levi tried to focus what little brainpower his big head had left. When Jeb took his cock back into his mouth and rubbed his thumb over his taint, Levi groaned wantonly and squirmed. With the crook of Jeb's finger, stars exploded behind Levi's eyes, and he gasped.

"Fuck." He heard a muffled chuckle from Jeb. He wasn't going to last much longer if Jeb did that again. "Don't or I'll come."

Of course, Jeb did it again, and Levi almost bucked Jeb off. Two fingers in, and Levi couldn't keep his mind on sucking, so he stroked Jeb's cock as Jeb fucked his hole, adding another finger. Levi hissed with the burning stretch. Jeb stopped moving and released Levi's cock from his mouth. "You okay?" Jeb didn't pull his fingers out, which was good because Levi wasn't sure if he'd let them back in.

Panting. Levi concentrated on slowing his breathing. "Yeah. It's just...."

"I know."

That caught Levi's attention. He knew as in he'd been fucked?

Jeb sucked Levi's cock and pushed fingers in and pulled them out with increasing speed. The burn started to diminish, and the stirrings of pleasure crept in. Not too bad, he thought, his breath hitching as Jeb hit that spot again. He couldn't wait any longer.

"Fuck me, now." Levi bucked Jeb off in one surprisingly smooth motion. Jeb got onto his knees. He ripped open the condom wrapper with his teeth. He rolled the latex down his cock, then liberally greased his sheathed cock with lubricant. Of course there would be lube there if Phillip was gay.

"If it gets painful, well, after the initial pain, tell me."

Initial pain. Levi knew the pleasure wouldn't come first. He wasn't sure why he'd begged for it, until Jeb started to suck him again, his pace increasing, until Levi grasped his head ready to unload his cum. That's when Jeb pulled off.

Struggling to catch his breath, Levi said, "Bastard." But he was ready to beg for Jeb's cock again.

Levi was unsure how to position his body. On his hands and knees? On his back? Should he ride Jeb? Levi was more nervous than he'd been seconds ago when he'd been ready for Jeb to stuff his cock into his ass.

Jeb, being the helpful Boy Scout he was, instructed Levi to lie on his back. He shoved a pillow under his ass. Jeb knelt between Levi's legs. Bending down, he placed his elbows on either side of Levi's head. Levi tensed expecting Jeb to shove his cock in, but Jeb kissed him slowly, languidly, rubbing their cocks together, thrusting gently. Levi wrapped his arms around Jeb's neck, his fear dissipating as the heat of their cocks touching spurred his hips upward. Jeb moved his lips to Levi's ear. "Can't wait to get inside you and feel you around my cock," he whispered, then bit down on Levi's neck.

Levi moaned. "Yes. Now."

Reaching between them, Jeb positioned his cock at Levi's entrance, continuing to suck on Levi's neck. When Jeb's cockhead started to stretch his muscle, Levi's entrance clamped shut.

"Push out against me and try to relax. It'll hurt at first, but just keep pushing until I'm inside. Okay?"

Levi nodded, trying to concentrate on relaxing. As he pushed, the head popped inside. The pain was immense, as if he'd rip apart at any second. Levi gripped Jeb tight, panting through the burn. Fuck, he hoped Jeb was right and that log splitting him in half felt good soon.

Jeb didn't move any farther. He kissed Levi and ran his hands through his hair, massaging his scalp. "I can't believe I'm inside of you. You're perfect." He kissed along Levi's jaw. Incrementally, Levi felt his body relaxing around the intruder. He experimented, bearing down and drawing in more of the shaft.

Searing pain flared again. "Wait."

Jesus, he wondered why anyone did this more than once. Had to be one hell of a payout in the end. Slowly, the pain eased, and Levi nodded to Jeb. With short staccato thrusts, Jeb worked his way farther inside, until his balls were touching Levi's skin. As he relaxed, Levi found some pleasure in having Jeb's cock in his ass, especially when Jeb latched on to his nipple. When Levi moaned, Jeb pulled out slowly and back in deliberately. The slide of Jeb's hardness against his muscle drew a hiss from Levi. Still, his ass couldn't decide to push the intruder out or allow it to stay. So far in was winning as Levi focused on relaxing. Would the discomfort ever end?

Jeb began a steady rhythm. Levi focused on the not-so-strange feeling of Jeb filling him up. Jeb hadn't stopped licking and sucking on Levi's skin since he'd entered. When he returned to Levi's lips, their mouths met, deeper and more passionate than any kiss they'd shared.

Jeb increased his pace, creating a swell of pleasure with the pain deep inside of Levi. He wrapped his legs around Jeb's thighs, lifting his ass to meet the thrusts, coaxing Jeb harder and farther. Levi groaned, his nerve endings completely overwhelmed. The small tingle in his groin expanded, swelling, and with the way Jeb's stomach rubbed over his cock, he was going to come.

"Feels so good."

"Hell yeah." Jeb pistoned his hips, his breaths shallow and jagged.

Between them, Jeb grasped Levi's cock, and Levi groaned with the dual pleasure. Jeb bit down on Levi's nipple, the pain spiking down into his groin. With one well-placed thrust, Levi grunted, then came, spasms jerking his muscles as his ass clamped down tight. Not long after, Jeb moaned, burying himself to new depths inside of Levi, emptying into the condom.

Levi let his legs fall to the bed, exhausted and sated unlike any orgasm in the past. Jeb kissed along Levi's jaw and cheeks, his chest heaving. Levi kept his eyes closed, floating in the warmth of the euphoric orgasm. Jeb's tender kisses completed the heavenly bliss, and Levi drifted off to sleep.

THAT BLISS was short-lived. Levi closed his eyes, and the next time he opened them morning had come. He sat next to Jeb on the couch, awaiting his doom. Thankfully, Jeb held his hand. Levi was terrified, but he did his best to hide his fear from everyone. Hank stood by the front door, the crystal hanging from his hand. With nothing to effectively block the crystal's energy, the next best thing was to take it far enough away to lose its effectiveness. Essentially that meant Hank was going outside and then across the yard. Wouldn't take much distance to stop the crystal's protection. Levi's stomach rolled in his gut. He hadn't eaten breakfast—something about an empty stomach being a good idea.

Phillip's reassurance that revealing his soul wouldn't kill him—even if he felt like dying—wasn't comforting. Once the horrid unveiling was done, Levi would be a whole human being once again. Levi wasn't sure why that thought scared him most. What if he wasn't the same person? What if it changed him?

"Hey, I'm right here. We'll get through this and then get Logan back." Jeb smiled gently, and Levi faked his in return.

Where would the lack of their connection leave them? Levi drew up images of earlier that morning. Of waking with Jeb wrapped around him, of Jeb's protests Levi would be too sore for sex, of crawling under the covers, mauling Jeb's hard cock, of pulling Jeb on top of him, wrapping his legs around his waist. Levi had needed the closeness, the desire, the bliss once more before they lost the influence of the crystal.

Their joining had been languorous, with gentle thrusts, neither rushing to orgasm. Faces inches apart, looking into Jeb's eyes, Levi had felt exposed and vulnerable, and connected. Gradually, Levi's orgasm had built while Jeb's gaze had been unwavering. After coming down from the high, Levi had become restless, needing to know what Jeb was thinking, what he was feeling. But how could he force Jeb to focus on him? He'd lost his son—again—and Levi didn't want to be selfish. God, how did people do this relationship crap? No wonder they acted like crazy psychos when they were in love.

Art sat on the coffee table in front of Levi, bringing him back to the present. "How're you doing?"

Levi blinked. "I'm… I don't know really." He surveyed his dad's face. The lines around his mouth and eyes were more pronounced, the strands of gray in his black hair more noticeable. Levi hadn't spent this much time with his dad, ever. "I'll be okay. How're you doing yourself?"

Art sucked in a breath, as if he hadn't expected Levi to ask. He was close to Logan, as close as Levi was to his brother. He had to be suffering and terrified over his kidnapping.

"Logan will be okay, Dad. I know it."

Art's grief escaped for a moment, and then he was back to his controlled self. "You boys…. You mean the world to me. I didn't hesitate in marrying your mother and taking you both as my own. I'm proud to be called your father."

Levi looked into his grayish-blue eyes, a bit darker than his and Logan's. He *was* their father, always had been there when it counted most.

"Same here, Dad." Levi touched his father's work-weathered hand.

Art cleared his throat. "We'll be right here. I won't let anything happen to you."

Levi was surprised he believed every word. He'd been sure his trust in his father had been destroyed.

Unsure if he wanted to know, Levi was surprised when he asked, "What's going to happen?"

His dad's hesitation told Levi it would be nothing good. "Hank will leave with the crystal, allowing Jeb's symbol to do what it was intended. Phillip doesn't have the books here to reverse any other way."

"Would it be less painful?" He was all for less pain.

Art touched Levi's knee. "Yes. You can wait on this, Levi."

He already knew the wait would be greater than he wanted. "No. I want to get this over with."

"Okay, Phillip can help the process go much faster."

Levi remembered the vision he'd had of Phillip, touching his forehead. Shit, he'd seen the future. He looked to Jeb. "This was our vision."

"I remember." Jeb lifted Levi's hand to his mouth and kissed the back of it.

"It'll be okay, Levi. You're a strong man." Art smiled, and Levi hoped that was true.

Noah came into the living room holding a fleece blanket, stopping to talk to Hank. Levi didn't even know the man could hold a conversation he'd been so quiet.

Levi leaned closer to Art. "Does Noah need to be here?" he whispered. He was about to embarrass himself to the high heavens, probably cry, even scream. He didn't need an audience. Art looked to the men across the room. Noah had been cold to Levi since their talk the day before. He shouldn't be there at all. But it seemed Phillip wanted him around.

"We need him. Things might get rough." And that was all Art said.

"You okay?" Jeb asked.

Levi nodded and boldly leaned in and kissed Jeb.

Pulling back, Jeb licked at his lips. "I'm right here to help. I'm not going anywhere."

"Thanks."

Levi's leg shook. Fear pulsed with each heartbeat and threatened to strangle him. Sweat popped out over his skin even though he felt cold.

Phillip finally came over, and he and Art both pulled out pocketknives and started to cut fleece blankets into long pieces. When they were done, Art circled behind the couch where Noah joined him. Phillip stepped in front of Levi. Behind him, Art lowered a twisted piece of the fleece blanket in front of him and stretched it across his chest.

"Lift your arms," Art said.

Confused, Levi did as he was told. Art pulled the blanket under his arms and over the back of the couch where he gripped one end. Noah gripped the other end.

"Why're you doing that?"

Jeb reached over and touched his cheek, taking his focus away from the others. Those dark brown eyes pulled Levi in. "Like Art said, it's going to get rough. If they tie you down with rope, you'll hurt yourself fighting. Hopefully, this way, we can keep you safe."

Levi watched Phillip tie his ankles together with a piece of fleece. It was better than rope, but the panic over being bound closed Levi's throat. This was going to hurt much worse than that last time with Jeb. He wanted to back out, but Phillip instructed Hank to leave. There was nothing left to protect Levi from the pain... from Jeb.

His heart rate tripled upon seeing Hank leave the cabin. "No... I can't... do this." Levi tried to get the blanket off his chest, but it was tightened.

"Levi, calm down." Phillip's voice was too gentle, too focused, too soothing.

Jeb cupped Levi's cheeks. "Deep breaths. You can do this. I'm right here."

Levi tried to take a deep breath, but the thought of the pain, of possibly losing who he was overruled Jeb's instructions.

"Jeb...." Levi managed to say between gasps.

"I don't think we should do this." Phillip's face had paled, and he appeared as scared as Levi was.

Jeb's gaze was unyielding. "Levi. It's going to be okay. Stay calm." Levi wanted to listen, but he couldn't hear past his fear of the pain and possible death, of the pressure already building in his head.

"No, it has to be done. Do it quick." Art held the blanket taut. "Before he totally freaks."

"Levi!" Phillip shouted, startling Levi into ceasing his struggle momentarily. "Just remember I didn't want to do this."

"Just do it!" Levi heard his dad shout.

Phillip touched his fingertips to Jeb's forehead, taking Jeb's gaze from him. Grasping for anything, he recalled after Phillip had touched his forehead in the vision everything had gone black. Sweet Jesus, maybe he'd be out for this.

Please knock me out.

Phillip touched Levi's forehead, muttered several undecipherable words, and waited. Maybe taking the crystal away wouldn't be enough. Maybe he'd gotten used to Jeb's symbol. Pain ripped through Levi, negating those thoughts. He heard himself scream from a long way off as if every cell in his body were going to explode.

CHAPTER 25

LEVI CLAMPED his eyelids tight as the pressure in his head grew exponentially. But that was nothing compared to the dagger stabbing into his heart and twisting viciously, over and over. He felt as if he couldn't breathe, but he could hear himself screaming, so he had to be getting air. He struggled to move but was still pinned down. Voices shouted his name, the words morphing into a low drone. A screeching sound swelled in his ears, deadening any noise outside of his head. Even his screams, which echoed through the bones in his head, were muffled.

The tangy, coppery taste of blood filled his mouth and backed up into his throat. He gagged, drowning in his own blood. He wasn't supposed to die from this. White-hot searing pain expanded. Levi prayed for release from the utterly hopeless agony filling his body. He held on to that scrap of his soul that Jeb had woken, held tight to having a life with emotions, a life where he could live and love and laugh and be somewhat fucking normal.

Beneath the screeching, Jeb called to him, demanding he fight back. Levi gritted his teeth, clamping down on the screams, waging the battle of his life, finally fighting for something rather than against it. He fought for his soul.

A blinding light filled the black field behind his closed eyes. The light sparkled and hummed and was as familiar as his own voice, his own thoughts. The humming expanded through his head, tingling and crackling with life and every emotion he'd been denied his entire life. The light was overwhelming, enriched with a rush of feelings, which appeared as colorful entities against the white light. The pain diminished, and his fight lessened. The screeching noise subsided to the dull roar of the blood rushing through his veins.

The strong taste of blood in his mouth roiled his stomach and gurgled up into his throat. He gagged. "Gonna puke."

The pressure across his chest loosened. He leaned forward, heaving until his stomach emptied, horrified he was puking on the floor. A solid hand rested on the back of his neck. When he'd puked out his stomach, intestines, and, he was pretty sure, his toes as well, a cool cloth wiped at his face. With a shaky hand, he took the cloth and buried his face in the cool dampness.

"Here. Clean out your mouth." A cup was placed in his hand. He sipped and swirled the icy goodness around. "Now spit." A small garbage can appeared before him, smelling of putrid stomach acid and blood. Well, at least he hadn't puked on the floor. He swished the cool water and then spit into the can. He drained what remained in the glass, handing it off to someone. A red pile of fabric on the coffee table caught his attention. It was the shirt he'd been wearing now covered in blood, but he couldn't care.

Arms wrapped around him, and he was pulled against a hard chest. The smell was all Jeb, and he burrowed into him, totally wiped out but alive.

"You okay?" Jeb whispered in a shaky voice, rubbing his chin over the top of Levi's head.

Levi exhaled. He didn't hurt anywhere, except for the rawness in his throat. He didn't feel any different except… there was something he couldn't name yet in his chest and his head.

"Good. Tired."

"Get some rest. We don't have to leave for another couple of hours."

Levi couldn't have stayed awake if he tried.

LEVI'S FIRST thought when he woke: *Is it over?* His second thought was that he'd been run over by a truck.

His entire body ached as if he had the flu. He recalled throwing up, but had the horror ended with him having his soul back? When he shifted, a hand squeezed his shoulder. When he opened his eyes, his head pounded. When he tried to sit up, his chest ached, and he rubbed at the soreness. Jeb was no longer with him on the couch. Art knelt before him and helped Levi to sit up. As he rose, the room dipped and spun, then settled. Levi looked around the room but didn't see Jeb. He tried not to read anything into his absence.

"How do you feel?"

"My body hurts. Feels like someone punched me in the chest, but I'm okay. Did it work? I mean, is it done?" Because if it wasn't and he had to go through that again, he'd live without a soul, thank you very much.

"Done and over," Art said.

Phillip and Noah stood off to the side. Noah's frown of disgust was something he didn't need. Phillip's look of skeptical anticipation made Levi feel as if he should say something but….

A crushing sadness washed over Levi, followed by fear swelling in his chest, pushing outward. The intensity encompassed every part of him, physical pain as well as emotional, and that pain had a name—Logan.

"We have to get Logan." Levi was near panic. His eyes stung, and he couldn't believe he was going to cry. He sucked in a breath, wanting it all to stop.

Jeb came in from the kitchen. Levi smiled upon seeing him. If not for the frown on Jeb's face, he would have leaped up and ran to him. "What's going on?" he asked, looking between Phillip and Art.

Phillip's expression remained neutral but tinged with concern. "Now that your soul is unmasked, you're experiencing the full brunt of your own feelings and emotions for the first time ever. They may get… intense until they even out."

"Seriously?" Levi wasn't sure if he wanted to feel this deeply, with such clarity, absent of the echoing ghostlike emotions of the past. Shit, if this was how people felt every day, how did they make it through the day? "I've felt emotions for the past few days, but…." Art nodded, but the concern never left his face. "It was nothing like this."

"What you were feeling was real. They were your emotions but on a lower level since Jeb's symbol still affected you. The crystal blocked out the majority of the energy. You'll adjust, and from this day on you're a normal guy who…."

Phillip's voice faded, and Levi's vision blanked out into a field of gray. When it cleared, he was no longer in the cabin but a large room that looked like a basement. The windows were small rectangles near the top of the walls. The floor was concrete painted gray. In the air was a musty smell.

Jeb stood in the middle of the room, his usual scowling sneer replaced by what looked like a combination of fear and mortification… and maybe even hope. His eyes were on Dr. Winston. Other people were in the room but were hazy and unrecognizable. Dr. Winston's eyes blazed with fury as she threw something into a bowl on the table before her. The action sent out a blast that hit Jeb, throwing him across the room. His head smashed into a metal pole, the crack of bones filling the air, and then he crumpled to the floor. Rushing to Jeb, Levi dropped to his knees over Jeb's lifeless body. Blood pooled beneath his head. His eyes were open, fixed in a vacant stare. His chest was still. Dead. Levi's thoughts whirled. He was going to throw up. He tried to reach for Jeb, to help him, but he couldn't no matter how hard he tried. Opening his mouth to shout for help, nothing came out. Grief as big as an ocean smashed into him.

Opening his eyes, fingers snapped before Levi's face, and he was back in the cabin. He blinked repeatedly.

"Hey. You back?" Phillip knelt before him.

Levi glanced up, grateful to see Jeb very much alive. Levi swallowed hard. "Yeah… yeah." He shuddered and wrapped his arms around his stomach and bent over.

"What did you see? It was a vision, right?" Phillip asked.

Yes, another vision, and Levi knew he'd seen Jeb's "fate." The vivid clarity of the scene and resulting emotions roiled Levi's stomach again, but he didn't have anything left to throw up. Jeb's death had been as real as anything he'd ever experienced. Nothing like thinking you'd lost someone to clarify how you felt about them.

"You have to teach me how to block them," Levi whispered, hating the pleading tone in his voice.

Phillip pulled him into a hug that Levi wanted to fight, but he didn't. "I'm so sorry. I didn't want this for you."

With that, Levi pulled away. He'd asked for it, right?

"Who did you see?" Art asked. Not *what* but *who* since that was one of his gifts, right? To see people's fates.

Levi looked up at Jeb, who was standing off to the side. Levi wondered why he wasn't coming to him.

"You."

Levi's pain wasn't only emotional but physical, seeing Jeb dead. He was sure if he looked down he'd see his own heart spilling out onto the floor.

Jeb's eyes widened. He paled slightly, but then his expression turned neutral. His lips thinned. "Hope it was quick."

"Don't say that!"

"Didn't you say that a vision isn't written in stone?" Noah had interjected a bit too enthusiastically. "Phillip, you said that what you see can be changed, right?"

"Sometimes. Tell me what you saw."

Levi told them about Dr. Winston, the bowl, and the explosion that caused Jeb to be thrown across the room. Levi would never forget the sickening thud of his head connecting with the metal. An ache pulsed steadily in his chest, something past want, past desire, past lust where Jeb was concerned. How had he let himself get so attached?

"Do you think she was purposefully trying to hurt Jeb?" Art asked.

Levi didn't have to think twice and nodded.

"Okay, so we keep her from accessing any of her spells," Jeb stated as if there wasn't any other option.

"*You* can't go." Levi couldn't watch him die.

"Hell yes, I'm going. She's been lying to me since I met her. She could be the person responsible for killing my family, my…." Jeb swallowed hard. "For killing my son." Jeb's anger and hate marred his expression, twisted his lips, turned his eyes dark. "I don't care what you saw. I'm going, and I'm going to make her pay for what she did."

Levi didn't say anything more. Jeb's goal for the last two years had been finding his son. Knowing he was dead had turned that to revenge. Levi knew he wouldn't back down, not even for him.

"She will pay, but with judgment from the council. We aren't vigilantes." Art's imposing stature punctuated his statement.

Not swayed, Jeb pointed his finger at Art. "Screw the fucking council. I don't give two shits about them. They took my son's soul. And when he was taken and killed the council did nothing, didn't even come to me after it happened. Maybe if you had, you would have seen the symbol on my chest and maybe my son wouldn't be dead! They have your son, Art. What if he's dead? What if they killed him? Would you stand by and do nothing but drag them before the council?"

Levi's knees went weak thinking of Logan dead. Another wave of fear and grief, and he fought to lessen the attack.

Art visibly clenched his jaw, the muscles bulging from the pressure. "I'd kill the fuckers."

Jeb nodded resolutely. "Then we have an understanding."

If Jeb exacted revenge, nothing good could come from the act. Nothing would bring his son back, and nothing he said would change the grieving man's mind. But still he had to try. Still had to keep him from crossing that line.

"Don't do this, please." Levi wasn't above pleading. "We can find another way. I won't lose you to revenge."

Only a few feet apart, their distance felt as wide as a canyon. He felt as if Jeb were already slipping away from him, those protective walls being reinforced.

"I've been waiting two years for this. You can't ask me that."

Because you don't have the right was what Levi had heard loud and clear in Jeb's tone. Levi didn't have the right because he was only a fling… a convenient fuck. With the crystal gone, his soul restored, Levi's greatest fear had been realized. It was over.

Phillip intervened. "Let's just get the information we need today. My friend texted me and still hasn't heard from his contact yet. He's sure something went wrong. He's going to meet us in Crown Point. The plan we worked out will be put into place. He has backup waiting if we get into trouble." Phillip looked to each of them, and then his gaze landed on Levi. "Are we ready?"

Agreement came immediately from everyone except Levi. Was he ready to face the woman who'd lied to him, deceived him, took his brother? Whether or not he was ready, he couldn't run away, couldn't let Jeb go in there and possibly get killed.

Levi gave a sharp nod. "I'm ready."

"Then let's go." Phillip picked up his hunting rifle and handed it to Art, and they left the cabin.

As they took the path to the boat that would take them to the parking area, Phillip stopped Levi as the others continued. Levi gave Phillip a questioning look. He was silent, his eyes darting around Levi's face. His body appeared stiff, guarded. He rested his hand against the side of Levi's neck, a very fatherly gesture. Art had done just that whenever he had advice to give, or worse, was gearing up to deliver bad news. Whatever Phillip wanted to say, there appeared to be a war raging in his eyes.

"Despite my absence, I've always been looking out for you. I've always known what was going on in your life, always searched for a way to give you the life I never had. I know I hurt you because I left you boys, and Art and your mother hurt you by keeping the truth from you. I can't imagine the anger you feel because of what we did, but…"

A cold breeze pushed at them, and Levi shivered. Phillip squeezed the side of his neck gently, and Levi appreciated the gesture. Phillip's gaze intensified, his eyes pinning Levi where he stood.

"If anything happens… I mean, if you feel as if something is trying to take you over, like fear or anger or hate or… anything too strong…."

What the hell? Levi wanted to back away, but didn't.

"I know it sounds crazy, but the dam, the one your counselor helped you to build…. Did it help you?"

The counselor who wasn't really a counselor but someone who'd been hired to help keep his soul hidden. Levi nodded because it had worked until Jeb had shown up. "You know about the dam?"

"Hey, let's go!" Art shouted from the boat. Levi looked back to see them all staring expectantly. Yeah, and he couldn't miss the glare Noah was giving him.

"That dam can still protect you, keep you in control, hold back whatever you want to hold back. Don't let your anger for me stand in the way. It's not what's important right now. Don't ever doubt that the dam is strong. That you are strong, so use it. Okay?"

Weird conversation. "Okay. I'll remember."

"Good. Good." Phillip smiled wanly. "I know I lost any right to be your dad, but I hope someday you can forgive me and we can have some kind of a relationship."

Levi didn't need to forgive him yet, because he was still a stranger. Before he could answer, Phillip placed a kiss on his head and walked to the boat, leaving Levi to wonder what exactly Phillip had been alluding to.

THE RIDE to Crown Point was silent. Phillip drove his SUV. Art sat in the passenger seat while Jeb sat as far away from Levi as was possible on the back seat. The chasm between them had grown. Jeb had shut down completely, distanced himself from Levi. What Levi didn't know was the reason why. Was it because of the vision of his death, or had Levi's premonition of the crystal being responsible for Jeb's interest been true? Either way, Jeb felt totally lost to him, and that was as good as a physical ache in every cell of his body. Fuck the emotions. He'd like a bit of happiness, please.

As they turned onto the road heading to the house, Levi concentrated on breathing and suppressing his fear. With his emotions having a mind of their own, he didn't want to be submerged in them and be useless. Whatever happened, he had to focus enough to get Logan out and keep Jeb safe.

With that thought, he was thrown back into the vision. This time he was carrying something heavy, running from the basement. He could see Phillip and Art, but not what he carried. What was so important that he'd leave them all… leave Jeb? Again, Jeb's fate played out with the same results.

Levi startled hard in his seat, gripping at his thighs. He blinked rapidly, forcing his eyes to focus.

Jeb glanced at him, frowning, and then his face softened. "Are you okay?"

As if he really cared.

Levi nodded curtly, desperate for Jeb to open up, say he cared, say that what was between them had been real. A simple question could give him some peace of mind, but Levi couldn't bring himself to speak. That was his loss. And that would be the only thing he'd be losing. He'd make sure Jeb didn't die. He meant something to Levi. More than he should.

Since Dr. Winston didn't know they were on to her deception, Jeb and Levi would go in first. Phillip and Art would meet up with Phillip's friend. Levi and Jeb would try to uncover what Dr. Winston was up to. The cavalry would arrive shortly after they'd entered. Hopefully they wouldn't be too late.

Phillip and Art got out by the road where Jeb took the driver's seat and Levi the passenger.

Phillip leaned into Levi's window. "As we planned, we'll meet up with Hank and Noah after they scout out the back of the house. My friend will come in from the lake side, with backup at the ready. Stall Dr. Winston until we can find a way in. If this woman is a Seer, she'll immediately know that you have your soul back. Say anything to keep her busy. If she doesn't notice your soul, then find out anything you can without tipping her off."

"Okay." Levi touched Phillip's hand, and he smiled.

When Phillip moved away, Art leaned in and kissed Levi on the forehead. "Be safe, and don't do anything stupid."

Levi chuckled nervously. Doing something stupid was his trademark. "Yes, Dad."

Art stepped away, and Jeb drove up the dirt driveway. Overgrown trees brushed against the sides and roof of the car. Jeb parked in front of the old colonial-style house, which could be seen from the main road. As a child, Levi had been convinced the spooky house was haunted. Now, he prayed Logan was behind its aged walls. If he wasn't....

"Come on." Jeb put the SUV into park, avoiding looking at Levi. They exited, and when they met in front of the car, Levi grasped Jeb's wrist. Jeb's scowl didn't put Levi off.

"Jeb, I—"

Jeb gently removed Levi's hand from his wrist, only increasing Levi's agony. "I can't do this right now." Was that regret Levi saw in his eyes?

"Well, I can. No matter what happens in there, you're walking out alive, and then you *will* talk to me." Levi left Jeb where he stood and stalked to the front door.

Before he could knock, the door opened. A man no taller than Levi with shorn black hair gestured them inside. What he lacked in height he made up for in girth. His biceps stretched the arms of his button-up blue shirt. Definitely there for muscle, which made Levi even more nervous. Once Dr. Winston saw Levi, she would know he'd gotten his soul back—if she was a Seer—and hopefully Phillip and Art would get inside quickly.

They entered a large living room to the left, which matched the colonial style of the house. Dr. Winston stood alone in the middle of the room before a table filled with bowls and herbs, candles and crystals. They weren't in the room where Jeb had died. Something wasn't right, but Levi couldn't say anything to Jeb. The muscle who'd let them in stood off to the side, with a menacing glare, as if that wasn't cliché. Levi wondered if it was just the two of them.

When Dr. Winston saw them, she exhaled noisily and smiled. "Thank the gods you're both okay." She circled the table and raised her arms.

For the first time, Levi could see her smile wasn't quite as sincere as he'd previously thought. When she hugged him, Levi cringed but didn't react. He faked a smile as she stood back and looked him over. She didn't say a word. She had to see that his soul had been returned, right? Phillip had assured him that even the lowest level Seer could. He needed her to be a Seer who was trying to help him, negating their suspicion of her. If not, then she'd played him, and the resulting vulnerability was something Levi didn't want to feel.

Levi glared at her but quickly schooled his features. Jeb didn't flinch, not even a muscle, upon seeing her lack of reaction to Levi.

"On the phone you said you knew Logan's location." Jeb's level tone was impressive given the anger he had for the woman. The neutrality in his expression reminded Levi that Jeb didn't let others see what he didn't want them to see. And that gave Levi hope. Possibly he was hiding what he felt for Levi… or maybe not.

"I have located Logan." She gathered items from the table.

Levi covertly wiped his sweaty palms on his pants. "Where is he?" Levi was frustrated by her lack of answers and attention. Why hadn't she mentioned seeing his soul?

Before she could answer, Jeb asked, "Who has him?"

She seemed rattled for a moment but gathered herself. "A radical group called the Righteous."

Levi hoped she truly was trying to help.

"I know who they are," Jeb said succinctly.

Her gaze snapped to Jeb. "Then you know what they stand for."

Jeb dipped his chin, confirming he did. Other than that, he hadn't moved, not even a twitch. His gaze never left her face. The tension between them filled the room. Jeb seemed to be freaking her out.

Levi moved closer to the table to get her attention. "They're a powerful group of people who hate those who don't have souls, and Seers and Keepers as well." He increased the distress in his voice, wanting her to focus on his fear. "They want me, don't they? That's why they have Logan, isn't it? What're they going to do to me?"

She appeared to be contemplating her response, and then her face pinched and soured with what appeared to be disgust. "Those lunatics aren't as powerful as they would have people believe. They're motivated by hate, by their misguided beliefs that Seers and Keepers are tools of evil for removing souls. They believe that those without souls should be dead." Disgust morphed into a grin that rocked Levi's hope for her innocence. "I have to agree."

Levi sucked in a breath. "What?"

"All in good time."

Jeb took a few steps closer to her. "You're with the Righteous?" Levi could see revenge brewing in Jeb's dark eyes. If he did anything rash, Levi might never get Logan back.

"You'll know soon enough. Now, how about you both sit and wait for our guest to arrive?" Her gleeful sneer sickened Levi.

Jeb raised his brow. "Guest?"

"Come now, Jeb, don't play dumb with me even though you're an idiot." Levi had never heard a harsh word spoken by the professor.

Jeb no longer hid his scowl behind his neutrality.

She looked to Levi. "Your father, of course. Well, the biological one. This has been a long time coming, and I'd like to thank you for leading Phillip right to me. We have unfinished business."

Levi couldn't have been more stunned if she'd told him she was an alien from the Andromeda galaxy.

"My father? What do you want with him? And where the hell is Logan?"

Rage covered her face in the blink of an eye. "I'm in charge, and I'll tell you what I want when I want!" Her screech ran right through Levi. He glanced at Jeb with a what-the-fuck look, which Jeb returned.

Dr. Winston ran a hand over her hair, then rested her hands on the table. Levi believed she was one freak-out from the looney bin. She'd always been so together, so rational. Really, if she was behind all of this, then it shouldn't be hard to end it right there given her instability. When she looked up, she'd returned to the calm and collected person Levi had known.

"Where your brother is doesn't matter. Maybe he's dead."

Levi growled and went after her, but Mr. Cliché grabbed him and threw him back. That incited Jeb into action, and the men went at it until Dr. Winston threw something into a bowl. The resulting pop stopped them both. In that moment, the man drew out a gun and pointed it at Jeb.

"Enough! I won't have some grunt messing with my plans." Dr. Winston pointed at Jeb, those annoying bangles clanging with each move. Yeah, Levi wanted to make her eat those. "Besides, Jeb you're not really that important to my plans, but Levi, Phillip, and oh, someone quite important to you, Jeb, are."

Jeb's snort was loud and amused. "Everyone I care about is dead or already in this room."

Levi's stupid heart jumped at that admission.

"Don't count your chickens, Jeb. No time like the present." Dr. Winston smiled the smuggest smile Levi had ever seen. "Sophia, can you bring our little prince in here?"

A door to the left opened, and a woman with short black hair entered the room carrying a toddler, a boy with dark curly hair and huge brown eyes who looked to be around two or three. When the child saw Jeb, he smiled with delight. "Daddy! I want my puppy."

If words could have struck someone dead, Levi was sure Jeb would have dropped right there. In fact, Levi was sure Jeb had quit breathing all together until he gasped, "No."

The fear on his face was an expression Levi had never thought he'd see on the stoic and fearless man.

"Jeb, meet your son, Connor."

CHAPTER 26

LEVI DIDN'T know what to think. Could this really be the presumed dead Connor? Or was Dr. Winston trying to control Jeb with something she knew he couldn't sacrifice? And how would he even know to call Jeb "Daddy"?

"You're lying! My son was kidnapped by the Righteous and killed!"

Her cackle filled the air. "Kidnapped by the Righteous, but not killed. I should know. I told them where to find him, then took him before they could harm him."

"Daddy, my puppy." Connor looked to Sophia who smiled and nodded.

Jeb stared at the child, speechless, face quickly paling, hands twitching at his side. He regained himself and glared at Dr. Winston. "I'll fucking kill you for trying to pull this shit on me."

Dr. Winston gave a mock gasp as she ran a hand over the fake Connor's thigh. "Such language. You don't want to teach your son such naughty words now, do you?"

"Want Copper." Connor looked to the floor as if hoping to see the puppy there.

"Your daddy will get Copper soon if you're a good boy," Sophia said, and Connor grinned. What was the deal with the dog?

Jeb didn't respond. His face twisted with confusion and anger until he looked at the boy whose eyes were wide. Jeb schooled his features and appeared less scary.

"He's not my son. He was taken as a baby. He doesn't even know me." Jeb's lips had barely moved as he'd gritted the words out.

"And yet he appears to know you're his daddy. Let's see. Maybe a story is in order. Once upon a time, a Seer I'm acquainted with—" She paused and her brow raised. "Do you know how hard those Seers and Keepers are to find? Being a professor certainly has its perks. Say you need anything in the name of research and advancement, and people will fall for anything. You know once I got my hands onto a Seer, I held on to him. Threatened his family or something." She waved her hand dismissively. "Anyway, this Seer had a vision, a very important vision about the birth of a boy, a very special boy."

Levi glanced between Connor, intent on calling Jeb "Daddy," and Jeb, caught between disbelief and hope and "kill the bitch" anger.

"This is your son, Jeb. He's a rare type of Keeper born on a powerful nexus of energy. He has the innate powers of a Keeper and the ability to harness the power of souls he doesn't even hold. With this concentrated power, he can open gateways and bring forth powers locked behind other dimensions."

Levi grimaced. "What have you been smoking?"

Dr. Winston's head snapped around, and her icy glare wiped the grimace from Levi's face. Fuck, she could be scary.

"You doubt me?" She stomped to Levi, bangles jingling, sneer widening. "Others have doubted me, and believe me…." She was right in front of him, face inches from his, eyes narrowed. "It didn't work out too well for them."

"Hey!" Jeb's shout caused Dr. Winston to turn toward him. "I don't care who you think this kid is. He's. Not. Mine."

"Of course he's your son. But if you won't believe me, maybe you'll believe someone else. Get them downstairs."

Mr. Cliché and Sophia, with the supposed Connor, herded them toward a hallway while the kid said, "My daddy. He got my puppy."

Behind the door was a set of stairs going down. Levi swore he could hear Jeb's teeth grinding as they descended. Levi had to admit the kid resembled Jeb, but then it shouldn't be too hard to find a kid with dark curly hair and brown eyes. To get him to call Jeb daddy had to take some work. Levi was sure the promise of that puppy had helped.

At the bottom of the stairs, they entered the room Levi had seen in his vision. Metal pole and all. He was close to freaking out. It was pretty clear Dr. Winston wasn't planning to have tea with them. They needed help. Where were his dad and Phillip?

As they moved farther into the room, Jeb stopped quick. "Milo?"

In the corner, Milo was tied with a myriad of ropes to a wooden chair. A large man stood behind Milo as if he might escape. Milo's face was a mass of dark purple bruises. Dried blood was crusted at the corner of his mouth and around his nostrils.

"I-I'm sorry, Jeb. She made me do it. I didn't want to…. From the beginning, I tried to stop her."

Dr. Winston raised her hand, and Milo cowered like an abused dog. "Tell him right now." Milo's entire body visibly shook. What had he done to incur her wrath?

Milo seemed hesitant, but another threat from Dr. Winston and he spilled. "He's Connor. He's your son. I've taken care of him since he was taken from your house. He's such a special boy, powerful. She made me show him pictures and videos of you so he'd know who you were. I had to tell him when you came you'd bring his dog, Copper, that she made up." Milo choked on his words, his eyes becoming glassy. "She made sure that he knows who you are so you... so you would do what she says." His eyes widened. "But you have to stop her before she—"

With a backhand from Dr. Winston, blood flowed from Milo's lip again. "Shut your mouth, you fucking traitor."

Promised the kid a puppy to play him. Damn, the lady was pure evil. Levi moved closer to Jeb who stared at Connor again, as if trying to decide if he should believe Milo, believe he finally had his son back. Then it clicked. What Levi had been carrying as he'd fled the room in his vision. Jeb's son. Then Jeb had been killed. Died saving his son. Levi wouldn't let that happen. They desperately needed help. Everything was fucked-up to an extreme.

There was a scuffle in the stairway. Phillip and Art were pushed into the room at gunpoint by a man and a woman, both providing more muscle. Levi wanted to scream at them. Where was the help they were supposed to have? Phillip and Art both froze when they spotted Dr. Winston. Their eyes widened and mouths dropped open.

"Helen!" Art roared.

"Hello, brothers-in-law. Long time no see. Phillip, I see you got my message that your sons were in danger. I knew you'd rush to their aid." She snorted. "Glad to see you have some sense of loyalty to family. Gods know you never showed me any."

Helen? Brothers-in-law?

"Give me my son back!" Phillip's face twisted with his rage, his body tense and ready to react.

The woman behind him must have sensed the same thing. "You take a step, I shoot."

"Aunt Helen?" Levi asked looking to his professor... his relative.

She grinned. "That would be me. It's taken me twelve years to put together this little family reunion. And here we are. Let's not waste any time."

She rounded the table that was covered with the items of her supposed craft—whatever that was. She picked up a bag of blue powder and looked to Milo. "Has his soul been returned?"

Milo glared at her mutinously. "Don't do this."

"Shut up, or I'll kill your sister and your entire family!" That definitely shut Milo up.

"Helen, what in the hell are you doing?" Phillip went to move when Art put up his arm to stop him. Phillip scowled at his brother until Art gestured with a sharp tilt of his head to the woman behind him. Phillip crossed his arms.

"Your son is nearby, but you do anything to interrupt my work, and he'll die." Again she looked to her "teaching assistant."

"Milo, answer me. Has his soul been returned?" Helen grabbed Milo's hair and he yelped. Blood covered his chin, dripping onto his shirt. He looked like the victim of some horrible accident.

Milo nodded, resignation and regret crossing his face.

"So you really aren't a Seer." Why was that fact so hard for Levi to believe? Because he'd trusted her.

Art growled. "A gold-digging, cheating whore, but not a fucking Seer."

Dr. Winston—Helen—flinched.

"Is that what this is all about? Some lame attempt at revenge because you were forced out of the family after Ray died? Maybe you shouldn't have spread your legs for everyone in town!" Phillip's rage reached out and hit Levi solidly. He grimaced. Something stirred in his chest, something electric and hot.

Levi looked at Phillip, but all of his attention was on the woman who'd been married to his deceased brother. Levi scrambled to think of something, anything to get them out of there. Milo's movements caught his attention. Moving his head to the left, Milo seemed to be trying to tell Levi something. His lips moved, but the swelling made his words unintelligible. It was like a bad game of charades.

"Revenge is so passé. This is about power. Revenge is just a nice side dish."

Art scoffed. "You set all of this up all by yourself? That's surprising since you couldn't even balance your checkbook last I knew." He chuckled and crossed his arms. "No way, Helen. Who're you working for? The Righteous?"

"They're working for *me!*" Helen's bellow bounced around the room, and Levi jumped. Fuck, if his heart beat any faster something was going to blow, an artery, a valve, something.

"What?" Phillip's tone rose with his disbelief.

Helen paced behind the table, wringing her hands. Maybe she'd lose it and.... Well, she'd probably kill them all. Levi shuddered. But Helen appeared to have pulled herself back together as she stepped up to the table. She surveyed the assorted bowls, dried plants, and bags of colored powder. Levi's breath caught in his throat. Déjà vu hit him like a Mack truck. Helen behind the table, the silver bowl, Jeb right where he'd been before.... How could he stop his vision from becoming reality? He watched her intently for the slightest movement toward that silver bowl. In his periphery, he watched Jeb for movement. Levi figured he could tackle him if he tried to go after Helen.

"They're a bunch of idiots who don't know their hands from their asses. Until I came along, they didn't even know about Levi or Connor."

That got Jeb's attention. "You told them about my son. You're the reason my brother and sister-in-law were murdered!"

Levi knew his vision was playing out. "Jeb, no! Dad! Now!" He pointed to Jeb.

"I'm gonna fucking kill you!" He started for Helen. Levi's chest seized, and he froze where he stood. Some fucking hero. The guy behind Milo was fast—really fast—and he tackled Jeb to the ground. Had Levi's shout changed Jeb's impending death? Really, he didn't care. He closed his eyes, as the tension in his muscles let lose.

Jeb bucked the man off and was on top of him in a flash. They threw punches at one another.

"Knock it off!" Helen's shriek went right through Levi and didn't stop the men as they punched and slapped. Art and Phillip stood back and did nothing as Jeb pummeled the man.

"You're ruining my plans!" Helen stomped around the table and went to where Sophia held Connor and grabbed him. Connor started to shriek and howl.

"Don't!" Milo struggled against his restraints, fear for Connor all over his face. "You're hurting him!"

That caught Jeb's attention as Art tried to pull Connor from Helen's arms. "Let go." He grunted as they played a game of tug-of-war with the kid.

Jeb jumped up, but before he could move, the man on the floor lifted his hand. "Freeze!"

"Jeb, he's got a gun!" Everyone turned to Levi, then to the man on the floor. Art released Connor, and whatever Helen was doing to the boy ceased. He whimpered as tears rolled down his cheeks. Poor kid.

"It's about fucking time, David. Get up and do your job," Helen said.

So, Mr. Cliché had a name.

David sneered but got up, gun still drawn.

"If anyone even moves, my dim-witted guard will put a bullet in you."

David grunted. She had to be paying him a shit ton of money to put up with her. Helen shoved Connor back into Sophia's arms.

"Okay. Enough of the nonsense. Phillip, do you know what you get when you sacrifice two rare Seers who are bound to a *Magnificiando*?"

Phillip blanched, and his fear ran through Levi. He was pretty sure he didn't want to know the answer to that question. He had to get to Milo, but the man guarding him wouldn't let that happen. Jeb wasn't available to help, his brown eyes gazing softly on his beautiful son, who called out playfully to Milo. The kid seemed totally unaffected by the situation.

"There hasn't been a *Magnificiando* birth in over a hundred years," Art said. "If there had been, the council would've known. A disruption of energy that large would have been detected by at least one Seer."

Helen smiled so sickeningly sweet that Levi wanted to punch her in the face. "A Seer did predict the birth." She went to Milo, who cringed, eyes intent on Helen, no doubt waiting for the strike. When she patted his bruised cheek, he winced. "Isn't that right Milo? Best investment I ever made." She turned to the room. "I have a penchant for rare and powerful things. And I've spent a great deal of time acquiring them. You and Levi, the *Magnificiando*. And Milo here is a Gemini Seer, half of a whole that includes his twin sister, able to see the future and the past." The surprised expressions on Phillip's and Art's faces said that had to be something important. Levi didn't care if Milo was the Easter Bunny as long as they all escaped.

Helen sneered as she looked down on Milo. "Unfortunately his sister is too feeble minded to use her powers. But Milo here is very capable. He predicted Connor's birth. Luckily, he was under my control when he did. After I convinced the kid's mother that I was a Seer and his flawed soul needed to be saved, she brought him to me, and I blocked his soul, much like you did with Levi's. I didn't want other Seers or Keepers to see what a powerful specimen he is and try to take him. By the way, thanks for that info on hiding a soul."

"I never told you what I did to Levi," Phillip said. His rage had lessened, but anger still pulsated from him.

"No, but Ray did. He even shared your books with me when I told him I was interested in his mother's craft. He never could resist giving me anything I asked for."

"He was a fucking idiot was what he was," Art said of his late brother.

"Can't argue that." She really was one cold person.

"How did you know Levi's soul was still hidden and hadn't been removed? No Seer would know that, even your captive Seer. They would see his lack of a soul and couldn't tell if it had been removed or hidden." Phillip's tone was condescending, and that riled Helen.

"You think I'm stupid, don't you? I know all of that, which is why I used Jeb as my litmus test. Had that symbol carved into his chest with the plan of using him on Levi once I'd lured him to Plattsburgh State."

Levi closed his eyes. "Fuck." Jeb stared at her, not blinking.

"I knew I would use Jeb to get to Levi since they're both faggots."

Jesus, had everyone known he was gay?

Jeb stabbed his finger at her. "Fuck you! I'm going to hold you down and fucking carve you up and listen to you scream!" Jeb didn't go for her, though.

"You'll be dead when I'm done with you." Helen's face twisted in rage. "You're nobody."

"Jeb, please." Levi needed him to remain calm.

"Yeah, Jeb, listen to your boyfriend and shut up."

Levi waited. Jeb didn't move, but Levi could see his rage gaining momentum.

"Now I just need to unmask the kid's soul so I can bind the three of you together. Shouldn't take but a few minutes to get that soul front and center. Then we can move onto the real fun."

She couldn't mean to put Connor through the same hell Levi himself had gone through by returning his soul. He really had to stop her.

"You don't know what you're talking about." Phillip crossed his arms. "All of that is pure myth. There is no *Magnificiando*. Sacrificing the three of us won't get you anything but life in prison."

Jeb's head snapped to Helen, then back to Phillip. "Who're you talking about? Who's a *Magnifan*—whatever you said." The wild look in his eyes scared Levi into thinking Jeb would do something stupid, like get himself killed.

Phillip sighed and ran a hand over his gray hair. "Connor."

CHAPTER 27

JEB CLENCHED his fists at his side. "What about Connor?"

"Helen seems to think he's a *Magnificiando*."

"What is that?" Jeb asked.

Helen snorted but ignored Jeb. "I know he is. Milo can attest to that."

"And why should we trust him? He's lied to me since I met him. He's had my son all this time," Jeb said, scowling at Milo.

"Because I said so! And Milo didn't have your son. I did. He's a *Magnificiando* whether you like it or not."

Jeb looked to Phillip and Art. "What in the hell is that?"

With reluctance Phillip said, "A Keeper, but a very rare one, with the ability to harness a soul's power, even though he isn't holding them. The *myth* is that using that borrowed power, the Keeper can bend the fabric of space and time, opening dimensions, which can bring forth powerful abilities. But it's all a fucking myth." He glared at Helen. "Don't you get it? Not everything in those books Ray gave to you was true. Killing us won't get you what you want."

The way Jeb's muscles twitched, his stance, his enraged expression, Levi knew Jeb was once again going to try something that could get himself killed. And he was right. Jeb charged toward Helen, eyes blazing with fury. "I won't let you hurt my son!"

Helen turned to the table, grabbed something, and raised her hand above a silver bowl. Shit! He'd been wrong. This was his vision unfolding before him. Phillip and Art both lunged, grabbing Jeb as he passed, their bodies crashing together and landing in a pile on the floor. Helen dropped what was in her hand. "Enough of this!" In the chaos, Levi went to Milo.

"You need to get Connor out of here. Phillip's right. What she's doing isn't possible. She's going to kill all of you for nothing."

Levi gaped. He couldn't just flee. Most of his family was there, Jeb and his son, and there were guns. And what about Logan?

"She'll hurt them. I can't...."

Milo's face hardened. "She's going to kill them anyway. If both of you get out of here, she's going to have to look for you. That gives us time to get some fucking help."

Levi clutched at his hair. She needed three of them—Phillip, Connor, and Levi. Now he knew why he'd run with Connor in his vision. And that could end in Jeb's death as well as his father's and Logan.

"Help me think of another way. She hasn't unmasked his soul yet. Maybe I can—"

"Listen to me," Milo said through clenched teeth. "His soul *isn't* hidden. I removed it and placed it with a Keeper I trust. I couldn't let her ever get to it. She's going to do the spell, and she's going to ask me if his soul is back. Either I tell her it's there and you three die, or I tell her it's missing, she loses it, and we all die. There aren't many cylinders firing up there."

Levi was about to agree when someone grabbed his hair. He was yanked away from Milo. He swung out and connected with Helen's arm, but she just pulled harder, bringing tears to his eyes.

She pushed him against Phillip, who wrapped his arm around Levi's shoulder.

Levi's dad knelt on the floor, the large man holding a gun on him. Jeb stood back as Sophia held a knife—a fucking pointy knife—at Connor where he sat on the floor crying.

"It's okay, Connor, sweetie. Don't cry." Jeb's attempts to soothe the kid fell short.

"Stop crying!" Helen grabbed the child roughly off the floor and shoved him into Levi's arms. The toddler screeched and arched his back, and Levi nearly dropped him.

"Connor, buddy, calm down." Levi knew nothing about kids. "I'll buy you a pony if you stop. A race car? Oh wait, a puppy?"

That got his attention. "Puppy! Daddy, my puppy."

"Yes, Daddy has your puppy."

Helen chanted, filling that silver bowl with herbs and crystals and powders. Levi held Connor tight, unable to believe his psycho aunt was really going to sacrifice them for her own greed. Like Milo said, she was a few cylinders short. Someone would end up dying no matter what.

As Art tried to reason with Helen, movement in one of the small basement windows caught Levi's eye. He looked around the room, but no one was paying attention. Looking again, he saw Noah peering in the window. Fucking Noah. Levi took back every bad thought he'd had of him.

Noah held up ten fingers, mouthed some words and then pointed to something in his hand. Levi had no clue what he was doing. He really needed to play charades more often. Holding up ten fingers again, Noah mouthed a word, and Levi thought he'd said, "seconds." Noah covered both of his ears. Levi shrugged. Noah rolled his eyes and started counting down with his fingers. Shit, ten seconds until what?

"Phillip. Something's going to happen," he whispered. "When it does I'm running with Connor. You tackle Jeb. Don't let him get near Helen."

Glass shattered, and Helen stopped chanting and her head whipped around. She spotted Noah and yelled to her minions to stop him. Noah's hand came through the window and opened. Something red with an orange glow fell. Three M80 firecrackers were on the floor, their fuses burning down quickly.

Levi crouched and covered Connor's ears. The ear-splitting pops from the M80s ripped into Levi's, and a high-pitched whine filled his ears. Everyone ducked and fell to the floor. Levi couldn't hear anything, except for Connor's muffled shrieks. He had to get Connor out of there.

Levi wrapped the screaming Connor in his arms and barreled for the stairs. When he reached the top a man staggered into the room. A trickle of blood ran down his temple. Levi froze when the man saw him.

"Stop!"

Levi didn't listen. He ran to the right and threw open the french doors, stumbling onto a stone patio. He bolted down the steps and into the field behind the house, the setting sun lighting his way. His feet sunk in the mud of the boggy soil, and with Connor's added weight, he was going too slow.

"Noah!" Levi had to scream to compete with Connor's terrified wailing.

"Stop!" Over his shoulder he saw the man chasing them.

If he thought Levi was stopping, he was fucking stupid. Ahead of Levi was a copse of trees. The lake wasn't too much farther past that point. He had no idea where he'd go when he got there. He just knew he had to keep running.

In the distance, voices called his name and looking back, he saw the man was gaining on him. Of course, he didn't have a toddler hooked to his hip. Another look behind him, and he saw another person coming behind the goon.

Jeb!

If Levi could just evade the man until Jeb caught up…. But already his legs were getting heavier, and his chest heaved. Connor at least had stopped screaming and was babbling about the puppy again as he was bounced around.

"I'll get you two puppies if we get out of this mess."

Connor clapped and chanted about two puppies. When they reached the stand of trees, Levi tried to avoid going in a straight line. Through the branches and emerging leaves was the grayish-silver of the lake. Soon he'd run out of land. If he went left or right, he'd be back out in the open of the field. Hopefully, Jeb would get to them and be able to stop the man. Then what? What was happening with his dads? He had to focus on keeping Connor safe for Jeb.

As he neared the lake, darkness obscured the ground, causing Levi to trip over rocks and branches, Connor's weight pulling him off-center. He almost fell several times but continued running until his vision grayed. He fell to his knees, and everything went dark.

He saw himself running with Connor, and suddenly there was no ground. They fell into the darkness, their bodies smashing into the rocks at the water's edge below.

Shit!

Levi opened his eyes. His knees were on the edge of the cliff, the rocks barely visible below. He clutched Connor and scooted back, his heart racing and banging against his ribs.

More of a warning next time would be nice, he thought as he wiped a shaky hand over his sweat-soaked forehead. "That was too close."

"Don't move."

The deep voice rattled Levi's nerves. Levi closed his eyes for a moment, then looked over his shoulder. Of course the man who'd been chasing him had a gun. Where was Jeb?

"Stand up and turn around."

Levi set Connor on his feet and then stood facing the man. He took Connor's hand in his.

"Back to the house." He motioned them forward. Levi's legs shook, and his feet wouldn't move. "Now!" The man stepped closer.

Connor started to cry and yanked on Levi's hand, knocking Levi out of his frozen state. He spotted Jeb about a hundred feet away, partially hidden by a tree. If he came out, the man would shoot him. Glancing down at Connor, who screamed and tried to climb his leg, Levi saw a rock near Connor's feet. Just big enough to hurt. Fuck, Levi was the one who was probably going to get shot.

"Calm down, Connor," Levi said, his voice as shaky as his legs.

In the guise of picking up Connor, Levi bent and in one fluid motion scooped up the hefty rock and chucked it at the man who twisted and stumbled. Without hesitating, Levi picked up Connor and sprinted to the right along the cliff. A gunshot rang out, and Levi hit the ground, covering Connor with his body. There were grunts and shouts, and Levi caught sight of Jeb struggling with the man. Both of their hands wrestled with the gun above their heads. Jeb was larger and no doubt stronger, but if he lost the gun he'd lose his advantage. The Fates had failed to show Levi a horrifying vision starring Jeb's death. Levi hoped that was a good sign.

Jeb grunted and swung down, forcing the man to bend at the waist, pointing the gun at the ground. With a sharp jab, Jeb's elbow connected with the man's jaw. He stumbled back, releasing the gun as he did.

There was a shout, and Noah and Hank sprinted from the trees. Jeb held the gun on the man who scowled. Jeb's chest heaved, and a trickle of blood flowed from his nose. Levi stood, and Jeb glanced in their direction, but he didn't look at Levi. He looked to Connor who lay on the ground sobbing for Milo. His face was a blank slate, but Jeb's eyes showed the pain of rejection.

"You guys okay?" Noah yanked the man from the ground and pinned his hands behind his back.

"Yeah." Jeb handed the gun over to Hank who stuffed the weapon into his waistband. From his pocket he pulled out—Levi squinted in the growing darkness—a zip tie. He secured the man's wrist, then relieved Noah of his prisoner. They headed in the direction of the house.

Tentatively, Jeb approached Levi and Connor, but his eyes were focused on his son.

Jeb crouched a few feet away. "Hey, buddy, it's okay. I'm here and you're safe." Jeb's voice cracked, and he cleared his throat. "Remember I'm your d-daddy."

Connor's cries quieted to whimpers, but he didn't move from Levi's side. Jeb held out his arms. Still, Connor eyed him suspiciously, sniffling. Despite the smile on his face, Levi could see Jeb's resignation. "It's okay, buddy. I can take you to Milo."

Connor's lip quivered, and he ran into his father's arms. Jeb's expression of joy and love lifted the corners of Levi's mouth. Jeb crooned to Connor, walking away and leaving Levi on the precipice of sorrow. He rubbed his chest as he watched Jeb getting farther away from him. Apt analogy there. He should be thrilled for Jeb, but Levi couldn't stop the gnawing ache in his chest. The bond created by the crystal was really gone. And damn, didn't that just kick up a storm of emotions from Levi's restored soul?

Noah touched Levi's arm, and he jumped. When Levi looked around, they were alone. "You okay?" Noah asked. "Are you hurt?"

Levi didn't shake off Noah's arm and didn't know why. "Where's my dad and Phillip? Are they okay?"

"Yeah, we were able to get Dr. Winston and her goon squad shut down."

Levi closed his eyes, and his legs began to shake, moving through his body. No matter how he tried, he couldn't stop the tremors.

"Hey, Levi, are you okay? Look at me." Noah tightened his arm around his shoulder.

Why was Noah being so nice to him? Levi was too tired to think about anything. He felt soon he was going to crash hard. The last week was too much. Restoring his soul, a biological father and a psycho aunt, being on the run, their lives in danger, Logan….

Fuck, Logan was still missing, probably being tortured by the Righteous. "Noah, we still don't know where Logan is. She didn't have him. She—"

"I think if you head back into the house, your search will be over."

"What?" Hope fluttered in Levi's chest.

Noah smiled with his entire face. He appeared almost giddy. Levi couldn't deal with Noah's fluctuating moods. He just wanted to see Logan. "He's in the house."

Levi's heart notched up a beat, adrenaline pumping again and chasing away his exhaustion. "He's really here?"

"Go to the house."

Levi sprinted through the trees and into the field where he dashed past Jeb and Connor. He sprinted through the front door and into the large living room, where he skidded to a stop.

What the hell?

CHAPTER 28

MEN AND women dressed in matching white jackets and black pants stood at the edges of the room, guns in hand. The red emblems on their jackets matched the one Phillip had said belonged to the Righteous, almost identical to the one on Jeb's chest.

Levi's fathers were on the large sofa along with Milo, their hands and feet bound before them and mouths gagged. Levi didn't see Logan anywhere. The one person he did see froze the blood in his veins.

The white-haired elderly woman raised her bony finger and pointed at him much as she had when she'd called him *senz-anima*. Her steely gaze cut through to Levi's recently restored soul. If a finger could kill, Levi was sure he'd be a pile of dust.

"Welcome, Levi. I see your soul has been returned. Now you can finally be of use to us."

The woman leveled a harsh, knowing gaze at him, her silver hair neatly gathered at the nape of her neck. She wore a white priest-like robe with the Righteous symbol stitched in red on the front. Levi shuddered as he recalled her prophetic words.

Levi backpedaled but was stopped short when he ran into something... no, *someone*. Noah shoved the gun he held into Levi's back. That was the second time the bastard had pulled a gun on him.

"What're you doing?" He was like a hot and cold running ally.

"Noah, you've done well. You will be highly rewarded for your allegiance to our cause," the woman said, her tone almost loving, a direct opposite to her hard exterior.

Phillip screamed into his gag. His wide eyes narrowed on the man he'd called "son."

"You're with this sick group? What the fuck, Noah?"

"Because people like you and your father are disgusting. You contaminate the world trying to save souls that aren't worthy, fucking up the world for the rest of us." Levi imagined Noah was probably someone who should have had his soul removed.

"You're holding a gun on me, and you think I'm disgusting. You didn't think I was too disgusting when you had your tongue down my throat!" And that thought made Levi want to rinse his mouth out with gasoline.

Noah's face scrunched up as if he'd eaten something rotten. "And I hated every minute of it, but when you're on a mission you may have to lie with the enemy."

"But if you knew where Phillip and I were, why didn't you just kill us? All of this shit with Helen doesn't make sense." Levi looked to Phillip, who apparently had the same thought.

"Death would be too good for you." Noah grinned and pushed Levi back into the center of the room.

Levi tripped and went down hard on his hands and knees in front of Milo. Art and Phillip both struggled against their restraints, muttering through their gags without success. Art's eyes held a murderous rage as he tried to get to Levi. A man behind him held him firmly by the shoulder.

Connor screeching at the top of his lungs took the attention of most everyone in the room. Jeb entered carrying his son. One of the women in white and black held a gun on them. "This one tried to sneak off."

Damn, if Jeb got away he could have brought help, Levi thought.

Jeb took in the scene, and then his gaze fixed on Levi, and he started to cross the room, ignoring the woman's command to stop. The steely determination on his face made Levi's heart jump. Before he could reach Levi, the woman brought her gun down against the back of Jeb's neck. Levi lunged forward as Jeb dropped to his knees. He held Connor tight, though, and Levi sighed with relief that he hadn't dropped him.

"Fool!" The elderly woman pointed to the woman with the gun. "Do not harm that child! He's needed to proceed!"

The woman grimaced slightly and stepped away from Jeb. "Yes, Priestess."

Priestess?

"Jeb, give me Connor," Levi whispered as Jeb swayed on his knees. Levi feared he would pass out and hurt his son. Connor cried harder for Milo. Even mentions of the puppy did nothing. Jeb released his son to Levi willingly. Levi then turned to Milo. Connor jumped into Milo's lap and curled up against him. His fear and confusion no doubt had fueled his fit.

When Levi turned back, Jeb wrapped him in his arms.

"You okay, kitten?" Jeb asked.

In the midst of the danger, Levi relished being in Jeb's arms again. "I should be asking you that." Levi choked on his words, fighting tears. Maybe he meant something to Jeb after all. "Are you bleeding?"

When Levi tried to check the back of Jeb's head, Noah stepped up behind Jeb. "Enough!"

He tried to yank Jeb from Levi, but Jeb turned on Noah and knocked the gun from his hand. Within seconds, he had Noah on the ground, punching him. Swiftly, he was lifted away by a large, bald man and another woman who was small but strong and quick. They both held the struggling Jeb.

Noise filtered up the stairs from the basement. A shriek was followed by Helen entering the room. She struggled against another uniformed woman with short red hair and colorful tattoos crawling up her neck.

When Helen saw the priestess she stopped, her face flushing red, her eyes narrowing. "What're you doing here, old woman? I told you to stay away. I have this under control."

The priestess maintained her stony expression. Her dull gray eyes showed no reaction to Helen's words. "You're not in charge. You almost ruined everything, you stupid woman. *You* are no longer necessary to move forward."

"What? Without me you wouldn't have everything needed for the sacrifice. I'm the one who set everything in motion, who gave you the information about the *Magnificiando*! I'm the one in charge here!"

If the woman's rage grew any higher, Levi thought her head might explode. The bald man stepped toward Helen, but the priestess shook her head, and he ceased moving.

"You, my dear Helen, were nothing but a bit player in a game much larger than anyone in this room. Well, except for myself and Levi."

Levi froze as all eyes focused on him. He was pretty sure her statement didn't mean anything good for him.

"While you may believe you held information I found valuable, I, in fact, knew all of the information you presented me with as well as information no one else in the world is privy to. While you were busy setting events in motion that I needed to occur, I was planning for this day."

She smiled, and the wrinkles gathered in her cheeks and around her eyes. Her appearance reminded Levi of a grandmother who might knit mittens for her grandkids, bake them cookies to spoil their dinners, and sit with them and read books. But apparently looks were deceiving, and this woman was closer to an Italian mob boss. A godmother instead of a godfather.

She pointed to Art and Phillip. "Remove their gags."

As soon as they could, they both let loose a string of threats and warnings.

"Shut the hell up now!" Definitely not grandmotherly.

They obeyed. Phillip regained his composure and spoke. "You can't do this, Concetta. You know this sacrifice is a myth. Sacrificing us will only lead to our deaths and nothing else."

"You can't do this! I made this happen, and I deserve—" Helen was cut off when the red-haired woman covered her mouth.

Levi was stunned. "You know who this woman is?"

Phillip glared. "Concetta was second in charge on the council many years ago, but a difference of opinion caused her to leave. Who knew that difference was just the tip of the iceberg? You're the person we've been fighting all of these years? You lead the Righteous?"

"Created and led."

"You're fighting against your own kind and killing innocent people! We're trying to help people and make the world better!"

Concetta snorted. "A better world, Phillip? Those souls you're supposedly saving through extraction are no cleaner or any less flawed, any less evil, when they're returned. Those inherent flaws are being regenerated through generations, passed along from parent to child, only for that child to pass those flaws and abnormalities on to their offspring. The human vessel doesn't have the ability to influence the makeup of the soul." She raised her hand to the roomful of people. "All human souls are predetermined, fixed in every one of us. No matter how good and respectable that person is, the soul doesn't change."

"That rhetoric was old when you were infecting others with that nonsense," Philip said. "This is about people's lives. You can't just kill them off because you don't like their souls."

Concetta looked down her nose at Phillip with disgust. "You never could see past your own ego. You have always led by your stagnant beliefs, unable to see past what you understood to be true even when others brought different ideas and information to the table. You even allowed your brother, who isn't a Seer or a Keeper, onto the council."

Phillip clenched his jaw, and Levi could see the rage in his eyes. "The humans needed representation. Seers and Keepers were closing themselves off from those they were helping, forming their own ways of doing things, their own rules as if they were gods."

"We're all playing gods, deciding who to extract a soul from and when to return it." Concetta waved her hand at Levi and Connor. "Everyone falsely believes that extracting and then returning a soul to a mature body can nullify what was present at birth. But that discordant energy continues to infect those around them, causing the chaos and instability of the world today. They must be cleansed from the Earth, from ever existing. And I will accomplish this with a creation of your own."

Levi frowned. Phillip's creation…? Oh. Why couldn't they just leave him alone? He was over being their frickin' prize.

"But what you're doing here won't change anything. Even if this sacrifice was valid, the result would only be one person endowed with the power to be an upper-level Seer and Keeper. Nothing more. Nothing to influence and change anything you're talking about." While Phillip's pleas were impassioned and sincere, Levi could tell Concetta wasn't swayed.

Her brow lowered. She placed her hands on her wide hips. "Do you take me for a fool? Of course this sacrifice won't work, and what would I need with such a foolish outcome as that? I won't be sacrificing anyone."

Levi wanted to sigh with relief, wanted to tell every one of his nerves to stand down, but they weren't being held at gunpoint for nothing.

"Then what the hell are we doing here?" Art asked.

Levi's attention was caught by the change in his dad's demeanor. The hard edge to his jaw, the fiery sharpness in his eyes, the rigid resolve, the fierce determination. Even though he was taller than the average man, his dad had never been imposing. Until now. Plain, old predictable Art Reed had been replaced with someone who screamed fuck off. Shit, if he'd pulled that personality out at home, Levi would have scrambled to obey every rule.

Concetta didn't answer Art's question. Instead, she turned and approached one of the men standing along the wall. He held a massive book. She took on the heavy tome, which looked enormous against her small frame. She returned to stand before Phillip and Art. Holding up the book, she silently looked to Phillip until his eyes widened.

"Is that—?" He shook his head, his jaw dropped, his forehead creasing, his jaw tensing.

She gave him a self-righteous smile. "Yes. It's the *Book of Mattavius*. You were dead set against its existence, if you recall. Maybe what you've been taught isn't as accurate as you've boasted."

Levi wanted to listen, but Milo tapped Levi's thigh with his bound legs. Connor was nodding off and leaning precariously close to falling. Milo was helpless to stop the toddler from crashing to the floor. Levi inched closer to Milo.

"Connor, lie down, buddy." Levi coaxed him to shift his position.

Connor gazed at Levi with half-closed eyes and said, "Puppy?" Levi smiled gently and nodded. Being so close, he noticed Connor had Jeb's dark eyes and bow-shaped lips. When Connor held his arms out, Levi picked up the tot. His little arms circled Levi's neck. His head rested on Levi's shoulder. The boy was so small, so vulnerable, and Levi's heart had been stolen already. Stolen by father and son. Levi peered over at Jeb. His expression appeared soft, but no other emotion escaped.

"That's not true!" Levi's head snapped to his dad.

Levi hadn't been paying attention to what was being said, but the information had stirred his fathers up, as well as Milo, who couldn't voice anything but muffled grunts.

Concetta closed the book soundly and handed it back to the man. "I can and I will. Not only will I rid the world of the flawed souls by ending the lives of those who are infected. I'll destroy the souls themselves."

"You can't destroy a soul," Phillip said. "They move on to whatever afterlife awaits."

"They move on and continue to affect the energy of the universe. And no, I can't destroy a soul. I don't have that power. No one does, except...." She turned slowly and leered down on Levi. "Your own flesh and blood."

That set Phillip off. Jeb freed himself from his captors. The general chaos that ensued ended with them all hog-tied, gagged, blindfolded, and thrown into separate cars.

AFTER A short trip, where Levi was fully able to appreciate the terror of their situation, he was removed from the vehicle, thrown onto a hard floor, and then a door had been slammed. Still blindfolded, he had no clue exactly where he was, no clue what they'd done with Jeb or his fathers... damn. Phillip's reaction to Concetta's prophetic "No one does except..." and then that cold, malicious stare that had cut through to Levi's own soul didn't bode well for any of them, especially Levi. He wasn't sure what Concetta, the bat-shit crazy priestess, had meant by destroying souls, but it sounded final. How was he supposed to do that? He hadn't even seen anyone's soul yet, which by the way, shouldn't that have come with the release of his Seer and Keeper powers? Why hadn't he asked more questions of Phillip? He'd been so freaked by seeing fates and the future and the return of his missing biological father and Jeb having a son that he'd glossed over the owner's manual.

He moaned and rubbed his cheek against the floor, which was smooth and hard. For some reason, the fact it wasn't concrete gave him a mild sense of relief. He chuckled morosely. Didn't matter if he was in a scary, dank basement or a room in the grandest house on the lake. He was still a prisoner, still the fodder for some mad woman's plan to kill souls. Apparently, she was already a murderer, killing the soulless as well as her own kind.

Levi was exhausted, but his mind whirled, trying to make sense of the past couple of weeks, which was fruitless. No matter what had happened, the focus was on getting away from the Righteous. All Levi could do was wait for that right moment to escape and get help. If he did, what would they do to his fathers and Jeb? To Logan? Was he even at the same location? Levi feared for all of them. What if they were deemed useless? Unnecessary? What if their souls were destroyed? Did that mean it would be as if they never existed?

His shoulders ached, and his mouth was dry and sore from the rag stuffed into it. He was still without a plan to escape the shit that seemed to follow him like a mangy dog. Even though he fought it, the fatigue won over. He drifted off into a dream-laden sleep where he was free but still totally alone.

CHAPTER 29

A NOISE startled Levi. With his eyes still covered and his grogginess, he wasn't sure if he was still asleep. Slowly the fogginess cleared, his thoughts ordered, and the full reality of his situation returned when he tried to move his bound arms. He cried out into his gag as a sharp pain pierced his shoulder. His arms were numb, and hell, they were going to hurt when, or if, he was freed.

Another noise was followed by a shuffling sound. Levi lifted his head from the floor and listened closely. A door closed, but the sound continued.

"Sit here, buddy," a voice whispered.

Levi tried to speak but only managed sharp grunting noises. He thrashed despite the pain, trying to get the person's attention.

A hand rested on his arm, and Levi fought harder.

"Levi, stop." He ceased his struggle. "I'm going to take your blindfold off and the gag." Thank God, it was Milo. Had he escaped? Levi latched on to the thought he was there to free him. Hot breath caressed his ear, and Milo whispered, "I need you to be very quiet. There's a camera. They can see us and hear us. Do what I ask, please?"

The fear was front and center in Milo's voice. Levi nodded.

First the blindfold came off, and Levi blinked repeatedly, trying to focus. The room wasn't bright, but even the small light on the nearby table was hard to take. The gag was removed, and Levi worked his jaw, his mouth so dry he couldn't speak.

Milo moved behind Levi. He cut the plastic ties holding Levi's wrists and ankles. There was no instant relief. Levi rolled onto his back, his arms dead and useless at his sides, his legs heavy weights. Maybe he'd been bound too long and they'd never work again. That thought had come too soon. The blood rushed back. Tingling filled his limbs, and then his nerves painfully flared as if thousands of electrified ants were running over them. He rolled onto his stomach as he gritted his teeth. Milo rubbed the skin on Levi's arms, which did little to relieve the agony.

"Fuuuuuck!"

A giggle to his left caused Levi to turn his head.

Connor sat on the bed a few feet away, clutching a blanket and something that looked like a mutated stuffed dolphin. A bed. They couldn't have thrown Levi on the soft mattress instead of the floor. He was sure he'd have bruises from rolling around on the hardness.

Resting his forehead on the cool floor, he panted through crackling and tingling, his arms regaining their blood supply. He flexed his muscles as they came back under his control. Connor babbled about a black puppy with white spots to Levi. He nodded and tried to smile, so ready to find a puppy so Connor could talk about something else. Jesus, had his captors focused his entire life on that puppy? Shit, did a puppy really exist somewhere? Cruel fuckers messing with a kid.

Levi slowly rose to his knees with the aid of his arms, shaky but working.

"Better?" Milo asked.

Levi rubbed his left and then right arm. "Yeah. Thought for a moment there I was going to need several amputations." That was something he wasn't anxious to feel ever again.

Milo still looked like hell. The reddish-purple bruises still covered his face and his neck, then disappeared under his T-shirt. His eyes were swollen, and several cuts on his lips had scabbed over.

Levi tried to stand, wobbled, but then steadied himself, making it to his feet. Damn, he had to piss like crazy. "Where are we?" Levi continued to shake his arms. The room was a basic nondescript bedroom with a dresser, nightstand, blue bedspread, and curtains that could be found in any house. "We have to get out of here."

As the last word fell from his lips, Milo flew at him, wrapping him up tight. Levi sputtered, his newly working arms flapping. He'd never been close with Milo, so what was with the bear hug?

"I told you they're listening," Milo whispered. "There's a camera up in the left corner behind you. When the red light is on, they can see and hear everything. If they think you're going to resist, they'll hurt your family, including Logan."

Levi tensed but played along and hugged Milo back. "Is Logan here?"

"He's here. Exactly where here is, I don't know. I've never been to this house before. But listen, they've given me information for you. You have to agree to what they tell you, Levi. You have to because they won't hesitate to hurt someone you love to get what they want."

Milo broke the hug before Levi could respond. "Is my brother okay?"

"I haven't seen him, but they said I could tell you that he'll remain unharmed as long as you agree to the information I am going to give you."

"But...."

Milo shook his head and sat next to Connor, who snuggled against him. Levi's anger flared momentarily. Somehow Milo had taken part in kidnapping Jeb's son and possibly killing his family. Even if he had been threatened by Helen and had incurred her wrath, Levi didn't know if he could trust the man. What if he'd been a patsy for the Righteous to help Helen get what they wanted from her?

"You're probably wondering how your family is?"

"Yes."

"Your father... I mean fathers, and, as I said, Logan are safe as long as you cooperate. Jeb too. They're in rooms similar to this one. They'll be taken care of as long as you do what they ask."

The fearful expression on Milo's mottled face said he was either worried Levi wouldn't cooperate, or, even if he did, none of them would be okay when everything was said and done.

"Sit." Milo motioned to the bed.

"Can I take a piss first? If not, the bed will need to be changed."

Milo pointed to the bathroom. Levi sprinted, fishing his dick out of his pants. Relief was immediate when he released a stream into the toilet. He felt about five pounds lighter. A quick shake, and then he tucked and zipped. As he washed his hands, he surveyed the full bath. No cameras were visible. He tried the window, but it appeared to be screwed shut. He'd get them out of there one way or another. He might not be strong or have any skills, but he was determined to succeed. He'd had enough of this shit.

He found Milo on the bed, tickling Connor who laughed in deep, gasping breaths. Milo's face was alight with joy as they played. He may have raised Connor, but did he think that made the boy his?

"That's Jeb's son." Levi blurted out the truth without thought.

Milo's expression fell flat, and his joy fled. "Yeah, don't think I don't know that. I've spent the last two years telling Connor all about his father, showing him videos and pictures and telling him stories about Jeb, all the while I raised him, cared for him, taught him everything." He averted his gaze to Connor. Levi could tell the boy loved Milo as much as Milo loved him. "Let's just get this over with."

Milo pulled a folded piece of paper from his back pocket. Unfolding the letter revealed handwriting.

"Did you kill Jeb's family and take his son?" Levi was blunt, but he wanted answers.

The question seemed to surprise Milo, who frowned. "Do I look like I'm doing this of my own free will?"

"How would I know? You were helping Dr. Winston. Why didn't you try to stop her, try to get help? You've had two years. Maybe if you'd done something, Jeb's family would be alive." Levi wanted to blame someone, and Milo was close to everything that had happened.

Milo wiped at his forehead. He chuckled in a flat tone. "I didn't know what she was planning at first. And Dr. Winston threatened to turn my twin sister over to the Righteous if I didn't help her. As she said, Ranae is a Keeper, but she isn't very powerful, plus she has cerebral palsy due to complications at birth, so she's in a wheelchair." Milo looked up, and Levi felt like a fucking heel. "Me, I'm a Keeper and can have visions of the future. My sister is small and has medical issues, so she can't handle the stress of holding souls. I had to protect her. I tried everything to sabotage Dr. Winston without her finding out what I was doing." He took in a huge shuddering breath.

"Six years I've been under her control while she used me to find other Seers and Keepers. I didn't give her anything specific to go on. I kept information about my visions vague, even though, being a Gemini twin, they can be quite clear. I never told her when I encountered another person from the community. But sometimes she got information out of me."

"But you told her about Connor."

Milo ran a shaky hand over Connor's hair, which was wavy like Jeb's. "I never would have told her about Connor's birth, but she was with me when I had the vision. It was unlike anything I'd ever experienced before. I heard of other Seers having epic visions, but man, you just don't know what they mean until you have one yourself. The energy and power was massive and totally took over me. I was so out of it and was babbling bits and pieces of his birth and his powers. When I finally came out of the vision, I was strapped to a table. And s-she… she… fuck," he whispered. The ghastly expression on Milo's face didn't need explanation for Levi to know how bad it had been.

He furrowed his brow. "I promise I didn't know about her plans for Jeb's family until it was too late. It was also the first I had heard of her having ties to the Righteous. By the time I got to Jeb's house, his brother and sister-in-law were dead, Connor was gone, and Jeb was dying. The only reason he lived was because I called 911."

Levi closed his eyes, grateful Milo had been there. "I'm sorry."

Milo nodded, but he probably knew, as Levi did, that the words held little meaning with so much already lost.

"I have to read this before they get huffy." He lifted the paper and read with a wavering tone. "Welcome to your destiny, Levi. You have important work to do. Listen well to the following instructions because the health and safety of your loved ones depends on your cooperation."

Levi nodded unconsciously. He'd listen, but the first chance he got, he'd do anything to save them from that cult.

"You are more than a Seer and a Keeper. While your father believes you to be like him, you're much more than that. You have the potential to become an amazing tool. One that brings forth harmony and peace. You can help move our planet into a new era. Imagine a world where a high level of morality is the norm, where people work for the greater good as a whole, where there is a collective community and the selfish I and me don't exist."

Levi grimaced. Whatever he'd expected to hear, this wasn't even close. Where was the talk about taking down the evil, eradicating the unworthy, the flawed? This actually sounded nice. Had he misunderstood what Concetta had been talking about earlier? Had his fathers been wrong about Concetta's goal?

"I don't understand. What's so wrong with all of that?"

Milo looked up from the paper. He nodded enthusiastically and smiled too wide. "Sounds great, doesn't it?" His eyes widened, and Levi realized he was supposed to nod in return. He also knew that Milo knew more than he could say.

Levi nodded. Milo continued reading about harmony and a better world for everyone, a utopia that Levi himself would sign up for in a second, if it were true. Every story he'd read revolving around utopias had never ended well for the inhabitants, as if true perfection and happiness were impossible.

"You will offer yourself up in servitude to humanity. You alone can help society to reach this pinnacle of harmony and enlightenment."

Oh yeah, there was the catch. What the hell was he supposed to "offer"?

"You have been born with the ability to combine powers, harness the energy in another rare Seer, to become a vessel for the Judge. No one has seen the likes of this power in millennia. You will be the vessel for the savior of a world where foul, tainted souls flood the world with their discordant energy, leaving the rest of us to live in their chaotic aftermath."

There it was. Kill the souls.

"With those powers, we will begin on a journey to eradicate hatred, extinguish evil, and help humanity to live in unity. Your journey begins tomorrow, and you will be a liberator and redeemer for all humanity. You, Levi, are comparable to the Second Coming of Christ. A savior, and your time has come to greet the world."

Levi gaped as Milo folded the paper and held it tight in his grip. Did she just refer to him as Jesus Christ?

"What the fuck?" he mouthed unable to fathom the crazy that went into believing he was anything but an emotionally stunted nineteen-year-old gay man with daddy issues and low self-esteem.

"Who's this other Seer I'm supposed to harness these powers from?" Was it his father? What did harness mean?

Sadly, Milo looked to Connor. Again, he ran his hand over Connor's soft curls as the boy sucked his thumb and played with his dolphin.

Levi clenched his jaw. Not sweet Connor. Maybe using his powers would mean something like borrowing them. He'd access them, and the kid would be fine. No harm.

Right.

"What will happen to Connor if I harness his powers?" What in the hell would happen to him?

Milo shook his head slowly. Not a verbal answer but a confirmation that it wouldn't be good.

"You have to answer one question." Milo chewed on his bottom lip. "Your answer will determine what will happen next."

The craziness Milo had read to him was fresh in his head, and still he had to ask. "Which is?"

"Agree, and what was written will move forward smoothly. Refuse, and your family members will be brought before you, one by one, and tortured until you either relent or they die."

What kind of choice was that? What the fuck was he supposed to do? Milo had told him to agree to everything. So he did.

"Yes."

Milo pierced him with a heavy, almost hateful glare, then deflated. "I was afraid you were going to say that." Milo turned to Connor, his lip quivering. Milo stroked Connor's cheek lovingly, almost reverently, then leaned over and kissed him gently on the forehead. "You be good for Levi, just like I told you, okay?"

Connor nodded. "'Kay.'"

As Milo stood and was going toward the door. Levi panicked. "Wait, what do you mean be good for me?" He wasn't going to leave him with Levi, was he? Oh, hell no.

Milo crumpled as if his legs couldn't hold him. He stayed on his hands and knees. Levi crouched next to him, ready to help. When Milo turned his head to face Levi, his fierce expression was startling.

His eyes were wet, his mouth tight as he whispered. "Get both of you away from here. Don't stop to think. Take Connor and get the fuck out of here. You have the blessing of every one of us, including Connor's father. Before it's too late for you and him. We're only a few people compared to the world on which she wants to unleash hell. We're working on a way for you to escape. When it comes, don't hesitate. Just grab Connor and fucking run."

Milo knelt, then grabbed Levi's wrist, turned the palm up, and slid a folded note into his hand as the door flew open.

The red-haired woman rushed in, face twisted with rage, and backhanded Milo. His head snapped to the side, and he fell back against the side of the bed. Connor let out a screech.

Levi lunged for the woman but found a gun shoved into his face. "Back off, freak." She grabbed Milo by the shirt with her free hand and dragged him from the room. The door slammed and locked.

Levi was too stunned by Milo's directive to move. He'd said Concetta wanted to unleash "hell," and he was the messiah who was supposed to be front and center of some kind of Armageddon.

Deep breaths, Levi. Get it back together. You only have to flee this hellhole and leave most everyone you love on Earth behind to save a bunch of fucking strangers.

He laughed out loud. "That's all."

Unable to ignore the wailing child, he dropped the letter onto the table beside the bed. He scooped the crying Connor up and bounced him on his hip. He cooed soothing words to the kid, but he so didn't know what to do with him.

"Hey buddy, it's okay. Shhhh…. Remember the puppies. Two black-and-white puppies. They'll be yours soon." He continued to wail, the sound eating into Levi's skull. He was ready to fucking lose his mind.

He turned and stalked to the center of the camera's view and shifted Connor to his other hip. The red light was still on. Good. He had some information of his own for the faceless assholes watching. "Listen up. I'll do what you want, but I want to see my brother first. Do you understand? I want to see Logan, or I'll find a way to slit my damned wrist or hang myself or somehow fuck myself up so badly you won't get what you want."

With that, he stomped into the bathroom and slammed the door. He sunk to the floor with Connor, whose crying had turned to shuddering sobs. Would Levi carry through on his threat and kill himself? It was the sanest decision he could fathom in the most fucked-up situation.

CHAPTER 30

LEVI STRETCHED out on the bed. Connor slept beside him wrapped around his dolphin. Shortly after his tirade to the camera, Levi's room had been infiltrated, and anything that could remotely be used to harm himself had been removed. Shoes, sheets, lamps, and anything with a cord. Yeah, they were thorough, but they hadn't checked above the curtain rod in the bathroom that held a short valance. He'd placed his socks up there, his long socks. They'd never even questioned where they'd gone and most likely had assumed he hadn't worn any.

They had also brought Levi and Connor a decent dinner. Levi had some kind of casserole with chicken and rice. Connor had mac and cheese. After that, Levi had taken it upon himself to bathe the tot who was quite amused with the bubbles. Levi even caught a quick shower himself although he had to put on the same dirty clothes. Getting them ready for bed, he'd found the folded paper Milo had given to him. He opened it to read again and something fell onto the floor. Two things actually. A slip of paper and a bundle of what looked to be dried sticks and leaves wrapped in twine. On the paper was a phone number and a message.

If you get out, call this number, leave a message w/ your location and say, Ho perso la camicia a Freni e Frizioni. Trust this man. He will help you disappear. Hide this spell bundle on your body for protection. Please be safe. Phillip.

They really did expect him to disappear. He still didn't know how, or if, he could do it. And what about his mom? Wasn't she in danger? He had to decide what to do. If he didn't leave, what would happen? The video camera never ceased watching him, its red, glowing eye a reminder he was on display. He tried to formulate a plan to escape as Milo had instructed. When it came down to a decision, could he leave his family, leave Jeb who'd held him so tenderly and called him kitten (which Levi had to admit had grown on him)? His affection had been apparent in every caress, every kiss, every thrust. But Jeb confused Levi to no end. Before they'd confronted Helen, Jeb's ice king personality had been doing the talking. When they'd been captured by the Righteous, Jeb had hugged him and called him kitten again. Levi wished he would make up his mind about how he felt.

No matter what Jeb decided—God, he wanted Jeb to choose him—Levi's new membership in the emotionally abled club was scary for a newbie. Emotions all the time, which weren't new to him, but amplified to the tenth power. Everyday he'd be schooled, learning new lessons on how to survive in the world with emotions (if he survived the Righteous that is). What he feared most was his first hard lesson would be the "break-up" with Jeb. He'd seen the mopey, tear-soaked aftermath of that phenomenon with Gia, and it had been horrendous…. Would he spend hours crying and eating chocolate? He shuddered.

Time to think of something else. Their slow and languid lovemaking that morning at the cabin had been torturous and passionate. Jeb's hard pecs and nipples had brushed against Levi's in an erotic dance of caresses. Jeb's languid thrusts, the slide of the silky skin of his cock, pushing into Levi until he could go no farther, their balls rubbing together.

Levi moaned and grabbed his cock, hard and leaking in his briefs, and remembered he was lying next to a sleeping toddler. "Shit."

He escaped to the bathroom and shut the door without turning on the light. Kicking his jeans and underwear off, he lay on the floor, eyes closed….

Sucking two fingers into his mouth, Levi pulled his knees to his chest and reached between his legs. Without pausing, he impaled himself on those fingers, needing to feel the intrusion. He closed his eyes, gasped as he pulled out slowly, then shoved his fingers back in. He shivered from the deliciously rough thrusts. He licked the palm of his other hand and stroked his shaft from root to tip, massaging the silky skin. When he opened his eyes, it was Jeb impaling him, Jeb stroking him to the rhythm of his thrusts, Jeb leaning over him, Jeb's brown eyes intent on his. So open and in the moment. Jeb's muscled arms held him over Levi, their faces close together.

Levi panted and twitched. "Fuck me, Jeb," he whispered.

Jeb growled and slammed into Levi, pulling out until just the head remained, and then shoved back in. So hard and so deep.

"Yes, yes." Jeb increased his speed, his angle. So full and tight and…. "Shit!" Levi's groin burned with the heat. His muscle clenched down tight on Jeb's cock. He needed to come so badly and knew words from Jeb would pull him over. Heated breath on his ear followed a bite on his lobe.

"Come on, kitten. Give it up."

Just that raspy voice in his head caused a tingle to race through him, contracting his balls. He slammed his fingers in deep as his hole strangled the digits. He held his breath, pushing hard, willing the cum out of his cock. Finally, a stream exploded across his stomach. He sucked in air, chest heaving, as pleasure rippled through his body. His hole pulsed around his fingers as cum fell in ropes on his chest and belly.

Removing his fingers, he slowly lowered his feet, his back cramped, his legs shaking. And that's where he stayed for the next hour thinking of Jeb, dreaming of a future that would more than likely never come, before he dragged himself from the floor and to bed.

MORNING CAME too soon, and Levi had yet to see Logan. They probably thought he didn't have the means to hurt himself. They were wrong. He figured if he tried to hang himself with his socks they'd stop him before he even figured out how.

So plan B.

The only window in the room had been nailed shut, like the one in the bathroom. The windows were single paned and the wood weak with age. He peered out and looked down, assuring an unobstructed fall to the ground from the second story. Yup, he could do some damage diving out, maybe even die. If he thought about it too long, he'd chicken out. He made sure the camera was on. Connor was safe on the other side of the room playing with the trucks that had been delivered with breakfast. Levi grabbed the bedside table, which was light, having only a drawer and four long skinny legs.

"Connor, it's gonna get loud, buddy. Cover your ears." He did as he was told.

Levi lifted the table and slammed it into the glass. The shattering sound echoed through the room as the lower double pane cracked. Another swing, and the upper glass shattered into jagged pieces, some still hanging from the frame. One of the table legs lay on the ground.

Levi hit the window again, enjoying the self-satisfaction of destroying something belonging to the Righteous. He dropped the broken table. Using the heel of his palm, he slammed into the wood until the window frame lay in pieces. Without stopping, he climbed onto the sill, then instructed Connor not to move. He gulped at the height and wondered why they'd allowed him to get to that point. Shit, were they going to let him jump?

The door opened and then closed before Levi could turn around. When he did someone was crouched on the floor on the other side of the bed.

"Logan!" Connor jumped up.

Levi lunged from the windowsill and into the room. "Logan?" He circled the bed and knelt before his brother. He caught Connor just as he was about to jump on Logan's back.

"Logan, are you okay?"

Logan nodded and spit crimson onto the floor. He wiped his mouth on his shirtsleeve. Levi didn't wait for him to get up and wrapped his arms awkwardly around his brother's head and shoulder. Logan coughed and sputtered, and when he looked up, Levi saw his nose and face were bloody and swollen. Connor's mouth formed an O.

"Thank God, Levi." Logan managed to get to his knees. Within seconds they were wrapped around one another. God, it seemed like an eternity since he'd last seen his brother. He didn't seem too beat up. Nothing long-term at least.

"Booboo." Connor scowled.

Logan smiled wide at Connor. "I'm okay." Logan's grin, despite being bloody, erased Connor's scowl.

"Okay. Logan play?"

"I need to talk with Levi. You go play with your trucks, and I'll be over soon?"

Connor smiled in return, then darted off and sat with his toys.

"You know Connor?"

Logan wiped at his face again, and blood coated the back of his hand. He scrunched up his face seeing the blood. "Yeah, we played whenever the goons got tired of dealing with him. Cute kid."

"He's Jeb's son."

Levi grimaced. "Whoa, yeah, guess they weren't wrong about that one."

"Yeah, it's shocking." More so for Levi. He surveyed Logan. "Are you really okay? I mean, other than bleeding out of your face."

Logan choked out a laugh. "I think they were pissed that you forced them to bring me here. Couple of quick smacks on the way. Douche bags."

Levi grasped Logan's shoulders and rested their foreheads together. "You okay, Crash?"

Levi choked out a laugh. "Yeah, Stay right here. Don't move." Levi went into the bathroom and wet a washcloth. Returning, he found Connor still playing and Logan had sat on the floor and watched him play.

Levi knelt before him. "Here. Lift your chin." Logan complied, and Levi gently wiped at Logan's face. Mainly his nose was bleeding, but his lower lip was split as well.

Levi concentrated on wiping the blood, afraid he'd lose it and cry like a baby. "I'm really sorry." He didn't know what else to say.

"It's just a little blood. They've tried a few times, but they can't hurt me. Tried to tell me they had you but could never prove it. I was so scared you were hurt or dead or...."

"Yeah, me too." Levi dropped the cloth on the floor. "This is all because of me, Logan. Me. Why the fuck is it always me who's messing up everyone else's lives? And do you know what Phillip wants me to do?"

Logan sucked in a breath, his blue eyes widening. "Phillip's here?"

Oh shit. So much had happened since Logan had been taken.

"Yeah. He didn't have anything to do with any of this, I mean other than me being like him, a Seer and a Keeper."

Logan rested his hands on his thighs and looked down. "What's he like?"

Levi realized he didn't have much of a clue. "I really don't know. I mean, I just met him. He said he never wanted to leave us, but the Righteous had found him. He had to leave, of course, to protect me."

"Stop it."

Logan's harshness snapped Levi's head up. "I.... What?" He frowned unsure what he was supposed to stop doing.

Logan leaned toward Levi, that big brother finger poking him in the chest. "Stop bringing this all down on yourself. You aren't responsible for what you were born as. You aren't responsible for our real father or this group of psychotic lunatics."

He wanted to blame someone else, but he was so used to blaming himself.

Logan scoffed and rolled his eyes, one of which was swelling. "Could you at least try?"

Levi cracked a smile. "Yeah, why not."

Grabbing the cloth, Logan reclined against the side of the bed and dabbed at his nose, which leaked a random drop of blood. "Ugh. Might be broken. Hope I don't end up with one of those crooked schnozzes, which just gets bigger with age."

"Phillip doesn't have a big nose, and I think you have the same shape."

Logan was silent for a moment. "What else can you tell me about him?"

Levi shrugged. "He seems like a decent guy." Levi bit his lip and looked away.

"What is it?" Logan pushed Levi's shoulder playfully.

"He told me he's gay." Why did Levi feel like he was the one coming out of the closet?

"Huh. Go figure. Looks like you have more in common with him than you thought."

Levi's heart seized, and in seconds, he was staring down on his brother. He had suspected. Levi feared his reaction.

Logan chuckled. "Don't have a heart attack and sit. Jeez, it's not like you're a secret serial killer or something. You're gay. So what? These days it doesn't mean much."

Levi wished he'd approached that fact so casually.

"How?"

"Remember Brett—"

"Oh, for the love of God. I follow one guy around, and you and Dad both think I'm gay, which I am, but one guy?"

"No, it was other things, subtle things that made me think. I can't remember what exactly. But recently, it was the way you looked at Jeb. The way he looked at you. How he talked about you when we went to get Phillip. Really, Levi, I don't care and neither will Mom. Dad knows. He's mentioned it to me a couple of times, but we don't care. And Phillip, well, we know how he feels."

"I know. You're right. It's me who needs to get used to people knowing." Levi sat and twisted his hands in his lap, then leaned his head against Logan's shoulder. He lowered his voice so they couldn't hear him. "Phillip wants me to run with Connor. Run like a coward and leave you all here."

"I agree," he whispered without hesitation.

"How can you say that?"

"Because I know what they've planned. Some of the goons here don't realize they shouldn't talk around me. Idiots. Heard them talking about the cellar and some hatchway. There are two ways to get there, and if you use the door off the kitchen, the hatchway is right at the bottom of the stairs. From the entryway, the kitchen is two lefts. Take the door to the right." Logan chuckled dryly, then rubbed at his chest. "I know because I got out of my room once when someone forgot to lock the door. Made it to the hatchway. Gail, the one with the red hair—stay the hell away from her if you can—caught me and used my ribs for punting practice."

Damn, Levi knew how crappy that pain could be.

"Run, little brother, and get the hell away from here. I think they'll be so busy scrambling to get you back that you'll have time to get us help... I hope." Logan must have seen the terror on Levi's face because his expression became harsh, almost angry. "You *have* to get both of you out of here because what they're going to do.... You can't...."

"Wow! Look at this cool sticker!" Connor stood and raised the truck he was playing with. He ran to Levi and dove into his lap.

When Connor's body connected with his, Levi's vision went black.

A loud screeching noise filled the air. Headlights illuminated the road before him. The car he was driving fishtailed. The speedometer registered over seventy miles per hour. Too fast for the dirt road they were on. Connor cried in the back seat. A car pulled up beside them and slammed into the driver's side, forcing them from the road. They collided head on with a pole, cutting through the car and obliterating their lives in a flash of metal and blood and shattered bones....

Levi gasped, trying to force any air into his lungs.

"Levi, what's wrong?" Logan helped him to his knees.

Oh God, the gory images continually flashed in his mind. The sickening sounds echoed in his ears. He opened his eyes and forced them to focus back on the bedroom.

"What was that?"

Levi looked to Logan, hope fleeing quickly. "If I try to run with Connor, we're probably going to die."

CHAPTER 31

LOGAN WIPED his mouth with the back of his hand. Then he turned them from the camera. "Why do you say that?"

Levi gave him the condensed version of what he knew about his supposed powers, keeping his voice low. He continued to shake and shudder from the intense vision.

"Not a superpower one would hope for."

"Right. Why not the ability to freeze time or teleport. No, I get to see people's deaths, including my own apparently."

"So, you just don't get into a car, right? Wait, you won't get far with a toddler in tow without one. Shit." Logan's brow rose. "Maybe you don't take him, because they need you both, right? Without one of you, they're still screwed."

"How do you know that?" Levi looked over his shoulder, knowing they were being spied on and hoping those watching couldn't hear.

"Again the talking heads. The head psycho is going to do some spell that binds your powers, and there's a lot more to it, but when they do that you're… well, you're going to be able to destroy a person's soul. I mean, not just send it to wherever but snuff it out for all eternity."

Letting the words settle like a layer of lead on his skin, Levi's only thought was psychopath. A killer, not only destroying—*murdering*—a person but wiping out their entire existence, their life essence, their energy. And without those people to procreate, whatever flaw was in their souls wouldn't be passed on. Their bodies wouldn't hang around to disrupt the fucking harmony of the world.

"There's something else I heard." Logan spoke even lower. "Well, two things. Apparently this spell is huge, I mean a gigantic drain of energy that will push out in waves, the kind of energy that Seers read in the soul. It's like a soul on mega-steroids. They said when it happens that all Seers and Keepers within a couple thousand miles will feel it and know something isn't right. Because of the magnitude, some Seers might actually be forced to have visions about the events as they happen. It might not mean much for us, but they're not going to be able to hide what they've done."

Levi huffed. One good thing, right? Of course, that would be too late to save him.

Logan hesitated, and the uneasy expression, the hint of fear on his face, told Levi the second something wasn't any better. "They're afraid something could go wrong to the point that it scares them. A couple of them were whispering about control and not wanting to be around if it all went bad. I don't know if that's the head psycho's control or your control. But from what I hear, that might not be better than the other option. So you really need to get out of here. Don't worry about the rest of us."

"Easier said than done. I'll try, but...." He hoped his cryptic message from Milo had meant that the bundle of whatever he'd given him would mess up the spell—hopefully not that control thing—because, at that point, it was his only ace in the hole. He had it tucked safely into his briefs next to his balls where it itched like crazy, but who would ever think to or want to check there?

The door opened, and the bald man, whose shoulders were as wide as the doorway, stepped in, grinning wider than the Cheshire Cat ever had.

"Show time, ladies." The woman with short black hair came in and scooped up Connor, who cried for his trucks. Levi was glad it wasn't Gail.

Logan leaned close to Levi. "Watch for the distraction, then get out. We aren't going to let them use you," Logan whispered. "Love you."

Levi choked on an errant sob as Logan was torn away from him. What was going to happen to them, and why did it have to all rest on his shoulders?

Well, fuck you, Levi. Get up and be a man.

Levi rose before Baldy could grab him. "Don't touch me." Levi growled at him.

Baldy growled back and pushed him into the hallway. Levi was pissed. He had no control over anything, but maybe he could delay the inevitable. He turned and, without a second thought, punched Baldy in the face, his fist exploding in pain, but he didn't stop. He raised his foot and kicked the side of the man's knee before he could recover. The man shouted and went down but quickly jumped to his feet, rising like a behemoth ready to fuck Levi up. Shit, it was going to hurt. He charged at Levi who swung out, but his fist sailed through the air in a wide miss.

Another guard tackled the bald man, who struggled to get out from under him. "Stay down. You can't touch him."

Baldy lay on the ground, his face red with rage as he glared at Levi.

"That's enough from you." Noah had snuck up on Levi, and before he could turn, Noah's boot connected with his back, right over his kidney. Levi's chest seized, and his legs buckled. He fell onto his hands and knees, his gut clenching tight.

Without pretense, Noah yanked him off the floor. The action allowed Levi to finally draw in a deep breath.

He wanted to kill Noah. "You're going to pay for that."

Noah barked out a harsh laugh as he pushed Levi down the hall. "You're in no position to do anything. It's going to be ironic, isn't it? Soon, you're going to be a weapon used to kill your own kind. Now that's justice."

The gun Noah had leveled on Levi was a reminder he should shut up, but why? Noah couldn't kill him. Concetta would probably skin him alive.

"What the hell is your damage? We aren't a danger to anyone. We aren't out to hurt people. What about you, Noah? Who have you hurt or killed lately?"

Noah ground his teeth and narrowed his eyes. "Me? You freaks are fucking everything up for the rest of us, making us live in a world filled with hate. People's lives get messed up or die because of your negative energy. My grandmother will finally get rid of everyone with fucked-up souls."

"Concetta is your grandmother? Well that explains your insanity."

As Noah raised the gun, Levi cringed.

Someone shouted from down the hallway. "Noah! Move it!"

Noah pursed his lips, probably thinking through the consequences of shooting Levi. "You'll get yours soon enough. Go."

Levi decided it wasn't worth inciting Noah's anger anymore. His back hurt like a fucker.

At the end of the hallway, Noah nearly shoved Levi down the stairs. He managed to catch hold of the railing and descended without further help from Noah. Logan and Connor weren't anywhere to be seen. At the bottom of the stairs, he didn't appear to be in the entryway as Logan had described. Even if he overpowered Noah, he had no clue where the kitchen was from there. He knew escape had been wishful thinking. If

Levi tried to run on Noah's watch, he'd no doubt shoot him in the leg or another nonfatal location.

They approached what appeared to be an exterior door. Levi was surprised when Noah directed him to go through it. Outside, several guards waited and followed behind. The house had a small grassy yard surrounded by thick woods. No other homes were visible through the trees. The steep slope behind the house was indicative of being on the side of a mountain. But where in Ticonderoga? Not many houses were located on the steep rocky slopes of the mountains there. Maybe they were in Hague?

They came to a broken-down, overgrown, and rusted chain-link fence that had been cut open. To the right, affixed to the links, Levi caught sight of a No Trespassing sign. The once-white sign with black writing was corroded with rust, but he made out the words "Republic Steel Corporation." Shit, they weren't in Ticonderoga anymore. They were about twenty-five miles north, probably in Mineville or in that vicinity. It had been over forty-five years since Republic Steel had run the mines—iron ore mines.

"The box was lined with iron ore. Blocks energy."

"...a gigantic drain of energy... will push out in waves. The kind of energy that Seers read in the soul... like a soul on mega-steroids."

No one would feel anything, know anything, if they went into the mines. The remaining iron ore in the bedrock would block the energy. Also, the mines were no longer safe, many having collapsed or filled with water long ago. Those that hadn't would most likely bury them alive under tons of rock with any kind of energy release. Maybe they'd all die before they could stop anything.

A short way past the fence, they came to the edge of a massive hole in the ground. The open mine was at least a thousand feet wide and over a few stories deep. At one time it had probably been deeper. Trees and vegetation covered the rocky walls, growing from large crevices. Near the top of that massive hole, someone had been digging or drilling. A large pile of rocks and dirt along with a few pieces of large machinery sat nearby.

"Climb down." Noah pointed to the hole.

Dizziness hit Levi immediately when he looked into the pit. His stomach lurched and rolled. Heights were so not his thing. He spotted what Noah was pointing to. Ten feet down, there was a narrow rocky path leading to a large hole in the side of the mine. Two rock outcroppings served as large steps to get there. One slip, and it was all done.

Levi crouched and scooted to the edge, carefully sliding off. The first rock was about five feet down. If he wasn't such a wimp, he probably could have jumped. His pulse raced, sweat prickled his skin, his legs and arms shook. Not a great combo for a rock climbing expedition.

"Jesus, speed it up. You always were such a fucking sissy boy."

Yeah, he'd hurry up just so he could become their weapon. This was his chance. He could jump and end it all, die as his body smacked against the jagged rocks, slammed into the thick trees. He paused, contemplating that possibility. As he stared down, he tried to focus on having a vision to see if he would die immediately or lie at the bottom of the pit a broken, living mess, but nothing came. When Noah grabbed his arm, Levi yelped and scrambled to grab hold of anything. Luckily, Noah held him tight because his foot slipped.

"Calm the fuck down."

Levi fell back onto his ass. With a stern look from Noah, he sucked in a breath and continued to slide until his feet were firmly on the path. If you could call it that. At its widest point, it was less than a foot wide. He shuffled along, avoiding looking down, swallowing repeatedly until they reached the large hole in the side of the pit. Levi practically dove inside, grateful to be anywhere but on that path.

The entrance was tall enough for an average-size man to walk through. He blinked to adjust to the dim light. The cave-like space opened up inside into a large area less than ten feet high. The room glowed from candlelight and lanterns. The walls and ceiling were a combination of jagged and smooth rock. The air temperature dropped inside, and Levi shivered. Being safely inside did little to calm Levi's fear-ravaged mind and body. Carving out this fucking den to unleash hell on earth had been no small undertaking. Levi feared nothing could stop what was about to happen.

Everyone Levi loved, or wanted to love, was seated on the floor around a raised wooden platform. Art and Phillip and Logan were on one side seated against the stone wall. When Levi caught their attention, they each gave him some sign of reassurance. Levi grimaced to hide his fear, but he was sure he hadn't been convincing. Logan nodded confidently at him. Levi nodded back in acknowledgment.

Across from them, on the other side of the platform, Connor sat on the floor at Gail's feet. Jeb was a few feet away from his son. Surprisingly, they were all unbound, and Levi had to wonder exactly why they were there. Milo was the only one unaccounted for. Many of the guards from the house stood around the stone room, but none inside the cave appeared to have guns. Only the two who were visibly guarding the entrance held them.

"Levi." Jeb tried to get up, but Baldy pushed him back down. With a twist of his body, Jeb was able to free himself. He nearly tackled Levi with his hug. Levi gripped Jeb tight, refusing to let go while Baldy tried to separate them.

"Stop. Let them have their moment, given it will be the last time they'll see one another." Concetta stepped up onto the altar-like structure where a wood table set. Her robe was now black and had that same annoying red symbol. "Besides we're waiting on the last person to arrive. Until he comes, we have to wait." Baldy released Jeb with a growl. Levi buried his face in Jeb's neck, his heat, his smell, his grip comforting, and Levi fought to keep from shattering right there. He'd never had to be this strong, never had to be the one to carry everyone else. But he would because if he didn't, they would all die. Why hadn't he killed himself when he had the chance?

"I'm going to get us out of this," Levi whispered.

Jeb's grip tightened. "We have a plan. When I signal the others, we're going to charge the entrance and take out the guys with the guns. You grab Connor and run."

"No, they'll kill all of you."

Jeb exhaled. "I have to save my son." His voice cracked. "You both mean too much to me to watch you being used by these sick people. I'd rather die trying to save you both." Jeb placed his palm beneath Levi's chin, and then raised his head, forcing Levi to look him in the eyes. They were ravaged by fear and anger. Jeb whispered close to his ear. "Please, Levi. Please, save him."

Levi wanted to say yes, and he almost did, because he'd run out of ideas. Even with the bundle from Milo secured in his crotch, this wouldn't stop, just possibly take some horrifying turn. But Milo had been so sure that this would be better than the alternative.

Levi squeezed Jeb and placed his mouth close to his ear. He had to say what was in his heart before it was too late. "You're the best thing that ever happened to me. You made me feel for the first time, and I'm grateful. So grateful even if you don't feel the same."

"Ahh, finally," Concetta said in a pleased voice. "Our guest is here, and we can finally begin."

"Dario?" Phillip's mention of Dario confused Levi. His father gasped. "What are you.... No."

CHAPTER 32

LEVI PULLED away just as Jeb began to say something. Levi turned hoping he'd heard wrong. No. Dario Alberici, the man Levi admired, loved like a father, stood at the mouth of the manmade cave. Gia's only living parent. Levi said the only thing that could come from his confused mind. "Dario, what're you doing here?"

"You!" Jeb tried to push past Levi. "You son of a bitch! I'm going to kill you!"

"Stop him," Concetta told the guards.

Baldy and Gail grabbed Jeb's arms as he fought for release.

"You lied to me!"

Phillip stood, bringing more guards forward. "What did Dario do, Jeb?"

Jeb sneered. "He's the person who told me he was Devon Adessi with the council. He came to the hospital with Milo."

"Dario is from the council." Phillip looked to Dario. "But you never told me you visited Jeb." Dario's silence only pushed Phillip's anger. "Dario, answer me?" Still nothing from the man who looked to Phillip with a blank expression. "What did you do? I trusted you." A guard held Phillip back as he struggled to get to Dario. "You're a Keeper, bound by the rules of the council. You took an oath. You betrayed us. You betrayed me."

"Phillip, calm down," Art said from behind him.

"Dad, what's going on?" Logan jumped to his feet appearing ready to defend his family.

Dario glanced to Phillip, his face emotionless except for the twitch in his jaw. "You should be more careful who you trust, old friend."

Friend?

"Are you prepared to perform the ritual?" Concetta asked ignoring the drama unfolding before her, an impatient glare marring her face.

Dario nodded. His gaze went to Levi who tried to see the caring father, the loyal husband, the family man. But nothing resembling the man Levi had thought him to be was there. Dario was going to do this to Levi, to his family. It was too much to fathom.

Concetta stepped up onto the altar. "Bring the boy."

Gail grabbed Connor, who was amusing himself with his truck, and set him on the table.

"Don't do this," Levi begged. "Please, Dario. What about Gia?"

Dario flinched.

"Is there a problem, Mr. Alberici? I believe we have a signed contract. You return the soul to the child, and I release the soul of your wife."

"What?" Phillip's face paled further.

Levi looked to Dario. "She has Cara?" But Cara, she'd died. How could she have her soul?

Dario stepped up to Levi and grasped him on both sides of the face. "*Figlio mio*. You're like one of my own and so special. All that I've done was meant to bring you to this day, to the salvation of the world."

"How could you do this?"

"And I love you like my own flesh and blood."

But he didn't if he was going to allow Levi to destroy anyone.

"Please, help me," Levi whispered in a last bid to stop the man.

"Get away from my son!" Art shouted. A scuffle ensued, voices rose, but Levi was too lost in Dario's betrayal to pay attention.

Dario kissed Levi's left cheek, and then the right, where he lingered for a moment. "*Ho perso la camicia a Freni e Frizioni.*" The words were barely whispered on a breath, and then he pulled away.

Levi recognized the words from Phillip's note, to identify the one person who could help him. But this was the person who'd betrayed his father and wouldn't help. Why had he spoken the words to Levi?

"You're the one to save us, but to save us, you must first save yourself."

Levi grimaced. "I don't understand."

"You will. Be ready, for when I am done returning Connor's soul, you will step up and do what you need to without hesitation." Dario leaned in again and kissed Levi's forehead, grasping his hands at the same time. "I swear on my Cara's soul."

Dario pressed something hard and cool with what felt like a thin rope into Levi's palm. He turned and walked away. Levi hid the hard object in his clenched fist. Just what Dario was about to do, Levi had no clue, but he'd sworn on Cara's soul, which was serious shit. Was he swearing he'd do what he was there to accomplish or that he was on their side? Levi prayed it was the latter.

Dario stepped onto the platform and removed his coat.

Phillip was still demanding answers from Dario. Concetta raised her hands. "Silence! Or I will dispose of those unnecessary for this ritual!"

Jeb stepped toward the altar, toward Connor, with an expression of determination. Levi stuck out his hand hoping to stop him. Baldy was ready to snatch him if he tried anyway.

"Wait. Please, trust me." Levi mouthed the words.

Jeb narrowed his eyes and growled but stopped moving. Levi knew it wouldn't be for long, but he had to see what Dario was going to do.

"Levi, please come to the edge of the platform, there." Dario pointed to the spot across from him. "We need to balance the energy in the room. Phillip, here next to me, please. So many Seers and Keepers and, well, other entities in such a small space." Dario actually chuckled and appeared relaxed, but Levi noticed a break in his voice, a bead of sweat running down the side of his face.

"Phillip, *here*, please." Dario pointed to the area next to him, but Phillip continued refusing to move. A guard was nice enough to assist Phillip to the spot Dario had indicated. He was within an arm's length from Dario.

"And, Jeb, since you're the boy's biological father, you stand next to Levi. Your energy is also in play here."

Without hesitation, Jeb stepped beside Levi. Probably anything to get closer to Connor. When Jeb reached out and squeezed Levi's arm, the movement was so unexpected. Jeb's trust in him was like a shot of bravery.

Dario rested his left hand on Connor's chest. Would Connor scream as he was torn apart by the reentry of his soul? No one as small as Connor should have to feel that. Maybe it was different returning a soul than unmasking one.

"Wait!"

Dario raised a questioning brow.

"Don't listen to him." Concetta glared daggers at Levi.

Dario didn't move or avert his gaze. "*Figlio mio?*"

"I don't want you to hurt him. It's going to hurt, right?"

Dario smiled. "No. Connor won't feel a thing. I promise."

"Enough. Get on with it." Concetta looked as if she were ready to strangle someone.

Dario lowered his head. "I, Dario Alberici, Keeper of the soul of one Connor Jebediah Monroe, deem the soul of this child worthy to be returned to him." Dario muttered more words that weren't anything close to English, his hand never leaving Connor's chest. He paused and frowned, cocking his head to the side, his gaze still on Connor.

"What's wrong?" Concetta's annoyance increased.

Dario lifted his head, and his gaze landed right on Levi. "Something's blocking the energy in here. Something…." He stepped down from the platform. Circling behind Phillip, Dario returned to Levi. He raised his hand in the air about six inches from Levi's body moving in circles. His hand stopped near Levi's groin. He swallowed hard.

Turning his hand palm up, Dario raised a brow. "Hand it over."

"What is it?" Concetta asked, her eyes afire with irritation.

Levi gaped like a fish. Dario's hand remained extended. What did he want? Was it what he'd given Levi himself or what was in his pants? When Dario's gaze fell onto Levi's groin, he knew which he was referring to. "Give it to me."

Levi hesitated until Noah grunted. "Take it out, or I'll take it out for you."

Yeah, no one but Jeb was getting near his crotch. Levi stuffed his hands down his jeans, which gave him the opportunity to leave Dario's gift there. Although Levi wasn't even sure he should keep anything from Dario.

He struggled and managed to pull out the bundle without major damage to his junk. He set it on Dario's palm. He smirked.

"Bring it here." Concetta extended her hand. When Dario handed it over, she snickered. "Did you really think this amateur attempt at channeling energy would stop me?" Her haughtiness was at an all-time high.

The odds Dario was for their side were dropping fast. He glanced to Logan who looked ready to pounce on command. His dad appeared to be monitoring both Phillip and Logan, possibly in case they tried anything stupid. When their eyes met, Art managed a smile and a nod, a loving gesture, causing Levi's eyes to burn. What if this was the last time he saw his dad and Logan and Jeb and Connor and Phillip? He'd lost confidence anything would turn out right. Even if they did get out of this, none of them would ever be the same.

Dario returned to Connor and began the ritual. A low, resonating hum filled the air. Levi looked around for the source until he realized the sound was everywhere at once. The vibrations filled his chest, his arms and legs. The hair on his head lifted slightly as if charged by static electricity. Concetta chanted under her breath as well, her arms raised high like a priest in sermon. Levi blinked. Was he seeing things? Dario's hand glowed. Connor laughed as if he were being tickled. Nothing like Levi had imagined.

The humming amplified, disturbing the air and running across Levi's skin. He swallowed repeatedly as his stomach turned, and his anxiety threatened to pull a scream from his throat. Something pushed into his mind, something familiar, unwelcome, unsettling, and dark, like the menace that had caused his dam to crumble and crack over the years. Every muscle in his body stiffened. And then he knew what was happening. While Dario was returning Connor's soul, Concetta was performing whatever ritual would change Levi into her soul murderer.

He tried to get the others to see what she was doing, but his throat was locked down. He flapped his arms, hopelessly rooted to the spot he stood. Jeb reached for him, but a sharp sting of electricity sparked between them. Jeb snatched his hand back.

"Levi!" Logan tried to move, but he appeared to be hindered by whatever electric force filled the air.

"Dario, you have to stop this." Phillip pleaded with his voice and his eyes, trying to stop his supposed friend. Levi didn't know what to believe about Dario.

Dario stopped mumbling the foreign language and looked to Concetta, noticing what the priestess was doing. "Concetta, you have to wait for the soul to be returned." But she continued chanting despite Dario's warning. In the closed-off rock room an impossible wind swirled through the air, and electricity crackled above the hum. "Stop, or you'll screw it all up."

"I know exactly what I'm doing. Don't stop, or I'll never release your wife's soul." She closed her eyes and chanted louder.

Dario continued. Levi wanted to plead as their eyes met, but his voice still failed him.

"Put the amulet around your neck, Levi." Dario struggled to keep his hands on Connor's chest as sparks popped around his hands. "Do it to save their souls."

How could he trust Dario? He'd lied to them all.

Slammed hard enough to jolt him physically, that familiar force spilled into Levi's mind. Expanding and threatening to tear him apart from the inside, the entity clawing from the endless depths of his subconscious and universal void. He fought the emergence, fortifying his dam—concrete and steel—thick and high to keep the darkness back. Energy arced from Levi toward Concetta, resulting from his defiance to accept her will.

"Don't fight me, boy! I'm much stronger than you, more practiced in my craft, and hold the energy of hundreds of souls. You're no match for me." Concetta laughed as another arc of energy connected them. The force in his head grew exponentially.

Jeb tried to grab for Levi again with the same shocking result.

Across the room, Art's frustration was apparent as he watched helplessly. Levi wanted to reassure him but was in a battle for his life. That cryptic conversation he'd had with Dario at his house now made sense. He'd told Levi to go with his heart. And he did. He yanked out what he'd placed in his pants and pulled it over his head. A round, shiny black stone carved with small symbols rested on his chest.

Dario shouted his remaining words, then reached out and grasped Phillip on the shoulder. His other hand thrust out, palm out, at Levi. "Phillip, give your souls to your son." Phillip appeared dazed and confused, unmoving, until Dario shouted again. "Now!"

That shook Phillip out of his head. He raised his hand toward Levi. Energy arcing from them both hit Levi hard in the chest. The searing heat, the expanding mass, pushed against his ribs. His breath caught. His heart seemed to stop. He was filled until he was sure his ribs would shatter. Light flashed from his chest, a light so pure, so angelical, so filled with love, that he reveled in the unearthly feeling.

Jeb begged Phillip and Dario to stop.

Dario removed his hand from Connor. He raised the hand, palm up again, at Concetta. Another spark, and she was part of the current running through them all.

"No! Stop!" Concetta tried to move but was trapped. The souls she'd held poured into Levi.

"D-Dad... I can't... I.... Too much." The pain grew, and he visualized his chest splitting open, peeling back, and exposing his organs.

"Jeb, put your hand over the stone. Do it now!" Phillip seemed to have figured out Dario's intent.

Without hesitation, Jeb slammed his hand over the stone. An explosion of sparks sprayed from Levi's chest and visibly raced up Jeb's arm. Another surge of energy funneled into Jeb, and the pressure in Levi's chest lessened.

"You have the power within you to contain it." Art tried to go to him, but a guard pushed him back. "Build up the dam, Levi. You can beat this."

Concetta continued to scream. Dario reached out and grabbed her arm. Levi looked to Jeb who wore an expression of amazement, of wonder, as sparks covered his body. A pathway opened between them, and Jeb's affection for Levi poured through. Then Levi was thrown into darkness.

When he opened his eyes, Logan stood before him pleading, begging, terror covering his face. "Levi, please, don't."

A malevolent darkness stained Levi's soul, a need to destroy, to cleanse, to consume. He pressed his hand against Logan's chest. With a ravenous hunger, Levi absorbed the energy from his brother's soul into his body, feeding his need, adrenaline rushing, a high like no other. Logan's eyes closed, and his body fell to the ground in an unmoving heap.

He needed more.

More.

Next Phillip, then Art. He consumed their souls, extinguished their lives in the blink of an eye. No remorse. No grief. No mourning. Killed them. Darkness ate away at his humanity, his soul, an eternal void, a thousand times more barren and hollow than he'd ever experienced. His single-minded purpose: fill the darkness, which could never be sated.

As his hand pressed into Jeb's chest, Levi fought to stop. Jeb stared at him, the heartbreak of Levi's betrayal etched forever into his expression, a reality so utterly devastating that Levi felt a sliver of pain, of loss. Then he killed the one person who meant so much to him. The person he loved.

CHAPTER 33

WHEN LEVI opened his eyes, he screamed. He'd killed them! Oh God. Logan, his father, Phillip, Jeb. He flailed against the weight on him, trying to escape as if that was the source of his pain.

"Levi, stop. Whatever you saw, it was only a vision. Just a vision." Phillip grunted as Levi struggled, needing to escape, end his existence, and ferry away the evil within.

"Come back to me. Open your eyes." Jeb rubbed his palm against Levi's cheek. He loved Jeb's touch.

Levi's vision focused. Jeb leaned over him, along with Art, Logan, Phillip, and Dario. How did he get on the floor? The vision slammed into him without restraint. He struggled to get away from the men. Where was the darkness, the insatiable need to consume souls? They all released him, and he scooted back, fearful he'd kill them just as he had in his vision.

"Hey, it's okay. Levi. Calm down." Jeb followed Levi.

"What did you see?" Phillip asked several times, his voice thready with desperation.

"G-get away from me!" Levi kicked at them.

The guards in the room stood back, their faces pale and terror filled. Oh God. The ominous foreboding intensified, and it was coming. The judge would devour their souls and, unsated, would go on to destroy the world.

"You all have to run! Get away from me!"

"Levi…." Jeb put his hand on Levi's leg, but Levi couldn't be touched. He was infected with the darkness. He'd turn on all of them, use their trust to kill them. His fate had been sealed.

On the floor behind Jeb, Connor cried, tears streaming from his eyes, too scared to move.

"Get Connor out of here. All of you need to run. I can't stop it from coming."

When Levi backed into the wall, he rose to his feet. Voices echoed in his head, so many voices. Energy coursed through him, so hot, so enticing.

"The souls…. They're…." He couldn't clear his head.

Dario stayed back, which was smart. "You've taken on a lot of souls at once. It's going to feel strange. The energy is massive, which is why we've connected you to Jeb. You're going to need the energy—"

A loud scream rent the air. An enraged Concetta pointed at Dario. "What have you done? You've given him the energy of hundreds of souls! He won't be able to control them with *il Giudice* in him. He'll feed off of our energy, kill us all. He has to be stopped!"

She raised the gun at Levi. Dario jumped at her. When the gun went off, Dario jolted and went down, blood spilling from his gut.

The pressure in Levi's head increased upon seeing Dario hurt. Darkness, an echo from his past, rushed in. Familiarity came with the darkness, like an old memory trying to surface, lurking, testing the boundaries, waiting to be recalled. Energy crackled over the surface of Levi's skin, white-hot sparks that failed to burn. The energy expanded, reaching jagged fingers above him, dancing over the rock ceiling, trapped by the surrounding iron ore. Concetta dropped the gun as a blast of energy zapped her hand. The terrified guards fled the cave, leaving their leader behind to save herself.

Levi's skin, bones, and muscles were engorged with power. With need. With want.

He looked to Phillip and narrowed his eyes, recalling his father's conversation on the phone in the cabin. "You knew this would happen?"

Phillip shook his head. The extreme shock should have told Levi he hadn't. "No! Dario…. He had a vision years ago. He told me…. He didn't tell me all of it." Phillip looked down at his friend, bleeding on the rocky floor.

Logan held his shirt over Dario's wound. Dario moaned, skin pallid, eyes unfocused, but he managed to speak. "C-couldn't… tell. You w-would… have… messed it up." He sucked in a breath and squeezed his eyes. "H-had to get to here."

Another surge filled Levi and he gasped. Connections branched inward, sucked into that void. So much power. Intoxicating.

Art looked to Phillip and then Levi. "What the hell is he?"

Phillip wiped at his mouth. "What Concetta said, a recreation of an ancient judge and jury, an entity that can kill a soul. And with the energy we gave him. I don't know how to stop him. I don't know what can."

Logan's pained expression squeezed Levi's chest. And Jeb. He'd never know if....

"Levi can... stop it... build the dam." Dario coughed and wheezed. If he died, Gia would be alone. Levi couldn't let that happen.

Art didn't fear coming closer. Levi cringed at his proximity. "That's right," he said. "You had the dam to contain the fear and the anxiety. This is no different. You're powerful, too powerful, and unless you contain it, the Judge will only get stronger and take over. If you even ta...."

His dad's voice faded. The distance between Levi and reality expanded. He knew whatever his dad said was important. But he couldn't hear him. Another swell of darkness, and the hunger appeared. Urgent. Voracious. Levi turned to Concetta. Her soul shone bright within her chest, its beauty marred by ugly, dark spots. The energy pouring from her soul was gray. Information rushed through Levi's brain. Damaged, depraved, immoral, corrupt, unworthy. The need to consume that soul was like a thousand pounds of pressure in every cell, whispering promises of eternal life, power, supremacy, if he just surrendered completely to the darkness. He had to judge her.

He had to judge them all.

"No." He clutched his head in his hands. He had to fight for his humanity. He lacked power to strengthen the dam. What he had to battle was too massive for a fucking human. He needed....

Surges pounded him relentlessly, the pull greater than that of a hundred suns. Energy coursed through him, readying the vessel....

I am not a vessel!

While his head battled the darkness, within his chest, souls combined, joined, coalescing into a dazzling, dominant sphere he could visualize in his chest.

"Levi!"

Levi's head whipped around to Jeb, whose eyes widened. He stepped back. "Fuck." Was he afraid? Jeb searched Levi's face, and then his usual confidence was restored. "You've gotta do what they said and stop this from taking over. I need you."

Roaring in Levi's head drowned out Jeb's pleas. Levi's vision partially whited out. Energy flowed over his body creating a protective layer, like a second skin. Levi felt invincible.

A shot rang out. Something bit into his back. He whipped around. Noah, gun in hand, appeared terrorized by his failure. The bullet lay at Levi's feet. A growl erupted from Levi. His hand raised without thought on his part. A bright stream of energy shot from Levi and slammed into Noah. Tossed like a doll, he smashed into the wall and crumpled onto the stone floor. Unconscious or dead. Levi didn't care.

Grinning, he turned to Concetta, as the wrongness of hurting Noah was quickly crushed. She crouched in the farthest point of the cave. Fear burned in the gray of her eyes, her expression that of someone facing imminent death. And Levi would be her judge, jury, and executioner.

The dam crumbled.

"Levi! Don't do it. Phillip says if you take even one soul there'll be no turning back. You'll be taken over and lost." Jeb tried to touch Levi's arm. A crack of electricity, and he stumbled back.

All Levi needed was one soul.

One.

Just one to fill the aching hollow. No. The void was endless, its need unquenchable. There would never be enough souls.

"Fuck!" Levi teetered on the edge of a gaping abyss. Fall, and he'd be lost to a mindless killing machine murdering those he loved. Murdering everyone until there was no one left.

He forced his focus on Jeb. He struggled to keep him foremost in his mind, see him, and not just a soul to consume.

Levi was so hungry.

No. stop!

Build it.

Levi turned his focus inward, on concrete and steel forming, building inch by inch, thick and unyielding, higher and higher, fighting against the darkness desiring to consume him. If that happened, no part of him would remain. The entity waged a war against Levi's effort. Cracks ran through the concrete, continuing to crumble despite his struggle. Soon all traces would be gone.

A cacophony of voices he'd never heard before rose in his head. Voices and energy. Power. And if he willed so, that power was his. He drew on the brilliant, primordial energy, connecting with the hundreds of souls sharing his body. Gathering strength, he pushed against the darkness, mending, and building his wall higher, thicker, wider. Fathoms of impenetrable, fortified victory.

He could still fail. "Get out!"

His family, Jeb, all stared at him with confusion and terror, hopeless to help.

"You have to get out! I'm not sure if it will hold!"

That sent his fathers scrambling into action. They raised Dario from the floor. Pausing, their eyes pleading for him to win. He couldn't disappoint them.

"It's your choice." Jeb stood beside him, Connor in his arms. Jeb's son. His flesh and blood.

Connor raised his hand to Levi's chest. "Mine."

Confused, Levi blinked, then realized what he meant. Shit, Connor's soul resided within Levi. Innocent and pure and lacking judgment, so brilliant and so open to love.

"It's your choice, Levi. Make the choice to stay with us."

Levi didn't argue with Jeb that none of this was his choice. If he could, he'd choose to stay. "Jeb, get out of here."

"No. I can't leave you here alone."

Logan grabbed Jeb's arm. "We have to leave."

Jeb shook his head. "Take Connor."

He kissed his son and handed him to Logan. Logan took the tot but hesitated. With a sharp nod, Levi told Logan it was okay. He grasped Levi's shoulder. "Love you, Crash. Go get 'em." He raced from the cave.

"Jeb, you have to go. Please, get out. It's coming."

He shook his head.

Levi rested his palm on Jeb's chest, feeling his heart pounding wildly, pumping life through his veins. Their time together flashed through his mind: the adversarial arguments, the lust-filled attraction, the quiet, caring moments, the laughter. Jeb grasped Levi's hand, holding on for dear life. If this was good-bye Levi needed more time, but time had run out.

"Jeb. Listen to me. I'm going to beat this thing, but I need you to go—"

"I can't leave you."

Another pounding surge. A deafening roar. Levi's arms raised and stretched out from his body, at shoulder height. Burning heat shot through him, the pain expanded, causing him to cry out. When the energy inside him discharged from his body, nothing in proximity to him would live.

"If you don't go, then you'll die and leave me alone. I'm pretty sure I love you, and I won't get to tell you that. When I win, I'm so going to need you."

Jeb whimpered, and then his glassy eyes widened as a magnificent white light surrounded Levi. Fuck, he was glowing.

"Holy shit." Jeb's mouth dropped open, his unbelieving gaze on Levi's glowing body. Then he snapped his mouth shut. His agonizing dark eyes seized Levi. "You'd better win, you son of a bitch." Jeb grasped Levi's face and kissed him, rough and possessive. Jeb broke the kiss, leaving Levi panting. With one last look, Jeb sprinted from him.

Levi ignored the fact that he might never see him again.

Pain ripped through Levi's chest. He doubled over, the agony gripping him hard. A burst of light shot across his vision. He screamed as roaring thunder filled his head. Hundreds of voices chattered at once, the sound overwhelming.

It's your choice.

"Fuck you!" Levi screamed.

The entity bellowed its displeasure but appeared to shrink back momentarily. The darkness surged back, fighting to take root, live within Levi's skin. Levi fired back with the innate energy he'd gathered from the souls he housed. Pure energy that powered everything in existence. Relentlessly, their battle surged and expanded and broke, like two monstrous waves crashing into one another. Building pressure clenched Levi's teeth as each clash swelled to new height and then collided again. Born from each collision was power and energy of monstrous proportions Levi would fail to contain much longer.

He needed an edge. A weapon. His search brought him into the depths of his own soul. There, he found an orb of pure light, of such beauty, no human had ever encountered. A window into some magnificent heaven. Contained within, the energy to create a thousand universes, containing the origin of time itself. Levi gasped and then literally grinned.

Now he could get down to business.

CHAPTER 34

"COME ON, you fucker! Fight me!"

Levi grabbed hold of that divine power. Within he saw the very beginning of time, the explosion busting outward in magnificent waves, energy coalescing, building, expanding, stars and planets, the first soul, the first life. Harnessing the energy, he attacked. The surging battle built into a raging war older than time itself, symbolized for eons as that between good and evil. Energy discharged from his body, radiated into the rocky walls, and the bedrock surrounding him, effortlessly penetrating the earth.

Levi screamed, and the entity roared. Energy crashed and burned and built again. Neither side showed signs of faltering. Levi thought of the people he loved, his need to continue on with them. The meaning of his life, of all life.

Love.

He was in love, and that would win every time.

And with one last magnificent surge, the energy expanded outward, blasting apart the bedrock, metric tons of earth moved. Levi's dam impenetrable, solid and fortified, the darkness screeched and then fled his mind.

Levi dropped to his knees. Chest heaving, body shaking uncontrollably, his head pulsing.

Damn. He'd won.

Large chunks of rock and dirt rained over him. He covered his head, but nothing touched him. Rocks bounced away as if he was covered by an invisible force field, and he had to laugh, fucking laugh out loud.

Standing, he staggered back. A foot away, a newly formed cliff fell off into a chasm reaching far into the earth. The pit, now twice its size, curved around the tiny remnant of rock floor he stood on.

"Fuck!"

He spun around expecting to be stranded on that shelf. His eyes widened seeing the ground behind him untouched. To his left a swath of trees had been felled. Turning back, he wiped a hand over his mouth. "Shit." Destruction that massive wasn't going to go unnoticed.

And in the center of that massive destruction, he'd survived.

Dust filled the air but was clearing quickly. With a short jump, he was on solid ground. He snorted seeing the path he'd feared earlier. Having battled the ultimate evil with a weapon of ancient energy, that path was small shit now.

He had to find his family, fearful for their safety, and headed down the hill.

"Jeb!"

No answer.

"Dad! Logan!"

Surrounding him, only trees and brush met his eyes. The woods were eerily silent.

"Jeb? Dad? Logan? Anyone here? Phillip?"

Where were they? God, he hoped the Righteous hadn't taken them again?

Remnants of the energy he'd harnessed still ran through him, causing his muscles to twitch and jump. The chatter had disappeared, but the souls remained. Many stirred with a restlessness that crawled under Levi's skin. He'd have to find out how to stop that annoying feeling.

"Levi!"

Levi's heart leapt hearing Jeb. He plowed through the underbrush toward the voice, ignoring the sticks scratching across his exposed skin. "Jeb!"

"Levi!" Jeb sounded hopeless, wrecked. Couldn't he hear Levi?

Levi tripped and stumbled but kept on.

A volley of voices called to him. Around a thicket, he saw Jeb being held back by Art and Phillip.

Levi's heart leaped, and he grinned wide as he stumbled over sticks and twisted vines. Everything could have gone so horribly wrong, but Jeb was there. As he got closer, a glowing light in Jeb's chest emanated outward in a burst of colors. So beautiful.

Why weren't his fathers letting Jeb go? Did they think he'd lost? Levi's gaze caught with Phillip's. Slowly, his pained expression faded and his despair and suspicion fled his face. He said something to Art, whose relief was palpable. They released Jeb, and Levi leapt at him. Jeb caught him in his arms.

"Thank God. Thank you. Thank you." Jeb buried his face in Levi's neck. Tears burned Levi's eyes, and he didn't give a crap if he cried. Jeb lifted his head and cupped Levi's cheeks. "Are you okay? I thought...."

"I'm okay. I'm here. I'm here," Levi whispered. Jeb held him. Everything would be okay.

"Levi." Art choked on a sob. His eyes watered, his hands shook, and his chin quivered. He was a mess. Levi released Jeb and hugged his dad as he sobbed. "It's okay, Dad. It's gone. We did it."

"Jesus, Levi. Are you okay? Are you hurt?" Art pulled back, sniffing, as he checked Levi's body for injuries.

"I'm okay. Really." The reality of that statement was unfathomable to Levi, but he'd wonder over the magnitude of what he'd done later.

Art smiled tremulously. "I can't believe you did it. I don't know how, but you did. I'm so proud of you."

Levi smiled with appreciation. "Thanks."

Phillip stood off to the side seeming unsure what to do. "You did so good." His voice shook, and to Levi, he felt a million miles away. He didn't like it.

Levi wrapped his arms around Phillip. With a grateful sigh, his father returned the hug. They had a long way to go, but they'd find a way.

Pulling back, Levi searched for Logan. Many of the Righteous were scattered about on the ground stunned, unmoving, their expressions ones of confusion, anger, grief. Maybe they were lost in the realization they'd been fighting on the wrong side. Others definitely weren't that remorseful, their hands and feet bound, their scowls showing they believed in what they had done. Gail screamed at those not bound to grow some balls and fight. Concetta sat silently, her hands tied at the wrists, her gray eyes gazing far off. Beside her, Noah lay, still unconscious, which probably didn't bode well for him.

Levi spotted Logan kneeling over Dario. Levi raised his brow, seeing Baldy kneeling across from Logan, cleaning the wound. Dario was so pale, but his eyes were open. His teeth were clenched, and sweat poured off his forehead. Gia was going to kick their asses.

Levi turned an imploring expression to his fathers. "We have to get him to the hospital."

Art went to Levi and peered down on Dario. "We've called for an ambulance. A few people headed down to get something we can use to carry Dario down to the house. We'll get him out of here as soon as we can, son."

Levi nodded and then knelt beside Logan, who had his head down. "Logan." His brother flinched but didn't move. "Logan?" Still nothing. Logan visibly shook, hands fisted on his thighs, head down. His eyes were shut, but tears managed to escape. Levi touched his arm.

"Logan, are you okay?"

Logan nodded. When he looked at Levi, his eyes were filled with pain.

"I'm sorry," he whispered.

That was unexpected. "You're apologizing for what?"

Logan swallowed hard. "You... I couldn't protect you. I was...." He chuckled with the most defeated sound Levi had ever heard. "I was going to save you.... Get you out of there, but...."

Levi laughed and pushed Logan, knocking him off-balance.

"Hey!" Logan ended up flat on his back.

Levi pounced, straddling Logan's hips. He pinned Logan's wrists above his head. The confusion on his face was amusing.

"I'm a big boy now. See? All grown up. You don't have to keep protecting me."

Logan licked at his lips. Being Levi's protector for so long, could Logan stop? Levi doubted it, but everyone needed someone to watch their back.

"So you think you can run with the big boys now?" Logan's neutral expression was belied by his twinkling eyes.

"I think I proved myself worthy."

Logan pursed his lips. "Perhaps, but...." Logan bucked his hips. Levi flailed and fell to the side. His mouth opened in a silent laugh as Logan's fingers dug into his side. Fuck, that worked every time.

"Hey... stop that roughhousing boys." The voice was weak but had scolded Levi many times.

Logan relented. Levi got to his knees, crawling the short distance to Dario. Phillip knelt next to the person he'd called an old friend. The concern on his face was unsettling.

"There's an exit wound in his lower back," Baldy said, his attention on Phillip. "The bleeding has slowed, but internal bleeding and damaged organs are a concern."

"Why should we trust you? You're part of the reason we were almost killed!" Levi wanted to do just that to them all.

Baldy's lips thinned, not from anger, possibly shame. "You're right. We listened to her, and that's on us. We thought.... Concetta, she didn't tell us the whole truth. She vilified you all, made you out to be hidden monsters waiting to destroy us. She showed us shit that we couldn't help but believe. I thought we were fighting evil. Seems that we were the evil."

"*Figlio mio.*" His voice was so weak.

Levi looked down and smiled. "Hey, Dario."

"So proud of you. If I don't... please, Gia and Rachele. Be there for them."

Levi shook his head. His chin quivered. "Oh, you're not leaving me to face the wrath of Gia alone."

Dario choked out a laugh and winced. "Such a strong girl." Dario's gaze fell on Levi's chest. "You shine so brightly."

Levi looked down. So many souls within him. One stood out among the others.

Cara.

"She's here," Levi whispered. "I can give her to you. To say good-bye."

Dario choked on a sob. "On Earth we've already said our good-byes. But... let me feel her one last time."

Levi guided Dario's palm to his chest. Dario closed his eyes as did Levi. The energy tickled as he connected with his wife's soul, their love overwhelmed Levi. So beautiful. The connection was severed when Dario's hand went limp. Levi's eyes popped open. Dario's head had fallen off to the side.

"Dario?" His eyes didn't open. Tears blurred Levi's vision. "What's wrong?" He looked to Phillip. His heart raced, fearing Dario was gone.

Phillip's hand shook as he placed two fingers on the side of Dario's neck. When Phillip didn't confirm one way or another, Levi's stomach rose into his throat.

Finally, Phillip huffed. "Bastard passed out."

Levi lowered his head. Damn, he couldn't take much more. A hand patted Levi's shoulder. Levi twisted around.

Connor stood behind him with Jeb. "Booboo?"

Connor had come through physically unscathed. "Yeah, but he's going to be okay." God, he hoped that was true.

Connor clutched his truck. Levi was unprepared when Connor rested his head against his shoulder. Levi gathered the boy into his arms and stood. Jeb smiled and wrapped them both in his arms.

"Thanks for choosing us," he whispered.

Levi was sure truer words had never been spoken.

CHAPTER 35

LEVI WALKED into the hospital with Logan. They rode the elevator to the third floor in silence. Jeb had taken Connor to the guesthouse for food and rest. Which was surprising since Jeb had literally gone pale, stuttering about his lack of kid experience, when Levi had suggested they go. Jeb had cared for Connor as a baby. How much harder could a two-year-old be? That question nearly had Milo rolling on the floor laughing at their lack of kid knowledge, and he offered to help. Jeb had reluctantly agreed. Art would bring Jeb to the hospital once Levi's dad did a hell of a lot of explaining to his wife.

They'd carried Dario and Noah down the mountain and loaded them into the waiting ambulances. Phillip had followed Dario to the hospital after he'd called the local sheriff, who was a Seer, as soon as they'd fled the cave. Damage control and cleanup was turned over to her. Concetta and the Righteous would face council law and punishment. No way would any court believe the evidence.

The elevator opened to a waiting room where Gia sat with Rachele. Seeing Levi, Gia grimaced and stomped toward him. His stomach flipped.

Shit.

She punched him in the shoulder hard. She hugged him. She yelled at him. "You goddamned stupid son-of-a-bitch. I should kill you."

"I know," Levi whispered.

"I should… I should…." Her voice wavered.

Levi placed his hand on her shoulder. "How's your dad?"

"He's lucky he got shot, because I would've beat the crap out of him. What the hell is wrong with you men? You don't have a brain cell to share between ya. I mean you could have told me, Levi! I freaked when Noah took off with you. I called my Dad. He told me to stay put. Why the hell I listened I don't know. Now I find out…. Seers and Keepers and fuck!"

"I really am sorry."

She crossed her arms and huffed. Her expression told him how annoyed she was, but Levi could see the fear she'd never show to others. She bit at her lip. "*Papà* says you have my mother's soul. Is that really true?"

Levi nodded and wobbled a bit, nearly falling, but Logan was there to steady him.

"Neat trick. Next time do it while you're sitting." Logan led him to a chair and sat him down. "You should be home sleeping."

Yes, he should be home with Jeb. Why had Levi convinced him to go home? He needed Jeb.

Levi slumped in the chair. The exhaustion was taking over. "I have to make sure Dario is okay."

"They just moved him to a room," Rachele said, sitting next to Gia. "The doctor said the bullet didn't hit anything major, but he lost a lot of blood." She sniffed. "He'll be okay, though."

The elevator opened. Phillip stepped out, carrying a tray loaded with food and drinks. Seeing Levi and Logan, he nearly tripped over his own feet.

"Whoa, there." Logan took the tray and put it on the side table. "You and Levi going for the record to see who can fall down first?" Logan smiled.

Phillip smiled in return.

Each shifted, stuffed their hands in their pockets, and looked around the room doing that chewing on the side of their lip thing. Logan did that when he was nervous.

Gia hit Levi's arm. "Shit, it's almost like mirror images. They even have the same mannerisms."

She was right. Logan had lived with Phillip his first two years of life. Maybe he picked them up then.

Logan finally broke the painful silence. "So Levi is kinda wobbly. I'm thinking he needs to eat and rest. Maybe between the two of us we can do something about it?" Logan raised his brow.

Phillip smirked.

Gia inhaled sharply and pointed. "Holy shit, that's your brother's cocky smirk."

"I think we can." Phillip put his hands on Logan's shoulder, and they turned their attention to Levi.

Levi huffed in defeat. "I'll eat, but I'm not leaving."

"Sounds good. Get to it," Logan said and handed Levi a sandwich.

Levi grabbed it and reluctantly started to eat. Waiting for the doctor, Logan filled Phillip in on what he'd missed: school, sports, mischievous pranks, work, and Melissa. Phillip's rapt attention gave Levi hope that he'd stick around.

After a thirty-minute wait, the doctor appeared with an update. Dario was stable and, barring infection, would be home in a few days. He could have a few visitors at a time. Rachele and Gia grabbed Levi's hands and tugged him along to their father's room.

Dario sat up in bed, still pale but no longer looking as if he were minutes away from dying. The tearful, blubbering reunion between him and his daughters was touching. The girls both carefully snuggled against their father. Levi was grateful this moment could happen.

"You have questions, *mio figlio*. I can see it in your face."

Levi nodded, squirming under the scrutiny. Boy, did he have questions, like how in the hell had Dario gotten involved and what had he known? Why didn't he stop it?

Dario hugged his girls tighter. "I'll tell you everything, but first you will release Cara's soul."

"But I don't know how to do that. I mean I want to, but...."

Dario snorted and then grimaced no doubt from the pain. "I will guide you, and together we will send my Cara to the afterlife where she belongs. And later you'll release the souls you hold that are ready to move on. Have you felt their restlessness?"

He had, and he couldn't imagine years of that nagging internal itch. "But won't that kill the people they belong to?"

"Concetta collected the souls of many people at the moment of death. That's why she had Cara."

"But why—"

"Cara first, then questions."

"Okay. Are you all sure you're ready?"

"Yes," Gia said. "We said our good-byes before she died."

Rachele nodded as her eyes filled with tears. Levi took in a shuddering breath and looked to Gia, who smiled sadly, and then to Dario.

"Find her soul and pull her energy to the surface."

Levi concentrated, immediately finding the beautiful ball of energy. He coaxed Cara's soul to the surface. The pure love was no less dazzling, no less enchanting.

"I have her," Levi whispered.

"Repeat after me. 'Release the soul of Cara Alberici. Free her from this mortal realm and into the afterlife.'"

Levi repeated the words. His eyes rounded as an orb of light floated out of his chest.

"What's happening?" Gia asked.

"Don't you see it?" Levi asked in wonder.

Gia and Rachele both shook their heads.

"They can't see her, but I can. *Bellissima*," Dario said. With a choked, voice he whispered, "*Addio mia bella Cara*. Until we meet again."

The orb rose higher, the brightness fading until nothing remained.

Grief rolled in like a raging storm. A tear rolled down Levi's cheek. He swiped at it, but more fell. He was crying. Cara was gone. He'd missed her so much since she died, but did even more so now that he'd held her soul. His chest felt like he'd been sucker punched.

"Levi?"

His head snapped to Gia. "I said me and Rachele are leaving. You okay? You look… off."

"Yeah, I'll be out soon."

Gia kissed him on the cheek. "Go talk. We'll catch up later. Love you." And she and her sister left.

Levi's questions, which had been prolific, seemed insignificant after what he'd just gone through.

"Thank you for releasing Cara."

Levi nodded. "Did she really go to the afterlife?"

Dario shrugged. "I believe so, and I hope there we will be together someday."

Experiencing firsthand the energy of a soul, he'd believe anything possible.

Levi looked Dario in the eye. "I thought you were helping the Righteous to hurt us. I really thought you'd betrayed me."

"I thought the same thing." Phillip stood near the door. "Even now I'm not too sure how much I can, or should, trust my old friend."

Levi crossed his arms. "Just how old?"

"Since we were boys dreaming of saving the world and believing we could do anything, including fly," Dario said with a tone of sweet nostalgia.

That brought a quirk to Phillip's lips. "You were the one who thought you could fly. That broken leg was all on you."

"Ah, but who tied the cape around my neck?"

"It was just a pillow case."

"To me it was a cape, my friend."

Phillip stepped into the room and came to Dario's side, his face softening. "It was a cape." That didn't last long as Phillip drew his brows together. "You didn't tell me everything. You allowed me to put my son in great danger. I don't know if I can ever forgive you for that."

Dario flinched. "Understandable, but if I'd given you all of the information, told you what Levi was capable of, who he had to fight, you would have tried to find another way to rid him of the ancient judge. You would have done anything to spare him what happened like any good father would."

Levi shuddered recalling the mindless, voracious need for souls.

"You've told me he is like a son to you."

Dario smiled at Levi. "Yes, but I also didn't give a part of my own soul to create his. You would have protected him at all costs, your judgment clouded. You wouldn't have let him face the darkness."

"Of course not." Phillip scowled. "He could have died today. We all could have."

Levi laughed dryly. "You have no fucking clue how close that came to being true. What the hell was that thing? How did it get into me?"

Phillip raked his fingers through his hair. "Until today it was thought to be a myth. The Judge is neither living nor dead. It's a creation from the imbalance of energy of a war for that power. Long before the earth was inhabited by humans, it's believed intelligent entities, bodiless forms of energy like souls, once filled the universe."

Dario snorted. "About as intelligent as humans. In their quest for what they called 'pure energy,' their greed took over. Many wanted to control access to all energy while others wanted to stop those who did. From that power struggle, a war started where the pure energy was nearly decimated. It all came down to greed."

"Who won?" Levi asked.

"No one," Phillip said. "The war created tremendous amounts of negative energy, and despite that they still battled. The side effect of that negative energy was the emergence of the Judge. In order to survive, the Judge needed more of that negative energy. He absorbed those entities with the most negative energy. Think of them as morally corrupted by today's standards. Some were glad to get rid of those who were immoral and flawed. That meant less negative energy affecting others."

"And that's where Concetta got the story wrong," Dario said.

Levi knew where this was going. "Let me guess; the Judge destroyed them all."

"Almost. As less souls with negative energy became available, the Judge took others until he was even consuming those with no negative energy. The Judge had been unstoppable." Dario pursed his lips and scowled. "Same as it would have been if it had been unleashed here on Earth."

Levi shuddered thinking just how close that had come to being a reality.

Dario touched Levi's arm, then continued. "The warring factions had no choice but to join forces to destroy the Judge. To gain the advantage, they came to Earth despite knowing they would be trapped once they penetrated the atmosphere. The Judge followed. Despite their efforts, it couldn't be destroyed. In a collective attack, they were able to dismantle the Judge by each absorbing a part of its negative energy. The remaining entities were trapped and found refuge in living organisms. The entities became the idea of the soul. That's how the human race began according to Seer and Keeper beliefs."

Levi raised his brow. "Quite the story. But if they dismantled the Judge, how was I fighting it?"

Phillip took over. "Each entity took on a part of that negative energy, which resides in all souls. If even one piece is released, the Judge is rebuilt by absorbing the negative energy around it."

Levi rubbed at his temple. Another headache. "So why me?"

"Because you and Connor were born within the same lifetime, allowing Concetta to try and bring forth the Judge. Two rare Seers being born in the same time period, much less on the same day alone are astronomical odds," Dario said.

Levi's eyes widened. "We have the same birthday?"

Dario nodded. "Yes. As a member of the council, Concetta had access to Seers and their visions as they contacted the council to report them. She might have even had many herself that she never shared. Most Seers wouldn't have known if their visions were part of a larger scheme. In Concetta's role, she was able to piece those visions together. Put each piece into place. It's quite amazing."

Dario took in a deep breath. He looked exhausted. "And the *Book of Mattavius*, that was a myth as well. Where it came from, I don't know. Possibly it was a well-hidden secret of her Seer line. With the book she had the ritual."

"Forming the Righteous, she wanted the Judge to rid the world of flawed souls, believing they were the source of the evil and strife in the world today. Unfortunately, she didn't accept just how flawed her own is." Phillip chuckled. "The Judge got one look at her soul and thought, 'lunch.'"

They all laughed, breaking the tension.

"I still don't get why I was the chosen gateway. Maybe my piece of the Judge was bigger, or maybe my soul is flawed." Maybe he had been evil at birth.

Dario narrowed his eyes. The scary Dario was back. "We don't know why you, but understand there's nothing wrong with you. Your soul is quite spot free. If not, I would have removed it to keep the Judge from tapping into that. I've been working to guide you to this day since you were a child. I worked with your guide—your counselor—to build the power of your mind, to build you up in case you had to face the Judge."

"What do you mean 'in case'? You told Phillip it all had to play out." Which Levi still didn't understand.

"It did have to in order to shut the gateway for good. But I didn't want you to have to face the Judge." Levi could tell Dario held guilt because it had gone that far.

Phillip inhaled sharply and looked to Dario. "You gave Levi the souls Concetta held. If she didn't have them, she wouldn't have had the power for the spell."

Dario nodded. "That's why I had Milo give you the spell bundle I had him make. Concetta needed to hold it without being suspicious. I gave it to you, pretended to sense it, and handed it to her. It allowed me to pull the souls from her. But with so many, I had to create a pathway through me and Phillip, or your chest might have exploded. In the bargain you got ours as well."

Levi wiped his hand over his mouth, his mind reeling from the information. He was so ready for all of it to be over.

There was a knock on the door. Levi looked to Dario and raised his brow. Dario nodded.

"Come in," Levi said.

Art and Jeb came through the door.

Levi immediately ran into Jeb's arms. He so needed Jeb at that moment.

"Damn, I missed you," Jeb said into Levi's neck, arms banded tight around him.

"I missed you too. Is Connor okay?"

Jeb released Levi. "He fell asleep eating. Funniest thing I've ever seen." He chuckled. "He talks a lot. You know what he talked about the most?"

Levi cringed. "Oops. I may have promised him a puppy."

"Levi's wanted puppies since he was about two. That was all he ever talked about," Art said, passing by them into the room. He patted Levi on the shoulder, and Levi smiled.

"Never did get one, though, did I?"

Art rolled his eyes.

Jeb snorted. "No wonder he wasn't all that upset about me not having a puppy for him. That kid can have all of the puppies in the world after what he's been through."

"Good, because I think I promised him two."

Jeb didn't reply. Levi had hoped at least for a chuckle, but Jeb had focused his glare on Dario. Jeb's only movement was the ticking of his jaw. He was pissed.

"Care to tell me how long you knew my son was alive and where he was?"

Shit. Jeb might beat the crap out of Dario when he doesn't care for the answer he's given. Art and Phillip seemed to come to the same conclusion and moved closer to Dario.

Dario didn't show any fear. "I always knew."

Jeb growled. "Milo too?"

"Yes. Milo had the vision of Connor's birth, what he was, and came to me at the council. I had already had the initial vision of Levi. It all fell into place."

"You did nothing, and my brother and sister-in-law were murdered!"

Dario shifted. "We didn't know about that. By the time we figured out what was happening, they were already dead." He closed his eyes and grimaced. "Connor was already gone. Milo found you unconscious and bleeding."

"And all cut up," Levi said.

"No." Dario looked down at his hands.

Jeb frowned with his confusion. "What?"

Dario looked to Jeb, and Levi saw the somber determination on Dario's face. "I cut the symbol into you."

Jeb cringed. "No. Helen said that she did that."

Dario was silent. His eyes on Jeb. "I made her believe it was her idea."

Yeah, that was the wrong thing to say. Jeb tried to get to Dario, but Art and Phillip intercepted and held him back.

"You son of a bitch!"

Dario flinched. Gia and Rachele raced into the room followed by a nurse.

"What the fuck?" Gia shouted.

The scowling nurse circled the bed and checked Dario's vitals. "There are sick people in this hospital. This man needs to rest. Everyone get out!" She pointed to the door.

Jeb stepped back, and Levi placed his hand on his chest, hoping to ward off any more attempted attacks.

Dario's pleading eyes asked Jeb to understand. "I had to put the symbol on you, Jeb. I needed you to stay away from Levi. You were just as important to Concetta for the ritual to work. You had to be present as Connor's father."

"You knew it, and you still let it all happen!"

"I'm calling security!" The nurse rushed out of the room.

"I got this." Art quickly followed her.

Levi rubbed at Jeb's chest. "Calm down. Dario did what he thought would stop all of this. He saved Connor."

Jeb glared at Levi, no doubt processing the reasoning. His face went slack, and he seemed to fold in on himself. Levi drew him close.

"I'm sorry, Jeb," Dario said. Gia tried to comfort her father. "When we visited you and had you work with Dr. Winston, it was so Milo could be near you and help keep the symbol stable. Connor was safe. Milo made sure he was well taken care of. Again, this had to play out."

"Play out? What if it had played out wrong? What if your plan didn't work?" Jeb asked.

"It didn't."

CHAPTER 36

NEARLY AT once everyone said, "What?"

"Well, it did up until I tried to return Connor's soul." Dario wiped at his mouth. "Concetta opened the portal early, accessing Connor's soul as I tried to return it. I had already opened the connection between us. When she started, I couldn't stop because those souls were her power. I had to get them out of her."

Levi shuddered. "It's a good thing you didn't stop. Without that extra energy…. Well, none of us would be here right now."

Jeb leaned into Levi, and he couldn't believe Jeb was with him.

Art returned to the room. "If we all leave right now, security won't kick us out. So, everyone move it. We can sort anything else out later."

"Let's go home," Levi said, and Jeb nodded in agreement.

"Dario, get some rest," Levi said and then hugged Gia.

As he left the room, Dario called out to him. "*Arrivederci, figlio mio.*"

"School on Monday, Levi. Don't be late!" Gia cackled.

Out in the hall, Levi paused and looked to Jeb who looked as tired as Levi felt. A shower and sleep were in order. "I want you to come home with me. You and Connor. We all need time to get our lives back into order, and we need support to do that."

Jeb immediately shook his head. "I can't. I have to—"

"What? Be a man? Do it all yourself? You have a new son, a toddler. Talk about jumping in headfirst. I have a house full of people who can help. I know you're all tough and everything but…." No more pussyfooting around, Levi thought. "I'm not going to be without you. You said I was the only family you had. Well, if I'm your family, then my family is now yours too."

Jeb didn't move or blink, and yeah, Levi just had to go and open his big mouth. He feared he'd pushed too hard.

"I will go with you on one condition. If your mother says I have to sleep in another room, you won't argue." Jeb's expression told Levi he was dead serious.

"What? Why?"

"Because I need to make a good impression on your family."

Levi slowly grinned. "Really, and why is that?"

"Someday I'm going to ask them permission for something, and I don't want to be turned down."

"Permission for what?" Levi asked as Jeb walked away without answering, a satisfied grin on his face.

Logan snorted and tried to walk by all nonchalant.

"Logan, permission for what? What would he need permission for?"

"Oh, Levi, so young and innocent. Maybe we'll tell you when you're older." Logan laughed heartily.

Levi swung at him, but Logan jumped back. "Still too slow." He stuck out his tongue and then took off.

Levi chased Logan into the waiting room where Art broke up their brotherly spat. "Yeah, things are getting back to normal. Everyone in the car. Jeb, we'll stop and get Connor. You're coming with us, no arguments."

"Yes, sir," Jeb said without hesitation.

Logan sailed into the elevator as the doors opened. They stepped in, and Art held the door as Phillip rushed down the hall.

"Why aren't you arguing with my dad?" Levi asked, mouth dropping open.

"Kitten, I wasn't arguing with you when you ordered me to go home with you."

Logan snickered. "Kitten? Seriously? *Meow*."

Art smacked Logan aside the head, as Phillip smacked him on the shoulder. "Ouch, Dads!"

Art gave him a stern look. "Should I mention what Melissa's pet name for you is, Pookie-bear?"

Logan pouted, face beet red, while everyone had a laugh at his expense.

"I have one question," Levi asked, turning to Phillip. "What the heck does *Ho persono il camicia* whatever the rest was mean?"

Phillip barked out a hearty laugh. "*Ho perso la camicia a Freni e Frizioni* means I lost my shirt at Freni e Frizioni. It's a bar in Rome where Dario and I spent time when we were there on council business. Let's just say we both have a competitive streak, and he literally won the shirt off my back. Someday I'll give you the details. It ended up becoming our code."

"So you really lost your shirt to Dario?" Logan asked.

"Yes, son, I did."

AFTER STOPPING to get Connor—plus an unexpected guest, Milo, who Art insisted come with them—they arrived at home. Phillip pulled in behind them but stayed on the phone, speaking with the council. Levi imagined he would be cleaning up Concetta's mess for months to come.

When they entered the kitchen, Levi's mother was already wrapped around Logan. "I'm good, Mom, really." When she pulled away, she peered at Levi. Damn, she looked like a total wreck, and her tears flowed harder.

"Hey, Mom."

She hugged him tight, blabbering on. "Are you okay? Did you eat? You need sleep. Have you slept?"

"Mom, I'm okay. We both are," Levi said, trying to reassure her.

The sorrowful look she gave them both was excruciatingly painful.

"I'm so sorry I didn't tell you the truth. Maybe if I had, none of this would have happened." Her voice shook as much as her body, and that's when Levi realized their dad had told her everything.

Logan was the first to speak. "There were a lot of people who didn't tell us what was going on. Not just you. And they had their reasons." Logan smiled gently. "I think you have to stick by those reasons."

Levi had to agree. They could be pissed off and angry, but after all that had happened, that seemed foolish. "Mom. It's not your fault. I'm the one who's sorry. I shouldn't have taken off when I did."

"I guess we all have a part in this," Art said, hanging his jacket.

"Maybe we should all cut ourselves some slack." Levi hugged her. "I love you, Mom."

"Love you too." She stiffened and then pulled away. Her mouth dropped open.

Levi and Logan looked to where she stared. Phillip stood frozen in the doorway, eyes wide.

Levi looked back to his mother. The hell and brimstone look she flashed his biological father was deadly. Phillip continued his fortified stand, not backing down.

"Phillip," she said curtly.

"Maggie."

Well, maybe it would take longer for some of them to be okay with one another.

Jeb held a sleeping Connor in his arms and had stood back. Levi could see the wariness and hesitancy in his eyes.

There was no better time than the present. "Mom." He took Jeb's hand, leading him to her. "This is Jeb, he's… umm." Fuck. What was he?

"So, this is the boyfriend," she said.

"Yes, ma'am." Jeb held out his hand, and she took it, not shaking it as Jeb had intended. He looked at their hands and swallowed. He was so nervous. "Nice to meet you."

"And this adorable boy must be Connor." Levi could tell his mother was already planning how to spoil him.

Jeb shifted uncomfortably. "Yeah. He's out like a light. I should get him to bed."

She raised a confident brow at Levi. "Well, at least one parent knows where their child should be. Art, I still can't believe you let Levi stay at the hospital for so long."

Art guffawed but quickly stopped his reaction upon seeing his wife's scowl.

Jeb chuckled, but the steely gaze from Art shut him down.

"Well, he's home now, isn't he?"

"Yes, dear, you did a good job." Her tone was only a bit condescending.

"Okay, Phillip and Logan and I are going to head into my office to go over some details." Art waved them on, and relief covered Phillip's face as he headed out of the kitchen.

"Right." She winked and smirked. "They'll be joined by Art's close friends, Jack Daniels and Jim Beam."

They all laughed, including Milo, who lurked in the doorway.

Levi's mother looked around Jeb. "You must be Milo. Come in, please, and welcome to our home. Now are you all hungry?"

They all shook their heads vehemently. "I think showers and bed, right guys?" Levi asked, to which they both nodded.

"Okay, Jeb, there's a cot in Levi's room for Connor. I figured you'd want him close."

Levi grinned at Jeb, who merely rolled his eyes.

"Milo, you'll be in with Logan. I hope that's all right." She grimaced. "I assume Phillip will be taking up space in the guest room."

Levi thought about defending his father, but he'd hurt her, and that was Phillip's bridge to mend, not his.

"Thanks, Mom." Levi kissed her on the cheek, and the others thanked her for her hospitality.

Levi showed Milo to Logan's room and then brought Jeb into his. Jeb laid Connor down on the cot and covered him gently. Levi was warmed by the love he saw in Jeb's eyes. He stepped closer and wrapped his arm around his waist. Jeb pulled him close just as Levi hoped he would. He rubbed Levi's arm, the touch soothing and so welcome.

"It doesn't seem real. He doesn't feel like mine. I don't feel like a 'dad.' I mean look, already he's spent his entire life living with someone else, kidnapped, watching people get hurt and, well, not the kid life he should have. What if all of this messes him up permanently? What if he didn't get enough *Sesame Street* or love or attention and he missed important steps? What if he grows to hate me for not being there for him, like some kind of repressed memory that jumps out when he's a teenager or an adult? He could suddenly think I'm the scum of the earth. And I'm not the best guy to raise a kid. What if I screw him up and—"

Levi kissed Jeb. Jeb flailed but then deepened the kiss and wrapped Levi up. When Levi released him, Jeb didn't speak, just stared into Levi's eyes.

"You sound like a dad to me."

"But what if—"

Levi shushed him. "Deal with the what-ifs as they come. He's a great kid, and you'll be a great dad."

Jeb smirked. "I'm gonna need some help, you know, with all of those puppies."

Levi hoped that was an invitation to something greater. "Puppies I can do. Now if you need parenting advice you're barking up the wrong tree, but I have a mom and a couple of dads who can probably give you sound advice."

Jeb cupped Levi's cheek, and there wasn't much Levi could do but be trapped in his gaze. "I meant it when I said that you were the only family we had. I know it's new, and we haven't had any of the normal relationship stuff. But...." He swallowed hard. "I do love you."

"Kitten," Levi said.

Jeb furrowed his brow and cocked his head.

"You forgot to call me kitten."

"I did, huh?"

"Yup."

"What do I get if I call you kitten?" Jeb's teasing expression lit up his face and ran straight to Levi's heart.

"Me."

Jeb grinned, apparently liking that answer. He leaned close. "I love you, kitten."

Damn, he'd never get tired of hearing that.

JAKE C. WALLACE started writing from a young age, but took a break for marriage, kids, and college (in that order). A few years ago, he rediscovered his passion for writing stories and ventured out into the brave new world of publishing. He has published several novels and short stories. Recently, his novel *Jerricho's Freedom* was a finalist in the Rainbow Book Awards.

At night and on the weekends, Jake writes about all things men, believing there is nothing hotter than two men finding and loving one another, whether for a night or forever. An avid reader of M/M romance, Jake loves a good twist of a plot, HEA, HFN, or tragic ending, and has over two thousand books in his library. He also writes what his best friend calls HUNKs (Happy Until the Next Kidnapping). In his daytime hours, Jake works with individuals with autism and behavior issues. He is owned by a beautiful partner, three kids, and two grandchildren. He lives in the Northern Vermont.

Website: www.jcwallacebooks.com
Facebook: www.facebook.com/jcwallacebooks
Twitter: @jcwallacebooks.com
E-mail: jcwallacebooks@gmail.com

Also from Dreamspinner Press

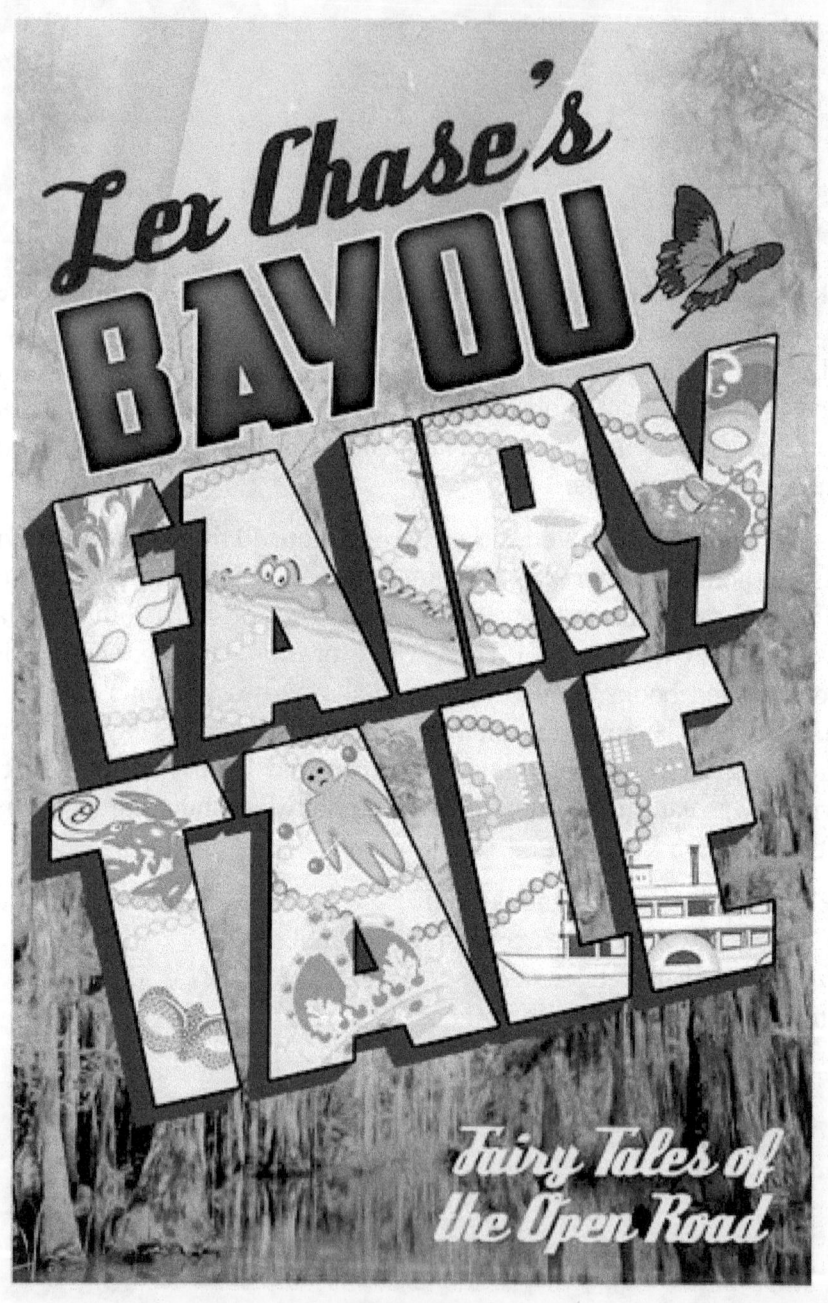

Also from Dreamspinner Press

Betrothed
A FAERY TALE
THERESE WOODSON

Also from Dreamspinner Press

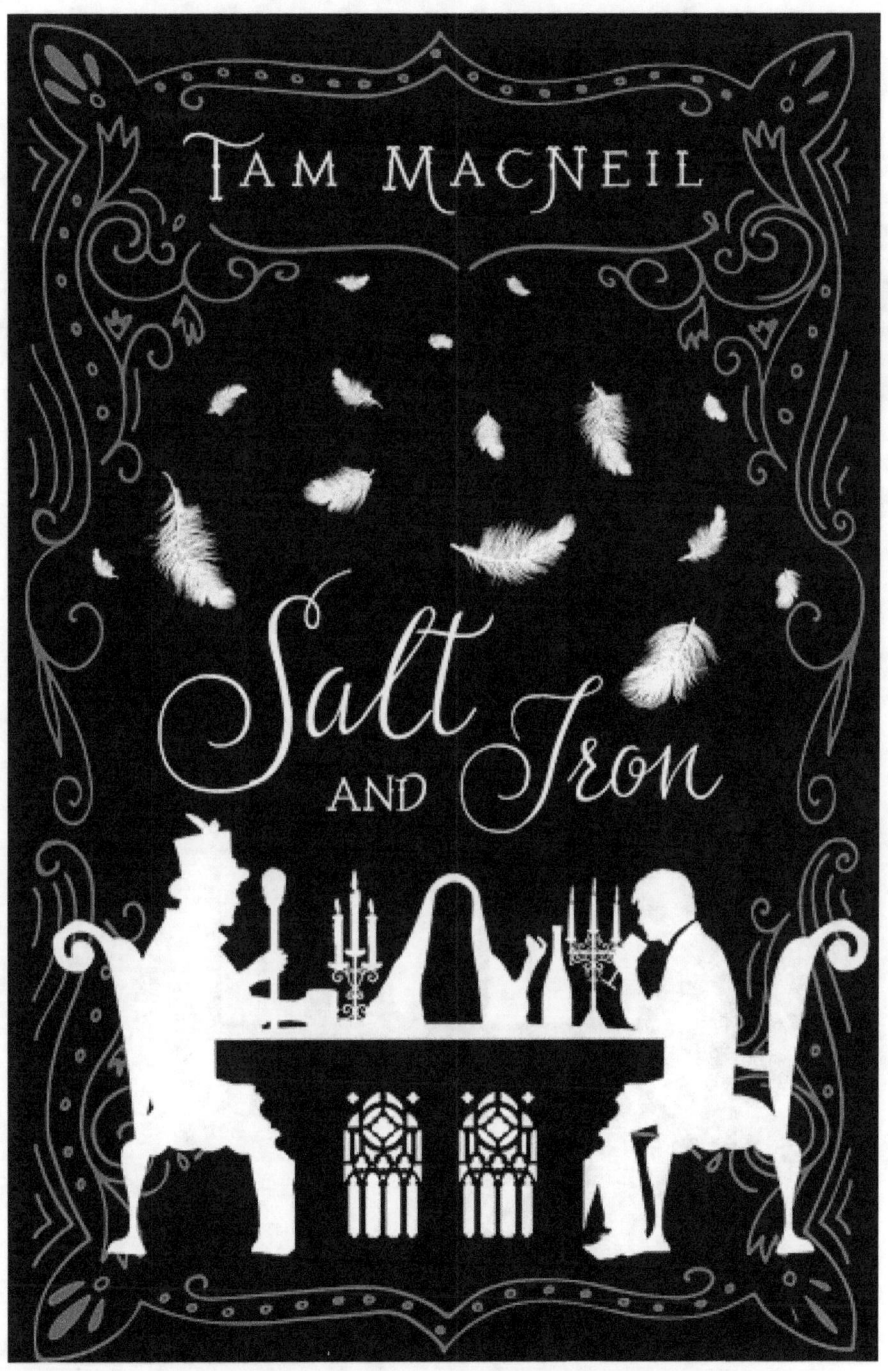

www.dreamspinnerpress.com